BAYOU

"I do not want your pity," Cord said in a chilly tone.

"I . . . maybe I wasn't offerin' my pity. Maybe . . . just maybe . . . I was workin' up to kissin' you."

"And why would you want to kiss me?" he asked in a hoarse whisper.

Delia focused on his mouth. "Maybe I wanted to thank you properly for the locket."

"Let me see your eyes. Look at me, Delia."

His commanding tone raised her lashes, but she had a hard time keeping her gaze on his.

"It is very dangerous to tease a man so."

"But I didn't . . . I wasn't . . ."

"No more lies. Just listen. I'm going to tell you something for your own good."

He kissed her cheek, then slid his lips to her ear. "Little girls who play with fire, sooner or later they get burned."

BLUE MOON BAYOU

KATHERINE COMPTON

AVON BOOKS NEW YORK

BLUE MOON BAYOU is an original publication of Avon Books. This work has never before appeared in book form. This work is a novel. Any similarity to actual persons or events is purely coincidental.

AVON BOOKS
A division of
The Hearst Corporation
1350 Avenue of the Americas
New York, New York 10019

Copyright © 1992 by Katherine Compton
Inside cover author photograph by Shaun Bynum
Published by arrangement with the author
Library of Congress Catalog Card Number: 91-92448
ISBN: 0-380-76412-1

First Avon Books Printing: August 1992

AVON TRADEMARK REG. U.S. PAT. OFF. AND IN OTHER COUNTRIES, MARCA REGISTRADA, HECHO EN U.S.A.

Printed in the U.S.A.

RA   10 9 8 7 6 5 4 3 2 1

For the real Netha Bea, my beloved mother,
who we still believe has eyes in the back of her head.

For Brittany Blue-eyes.

For Betsy, a kindred spirit who hears me
screaming across the miles . . . and responds.

For all the aunts and uncles, cousins, nieces,
nephews, in-laws, and out-laws
in my family. I love you all dearly.

The senses folding thick and dark
About the stifled soul within,
We guess diviner things beyond,
And yearn to them with yearning fond;
We strike out blindly to a mark,
believed in, but not seen.
ELIZABETH BARRETT BROWNING

Chapter One

Southern Louisiana, 1852

"**S**candalous?" Adelaide Abernathy, *Delia* to close acquaintances, shifted her weight on the marble bench, adjusting her hooped skirt. She hid a smile behind a sip of mint julep, secretly delighted to be the center of tittle-tattle in Boudreaux Parish. "Tell me true, Milly, did they honestly use the word 'scandalous'?"

Seated across the summerhouse, Millicent Mosely nodded, causing her dark ringlets to bob. "Mrs. Davenport did, and Mamma fussed all the way home from the readin' circle. She forbade me to be seen in your company. Why, she'd have herself a fit if she knew you were here visitin' today." A worried frown creased the young woman's delicate features. "Oh, Delia, why do you do such wicked things?"

"Now, now, Milly. You fret too much. You take common gossip way too seriously. When you get to be *my* age—"

"Delia, you're barely two years older than I am."

"Yes, but the years between eighteen and twenty make all the difference. You come to a point in your life when you're not so prone to

1

follow conventionality." Cocking her head to the side, Delia twisted one of her long blond curls around her finger. "What else did they say?"

"Really, Delia. You amaze me. Simply boggle the mind. *You* have *never* been prone to conventionality. Why, it was one thing when you walked out on the veranda at Cynthia's comin'-out and lit up a cheroot, but *this*—"

Delia rolled her eyes and set her drink on the small table next to her. Picking up her fan, she snapped it open, stood, and moved to the edge of the gazebo, presenting her back to her friend.

"Delia . . . dear, dear Delia," Milly said, then sighed heavily. "Don't you care about your reputation? Don't you care what people say? Heavenly days, it's as if you enjoy knowin' that tongues are waggin'."

"Of course I enjoy it," Delia commented, gazing at a pair of peacocks that paraded across the plantation grounds. "If it wasn't for me, what else would the old cronies at the readin' circle have to gossip about?"

A warm breeze blew through the gazebo, carrying the sweet scent of magnolias. Delia tilted her head and allowed the air to cool the base of her throat. The wind billowed her full, pale green skirt. Idly, she dragged a fingertip along the rosebuds embroidered on her neckline and watched a tall, dark-haired Cajun worker emerge from a neatly trimmed hedge in the distance. When he stopped beside the woodpile and picked up an ax, Delia observed his muscular build with mild interest, noting how tightly his rolled-up sleeves banded his biceps. He appeared fairly good-looking from where she stood. Of course, she was certain that upon closer examination his face would be lined . . . his hands dirty and callused . . .

"Delia." Milly's voice came from behind her, distracting her assessment of the Cajun. "About last night . . . you didn't *really*—I mean, you didn't permit Chauncy Bateman to . . . to—"

"To what?" Delia aimed a frown over her shoulder at her friend.

Milly blushed and clasped her hands in her lap. "Everyone saw the two of you slip into the garden. No one could miss Chauncy's embarrassment when you returned . . . almost a full half hour later . . . and . . . well, the state of your hair and gown suggested . . . suggested—" Milly bit her bottom lip. "Delia, I must admit the games you played to raise brows when we were younger were all quite amusin'. And everyone forgave you because your grandmother is who she is. But now that we're no longer children . . . well, there are just some things that are *unpardonable*."

Delia turned slowly and leaned against the large ornate column. "Millicent Mosely," she said, then set about fanning her face furiously. "How could you think such a thing of me? Why, you're my very best friend in the whole world. You know me better than anyone. I have plans to see the world, remember? Do you really think I'd set myself up to be trapped into marriage? Well, do you?"

Milly dropped her lashes.

Delia immediately felt a stab of remorse for speaking so sharply. Dear Milly's feelings were so fragile. "Oh, Milly, I didn't mean it like that.

You know I didn't." Pressing her lips into a tight line, she stilled the fan against her breast. "It's just that . . . well, Grandy's been at me again. She informed me she's havin' Miz Partridge and that nephew of hers from N'orlens to supper next week. I told her she can keep right on introducin' me to so-an'-so's nephew if she likes, but I'm *not* gonna change my mind about matrimony. I'll swan, Milly, it's beyond me why any intelligent woman would want to make herself liable to the trials of a husband. Why, it's no less than slavery."

Milly smoothed her skirt, her expression apprehensive. "Then what *did* happen with you and Chauncy?"

"I let him kiss me." Delia raised her chin a notch. "Of course, he did try to press himself upon me. They *will* try, Milly. *All* of them," she added with an air of authority. "But a good, sound slap will stop them cold. In fact, had anyone taken the time to notice, Chauncy's embarrassment was more likely due to the imprint of my hand on the side of his face."

Milly giggled, and Delia's lips twitched into a smile. "But don't you dare tell anyone the truth, you hear? Let them all believe what they will. Rumors keep this town from bein' so dull, don't you think?"

"Adelaide, you really are—"

"Scandalous?" Delia supplied with a lift of a brow.

"Precisely." Milly's laughter dwindled as her attention settled on something beyond Delia.

Delia followed her friend's gaze. The Cajun chopping wood was unbuttoning his shirt. Seemingly oblivious of Delia's or Milly's presence, he peeled off the sweat-soaked garment, let it drop to the ground, and resumed his chore.

"My, my, *my*," Delia commented, and absently fanned her face.

The man's broad, golden shoulders, glistening in the noonday sun, tapered down to a slim waist. His snug trousers settled low on lean hips. With each powerful swipe of the ax, his muscles flexed.

Delia edged the weight of one hip onto the rail and glanced at Milly. Her friend was apparently just as enthralled by the worker's good looks as she was. "Did you ever wonder, Milly," she said, casually eyeing the Cajun again, "why God would create a man like that, then place him b'neath our social station?"

"Delia!"

Delia cocked her head to find her friend's mouth pinched with disapproval.

Milly drew herself erect. "That's blasphemous."

"Oh, it is not. It's merely an observation, that's all. And you know good and well it's *true*. Why, we can look at him all we want, but neither one of us would ever actually speak to the likes of a Cajun hired hand."

Milly's frown softened. "But we could still look at him, couldn't we?"

"Of course we can. I won't tell if you won't." Delia winked. "Who is he, anyway? I don't recall ever seein' him b'fore."

"Oh, Delia, surely you recollect who he is. Cord just got back in town. Came around a couple of weeks ago askin' for work, and Daddy hired him."

"Cord?"

"Cord Kibedeaux," Milly said with a wave of her hand. "You remember, he's the one Mr. Grayson took in after that awful incident with his mamma and daddy—you know, when his daddy shot his mamma, then committed suicide? He just got out of prison a year or so ago," she whispered. "I hear tell he's been doing odd jobs around Baton Rouge and Lafayette since then."

Delia stared openly at the woodcutter. *Cord Kibedeaux.* If memory served her, he and his family had shown up in Boudreaux Parish the summer her father had brought her the doll from China for her ninth birthday. He'd been a tall, thin, raggedy boy of fifteen or so. Chauncy Bateman and the other boys had teased him unmercifully. Cord had simply walked by them with his head down, pretending to ignore the taunts and shoves. Looking back, Delia had thought he was such a coward for not standing up to them. At the same time, she had pitied the boy.

"I'm really surprised he had the gall to show his face around here," Milly said, peering above her drinking glass. "After what he did to old Mr. Grayson? That poor man has had his share of woe, hadn't he? Why, everybody knows how his daughter ran off with that Cajun gambler passin' through. I heard tell old Mr. Grayson was heartbroken for years afterward. Took Cord in outta the kindness of his heart, he did—after that nasty incident with Cord's mamma and daddy?"

Milly shifted her weight, then continued in a hushed tone. "Then Cord does him dirty. Poor man. Can you imagine stealin' from someone who was kind enough to take you in? You shoulda heard Mamma, Delia. She liked to have had a fit when Daddy hired Cord. But you know Daddy and that big, soft heart of his. He said the boy had done his time, paid his dues, and deserved a second . . .''

Milly's voice faded as Delia studied Cord. He looked so different—not at all like the scruffy boy she remembered from childhood. Nor did he resemble the handsome young teller who had later worked at Mr. Grayson's bank.

Cord's trial, Delia recalled, had caused quite a stir throughout Boudreaux Parish. Although Grandmother Abernathy had forbidden her to attend, Delia had slipped into the back of the courtroom anyway. Wide-eyed, she had quietly observed the ruckus, listened to the accusations, and heard Cord's ardent denials.

Delia watched Cord turn and reach for another log to split. Several white scars crisscrossed his tanned back, she noticed. A wave of nausea floated over her, and she closed her eyes.

She simply hated unpleasantries . . . detested discussing problems that could never possibly affect her safe little world. Up to this point, she and Milly had been having such a nice visit. Cord Kibedeaux showing up was surely going to spoil the rest of the afternoon.

''You do remember, don't you, Delia?'' Milly's voice droned on. ''The Kibedeauxs were the no-accounts who took up residency in that little old shanty, the one down in Blue Moon Bayou that everyone said was haunted. They hadn't lived there long, only a couple of months, I think, when—''

"Milly." Delia made a sour face at her friend. "Can't we talk about somethin' else?"

"Oh, but, Delia, just wait till I tell you what I heard!" Milly scooted to the edge of her seat and opened her big brown eyes wider. "I heard Cord is stayin' down at the bayou—in that same little shanty. I'll just wager the ghosts of his mamma and daddy linger 'round there day and night. Can you imagine livin' in that creepy old place? And you know what else?"

"Milly, I . . . I'm afraid I'm going to have to beg off for the rest of the afternoon. I've suddenly developed the most awful headache." Delia pressed the back of her hand to her forehead for effect.

"Why, you poor dear." Milly rose, moved forward, and caught Delia's elbow. "You do look ghastly pale. I hope it's nothin' serious. I s'pose I shouldn't have gone on and on the way I did."

"Nonsense, Milly. I'm sure it's just this heat." Delia felt guilty for playing her best friend false, but she didn't want to think about, much less talk about, the sordid details of a common thief's life. "I'll be fine if I just go home and lie down for a bit."

With a concerned frown, Milly nodded, then called out toward the house. "Lizzie! Tell Ol' Ben to fetch Miss Adelaide's carriage 'round front. And tell him not to dally, you hear? Miss Adelaide's feelin' poorly."

The following day, Delia hurried through the door of Sedberry's Millinery Shop with Millicent Mosely treading on her heels.

"I saw it first, Milly," Delia declared and

headed straight for the wide-brimmed straw hat in the window. She plucked it from the display, settled herself before the looking glass, and placed it on her head.

"Oh, Milly, it's perfect," she said as she tied the pale blue scarf into a bow beneath her chin. "It will match the dress I'm wearin' to the Norwoods' garden party. Isn't it just divine?"

Milly looked over her friend's shoulder into the mirror. "I s'pose," she murmured, then puckered her lips.

"You s'pose?" Delia tilted her head, admiring her reflection from different angles. "Why, just look how my eyes pick up the color. The scarf makes them look even bluer."

Milly bit her bottom lip and squinted at her friend's image. "It *is* divine," she said after a moment, then smiled with resignation.

Delia returned an even brighter smile. She removed the hat, then made her way with Milly to where the proprietor stood stocking the shelves behind a long counter.

"I'll take this, Mr. Sedberry." Delia set the hat on the counter. "And a half dozen of those white linen hankies you carry—the ones with lace, if you please. And let's see, what else?"

Delia's gaze shifted from the finery on the shelves to Mr. Sedberry's grim expression. "Is anything the matter, Mr. Sedberry?"

"I'm 'fraid so, Miss Adelaide." He tugged his lapels while straightening his tall, thin frame. "I regret to inform you that you no longah have credit heah."

Delia blinked. "I beg your pardon?"

"Your grandmother sent her man 'round this mornin' to me, and, I hear tell, to every other proprietor in town, forbiddin' us to extend you any more credit."

Heat crept up Delia's neck, burning her ears, setting her cheeks afire. Taking a deep breath, she glanced at Milly's white face, then narrowed her eyes on Mr. Sedberry. "This must be a mistake. A prank. Someone's just playin' a nasty prank. My grandmother will have whoever's at fault horsewhipped for this. Why, she'll have the hide—"

"Ain't no mistake, Miss Adelaide. I have the note right heah if you'd care to see for yourself." Mr. Sedberry thrust a white slip of paper forward. "It's in your grandmother's handwritin'."

Delia stared through a red haze at the signature she knew so well. It was all there in black and white. Her grandmother had indeed written the note. Agatha Abernathy was well known for her heavy-handedness in controlling the town. But Delia couldn't imagine Grandy placing her own granddaughter in such a humiliating predicament, especially when everything the Abernathys did was so widely whispered about.

Tears of anger blurred Delia's vision. Fury swelled inside her until she was sure she'd pop a corset string. Lifting her chin at an unusually high angle, she glared at the shopkeeper as if this were all his fault. "You put that hat behind the counter for me, Mr. Sedberry. I assure you I'll be 'round tomorrow to fetch it."

With that, she left the shop, slamming the door so hard that two hats fell off their perches in the display window.

* * *

"Grandy!" Delia yelled at the top of her lungs, storming into the large polished foyer. "Grandy!"

A round-faced black woman burst through the door that led from the kitchen. "Ho, now, missy," she said, drying her hands hastily on her apron. "What you hollerin' 'bout now? Land sakes, chile, you gonna wake d' dead."

"Where is she?" Delia asked, and moved forward in a wide, anything-but-dainty stride. "Where is she, Bess?"

Bess furrowed her brows, making the kerchief tied on her head slip slightly forward. "Wheah's who, Miss Delia?"

"You know who. Grandy. Where is she?"

"Don't you go gettin' sassy with ol' Bess, gal." Bess placed her hands on her broad hips. "You'd best calm down and tell me wha's got you all puffed up like a toad."

"I have to see Grandy, Bess. I have to see her . . . *right now*."

"Your grandmamma's entertainin' Mr. Baldridge in d' study." As Delia headed in that direction, Bess added, "But Ah'd wipe dat look off my face if ah was you afore you go in dere. You heah me, missy? Miz Abernathy ain't gonna like dat snippy face none a'tall."

Leaving Bess mumbling to the good Lord above, Delia marched to the study and swung the double doors wide without bothering to knock.

Grandy sat regally behind her desk. Thaddeus Baldridge, attorney-at-law, stood to the elderly woman's right, one hand on the high, ornately carved back of Agatha Abernathy's chair. Neither gave any indication of surprise at the interruption, but rather, appeared as though posed for a photograph.

Agatha's thin, pale lips curved slowly into a curt smile. "Come in, Adelaide. We've been expectin' you."

Delia rustled into the room, her skirt swaying, and braced her hands on her grandmother's desk. "I need to speak with you immediately, Grandy." She glanced at the attorney. "*Alone*, if you please."

"Now, Adelaide," Grandy drawled, "there's no need to be rude. Thaddeus is an old friend of this family. He's traveled all the way from N'orlens to be with us today. Why, he already knows everything there is to know about us." She patted her neatly styled silver hair. "You may speak freely in front of him."

Delia glared at Thaddeus Baldridge. She'd never liked the man. He reminded her of a crow. He was forever dressed in black. His nose looked like a beak. His dark, beady eyes were too closely set, and the right one twitched whenever he became overanxious.

"Very well." Delia tossed a crumpled piece of paper on the desk. "Mr. Sedberry said you sent this to him this mornin'. He told me right there in front of Milly that—"

"You are not to be extended any more credit," Agatha finished. "That's correct. Mr. Sedberry, along with every proprietor in this town, has been notified that I will no longer pay your accounts."

Delia tightened her jaw, fending off the rage mounting inside her. "Why," she asked in a controlled, even tone, "would you do such a thing?"

"To gain your attention, of course. And I did get your attention, didn't I? Sit down, Adelaide," Agatha commanded.

Delia looked into Grandy's steel-gray eyes for a long moment. Knowing full well defiance would only prolong her grandmother's silence, she seated herself grudgingly in the wing chair facing the desk.

"Well, you've most certainly gotten my attention, Grandy," she said, then folded her arms over her chest. "Now, you wanna tell me why you felt inclined to go to such humiliatin' extremes to do so?"

"It's comfortin' to know at least something humiliates you, Adelaide. I was beginnin' to worry about that." Retaining her stiff posture, Agatha exchanged a meaningful look with the attorney, then clasped her blue-veined hands together on the desk. "I don't relish havin' to do this, Adelaide, but you leave me no choice. You are no longer a child, yet you continue to act like one. It appears the discussions we've had about your behavior have gone in one ear and out the other. I warned you the last time we talked about the propriety of a respectable young lady of your station and that I would stand for no more nonsense. Yet you deliberately defy me."

Delia opened her mouth to protest, but Grandy stopped her with a raised hand.

"Not one word, Adelaide, till I've said my piece."

Delia had learned over the years when and when *not* to dispute her grandmother. The familiar glint in Grandy's eyes signaled this would be one of those times when no amount of argument would forestall the scolding about to be delivered. Settling back in her chair, Delia prepared to sit through another boring lecture. Idly, she set her mind adrift and daydreamed about the Norwoods' garden party scheduled for next week.

"Adelaide, look at me when I speak to you," Agatha said sharply.

Delia obeyed, but her thoughts remained elsewhere.

"You have pulled the last of your fiascos, young lady," Grandy went on. "As if gallivantin' around till all hours of the night with Lord knows who or how many, playin' brag, and smokin' cheroots in public weren't enough. Now this . . . this disreputable incident with Chauncy Bateman. I won't have it, Adelaide. I tell you, I simply will not have it." Agatha pounded her fist on the desk, bringing Delia upright in her chair. "Adelaide! Are you listenin' to me?"

Delia sighed. "Yes, Grandy. You were talkin' about Chauncy Bateman." Delia had heard that much. "I don't know what your gossipy old friends told you, but it's not what you think. It wasn't like—"

"I don't want to hear it, Adelaide. It doesn't matter whether you actually did anything or not. What matters is that you are on your way to ruinin' your reputation . . . *and* mine." Agatha tucked her chin and peered from beneath her silver brows. "You have a wild streak in you, Adelaide—just like your father."

Delia gripped the arms of the chair. She would *not* hear a word said against her father. It was true he only fluttered into her life every two or

three years, lavishing her with gifts and laughter
for a few days, then sailed off with a lighthearted
wave. And no, he wasn't always there when she
needed him, but Delia loved and admired him—
and hated it when Grandy spoke ill of him. "My
father—" she began in his defense.

"Is a gadabout," Agatha supplied, then pursed
her lips. "Traipsin' all over Europe, flittin' from
one high-society trollop to another . . . " Grandy's
voice trailed off and her eyes grew misty. "I love
Wendell. He's my only son, Adelaide, but I do
not excuse his treatment of you. Not that I have
ever regretted him leavin' you in my care when
your mother, God rest her gentle soul, passed on.
You were such a beautiful baby." Agatha's nos-
talgia faded suddenly and her stern expression returned. "But I've spoiled you. I now see a great
error on my part in indulgin' your every whim,
and I intend to make up for the damage I've done.
For the sake of my health and our good name, I
plan to see you nicely settled before I die."

Delia closed her eyes. "Grandy, we've been
over this a hundred times. Every woman doesn't
need a man in her life to make it complete. *I* certainly don't." Leaning forward, she gave Agatha
her sweetest smile. "If it will make you rest easier, I promise I won't go and do one more little
thing to tarnish the Abernathy name. Cross my
heart." Delia made an X on her chest. "See?
Now, if you'll just write a note to Mr. Sedberry
tellin' him you made a mistake, I might have time
to ride back into town and pick up the hat he's
holdin' for me. You're just gonna love it, Grandy.
It's—"

"I wish to see you married, Adelaide," Agatha stated dispassionately, as though she hadn't heard a word her granddaughter said. ''I can't go in peace until I do. You'll be twenty-one your next birthday, well past marriageable age.''

Delia's confidence that this was simply another scolding wavered slightly as she searched her grandmother's face. The old woman's expression was always grim. But there was something in Grandy's eyes, something in the tight set of her mouth, that bothered Delia. ''Now, now, Grandy,'' she said, then brightened her smile. ''Don't go gettin' yourself all worked up about this again.''

Holding her stern demeanor, Agatha arched a brow. ''That smile may have worked miracles in the past, Adelaide, but it's not goin' to sway me this time. I've made up my mind, and you will abide by my wishes.''

Delia felt the corners of her mouth flinch. She looked from her grandmother to the attorney. His right eye started to twitch.

A breathy little laugh escaped Delia as her gaze returned to Agatha. ''I'm sure you would tie me up, drag me to the parish priest, and have him marry me off to the first man who walked through the door if you thought you could get away with it. But you can't, Grandy. You can't *make* me marry.''

Agatha sniffed and lifted her chin. ''Oh, but I can. In fact, I've gone to great measures to see that you do.'' Turning to the attorney, she motioned him forward. ''Show her the agreement, Thaddeus.''

The man rounded the desk and laid a multiple-paged document before Delia. She glanced from the official-looking papers to her grandmother and back again.

"It's all very simple, Miss Adelaide," Mr. Baldridge drawled. "Let me explain. The first page states clearly that unless you marry before your next birthday, your grandmother will provide nothin' more for you than room and board. Nor will you inherit any of her assets when she passes on." The attorney pasted a placid smile on his face, but his eye was still twitching. "Miz Abernathy has indicated that if you fail to comply with her wishes, her estate and all possessions therein will be auctioned off and the proceeds donated to charity."

Delia stared at her grandmother in disbelief. "But my birthday is only a few months away."

"Yes, I know, dear. You may, of course," Agatha went on, without the least show of remorse over her decision, "marry the man of your choice. It shouldn't be difficult to select a suitable husband from the horde of young men you keep company with."

"However," Thaddeus Baldridge added, "your elected husband-to-be must receive your grandmother's blessin'." He set the first page aside and pointed to a paragraph on the second. "This clause concerns livin' arrangements and states that you must reside together as man and wife for at least six months"—the attorney cleared his throat—"to . . . ah . . . secure the possibility of providin' an heir."

Delia tried to say something, but the words wouldn't make it past her throat. All she could do was widen her eyes on her grandmother.

Grandy shrugged. "I cherish the thought of

bouncin' a great-grandchild on my knee before I go,'' she stated simply.

Delia closed her eyes, feeling overheated. ''I won't do it,'' she said through clenched teeth.

''Oh, I think you will,'' Grandy uttered in a calm, condescending tone that elevated Delia's temperature to a full boil. ''Especially after you consider the consequences—that you'll be penniless unless you sign this agreement.''

Chapter Two

Delia looked out her bedroom window, gauging the distance between the second-story room and the ground below. It wasn't high enough. If she jumped, most likely she'd only break an arm or a leg.

Leaning her forehead against the windowpane, she sighed. Outside, servants and slaves hustled about the plantation as usual, as if nothing at all were amiss. They moved like an army of ants, Delia decided, each performing the same tedious tasks as on the day before. The Abernathy Plantation ran like a well-wound clock. Nothing ever changed.

But in Europe . . .

Delia quirked one corner of her mouth. Surely in Europe life was different. Spontaneous, she imagined. Her father had indicated there were no set rules abroad, no yardsticks measuring propriety.

"Oh, Daddy, why aren't you ever here when I need you?" Delia whispered, and envisioned her father striding across the lawn.

Tall, handsome, graying at the temples, Wendell Abernathy oozed Southern charm. He possessed a dazzling smile and a carefree nature. Delia knew he deliberately flitted around issues of any real importance during his short visits. She never minded, though. In truth, she was much more interested in his frivolous accounts of Paris and Rome.

The image of the distinguished man, complete with top hat and cane, vanished suddenly and left Delia gazing at her own reflection in the glass. Watching an unchecked tear roll down her cheek, she clenched her fists against the windowsill. She would have been joining her father abroad in a matter of months had Grandy not foiled her plans with this silly marriage agreement. Of course, she'd never actually discussed those particular plans with her father, but she was certain he would welcome her company—especially if he knew what Grandy was up to. Why, he would be appalled to learn of Grandy's wicked scheme!

The idea of simply packing her belongings and running away fluttered briefly through Delia's mind, but she quickly reasoned she couldn't get far without funds.

Turning from the window, she glanced around the mauve room filled with porcelain dolls and French lace. Her gaze landed on the music box Grandy had given her last Christmas. Just for spite, she marched over, picked it up off the bureau, and hurled it at the door.

Delia stared for a long moment at the shattered pieces of the china figurine and listened to the last distorted tinklings of the sweet melody. Then she sank onto the edge of her bed and burst into tears. It had been her favorite music box. Now it was gone. Broken. And what had she achieved by breaking it?

No more than she had achieved two and a half weeks earlier when she'd thrown Grandy's favorite flower vase against the study wall. Nothing. All her screaming and crying the day Thaddeus Baldridge had presented her with the contract had done nothing to alter her grandmother's decision. Nor had any amount of pleading, begging, or hatefulness since, changed Grandy's final verdict.

Someone knocked softly at her door, and Delia swiped at her wet cheeks. "Never mind, Bess. I'll clean it up myself this time."

"Delia?" Milly called. "It's me. Can I come in?"

Delia rose, quickly tiptoed around the broken music box, and opened the door. "Oh, Milly," she said, tugging her friend inside. "It's been just awful."

Milly eyed the scattered pieces of china on the floor. "I knew somethin' was wrong. I just knew it when you weren't at the Norwoods' garden party. I've been dyin' to come over, but Mamma's been watchin' me like a hawk for the past couple of weeks. She's still goin' on about you and Chauncy and—" The small brunette paused and scrunched her nose. "My, Delia, you do look dreadful. Have you been cryin'? What on earth has happened?"

Delia ran a hand through her disheveled hair, then clutched her dressing robe closed at the base of her throat. "Sit down, Milly. You're not gonna b'lieve what Grandy's gone and done."

Milly gingerly seated herself on the bed. Her eyes grew wider and wider as Delia relayed the terms of Grandy's agreement.

"No," she whispered as Delia finished. "She wouldn't really do such a thing, would she?"

Delia returned to the window. Pulling back the lacy curtain, she stared out at nothing in particular. "Grandy already has done it. She won't give me a penny till I sign those papers. That's why I couldn't go to the garden party. I didn't have a decent hat to wear."

"You poor dear. That truly *is* awful." Milly gave her a sympathetic look, then stood, walked over, and offered her a hankie. "Here now, don't you fret too much. You know how your grand-mamma is. She'll give up on this silly notion. She always does. Why, Delia, you always get your way in the end."

Delia took the handkerchief and blew her nose. "I don't know, Milly," she said with a shake of her head. "I've done every wicked, nasty thing I could think of. I've thrown one fit after another. I've"—she glanced at the shattered music box—"broken things. Even a stem of Grandy's best crystal. I've refused to leave my room. I haven't dressed or eaten for three days. Nothin' has worked this time. It seems Grandy has her heart set on marryin' me off b'fore I turn twenty-one."

"Delia, have you tried simply talkin' to her?" Milly clasped her hands and pressed them to her breast. "I mean really talkin', not yellin' or anything, just sittin' down and havin' a civil conversation."

"Well, of course I have. I tried that last week." Delia felt a quick renewal of fury at the memory of the discussion. Agatha hadn't budged an inch. "It didn't do a bit a good. She just asked me if I understood that even if I married later on, she wouldn't provide me with a dowry." Delia's chin

quivered, and she folded her arms at her waist.
"I tell you, Milly, she knows she has me cornered
like a fox in a henhouse. I don't know how she
expects me to get by without the means to pur-
chase a new hat now and then."

Milly frowned and twisted her mouth to one
side. "There's got to be somethin' you could do.
What about your daddy? Couldn't he do somethin'?"

"I've already thought about that," Delia said,
then sighed. "I don't know precisely where he is.
And even if I did, it could take months to get a
letter to him. Besides, I truly don't know what he
could do. Grandy *is* my legal guardian."

Milly met her gaze levelly and forced her lips
into a tight line. "Adelaide Abernathy, I've never
in my life known you to back down from your
grandmamma. Now you come on over here and
sit down with me," she said, looping an arm
through Delia's and guiding her to the bed.
"We're just gonna have to put our heads together
and think. There's got to be some way to turn the
tables on Grandy."

Delia and her friend sat side by side in silence.
Delia hadn't thought of turning the tables on
Grandy. She'd been so busy opposing her grandmother, and applying her usual methods of ob-
taining whatever she wanted, that the idea had
simply passed her by.

Pressing her fist to her mouth, she closed her
eyes and considered the terms of the contract. *She
had to marry before her twenty-first birthday. She
could marry the man of her choice. Grandy had to
approve . . .*

Delia opened her eyes. Grandy's blessing. She
had to secure Grandy's blessing. A slow smile

curved her lips. "Milly? What do you think Grandy would do if I presented a no-account for her blessing?"

Milly looked at her askance. "A what?"

"Someone utterly shiftless." Delia swiveled on the bed and grasped her friend's hands. Excitement tickled her insides with the growing concept of thwarting Grandy. "What if I brought the most disreputable lowlife I could find to Grandy for her blessing and claimed to be just madly in love with him? What do you think she'd do?"

Milly blinked and seemed to consider Agatha Abernathy's reaction. "Knowin' your grand-mamma, I'd say she'd faint dead away."

"But she certainly wouldn't approve, would she?" Delia arched an eyebrow. "If I recall, the agreement does state that I can choose my hus-band. Grandy might find herself in quite a di-lemma if I brought her a man of questionable moral fiber and told her I'd have no other. Why, it's liable to cause her so much upset that she might be willin' to retire her efforts on this matter entirely."

Milly bit her bottom lip and nodded thought-fully. "It just might work. There's certainly enough riffraff 'round here. You got somebody particular in mind?"

"No," Delia said as she stood and started to pace back and forth. "Ol' man McGuire couldn't stay sober long enough to play along. Grandy would see through him in a minute. It'll have to be somebody more convincin'." Stopping her stride, she faced Milly and put a finger to her chin. "What about Alphonse Polite's oldest son? The one with curly hair? He's big and handsome. Now *he's* a troublemaker. Lands in jail every Saturday night, I hear.''

Milly made a face. ''He's also feeble-minded. Surely we can come up with a better prospect than that. But you *are* right about him needin' a certain amount of good looks. Otherwise, Grandy would never b'lieve you could honestly—'' Milly's eyes suddenly brightened and glazed over; then, gasping, she pressed a hand to her heart. ''Oh, Delia, I've got it! I don't know why we didn't think of him before!''

''Who?'' Delia asked. Stooping down, she caught her friend's forearms.

Milly looked up, and the smile in her eyes creased her lips. ''Cord,'' she whispered. ''Cord Kibedeaux. Oh, Delia, he'd be perfect.''

Delia straightened slowly and tapped a finger against her lower lip. Consorting with Cord would most certainly cause a sizable scandal—*and* furnish gossip that Grandy couldn't ignore.

Then again, truth be known, Delia had always been a tad curious about Cord Kibedeaux. There seemed to be an air of mystery about him. It might be rather interesting to find out what made such a wicked man tick.

With a lift of her brow, Delia returned her friend's sly smile. ''Why, Milly, I do believe you may have just provided me with the means of completely dissolvin' Grandy's hateful old agreement. By the time I'm done, she might feel obliged to pack me off to Europe herself.''

Cord took a bite of red beans and rice, rocked back in his chair, and propped his bare feet on the porch rail. The late afternoon sun shone eerily through the Spanish moss dangling from the canopy of twisted trees. It was too hot in the house. Though the air was still sultry, it was much cooler here in the shade where the porch overhung the bayou.

He breathed easier outdoors anyway. The two dingy rooms inside held too many bad memories. Too many ghosts floated about, even during the daylight hours.

Focusing on a crawfish that crawled slowly out of a hole on the muddy bank, Cord tried to veer away from thinking of the past. He hadn't returned to Boudreaux Parish to reminisce. *"Mon Dieu,"* he whispered absently and ran a hand through his dark hair. "I knew it was going to be hard to come back here."

But he hadn't known *how* hard until he'd spent his first night in the shanty, heard the voices, relived the pain. He'd taken to sleeping on the porch since then.

He hadn't expected a warm welcome from the people of Boudreaux Parish. He had anticipated the scorn he'd received the first time the Mosely foreman had sent him into town on an errand. Being called white trash hadn't affected him any more than it ever had. He was used to it. He and his parents had been called a hundred such names in a hundred different towns and parishes. And justly so, he reasoned.

Cord couldn't remember ever staying anywhere for longer than a month or two. He and his family had occupied one run-down shack after another. His father's crooked gambling and drunkenness and his mother's mad ravings had stirred up trouble wherever they went. If they weren't moved on by angry owners of neighborhood chicken yards, or by the local sheriff after an epidemic of petty thefts, Cord could always count on being dragged from his bed in the middle of the night the day before the rent was due.

But he wasn't leaving Boudreaux Parish before he got what he'd come for. He was no longer a scared little boy. They could say what they would, do what they would. He wouldn't let them run him out of town . . . not until he knew the truth. Not until Winston Grayson knew the truth.

"Miz Abernathy ain't gonna like dis," the old black man said, then rolled his eyes.

Delia gathered up her full skirt and stepped off the bank into the small, flatbed boat. "Well, if I don't tell anyone and you don't tell anyone, she'll never know, now, will she?"

Remaining on the shore, Samuel shifted his weight, then scratched his ear. "Ah don't know 'bout dis, Miss Delia. If you ax me, you ain't got no bizness goin' down to Blue Moon Bayou. Dey's gaters an' all sorts a bad an' evil—"

"Samuel, will you just hush up," Delia interjected, looking past him and scanning the area. "And get in the skiff before somebody sees us."

The man hunched his shoulders and glanced behind him, then, shaking his gray head, climbed into the boat and took up the pole. "Ah don't know why you wanna go an' do somethin' like dis," he mumbled as he pushed the craft away from the bank. "Mmm, mmm, mmm. Lordy, Lordy. Miz Abernathy finds out, she gonna have me skinned alive."

"Oh, now, Samuel, don't fret so." Leaning forward, Delia placed a hand on his arm. "Everything's gonna be fine, you hear? Just trust me.

My business with Mr. Kibedeaux is most pressin', or I wouldn't have asked for your help."

"Uh-huh." He bobbed his head. "Truss you. Uh-huh. Dat's jus' what you say de las' time you ax me t' do somethin' like dis. Mmm, mmm, mmm. Lordy, Lordy, Lordy."

The small craft cut a slow trail through the duckweed that floated on top of the murky water. Samuel continued to mutter under his breath while Delia kept a lookout for alligators along the bank.

She had probably overdressed, Delia thought as she smoothed her skirt over her knees. Her pale pink day dress couldn't be considered fancy by any means, but it certainly wasn't proper attire for these parts. Of course, she'd been aware of that fact when she'd put it on. She'd purposely worn it, though, because the neckline was becoming and the waist was snug. And the dress *had* gained its share of gentlemen's attention.

Delia nibbled at her lower lip and absently twisted a long blond curl around her finger. She did so hope Cord Kibedeaux liked pink. The outcome of her scheme would depend on him being agreeable. She and Milly had planned everything with the utmost care. Milly was going to spread the rumor that Delia and Cord had been meeting secretly in the Mosely stables ever since Cord's return. Delia would claim the reason she'd been against Grandy's proposal was because she and her Cajun lover had already discussed eloping. She would explain that after considering the matter thoroughly, she'd decided to confess her love for Cord and ask for her grandmother's blessing. Assuredly, Agatha Abernathy could never approve of such a union.

Delia's insistence that only Cord would do, would undoubtedly push Grandy into giving up altogether.

Delia set her sights on the thickening cypress trees and black willows ahead, and smiled. The plan would work as long as Cord played along. And she intended to use every bit of good old Southern charm she owned to make sure that he did.

The winding waterway narrowed, and the late afternoon sunlight faded, peeking sparsely through the vines and Spanish moss overhead. As they floated through the tunnel of vegetation, a sliver of misgivings over what she was about to do, suddenly seeped into Delia.

"Lissen," Samuel whispered, slowing the boat to a halt. He turned to Delia, his eyes wide and worried. "You hear dat?"

Delia furrowed her brow and heard someone faintly humming an eerie tune in the distance.

"Dat ol' witch be out an' about. Ah done tole you we shouldna come down here."

Delia had heard stories all her life about *Tante* Netha Bea. Some said she had been in Blue Moon Bayou forever. Many claimed to have seen her. But spying on *Tante* Netha Bea had been one dare Delia had never taken.

"Ah thinks i's bes' we be gettin' on home. Ain't nothin' good gonna come of dis if we's go any further. Ah gots a bad feelin' in my bones, Miss Delia. A real bad feelin'."

Delia frowned at the man's fearful expression. "You're just bein' superstitious, Samuel. There isn't anything to be afraid of. Why, she just an old Cajun woman, that's all. I'm sure if we don't bother her, she won't bother us none. Now let's get goin' . . . unless you want t' get caught out here after dark.''

Samuel hesitated, then shook his head, picked up the pole, and moved the boat forward.

The humming stopped as they neared a shanty that was set back from the bayou, but the steady creaking of a rocking chair filled the silence.

"Don't even looks at her, Miss Delia,'' Samuel murmured out of one corner of his mouth. ''She might give you de evil eye.''

Delia tried to focus straight ahead. Like a child being told not to do something, though, she couldn't stop her gaze from side-skipping.

The old woman sat rocking in the shadows of the porch, partially hidden by a curtain of gourds, herbs, and dried frogs that hung from the ceiling.

"I see you, *petite fille. Tante* Netha Bea sees you.'' The voice cracked with age and made the hairs on Delia's nape prickle. ''Me, I know where you're goin', yeah. Beware, *chère*. Take care. Meybe you gonna bite off more den you kin chew, *hein?*''

Tante Netha Bea's high-pitched cackle echoed into the bayou, and stayed with Delia long after they'd drifted past the witch's shack. Delia told herself the old woman was crazy. She told herself *Tante* Netha Bea couldn't possibly know what she was up to. Still, Delia couldn't seem to shake the foreboding that settled in the pit of her stomach when the skiff approached the Kibedeaux place.

The gentle swishing of water rousted Cord from his chair. He peered up the bayou and saw a boat coming, but a shroud of Spanish moss and vines made it impossible for him to detect who it was.

Slipping into the house, he closed the door and shuttered the windows, then stood to one side and peeked through a knothole. There were plenty of other Cajun families that lived further down the bayou. The skiff most likely belonged to one of them. But Cord wasn't taking any chances. Whoever had tried to get rid of him before might very well try to do so again. Cord fully intended to face that person—but in his own good time, and not until he had the evidence he needed to clear his name.

He watched the boat round the bend. He was more than a little surprised when a black man pulled it up beside his house and helped a well-dressed white lady onto the porch.

The young, blond woman stood by the railing for a matter of moments, warily assessing the shabby surroundings. Something was slightly familiar about her, but Cord couldn't put his finger on it. Furrowing his brow, he came to the swift conclusion that he'd probably seen her on the streets of Boudreaux Parish at one time or another. As a general rule, though, he didn't pay a lot of attention to ladies from influential families. Women like the one loitering on his porch were like gems in a jewelry-shop window. You glanced at them from the corner of your eye, admiring them as you passed by. Then you never so much as thought about them again. A hired worker didn't openly stare at a gentleman's daughter—not if he knew what was good for him.

And gentle-bred ladies didn't make a habit of

visiting the swamp. *So what the hell was she doing here?*

As if prompted by his impatience, she straightened the pink bow in her hair, then marched to the door and knocked. "Mr. Kibedeaux?" she called out. "Mr. Kibedeaux, are you in there?"

Cord seriously considered not answering. He wanted no trouble. He didn't need any complications interfering with his plans. His past experience in Boudreaux Parish was going to make snooping around difficult enough.

But when the young woman continued to knock and called him by name again, curiosity got the best of him. With reservations, he moved to the door and jerked it open.

"Yeah?" he said, hooking his thumbs in the waistband of his loose-fitting trousers. "What do you want with me, *hein?*"

Her blue eyes widened, and she took a step backward. Just when Cord thought she might turn tail and run, she squared her shoulders and lifted her chin. "I—" Her gaze skipped between his bare chest and his face. "Mr. Kibedeaux, I . . . my name is Adelaide Abernathy."

"Adelaide Abernathy," he repeated. *"The* Adelaide Abernathy?" *The same one whose grandmother owns damn near half of the parish,* he thought with a frown.

Cord knew it was impertinent for him to regard her without restraint. But he couldn't help himself.

Adelaide Abernathy had been a mere child when he'd been sent to prison. As Cord looked into her face, he saw her as she'd looked then— fair and freckled, with her nose perpetually tilted upward. On most of the occasions when he'd had the misfortune of crossing paths with young Chauncy Bateman and his friends, Adelaide Abernathy had been present. She had stood to one side during the confrontations, Cord remembered, fretfully twisting a long golden curl over her shoulder and eyeing him with a mixture of contempt and sympathy. God, how he'd hated her obvious pity.

Cord flexed his jaw, disengaging his thoughts of the past. That was then. This was now. The years had changed them both, it seemed. He'd long since grown callous concerning others' opinions of him. And Adelaide Abernathy had most definitely grown up.

Despite the fact that she still held her small, well-shaped nose at an annoying angle, she had the most perfect, delicate features Cord had ever seen. He'd heard her name spoken in reverent tones since his return. He had to admit, everything they said about her proved true. She had emerged into quite a beauty. Her eyes held a hint of deviltry, while her mouth looked rather vulnerable, and the contrast resulted in a pleasing effect. The seamstress-made dress she wore plainly exhibited the soft, shapely contours of a body that would make the saints sigh. Cord could see now why the locals referred to her as *la belle de Boudreaux Parish*, though he was more confused than ever as to why *la belle* would brave the swamps to seek him out.

She appeared to grow indignant under his scrutiny. Cord narrowed his eyes, purposely increasing the intensity of his stare. Her cheeks flushed with discomfort and she cleared her throat, and Cord figured he was about to find out why she had come. He also had the distinct feeling that whatever the reason for her visit, he wasn't going to like it very much.

Chapter Three

"I'd like to discuss a matter of business with you, if I may," Delia stated bluntly, attempting to keep her gaze from wandering once more over the man's well-formed chest and impressive shoulders. The day she had observed him at a distance from Milly's gazebo, she'd noted he was handsome. But she'd never dreamed he would be so striking at close range.

He was dressed like a hired hand, yet certainly didn't look like one. Nor did he speak like any of the other Cajun workers. Though a trace of accent lingered in his deep, throaty voice and his sentence structure was prominently Acadian, his pronunciation was clear. Then again, as Delia recalled, he'd been tutored during his brief stay at Winston Grayson's.

"Business?" He lifted one slanted, dark brow. "You must have the wrong Kibedeaux. Cleavus, he and his family, they live on down—"

"No. It's you I want." Delia tried to appear calm while she stared up at him. The man's bold appraisal of her when he'd first opened the door had unnerved her. But the way his dark amber eyes searched hers at the moment unsettled her even more. She focused on the raven-black hair curling below his earlobes, then shifted her gaze to his square, proud chin. It irritated her somewhat that his features held a certain arrogance that she had assumed belonged exclusively to the wealthy of Boudreaux Parish.

"I'd like to offer you work," she said, bringing herself around to her purpose.

He shrugged, then crossed his arms over his bare chest and propped a shoulder against the doorjamb. "You come here for nothing, then, mademoiselle. Me, I already have all the work I can handle up at the Moselys' plantation."

"This . . . would be different." Delia clasped her hands at her waist, took a deep breath, then forged onward. "I'd like you to pose as my fiancé."

His eyes glazed and turned a shade darker; then he dropped his thick lashes a notch. "This is a joke, no?"

Delia moistened her lips. She was extremely uncomfortable. By habit, she generally avoided disagreeable predicaments. This was one unpleasant situation, however, she couldn't turn and walk away from. Her plan to silence Grandy's wedding bells had already been set into motion. Milly was presently spreading gossip throughout the town. Delia desperately needed Cord's cooperation.

"Mr. Kibedeaux," she said, putting on her sweetest smile, "I assure you, my proposition is legitimate. All you have to do is to pretend to court me for a few days, possibly a week or two at the most, then stand before my grandmother and ask for my hand in marriage."

His short laugh left a trace of mirth on his face. "And I'm sure your *grand-mère* would like that."

"No. Actually, she wouldn't." The corners of Delia's mouth quivered, threatening to turn her smile into a grimace, but she quickly recovered her charming disposition. "You see, my grandmother is trying to force me into marriage, and I thought she might be reluctant to do so if I brought her . . . well, someone she couldn't possibly approve of."

Heat flushed Delia's cheeks, and she cast her eyes down at the plank boards beneath her feet. The words had come out all wrong. She hadn't meant for them to sound so condescending. Regretfully, she looked up at Cord, but found his reaction something other than she'd expected.

Amusement shone bright in his eyes, though it neglected to reach his mouth. *"Non,"* he said softly. "I do not think this would be a good thing for me to do. Not—" His gaze roved leisurely downward over the curves of her body. "Not that such a prospect wouldn't be . . . interesting."

"But I could pay you well," Delia said. Then, on impulse, she cocked her head and slowly ran a fingertip along the neckline of her dress. Such suggestive little motions had worked wonders on disagreeable young gentlemen in the past. "I could pay you very well," she repeated in a candy-coated voice and lowered her lashes for effect.

"Oui, I bet you could." One side of Cord's face lifted in a mocking grin. With a deep chuckle, he snaked an arm around her waist, fitting her snugly against his hard torso.

Delia swallowed a gasp. Bracing her hand in the middle of his chest, she eyed him cautiously and fought to control the frantic beat of her heart. He was merely calling her bluff, she told herself.

"Precisely how much would you pay, mademoiselle?" he asked, narrowing his devil-tinged eyes. *"Hein?* How much?"

Delia opened her mouth, then closed it. He'd played his card. It was her turn. But for reasons beyond her, her brain couldn't settle on a sensible answer.

"Well?" Cord persisted. "How much?" He dragged his thumb back and forth over the buttons at the base of her spine, making Delia tremble inside. "You would pay a great deal, no?"

"Yes, a great deal," Delia replied in a hoarse whisper, then cleared her throat, forcing herself to relax. She could win this game, she determined, if she remained calm and kept her wits. "I'll pay you . . . oh, say one-fifth of my inheritance," she said curtly. "Would that be fair?"

"Ah, *chère,* you disappoint me. You speak only of money, when you have so much more to offer." Cord shrugged, expelling a long sigh. "I must admit, I expected you to entice me with the promise of your precious virtue. But no. You do not even offer your kisses as a reward."

"Well, I—" Delia glanced to the side. "I s'pose . . . in addition to our financial arrangement . . . well, I s'pose you *could* kiss me from time to time."

"From time to time?" Cord tucked his chin.

Delia lifted one shoulder. "How 'bout if . . . if I allowed you to kiss me anytime you wanted? Would that do?"

"Hmm." Cord fixed his gaze on her mouth and furrowed his brow in concentration. "Me, I like kissing beautiful women, yes," he stated bluntly.

"But how would I know whether or not your kisses are worth my time and trouble, *hein*? Should I not sample what you offer before I make my decision?"

Delia stared up at him. The palm she held against his naked chest grew moist with perspiration. Part of her—the wicked part that generally pushed her past the line of propriety—awakened to the thrill of kissing this Cajun convict. The suffocating heat of the day suddenly became warmer, and she unconsciously wet her lips. "I don't b'lieve there'd be any harm in grantin' you that small request, Mr. Kibedeaux," she murmured. "I mean, after all, this is a business deal, isn't it? Nobody buys a mule without first checkin' his teeth . . ." Her voice trailed off, and she blushed with embarrassment at her choice of words.

Cord's eyes met hers briefly, then dropped once again to her mouth. "Ah, *chère*, you do tempt me. I am sure you would taste sweeter than the finest crop of sugar cane, but—" He shook his head decisively, and released her so abruptly that she teetered on her heels. "*Non.* You could not pay me enough, mademoiselle. Me, I have too many worries of my own, you see. I do not need the whole of Boudreaux Parish hunting my hide."

Delia could feel a wave of humiliation burn into her cheeks that filled her with undiluted fury. Balling her hands into fists at her sides, she charged toward him. "Of all the gall," she ground out between her teeth. "Yoooou . . . dirty, pigheaded . . . river rat! How dare you—"

"*Adieu*, mademoiselle," Cord retorted, then ducked into the shadows of the house and shut the door.

"Open up!" Delia shouted. "You hear me? You

get yourself back out here this instant. I'm not
through talkin' to you!''

''Perhaps not, *chère,* but I am through talking
to you.'' Cord raised his voice just enough for her
to hear, as he propped a chair beneath the doorknob. ''You go. Go home,'' he added. ''Do what
your *grand-mère* asks. A woman like you *should*
marry. A good husband would keep you from doing crazy things like coming to the bayou alone.''

Ignoring the woman's insults and the pounding at his door, Cord seated himself at the table
and poured a glass of wine. He toasted his judgment in turning the high-and-mighty Adelaide
Abernathy down. She was spoiled and demanding, a perfect example of the affluent of Boudreaux Parish. She represented a breed of people
who thought they were gods. Adelaide Abernathy and her kind treated people of less fortunate means like puppets. They sat upon their fat
rumps in their cozy, comfortable homes and expected everyone else to jump whenever they
snapped their fingers. And *la belle de Boudreaux
Parish* was no exception. She was no doubt accustomed to having her way.

Well, not this time, Cord vowed silently, and
filled his glass once more. He wouldn't perform
dog tricks for Adelaide Abernathy. He had more
important things to do. *Much more important,* he
mused, trying to turn his thoughts to Winston
Grayson.

But Cord found it terribly hard to concentrate
on such matters with the woman pacing back and
forth across his porch. He had consumed almost
half the bottle of wine before the pacing outside
died down, and finally ceased.

Slightly light-headed from the wine, Cord rose

and made his way to the window just in time to see Mademoiselle Abernathy climb into the waiting skiff. He watched the boat round the bend, then stepped out onto the porch. Lighting a cheroot, he inhaled deeply and blew the smoke out in slow measures.

"You can come out now, *Tante* Netha Bea," he called loudly, scanning the swampland to the right of his property. "I know you're there. You might as well come sit with me a spell." At the lack of a response, he added, "I have some good red beans and rice."

Tante Netha Bea seemed to materialize out of thin air, hobbling from the camouflage of twisted vines and trees. Cord gave her a hand up onto the porch, then helped her into a chair.

"I suppose you heard everything, *hein?*" he asked, placing the crooked stick that served as her cane within her reach.

Netha Bea scrunched her nose, emphasizing the legion of wrinkles that lined her face. "I hear you say you got red beans and rice, yeah."

Cord smiled and flicked his cheroot into the murky water of the bayou. He walked into the house, then returned momentarily with a bowl. As she wrapped her long bony fingers around the dish, *Tante* Netha Bea looked at him from beneath the folds of the shawl covering her head, and her black eyes sparkled. "I heard," she whispered. "Me, I hear tings before dey are spoken, you know."

Cord propped a hip on the rail, hooking his thumbs in the waistband of his trousers. "That Abernathy woman, she is crazy, no?"

"*Non.* Is you who is crazy, *T-boo.*" *Tante* Netha

Bea bobbed her head up and down, then took a bite of beans.

"Me?" Cord tucked his chin. "Why do you say that?"

"You should not have been so quick to send dat woman away, *cher.* You should have agreed to what she wanted you to do."

Cord chuckled and shifted his weight. "Oh, yeah. I should give Boudreaux Parish one more reason to hang me, *hein?*"

"*Mais oui.* How else you gonna find out what you want to know?"

Cord eyed the old woman skeptically. Though *Tante* Netha Bea often spoke in riddles, she generally had a good point hidden in her words. Upon occasion, she could be persuaded to elaborate, but only if moved to do so. "Sometimes," he said with a grin, "I think you truly are the *couillon* witch they say you are, instead of the *traiteur*, the healer, you claim to be."

"*Pooyie!*" Netha Bea exclaimed, then rolled off a string of Cajun curses. Composing herself somewhat, she shook her spoon at him. "Me, I'm no crazy witch, so you don't say dat no more, you hear? When you was a little boy, and I find you in the swamp crying, did I not take you to my house and heal your cuts and bruises? And those times your *mère*, she make you scared wit all those bad, wicked tales, did I not tell you dey was not true, *hein?*" Erecting her hunched shoulders, she squinted at him. "You lissen at me, *T-boo*. You lissen good. Did I not tell you once dat you did not belong here in the bayou? All you seek lies within the walls of those *grandes maisons*. Dat *jolie fille* who comes here to see you, she could help you, yeah. She offers you a way to walk among the ones who have the answers you want.''

Cord stared at *Tante* Netha Bea, absorbing what she said. There was a certain amount of shrewdness in her logic. He'd already come to the conclusion that whoever had framed him must have been influential enough to move about Winston Grayson's bank freely. Netha Bea's counsel made sense. Adelaide Abernathy *could* open doors that would otherwise be closed to him.

''Ahh.'' *Tante* Netha Bea nodded. ''I see you think about this, *hein? Ça c'est bon.* I am right, you know. Good tings will happen if you do this, *cher.*'' The old woman came closer to smiling than she ever had, and winked. ''I see *amour* in your future, *T-boo. Beaucoup d'amour.*''

''Love?'' Cord shook his head and laughed. ''Now I know for sure you are *couillon.* There could never be anything between me and Adelaide Abernathy—if that's what you're insinuating.''

''*Comment ça se fait?*''

''Because.'' Cord spread his arms wide and glanced around, amazed they were having this absurd discussion. ''Because Adelaide Abernathy is who she is, and I am who I am. That's why.''

''*Non.*'' *Tante* Netha Bea leaned forward and narrowed her eyes. ''You are not what you appear to be. I tell you this many times, *cher,* and still you do not lissen.''

Cord felt the muscles in his jaw tighten. Netha Bea had played this game before. He knew she wanted him to press her for answers now, but he deliberately refrained from doing so. She would only end up talking in circles again. Leaning back against the post that supported the roof of the porch, he crossed his arms and grinned. "Maybe I don't listen because I truly believe what they say about you being crazy."

Tante Netha Bea grasped her cane and pushed herself up out of the chair. "Me, I'm gonna go home now. You call me *couillon* two more times, yeah. You gonna talk like dat, *T-boo,* I'm gonna go home and pray the rosary for you."

Cord helped *Tante* Netha Bea from the porch despite her sharp protests. In her present mood, he didn't tell her that he didn't think the rosary would do him much good.

While he watched her disappear into the thicket of black willows, he tried hard to make sense of her prattle.

He had a hunch she knew more about his parents' death than she would admit. He also had an inkling that she had some insight about what had happened at the bank. But every time he had approached either subject, she had simply told him he must look for the truth himself.

Cord rubbed the back of his neck. He would not only look for the truth, he swore once more, he would find it. Though *Tante* Netha Bea had been vague, he supposed in her own way she was trying to aid him in his search. The old woman's idea to use Adelaide Abernathy as a means for Cord to move about the circle of society was worth considering. Perhaps he and *la belle de Boudreaux Parish* could do business after all. Perhaps they *could* make a fair trade.

"He up and closed the door right in my face, Milly." Delia stopped pacing long enough to light the lamp atop her bureau. A warm yellow glow chased the evening shadows from the room while she regarded her friend sitting on the edge of the bed. "Can you believe it? He closed the door in *my* face. He didn't even give me a chance to bat my lashes."

Milly shifted her weight and frowned. "Oh, dear," she said in a small voice. "This is just awful, Delia. Why, I've already told Cynthia all about the two of you. And you know how *she* is about tellin' everything she knows. I went all over town today, makin' snide comments about you and Cord Kibedeaux. Anyone who cared to listen could've heard." Milly pressed her fingertips to her cheeks and lifted her worried, red-rimmed eyes. "Oh, Delia, what are we going to do? I just never once thought about Cord turnin' you away."

"Neither did I," Delia said, then twisted her mouth and plopped down next to Milly. Bracing an elbow on her knee, she cupped her chin. "I still can't figure out where I went wrong."

Milly mimicked her friend's pose and was thoughtful for a moment. "You did smile at him, didn't you? I mean, not just your ordinary smile, Delia. You *did* try the one that usually has every male in the parish fallin' at your feet, didn't you?"

"Oh, I tried it, all right. It just didn't work this time. I even hinted that I might be willin' to barter my virtue for his effort."

Milly widened her brown eyes. "Delia, you didn't! You couldn't have promised—"

"Oh, calm down, Milly. You know I'd never actually do such a thing. Besides, when it got down to it, I only offered to let him kiss me whenever he wanted."

Milly's face paled. "Gracious," she murmured beneath her breath. "What did he say to that?"

Delia looked away. "I don't really want to discuss it, other than to say it was the most humiliatin' moment of my entire life."

"Well, I hope so," Milly remarked in a scolding tone. "Delia, you shouldn't tempt men like Cord Kibedeaux. He's different. He's . . . well, he's no gentleman. He's liable to insist you keep any bargain you make."

Delia smiled limply and patted Milly's hand. "I don't want you frettin' anymore about this, you hear? I got myself into this mess, and I'll get myself out of it."

Milly looked skeptical. "How?"

"I don't know yet." Delia sighed, then glanced at the ceiling. "But I'm bound to come up with a way by mornin' to change the man's mind. There has to be *somethin'* Cord Kibedeaux wants . . . somethin' that would convince him it might be in his best interest to go along with this."

Feigning a brightness of spirit for her friend, she raised her brow. "It's gettin' late. You'd best get on home b'fore your mamma comes lookin' for you."

Delia rose from the bed, looped her arm through Milly's, and walked her to the door. "Don't you worry none," she said as Milly stepped into the hall. "I'll think of somethin'."

Delia closed the door, leaned her head back against it, then let the cheerfulness she'd worn for Milly slip away. The town gossips were probably already spreading the rumors Milly had conjured up. The firecracker had been lit and the fuse was short. Delia didn't have much time left.

Moving away from the door, she sighed again. She had suspected Cord might be a little hard to persuade, but she hadn't been prepared for him to turn her down flat. Nor had she expected him to play havoc with her feelings.

Delia crossed the room and snatched a nightgown from her drawer. She was just going to have to set her mind to work, she decided. She would show Cord Kibedeaux whom he was dealing with. One way or another, she'd get even with him for embarrassing her as he had. By the time she was through with him, he'd be on his knees begging her to kiss him.

Without waiting for Bess to help her undress, she changed into her nightclothes, then sat down at her dresser and picked up her brush. She stared at herself in the looking glass and absently stroked her long, thick hair over one shoulder. Other men found her attractive. How could Cord have been so unaffected? she wondered. Why, most any of the gentlemen in Boudreaux Parish would have jumped at the chance to escort her about town for a few days.

Then again, as Milly had pointed out, Cord was certainly no gentleman.

Delia stilled her brush and narrowed her eyes pensively. She'd show him, all right. Tomorrow when she visited him, she'd wear a lower-cut dress. She would be an unmerciful flirt. She would run her fingertips up and down his arm. Before she was done, she'd have him purring like—

A sharp tap at the window disrupted Delia's thoughts. She turned toward the sound and listened harder. She was about to decide the wind had stirred a branch on the tree just outside when a small object struck the pane again.

Rising from her dresser stool, she cautiously crossed the room and peeked through the gap in the lacy curtains. Cord Kibedeaux stood below, the moonlight slanting across his upturned face.

Delia's hope climbed. Had he decided to accept her offer? Her heart picked up a furious pace as she hurriedly opened the window and leaned out. Lifting her chin a tad, she took care to appear annoyed rather than quite so anxious. "What on earth are you doin' here?" she whispered.

Cord dropped the handful of pebbles he held and quirked one corner of his mouth. "Me, I have been thinking, you know, about the business you spoke of this afternoon." He paused, then reached up and scratched his ear. "I think perhaps we can strike a bargain after all."

"A bargain?" Delia eyed his handsome features and felt her stomach quiver. "What kind of bargain?"

"Come out here and we will talk, *hein*?"

Delia curled her fingers around the windowsill, wondering how she could have ever thought of trifling with the man. Even from this distance she sensed something dangerous about him. She'd probably be safer locked in a closet for hours with Chauncy Bateman and his six hands than she would be alone for five minutes in the dark with Cord Kibedeaux.

"Of course, if you have changed your mind—" Instead of finishing the sentence, he merely waved a hand, then turned as if to leave.

"No! No," Delia said, a little more urgently than she would have liked. "I'll . . . be right down." Clutching her robe closed at the throat, she leaned forward to shut the window and frowned down at him. "How did you know this was my room?"

"I guessed," he answered with a slight grin. "Me, I just looked for the frilliest curtains. And when I see yours, I say to myself, this must be the one, no?"

Chapter Four

D elia slipped quietly out the servants' entrance with a tiny fluttering inside her abdomen. Apprehension seeped into her bones, making her footsteps drag as she made her way to the garden. For the first time in her life, she actually found herself weighing the outcome of her devil-may-care behavior. Always before, she'd merely acted on impulse. Worry over the consequences of her misdeeds had hardly ever bothered her. Although remorse occasionally reared its ugly head during one of Grandy's tongue-lashings, Delia's guilt never lasted long. But this current situation was a far more serious one than she'd ever found herself in before.

What, she wondered, did Cord Kibedeaux want in exchange for his cooperation? Had he taken more notice of her flirtatious ploy this afternoon than she had originally assumed?

She hesitated at the edge of the high-hedged garden. Wrapping her robe more securely around her, she hugged her ribs. What if Cord demanded more than a few kisses? And suppose he expected some sort of token payment—perhaps a demonstration of her willingness to go through with her part of the bargain . . .

"I was beginning to think you had changed your mind."

Delia flinched at the soft caress of his voice behind her. She whirled and skittered away from him.

Moonlight sloped across his dark, sculptured features, and Delia's heart picked up a frantic rhythm.

"I do not think we should talk here in the open," he suggested, glancing toward the house. "The moon is so bright tonight. Someone could see us. Come." He gestured for her to precede him into the maze of tall shrubbery. "We will move further into the garden, no?"

Delia stood rooted to the spot, eyeing him warily. "We can talk here," she replied with a slight inclination of her chin.

He quirked one corner of his mouth, though she couldn't tell whether he was smiling or smirking.

"Look, *chère* . . . me, I have no wish to be caught here in the middle of the night with you. If you want to talk, we will go into the garden, where no one can see us. If not, I will leave, *hein?*"

Delia opened her mouth, then shut it tightly. She wasn't accustomed to hired hands giving her ultimatums. But in this case, the man was right. A light shone from her grandmother's bedroom. Grandy often sat by the window late at night reading, and she might look out and see them.

Delia shifted her attention to Cord and took a deep breath. She had fended off advances from half the male population in Boudreaux Parish. If

Cord Kibedeaux tried to exercise his virility, she would very simply slap the fire out of him. "Very well," she said, then turned and started down the hedge-lined path.

He fell in step beside her, taking long, graceful strides. He did not attempt to touch her, yet his overpowering presence made her skin tingle just as surely as if he had.

"You are afraid of me, no?" His deep, vibrant voice broke the monotony of bullfrogs croaking from the lily pond in the center of the garden.

Delia looked at him askance, barely managing to keep her pace steady. The man was irritatingly arrogant, considering his shabby clothes. "No, of course not," she replied in a crisp, even tone.

In truth, she was at this moment more angry than afraid. She couldn't shake the memory of the way he'd held her, the way he'd taunted her into promising him kisses just so he could refuse her offer. After a few more steps, she stopped in her tracks and pivoted toward him, placing a hand on her hip. "Is this far enough?"

He surveyed the secluded surroundings briefly, then cocked his head and lifted one broad shoulder. "It will do, I suppose."

Cord took in Adelaide Abernathy's sparsely lit features, focusing on her pouty lower lip. She *was* afraid, he decided. She tried to hide it, but he detected alarm in her eyes, just beneath the surface of her glare. He had witnessed the same look in others' eyes often enough to recognize it for what it was.

For some bizarre reason, he was struck with the urge to assure this woman that even if he tried, he could never be able to reach the level of wickedness attached to his reputation.

"Well?" Obviously growing impatient, she shifted from one small slippered foot to the other. "You said something about a bargain."

Cord tried to ignore the odd commotion going on inside his chest, and shoved his hands into his pockets. "If you still wish me to pretend to be your fiancé, I will do so."

Delia narrowed her eyes suspiciously. "This afternoon you told me you wanted no part of any of this. May I ask why you've decided to take my offer?"

Cord shrugged again. "Me, I have always been poor, you know? I would like to see how the other half lives. You have promised to pay me well. Perhaps with the money, I will invest in my own business. Maybe I will meet someone within the circle of your rich friends who will want to make an added investment, *hein?*"

Delia almost sighed. Not one mention of kisses. He wanted money and prestige, not her virtue. She scanned his expression for alternative motives, but observed nothing more than honesty in his low-lidded amber eyes. Her wariness of him ebbed, giving way to another, stronger feeling that she couldn't quite assess. Something close to excitement filled her at the thought of secretly conspiring with this handsome convict. It was almost as if she were about to cross some imaginary boundary from which there might be no escape.

She couldn't suppress the thrum of her heart. She loved taking chances, and this was bigger than anything she'd ever dared do before. "I'll pay you five thousand dollars as soon as our little undertakin' is over and done with," she announced with a faint curve of her lips. "The rest

I'll have delivered to you in payments on a monthly basis. Will that be agreeable?''

Cord merely nodded, then spread his arms wide. "So. When do we begin this charade?''

Delia put a finger to her chin and considered the matter for a moment. "We need to be seen together as soon as possible,'' she said. "Are you familiar with the grove of live oaks beside the crossroads?''

"*Oui*, I know the place.''

"Good. You meet me there, say . . . oh, half-past ten tomorrow mornin'. I'll make up some excuse to assure no one accompanies me, and I'll drive the lightweight buggy myself. We can discuss the details of our agreement a little more thoroughly on our way to town.''

Cord inclined his head, and Delia eyed him carefully, hoping she wouldn't regret engaging the man for her purpose. His good looks alone would no doubt be enough to convince Grandy that her granddaughter had lost her heart.

"Tomorrow mornin', then, Mr. Kibedeaux.'' Delia assessed him from head to toe once more, then turned and started toward the house. "Mind you're not late, now,'' she called over her shoulder.

A slow grin emerged on Cord's face as he watched her leave.

With little time to spare the next morning, Delia raised the hem of her blue silk hoopskirt and hurried down the wide, curved staircase. Stopping at the landing, she straightened her matching bonnet, then held her breath and attempted to tiptoe past the open door of the library, where, as usual, Grandy would be going over the accounts.

"Adelaide?"

Delia froze in the middle of the doorway, her sharp intake of air a bit more than her stays would allow. Bracing a hand against her corset, she swiveled toward her grandmother and smiled innocently. "Good mornin', Grandy."

Seated behind her formidable desk, Agatha surveyed Delia's attire with a glimmer of approval in her keen gray eyes. "You're lookin' suspiciously well today, dear," she commented. "Are you goin' somewhere?"

"Why . . . yes. Yes, I am." Delia clutched her reticule to her waist, straightened her shoulders, and relaxed her stiff smile. "I thought I might have the buggy hitched . . . and go over to fetch Milly . . . and take some air. It's a beautiful mornin' for a ride, don't you agree?"

Expressionless, Grandy leaned back in her chair and ran her knuckles along the underside of her chin.

Delia focused on the parquetry floor to avoid her grandmother's scrutiny. "Well, um . . . I'd best be on my way," she remarked in a light tone, then cleared her throat. "Milly's expectin' me."

"Just a moment, Adelaide." Grandy's command foiled Delia's hasty getaway. Agatha leaned forward, picked up her quill, dipped it in her inkwell, then scratched a figure in the open ledger on her desk. "It's good to see you up and about," she said, concentrating on her accounts. "Since you seem to have forsaken your foul mood, I assume this means you've decided to heed my wishes. Am I correct?"

"Yes, Grandy." Delia glanced around the room.

"Good." Agatha made a slight gesture with her

hand, silently dismissing her granddaughter. "You and Milly have a nice visit, then, dear," she said idly.

Dallying with Grandy had delayed Delia. She arrived at the grove of live oaks some ten minutes later than she had intended. As she pulled back on the reins, slowing the buggy, she noted that Cord was nowhere in sight. She was harboring the worrisome thought that perhaps he'd grown tired of waiting when a man she hardly recognized stepped from the thicket of trees.

"Bon jour." Cord removed his gray stovepipe and swept into a low bow. One corner of his mouth curved upward as he straightened. "It is a pleasant morning, is it not?" he asked, lifting a hand toward the blue sky and sunshine.

Delia was incapable of replying. Her gaze slid from the black scarf tie he wore, down the front of his gray brocaded vest, and landed on highly polished boots.

As if he read her mind, he caught hold of the lapels of his long black frock coat. "What do you think, *hein?* My friend Papite, his wife takes in laundry and mending. She says the gentlemen she borrowed these from will not miss them for a week or so."

Delia met his whiskey-colored eyes and blinked. "You look just fine," she said, rather than granting him the compliment he obviously expected. Actually, she thought he was overly handsome. Dressed as he was, he could easily have passed for one of the prominent gentlemen who resided on Clio Street in New Orleans. But she didn't dare say so. She didn't hold with encouraging hired help to be prideful.

Pushing down her skirt she scooted over on the buggy seat and patted the space beside her. "Well? Climb on up here and take these reins. We don't have time to dillydally. The mornin' rush at the coffeehouse is gonna be thinnin' out if we don't hurry."

Cord's expression turned cold. He remained where he was for several long moments, staring up at her, unnerving her, with a hard glint in his eyes.

Then, in a sudden swift movement, he hopped up onto the seat next to her and took the reins. The horse and buggy lurched into motion at his command, jarring Delia backward, then forward.

Cord's breakneck pace tossed Delia about unmercifully. Fighting to keep the hem of her skirt from flying up and revealing an indecent amount of her pantalets, she aimed a deadly glare at her escort.

"Stop it!" she shouted. "Stop it this very instant, do you hear?"

Cord gave her a sidelong glance, then pulled back on the reins. He was hard put to withhold the smile tugging at the corners of his mouth when *la belle de Boudreaux Parish* turned her wrath upon him.

The effect of her fury was damaged by the fact that her bonnet was askew and a curl that earlier had been carefully placed now fell over one eye.

"Just what is the meanin' of this?" she asked in a breathless voice, shoving the hair off her flushed face. "Goodness gracious sakes alive, whatever is the matter with you? Are you tryin' to kill us or somethin'?"

Projecting an air of innocence, Cord arched a

brow. "You said we were in a hurry, did you not?"

She opened her mouth, then clamped her lips into a bitter line and pierced him with a look that would have made the saints tremble. As if no longer able to bear the sight of him, she swiftly devoted her attention to repairing her disarrayed appearance. "You know full well," Delia said as she jerked her bonnet into its proper place, "that I never intended for you to go chargin' off like a bat outta hell."

Cord laid a hand over his heart and feigned a most humble expression. "Mademoiselle, if I have offended you, I—"

"You *have*. Oh, you most certainly have! So . . . so you'd just best continue at a more respectable pace. Do you hear?"

"*Oui*," Cord answered with a lift of his shoulder. He flicked the reins, coaxing the mare into a gentle trot.

Delia set her nose at a decidedly superior angle. "From now on, I suggest you conduct yourself in a gentlemanly manner whenever or wherever we are. Do I make myself clear?"

"But of course."

Delia eyed him skeptically, inclined to believe he was actually patronizing her. Then again, he wouldn't dare. Surely a man like him—a hired hand, a common thief—would know his place.

Her gaze skipped over his remarkable profile to the pleats of his crisp white shirt, and a sudden, disconcerting thought struck her. In his present finery, Cord appeared as gallantly charming as any well-to-do plantation owner. And it wasn't just his tasteful clothing that gave him the illusion of being a Southern gentleman. There was something about the way he carried himself, something in the way he held his head, that produced an air of importance. Something blatantly undeniable, which Grandy's keen, steely gaze couldn't miss—that special quality that made a lady's heart flutter. Agatha Abernathy did so pride herself on first impressions. What if she were honestly taken with him?

Delia nibbled her bottom lip and stared at the marshy terrain rolling past the buggy as it went by her in a blur. The notion was completely absurd, she assured herself. Her grandmother might be swayed by Cord's appearance at first, but would certainly recognize his name upon introduction and recall his unsavory reputation. Grandy couldn't very well overlook his background, and would surely object to welcoming someone so disreputable into the family.

Brushing the matter aside, Delia surveyed Cord once more. In any event, his attractiveness would work to her advantage. Those fetching whiskey-brown eyes would prove very convincing indeed. By the time Delia added her portrayal of a lovesick female, Grandy could have no doubt that her granddaughter was completely devoted to the notorious Cord Kibedeaux. It would be up to Cord, of course, to supply the finishing touches, by assuming the role of the totally besotted beau.

Determined he should play his part most persuasively, Delia broached the subject with conviction. "Mr. Kibedeaux," she said, then waited for him to look at her. When he did, she found it greatly disturbing that she couldn't keep her gaze steady. She ended up focusing on her hands, which were folded in her lap. "Mr. Kibedeaux, I . . . I take it you've had some experience in . . . in *courtin'*."

One corner of his mouth quivered slightly. "Some."

Delia nodded, then cleared her throat. "Good. Well, then, I s'pose I needn't tell you that it is *vitally* important that my grandmother thinks we're . . . well, that she thinks you are just completely smitten with me. You do understand, don't you?"

"*Oui*, I understand."

"I mean, that is what I hired you for, you know. And if you show the slightest indication—any at all—that you don't truly care for me, Grandy will see right through you. She's very perceptive."

The sound of turning buggy wheels filled a long silence. Delia peered sideways at the man next to her, but couldn't decipher his thoughts. He was staring straight ahead, as if he'd removed himself from her presence.

With a startling suddenness he looked at Delia, regarding her with such intensity that she automatically eased away from him.

"Mademoiselle, no matter what you may have heard about me, know this—when I make a bargain, I honor it." Without warning, he reached out and laid a hand over hers, still clasped in her lap. "You may rest assured I will not fail you. I will play my part so well that your *grand-mère* will not for a single instant doubt my undying affection. You can expect satisfaction for the amount you are paying me. This I promise you."

He withdrew his hand from hers and returned his attention to guiding the horse along the lane that led to town. But the warmth of his touch lingered on Delia's fingertips and, after gradually trailing up her arms, settled in the center of her chest.

She couldn't name precisely what it was he'd done or said that produced the odd sensation inside her. She certainly hadn't anticipated integrity from an ex-convict. Maybe it was the sincerity in his voice that had moved her. Or perhaps she simply wanted to believe him because, rather than the sins of his past, she'd glimpsed hurt and loneliness in the depths of his eyes. Whatever the reason, she had the distinct impression that he *would* keep his word.

Delia watched Cord from the corner of her eye as they approached the edge of town. He was going to work out nicely, she decided, even though he seemed a bit uneasy at the moment. He sat beside her in a stiff, straight-backed, almost regal pose, appearing not to notice the reactions of the people they passed.

Delia, however, was all too aware of them. With somewhat mixed emotions, she observed the quick change of expression in the pedestrians' eyes as they flickered from her to her companion, then widened in surprise or dismay. Smiles rapidly vanished. Hands raised in greeting froze in midair. Usually Delia reveled in seeing these familiar faces register shock. But this morning, something that resembled annoyance towered above the satisfaction she'd always gained from her mischief-making.

She glanced Cord's way again and saw that he'd lifted his chin a notch higher and tightened his jaw. She hadn't considered how her ploy might affect him. Boudreaux Parish was a quaint town, fashioned according to the charming influence of New Orleans, though on a much smaller scale. With the exception of a single gaming hall, it lacked the larger city's sinful vices. The wealthy resided on cypress-shaded lanes and sugar plantations, in stately homes blending French and Spanish architecture. Distinguished inhabitants of the community dealt cordially with one another, and often looked the other way whenever misdemeanors were committed by one of their own. Yet the good citizens had preconceived ideas of the manner in which the world should be conducted. They possessed no tolerance for unruly slaves or troublesome members of the impoverished families from the bayou. Any lower-class offender was never forgiven, his crime never forgotten.

Delia could only speculate about the level of Cord's anxiety over escorting her in public view today. Outwardly, he appeared to handle the open contempt with a quiet dignity. Her suspicion that he wasn't nearly as composed as he wanted everyone to think made her slip a hand into the crook of his arm.

His muscles flinched beneath her touch. His amber gaze darted first to her fingers clutching his elbow, then to her eyes.

Delia responded to his perplexed expression with a smile. His lips began a slow curve upward. But she didn't know if he actually produced a full-fledged smile, because she was suddenly distracted by a short, stout, elderly woman leaving Sedberry's Millinery Shop.

''Mornin', Miz Pixley,'' Delia called out in a singsong tone.

The woman looked up, blinked, then placed a hand over her heart. Just for spite, Delia waved and scooted closer to Cord, causing Molly Pixley, one of Grandy's oldest and dearest friends, to re- act as though she'd swallowed a whole, unri- pened persimmon.

Chapter Five

Faldene's Coffee Shoppe buzzed with activity nearly every weekday morning. Styled after the cafes in New Orleans' Vieux Carré, Faldene's mainly attracted prominent plantation owners, local merchants, and slave traders.

Unescorted ladies wouldn't dare set foot in the establishment, but Delia had spent many enjoyable evenings in the rear gaming rooms. When the stakes were high, she'd never had a problem finding a willing gentleman to accompany her.

The rich aroma of coffee and sweet buns met Cord and Delia on the sidewalk outside. Grasping his elbow securely, she stepped through the door and displayed a smug attitude toward the people who paused in conversation. She didn't miss the heads turning as Cord led her to a vacant corner table. For her acquaintances' benefit, she aimed a warm smile over her shoulder at Cord while he pulled out her chair and seated her.

She noted then that her companion wore a dark expression. The sober arrangement of his features didn't waver when he sat down opposite her. His chin and shoulders remained at a prideful angle.

Anyone else in the room might have mistaken his rigid pose for arrogance, but Delia could almost feel the thick wall of tension surrounding him.

Ignoring the whispers and subtle nods cast in their direction, she reached across the table and laid her hand over his. Beneath her palm, his fingers curled into a tight fist. Then his hooded gaze met hers.

He regarded her in a manner that gave her a sudden chill and made her instantly withdraw her hand. She'd noticed this same look before during their few meetings. It was as if a wire netting veiled his eyes—a barrier he called forth, she suspected, not only to preserve his outward composure, but also to obstruct any glimpse of his true demeanor.

Yet Delia observed something else lingering behind his cold facade: a deep-rooted, ever-present sorrow that flickered now and then, despite his attempt to keep it hidden. The glimmer of pain in his eyes mesmerized her, held her prisoner, even though she longed to look away.

She nearly sighed in relief when a black waiter appeared at their table and diverted her attention. Lifting her gaze to the man, she pasted an overzealous pleasantness on her face. "Good mornin', Ira."

"Mornin', Miz Abernathy," Ira replied with a bob of his gray head, giving her a wide, bright grin. "We ain't gots no mo' king cake leff—I knows dat be yor favorites, but we gots a molasses muffin or two still warm from de oven."

"B'lieve I'll just have me a cup of *café brûlot*, Ira."

"Yes'm," he said with a nod, then looked at

Cord. "And what you gonna be wantin' this fine mornin', suh?"

The waiter's question temporarily interrupted Cord's study of Mademoiselle Abernathy. "Warmed sling, *s'il vous plait*," he answered absently, his mind preoccupied with how the woman across from him could alter her mood so quickly. Within the span of a heartbeat, she had changed from appearing wide-eyed and vulnerable to behaving like the typical Louisiana belle, bubbling over with Southern charm.

After Ira had ambled off to fill their order, Cord braced his forearm on the table, eyeing his beautiful companion thoughtfully. "Mademoiselle—"

"Delia," she said, then glanced around, leaned forward, and added in a whisper, "You must call me *Delia* if we're ever going to pull this off. All my dearest friends do."

Cord focused on the licentious painting adorning the wall behind her. He stared with an unnatural lack of interest at the trio of scantily clad, voluptuous women dancing in a circle. "Very well. *Delia*." Dropping his gaze to *la belle de Boudreaux Parish*, he dragged his knuckles along the underside of his chin. "It seems we have caused quite a disturbance here this morning, have we not?"

"Oh, I do b'lieve we have." A genuine smile curved her lips, and her blue eyes twinkled.

Her pleased attitude puzzled Cord. Either she actually enjoyed flaunting him as her disreputable beau, or she was a very good actress. Perhaps both. "Then this"—he made a subtle gesture toward the obvious scowls that surrounded them—"this, *chère*, is what you wanted to happen, *hein*? Forgive me, but I cannot imagine why you would wish to create such a scandal. Are you not worried you will tarnish your reputation?"

Delia laughed. "Oh, but you see, everybody hereabouts expects this sort of behavior from me. It's my nature. Of course, they all know my"— she cocked her eyes to the side for a moment— "my *little indiscretions*, shall we call them, are perfectly harmless. Folks don't hold nothin' against me. Leastways, not for too long. None of them could hardly risk fallin' from Grandy's good graces. Every single one of them owes her somethin' or another."

Ira returned and set two steaming mugs on the table. Delia gave the waiter a smile of thanks before he scurried off; then she shifted her smile to Cord. Lifting a white-gloved hand to the base of her throat, she fingered the small diamond brooch pinned in the center of her lace collar. "In all honesty, I do b'lieve folks would be sorely disappointed if I up and reformed. Why, they wouldn't have a thing to whisper 'bout after Sunday services. Not much of nothin' else happens 'round here. Gracious, this old town hasn't had its foundation shaken since . . . well, you know," she said, lowering her voice to a conspiratorial level, "since you robbed the bank." She glanced over her shoulder, then wet her lips and scooted forward in her chair. "Do tell me. However did you do it?"

Her bluntness caught Cord unawares, though he supposed he shouldn't have been surprised. Understandably, his reappearance in Boudreaux Parish had piqued her curiosity—along with everyone else's. He had half expected her to broach the subject at some point during their odd association. But he hadn't been prepared for her to approach the matter with such excitement shining in her eyes. Regardless, he certainly had no intention of discussing his past in a coffeehouse. "Mademoiselle Abernathy—"

"Ah-ah-aah. It's Delia," she corrected, raising a pointer finger.

"Very well, then, *Delia*—"

"Pardon me," she broke in again, furrowing her perfect brow. "But couldn't you say it with a little more feelin'? My name, I mean—you know, maybe just a tad more fondly?"

Cord tightened his jaw. He braced his elbows on the table, reached out, and took both her hands in his, pulling her forward until their noses almost touched. Disregarding her startled expression, he lowered his lids in a sensuous fashion. "Delia . . . *dear*," he said in a soft, breathy tone. "You have employed me for certain services, no?"

Her eyes wide, she gave him a staggering nod.

"I can tell you now, *chère*, I will respect your wishes. Whatever you desire me to do in accordance with our agreement, this I will do. But I will not talk of my private affairs with you, *hein?*"

Pushing out her lower lip, Delia wrenched her hands free, then flopped against the back of her chair. "I was merely tryin' to start a conversation," she whispered fiercely.

For reasons beyond his understanding, her sulky pose charmed Cord, made him want to smile when he would have preferred to keep a straight face. The woman pouted like a spoiled child whose toy had just been taken. Though he'd doled out more than his share of cynical grins, the occasions upon which he'd honestly felt like smiling had been few and far between in his lifetime. The urge to do so now disturbed him greatly, but he tamped it down as best he could and cleared his throat. "Perhaps . . . we could speak of other things, no? For instance"—he shrugged and spread his hands— "the threat of war? Me, I have heard that the Abolitionists—"

"Abolitionists? Hah!" Delia shifted in her chair and crossed her arms over her chest. "Damned Yankee insurrectionists. Why, if you ask me, if anybody's gonna start a war, it should be us. Northerners. Hmph. They wouldn't dare start a war with us. Fact is, they need us. Why, our cotton alone provides . . ."

Instantly, Cord was sorry he'd brought the subject up. His opinion differed drastically, but the woman's praise of Southern policy didn't stop long enough for him to debate the issue. She paused for brief intermissions to take a quick sip of coffee, barely allowing him time to squeeze a word or two in edgewise.

After fifteen minutes into the conversation, he gave up trying to state his sentiments. Instead, he leaned comfortably back in his chair, drank his warmed sling, and simply nodded agreeably at appropriate intervals. He even squinted, appearing to concentrate on Delia's every word, but behind lowered lashes he discreetly looked past her now and then.

Disapproving faces glared at him, emanating contempt. Cord could feel the hatred, the prejudice. But his skin had thickened during his years in prison, and he no longer felt the anguish of relentless spurn. In fact, he felt nothing at all. It was as if something had died inside him, leaving an empty space.

As he continued to survey the establishment, his attention returned time and again to an elderly gentleman seated in the rear of the room. The old fellow primarily kept his head ducked, except for a few fast glances he directed Cord's way. Cord studied his profile, marked the beak-like nose and hollow cheeks . . . and eventually a younger, more vital version of the man formed in the shadows of his mind.

John Hart. His name was John Hart, Cord remembered. He'd been a teller at the bank when Cord had been accused of stealing funds. Cord focused harder on the man, noting how the years had aged him. Hart had always kept to himself. Mild-mannered and efficient, he'd rarely spoken to anyone other than customers during working hours, except to utter a meek good-morning or good-evening.

Cord caught himself staring openly at the man. Hart, upon noticing he was being watched, donned his hat, rose swiftly, and headed for the door. He held his hand on the brim of his stove-pipe, hiding his face as he passed.

"M'sieu," Cord called out on impulse. "John? You are John Hart, no?"

The old gentleman froze for a split second. He glanced at Cord with undeniable fear in his weary eyes. Then he hurried from the coffee shop.

Cord stood, his long legs jarring the table.

"Goodness gracious," Delia remarked, steadying the mugs before they toppled. "What on earth—"

Tossing a few coins on the table, Cord grasped Delia's wrist and hauled her briskly through the door of Faldene's. He stopped just outside and looked up and down the street, but there was no sign of the old teller.

Cord paid little heed to Delia as she jerked free of his hold and set about straightening her bonnet. He was too preoccupied to give her obvious indignation much notice.

John had deliberately avoided him. But why? While Cord could hardly call his affiliation with the old man friendship, they had been on good terms at the bank. Hart had been one of the few people in Boudreaux Parish to ever treat him with respect.

"You mind tellin' me just what this is all about?" Delia gave Cord's coat sleeve a sharp tug. "Huh? Cord? Are you listenin' to me?"

Cord sidestepped her to get a better look at a man leaving the tobacco shop across the street, but then a carriage blocked his view. By the time the rig had passed, the man had disappeared.

Combing a hand through his hair, Cord set his hat on his head. On second thought, he figured Hart's uneasiness might have been a perfectly natural reaction. As a general rule, decent, upstanding citizens regarded ex-convicts with a high amount of apprehension.

Demanding her share of attention, Delia moved beside him and pinched his upper arm viciously.

Cord flinched, more from surprise than from the pain, though he was certain that even through the layers of clothing she had left a welt. Frowning, he glared down at her. "Why the hell did you do that, *hein*?"

"Well, I s'pose I get a tad irritated when people ignore me," she replied with a lift of her chin. "Now, are you gonna answer my question or not?"

"About what?"

Delia let go of a long, exasperated sigh, rolled her eyes, then perched her hands on her hips. "About why you jumped up and dragged me out of Faldene's like the place was on fire or somethin'. What in heaven's name were you thinkin', chasin' after poor ol' Mr. Hart, anyways?"

Cord looked at her speculatively. "You know John Hart?"

"Well, of course I know him. Everybody knows everybody 'round here."

"How well do you know him, *chère*?"

"Not well." Delia shrugged. "Nobody knows Mr. Hart very well. He's the quiet sort. Ever since he retired from the bank, he stays cooped up in that creepy old house of his. He takes a notion to go to Faldene's now and then, but—" She narrowed her eyes. "How come you're so interested in him?"

Cord relaxed his features. "I worked with him at the bank. I only wished to ask how he was faring these days." He then offered her his arm. "Should we not be on our way? Your *grand-mère*, she may be wondering where you are, no?"

Peering at him askance from under the brim of her bonnet, Delia curled her fingers around his elbow. "You hauled me out of Faldene's like a hooligan just so you could inquire after Mr. Hart's welfare?'' She closed her eyes for a moment in apparent vexation, then pinned Cord with a perturbed look. ''Do tell. Well, if you will recollect, you and I have a little business goin' on here at present. Might I suggest that in the future you conduct your cordial inquiries on your own time?'' She nodded toward the glass storefront of the coffee shop, clearly denoting they stood in full view. ''Land sakes, what's everyone in there gonna think now?''

Cord followed her gaze. Though his tall reflection and Delia's smaller one obstructed precisely what was going on inside, he sensed the nosy customers ogling them.

On the spur of the moment, to appease himself as well as the woman who'd hired him to play her lover, he caught hold of Delia's shoulders and pulled her against him. Lowering his face a hairbreadth away from hers, he looked deeply into her wide, alarmed eyes. ''They will think I am crazy in love with you,'' he whispered.

Delia stared up at him, and for the span of a stammering heartbeat she completely forgot they were being watched. Cord's amber eyes glowed with a savage inner fire. A fire that both excited and frightened her. Instinctively, she stiffened, then started to squirm.

''Shh,'' he murmured, his breath coming warm and soft against her lips. He laid a hand alongside her face. The gentle stroke of his thumb on her cheek stilled her. ''You did say I could kiss you whenever I wanted, did you not?''

''Yes,'' she answered in a weak voice. Her gaze dropped to his mouth, then jumped back to his eyes. "But not here . . . on the street . . . in public."

"Perhaps we should give everyone in Boudreaux Parish something to talk about, *hein?*"

Delia met his small, secretive smile, and slowly one of her own tipped the corners of her mouth. Her fingers unfurled against his chest. No doubt the whole establishment of Faldene's was pressing up against the inside of the window by now. Delia dragged her gaze from the glint of mischief in his eyes to his full lower lip. She wanted him to kiss her—and not only for the benefit of those craning their necks in the coffeehouse. Straining forward slightly, she angled her face to convey her wish.

The door of Faldene's swung open abruptly, and the sound of a deeply cleared throat stole Cord's attention. With disappointment settling into the pit of her stomach, Delia turned an angry expression on the portly, middle-aged gentleman who approached them.

Giving his lapels a sharp tug, the man pinned Cord with a fierce scowl. "Now lookie heah, boy," he drawled, his sideburn-covered jowls quivering with indignation, " 'round heah, we don't much cotton to no public displays of affection. Especially from some no-account like yourself. It's simply not tolerated and—"

"*Mais oui*, of course, m'sieu." Cord released Delia from his embrace so swiftly that she swayed in an attempt to keep her balance. "Forgive me if I have offended you, m'sieu," he said, sweeping off his hat and placing it against his chest. "Ah, but such a fine-looking gentleman as yourself must surely have fallen under the spell of a beautiful woman a time or two, *hein?*" Cord gave him a knowing wink, then gestured toward Delia. "A creature so rare and lovely as this would make a saint forget his manners, no?"

"Hmph," the man replied with a raking glance. "I'm certain you possess no such manners, boy. You're lookin' to be tar and feathered, you are." He shifted his gaze to Delia. "Miss Adelaide, does your grandmother know where you are and who you're gallivantin' around with these days?"

Heat climbed up Delia's spine and filled her head. "Mr. Witherspoon, might I suggest you examine your own conscience concernin' manners? Myself, I consider it in extremely poor taste for you to address my fiancé here as 'boy.' " Lifting her chin, she looped her arm through Cord's. "His name is Cord. Cord Kibedeaux. *Mr.* Kibedeaux to you. I'll expect you to address him properly the next time we chance to meet." Delia gave him a curt smile, then steered Cord around the man. "Good day, Mr. Witherspoon," she said without bothering to look back.

As soon as they rounded the corner, Delia hugged Cord's arm and broke into a fit of giggles. "Did you see his face? I thought his side-whiskers were gonna pop right off the way his jaw was swellin'."

She peered up and met Cord's gaze. He studied her with only a slight trace of humor in his eyes. "You think I'm simply awful, don't you," she stated rather than asked.

"*Non*," he said, then appeared to weigh the question more thoroughly for a moment. "No. Not at all. On the contrary, I admire the way you handle certain situations. Me, I have always tried to talk my way out of trouble. You . . . you, *chère*, meet it straight on with your fists raised, do you not?''

Delia ducked her head and bit her bottom lip. ''Grandy says I'm headstrong. She's always tellin' me I'm way too aggressive. Too . . . belligerent, as she calls it.''

''No,'' Cord said, drawing the word out with a teasing lilt. ''You? Belligerent? I don't believe that.''

''Well, I fear it's true.'' Delia sighed. ''And accordin' to Grandy, it's my failin' fault.''

''Ah, no. No, *chère.*'' He patted the hand she crooked in his elbow. Then he lifted one dark brow pensively. ''Me, I think being aggressive can sometimes be a good thing.''

''Do you really think so?''

''Oh, *mais oui.* People rarely take advantage of you, is this not true?''

''I s'pose you're right,'' Delia said, slowing her steps as they neared the buggy. ''I do recall one incident in particular when my belligerence came in handy. I socked Chauncy Bateman in the eye.''

Cord stopped beside the rig and grinned. ''Recently?'' he asked.

''Heavens, no.'' Delia felt her cheeks turn pink, and was instantly sorry she'd disclosed anything about the viler side of her nature. ''I was barely thirteen at the time.''

''I see.'' Cord caught her by the waist and lifted her onto the buggy seat. ''And Chauncy, he deserved this sock in the eye, *hein?*''

''He did,'' Delia replied, letting her fingers linger on his broad shoulders a little longer than necessary. ''He put a frog down the back of my dress. Actually, he deserved more than—''

Delia caught sight of a tall, lean figure striding purposefully toward them, and straightened in her seat. "Oh, my gracious, speak of the devil."

Chapter Six

"I swear, Chauncy Bateman seems to turn up everywhere I go," Delia muttered. She cast Cord a long, sideways glance. "Just nod politely. Maybe he'll pass on by with nothin' more than a mornin' greetin'."

"Me, I would not bet on that happening, *chère*," Cord commented dryly, assessing the familiar, frowning features of the sandy-haired young man who walked steadily toward them. Chauncy Bateman had grown in size since Cord had last seen him, but his foul expression of displeasure had not changed.

"I b'lieve you may be right on that account," Delia said, and patted the seat beside her. "You'd best hurry and hop up here. We just might be able to get goin' before he gets any closer."

Having no desire to fraternize with his childhood enemy, Cord rounded the rig, climbed in, and settled himself next to Delia.

Chauncy picked up his pace to match theirs. "Delia," he called out, then waved. "Delia, wait!"

She turned her face to Cord and rolled her eyes, then put on a sweet smile when Chauncy approached. "Mornin', Chauncy. I'm terribly sorry, but we're in a rush. We have this previous engagement that—"

"Oh, come now, Delia. Don't tell me you don't have a few moments to spare an ol' friend," he drawled, fingering the fringed top of the buggy. His pale blue eyes lit on Cord with contempt, then flickered back to Delia as if he'd completely dismissed Cord's presence. "Just what are you up to now, Delia?"

She arched her eyebrows innocently. "Why, whatever do you mean?"

"You forgettin' who you're talkin' to? You're up to one of your little tricks, sure as the world." He slid his gaze to Cord and back again. "I know you, my dear. Remember?"

"Not as well as you'd like to, I'd wager," she said with the hint of a smile.

His sober expression changed to one filled with ill-concealed desire. "That's no secret," he replied in a hoarse whisper. "The whole town is well aware of how I feel—" Glancing at Cord once more, he stopped short, then raised his voice in an authoritative way. "What are you up to, Delia?"

"Nothin' that concerns you. Now, if you don't mind, we really do have to be on our way. We're gonna be late if—"

"Oh, but I do mind." He grabbed her forearm. "And since this does concern me, whether you're willin' to admit it or not, I think you'd better tell me right here and now what you're doin' cavortin' with this . . . this white trash."

"Let go of me," Delia insisted, trying to struggle free of his grasp. "You're hurtin' my arm."

"Not till you answer me."

"Unhand the lady, m'sieu," Cord said in a deadly calm voice.

"You stay outta this, boy," Chauncy replied, keeping his eyes trained on Delia's face. "This here conversation is between Miss Adelaide and myself. Now, damn you, Delia, answer me, or so help me, I'll—"

In lightning-quick succession, Cord reached across Delia's lap, wrenched Chauncy's hand from her sleeve, and hit the man's shoulder, shoving him backward.

Chauncy's features momentarily registered shock as he stumbled away from the rig. Then his expression turned murderous. With his chest heaving, he doubled his fists and started forward. "You dirty Cajun scum," he hissed. "I'll teach you to mess with your betters."

"I wouldn't try it, m'sieu. I will not walk away from you as I did when I was a boy." Cord spoke in an unprovoked tone, but his lethal glare stopped Chauncy in his tracks.

Chauncy stood immobile for several long seconds, exchanging a look of animosity with Cord. Then he shifted his gaze to Delia. "Climb outta that buggy, Delia," he commanded. "I'm takin' you home."

She opened her mouth to protest, but Cord cut her off.

"The lady came with me, m'sieu, and she will leave with me," he stated, then flicked the reins against the mare's rump.

"You're beggin' for trouble, Cord Kibedeaux," Chauncy shouted after them as they drove off. "You hear me, boy? Big trouble!"

Delia leaned over and peered around the edge of the rig at Chauncy.

"And I'll be seein' you later, Delia," he hollered, shaking his finger at her. "We got us some talkin' to do, by God!"

She shrank back into the shady interior of the buggy and smoothed her skirt. From the corner of her eye, she looked at Cord. "Chauncy riles easily," she commented. "He'll get over it soon enough. Why, tomorrow evenin' at Cynthia Davenport's engagement party, he'll probably walk right up as if nothin' had ever happened and ask me to dance."

Cord made no response. He simply stared straight ahead, allowing the creaking carriage wheels to fill the silence as they rode along. He could think of nothing to say. Delia's knee knocked his thigh every time they rolled over a bump in the road, emphasizing his discomfort.

He blamed Chauncy for disrupting the easiness that had started to bud between Delia and him. He hadn't thought of Chauncy Bateman in years. He'd pushed all recollection of taunting youngsters trailing after him and calling him names to the far outposts of his mind. He'd almost forgotten the long Sunday dinners at the Batemans' that he'd attended with Mr. Grayson. Now a clear picture formed in his head of how Chauncy had glared at him across the polished dining room table. A mixture of degradation and jealousy had arisen in Cord as he'd stared back at the boy. Chauncy had taken everything for granted—all the things Cord had always longed for—including doting parents.

Cord focused on a row of trees laced with Spanish moss in the distance. His melancholy lifted somewhat when he remembered Winston Grayson. The old man had placed a hand upon Cord's shoulder from time to time during those Sunday suppers with the Batemans. Whenever he had looked up at the elderly gentleman, Mr. Grayson had always given him a reassuring smile.

Delia watched Cord on the sly. There was a spark of undeniable emotion in his eyes, though his expression was unreadable. He appeared to be far away in this thoughts. Meeting Chauncy, she figured, had no doubt conjured up bad memories. Chauncy had been the main instigator of the ridicule Cord had had to endure when his family first moved to Boudreaux Parish. Delia had never understood Chauncy's cruel need to taunt the less fortunate—no more than she'd understood why Cord Kibedeaux had simply walked through the gauntlet of shoving boys without lifting a finger to stop them.

When she looked at the proud angle of Cord's profile now, she could hardly believe he was the same impassive youngster who'd been bullied so long ago. Prison—life in general, perhaps—had hardened him. Delia couldn't imagine Chauncy pitting himself against Cord these days. Cord was only slightly taller, but broader through the chest and shoulders and obviously more muscular. Cord Kibedeaux was no longer the shabby young man who used to shuffle through the streets of Boudreaux Parish with his head down. He'd come back bearing an air of superiority and looked the people who'd once snubbed him straight in the eye.

"I . . . I'm sorry 'bout what happened back there," Delia said quietly, breaking the barrier of silence. "I truly am."

Cord slanted his gaze to hers.

"I mean . . . well, I suspected folks would stare

and whisper and such." Delia dropped her attention to her hands clasped in her lap. "But I never expected any of them to approach us like that."

"Did you not? I did." He studied her with a cold, distant glint in his eyes. "Tell me, what exactly did you expect, *hein*?"

"I don't know. I certainly didn't expect Mr. Witherspoon to walk out of Faldene's and bawl us out right there on the sidewalk and all." Delia idly twisted a curl over her shoulder. "And I never woulda believed Chauncy would actually insult you to your face the way he did."

Cord scanned the marshy terrain ahead. "There has never been any love lost between M'sieu Bateman and me."

"No, I s'pose not." Delia cocked her head. "He and those pack of wolves he called friends were awfully mean to you when you first came here—pokin' fun at you and everything." She sighed thoughtfully. "Boys will be boys, I s'pose. Always out to 'git' somebody. Before you, it was Bubba Riley. Poor ol' Bubba never has been right, you know. Chauncy and his bedevillers just naturally went after you cuz they'd heard your mamma was touched and your daddy stole things."

Delia's scalp tightened with embarrassment. Unintentionally, she'd repeated allegations she'd overheard as a child about the no-account Kibedeauxs. Guilt-ridden, she peered at Cord. He showed no offense, no emotion at all, in fact, at the mention of his parents' transgressions.

Nevertheless, she felt truly uncomfortable and searched her brain for words that might make amends. "Um . . . I mean . . . well, in my opinion, it never shoulda mattered whether your family was shiftless or not. Those boys had no call to torment you like they did." Fire burned the tips of her ears. She closed her eyes. "Oh, fiddlesticks," she murmured, then gave Cord a regretful grimace. "I truly didn't mean to say that your family was shiftless. What I meant was—"

"Make no apologies, *chère*." Cord glanced in her direction briefly, then resumed staring ahead as if something of great importance lay in front of him. "It is true, no? everything they said about my parents." He shrugged. "It was the same wherever we went. A month or two here or there. The constable was never far behind, moving us on. Me, I cannot fault children for merely quoting irrefutable hearsay recited by their parents. And, as you say, boys will be boys."

"Yes, but you and Chauncy are grown men now. Not children." Delia laced her fingers tightly together in her lap to keep from touching him with compassion. She had an inkling he might take any such gesture as a sign of pity. "Well, it was childishness, pure and simple," she said instead of reaching out to him, "for him to speak of you as he did today."

Cord gave her a bland look, his lids at half-mast, his eyes blank. "It makes no difference. I am used to the manner in which people talk to me, how they look at me. It is the way of things."

Delia marked the remoteness in his tone. It occurred to her that he accepted rude treatment as his due. The notion infuriated her, though she couldn't fathom why. *It is the way of things*, he'd said. Those blessed with wealth and position elevated themselves to a higher plane than those who weren't so fortunate. Delia had never thought much about it before, but she supposed she, along with her peers, *did* consider that slaves, servants, field workers, and the like were beings of lesser emotions.

Delia frowned, ashamed, yet not quite able to make herself feel differently. Other than ordering people beneath her about, she'd hadn't ever held much of a conversation with them. Cord had been the first Cajun she'd spoken more than two words to.

She eased back in her seat and idly viewed the draping black willows and red cypress trees as the buggy rolled past. A stillness settled between her and the man beside her. She could feel something vital within her changing, and she wasn't certain she was all that fond of whatever it was that was starting to happen to her. She liked her life the way it was. She'd been content to sit on the veranda and fan herself as she watched her world go by, unconcerned about the worries of the insignificant people who buzzed about the plantation unnoticed.

Delia observed Cord from beneath the cover of her lashes for the remainder of the drive, silently cursing him for her sudden mixed sentiments over the more common inhabitants of Boudreaux Parish. *Damn the man,* she thought. Cord Kibedeaux certainly did bring out the strangest feelings in her.

When they reached the crossroads where she and Cord had met earlier that morning, he reined the horse, then climbed down from the buggy. Nudging the brim of his hat, he gazed up at her. Sunlight pierced his warm brown eyes, revealing flecks of gold.

Delia stared at him, and her insides turned liquid. Regardless, she drew herself erect, refusing to let him affect her so. Swiftly scooting to the center of the seat, she snatched up the reins and made an intent study of the surrounding area to avoid looking at him again. "You be here just after suppertime tomorrow evenin', you hear?" She didn't bother to curb the edge in her voice. "We'll be going to Cynthia Davenport's engagement party, so don't you dare keep me waitin'."

"If you say so," he replied casually.

"I do." Delia glanced in his direction, but was careful not to meet his eyes. She was highly irritated at the way that low-lidded, devil-may-care gaze of his disturbed her. And she was quite sure he knew it.

"Good day, Mr. Kibedeaux," she said more than a little ungraciously, then snapped the reins and trotted off, resisting the urge to look over her shoulder.

Delia stared at the moth fluttering against the globe of the lamp on her dresser. She dragged her brush lazily through her hair, making comparisons between the moth's persistent suicide attempts and her distracting feelings about Cord Kibedeaux.

The man was dangerous. The slightest consideration of the two of them venturing beyond the boundary of their business relationship was as senseless as the moth flying into the white-hot flame. Yet with no more resistance than the tiny winged creature currently battering itself against the glass lampshade, Delia found her thoughts drawn toward the Cajun.

She had tried to push Cord from her mind by dwelling on the progress made that morning at the coffeehouse. She could well imagine her grandmother's reaction upon hearing the gossip that had no doubt already reached her ears.

But the elation Delia experienced over foiling Grandy's plans kept dwindling, replaced by surfacing visions of Cord's heavy-lidded, intense whiskey-colored eyes and cynical smile. His deep, sensuous voice had followed her home and had continued to annoy her throughout the afternoon. Even worse, all evening she'd caught herself reliving the few minutes during which he'd so brazenly embraced her in front of Faldene's.

Delia set her brush down abruptly, rose, and went to the open window. A balmy night breeze billowed the curtains on either side of her. The sweet scent of magnolias drifted up to her while she gazed at the dark silhouette of the gardens below. None of the gentlemen who'd vied for her attention had *ever* plagued her thoughts for an entire day. Indeed, she had never lost one minute's sleep over a suitor before.

She fingered the Valenciennes lace collar of her nightgown, thinking how irrational it was that the first man interesting enough to keep her up half the night was an ex-convict with a shady past . . . someone with no means whatsoever of actually winning her hand.

Delia closed her eyes and shook her head, trying to rid her mind of such a silly notion. She had no desire for Cord Kibedeaux, or anyone else for that matter, to pursue her with serious intent. She simply wondered what it would have been like if Cord *had* kissed her in front of the coffee shop.

She liked Cord. That was all. There wasn't a thing wrong with liking him, she assured herself. He had a quiet dignity about him. And she ad-

mired the man for rising above what he'd been—
what he was.

Delia yawned. It was hours past her usual bedtime. Making a mental list of all she had to do to
get ready for Cynthia Davenport's soiree tomorrow, she turned from the window and crawled
into bed.

She was bone weary, but her eyes refused to
close. She stretched out on her side and, unable
to quiet her brain, focused on the bright crescent
moon outside the window.

Perhaps part of her fascination with Cord Kibedeaux, she decided, stemmed from the poor
toss of the dice he had apparently been born with.
What little Delia had gathered of his history indicated he'd grown up with bad luck nipping at
his heels. Bad luck and bad blood certainly wer-
en't a very favorable combination, she concluded.

Shifting her weight on the down mattress, she
wondered what had brought him back to Boudreaux Parish. After all that had happened, why
hadn't he gone somewhere new, some place
where no one knew of his past and where he
could start fresh? He had no family in the area,
no ties here, no reason to return to a town that
despised him.

Or did he?

Cord flipped his cheroot over the porch rail. He
watched the tiny stream of orange light hit the
water and fizzle out. Cupping his hands behind
his head, he leaned back in his chair and gazed
at the glimmer of moonlight peeking through the
thick Spanish moss. A chorus of crickets and katydids hummed a constant tune. Knee-deep fog

hovered over the bayou and crept up onto the porch, swirling around his bare feet.

He inhaled a deep breath of the humid night air, experiencing a rare touch of peacefulness. For the first time since walking out of the prison gate, Cord felt truly free of the heavy chains he'd worn for almost a decade. Subconsciously, he rubbed his wrist, his thumb gliding over the scars from the iron manacles that would forever mark his skin. And never allow him to forget.

He'd been released more than a year ago, yet only recently had he sensed his spirit beginning to stir again. Not until now did he realize how young he had been when they'd shackled his ankles and shoved him into that dark, damp hell.

Cord closed his eyes and rolled his shoulders. *Eighteen. God, so young. So many years wasted.*

In a melancholy moment, he remembered how he'd kept his head down, avoided contact with the other inmates, and attempted not to antagonize the guards. He'd found out soon enough that his jailers needed no particular reason to raise a whip to a prisoner's back. They chose convicts on a whim to discipline as examples.

Cord had taken his turns at the whipping post in stride. His father might have contributed little else to his upbringing, but he had trained Cord well to withstand a beating. Cord had learned at an early age how to separate his mind from his body. Slipping into a reticent state, he had escaped to a place deep within himself . . . a place where nothing could hurt him.

A trickle of sweat rolled down the side of his face, causing a slow awareness of how tightly he was gripping his wrist. He loosened his hold and flexed his hand, allowing the circulation to return.

"It is over," he murmured to no one but the deserted bayou. "Over. In the past."

Once he'd gotten what he'd come for, he would leave this wretched town and all its memories behind. He would make a new life elsewhere . . . somewhere no one had ever heard of him.

But not until he found out who was responsible for sending him to prison.

Cord stared at the reflection of the quarter moon in the dark water. He'd replayed the morning's events over and over in his head. Perhaps John Hart's skittishness and hasty departure from Faldene's were relevant. Perhaps not. Either way, Cord had every intention of visiting the old teller as soon as possible.

A swishing sound drew Cord's attention, and he caught sight of an alligator rippling through the water, shattering the image of the moon on the surface.

Oddly, Adelaide Abernathy came to mind. In the same way that the alligator had disturbed the water, the woman seemed to stir the atmosphere wherever she went. What's more, she apparently enjoyed doing so.

He didn't care much for her superior attitude or the pretentious mannerisms she used on people. But there had been moments today when she had looked at him . . . and he'd felt as if her gaze had reached inside him and touched his soul.

For a matter of moments, Cord sat on the porch, listening to the frogs croak, and wondered if there could be more to *la belle de Boudreaux Parish* than met the eye.

Then he shook his head and laughed.

Standing up, he stretched his arms high over his head. "Ah, my friend," he muttered to himself, "these are crazy thoughts you have. It is time you get some sleep, no? Tomorrow we must work in the fields, and then escort *la belle* to her party."

With the trace of a grin lingering on his mouth, he turned and walked into the house to fetch a pallet for the porch. Once again, he had decided it was too hot to sleep inside. It was much too hot. And he was far too restless tonight.

Chapter Seven

"**M**mm-hmm," Bess remarked, giving Delia's pink, lacy skirt a last tidying tug. The plump black woman stepped back and surveyed her handiwork with a deep chuckle. "Yes, indeedy, Miss Delia. Yo shore 'nuff gonna turn heads in dat dress."

Delia peered around the housekeeper for a final glance at herself in the looking glass. She smoothed the upswept sides of her hair, then pulled one of the long curls dangling down her back over her shoulder. "You don't think the orange blossoms are a bit too much?"

"Adds jus' the right touch," Bess answered, eyeing the arch of white flowers adorning Delia's head. "Dose gentlemen-folk gonna be buzzin' 'round you like bees after honey tonight, chile."

Delia smiled her thanks. "What in the world would I ever do without you, Bess?"

"Ah don't know. But i's a good thing you gots me to hurry you along, or you'd never gets anywheres." Bess shook her head and chuckled again, then busily started picking up the discarded clothes strewn about the room. "You bes' get goin'. Yor grandmamma axed to see you b'fore you leave. She's havin' another one a her spells.''

Delia's stomach tightened. She'd known her time of reckoning would come. News traveled fast in Boudreaux Parish. Without fail, Grandy's gossipy old friends had no doubt reported the latest development in Delia's love life.

"Well, what you waitin' for?" Bess inquired, shifting a bundle of Delia's petticoats from one arm to the other. "Go on. Git. Lord knows you gonna be late as is."

Delia pasted a placid smile on her face. " 'Night, Bess," she murmured, then made her way out the door and down the hall to Grandy's room.

She inhaled deeply before she raised her hand and knocked at the door. Upon Grandy's summons, she entered with hesitant steps.

Grandy lay in bed, reclining on a mound of pillows, her face almost as white as the ruffled nightcap she wore. Her expression, however, appeared anything but frail.

"Evenin', Grandy. Bess said you wanted to see me?"

"Come closer, Adelaide."

Delia's nails curled into her palms as she moved toward the bed, noting the tiny lines of pain etched in her grandmother's brow. "Bess told me your rheumatism was actin' up again. Is there somethin' I can get you b'fore I go?"

"I didn't call you in here to discuss my ailments, Adelaide." Agatha's cool gray gaze took in every inch of Delia's appearance. "You're lookin' especially lovely tonight, dear."

"Thank you," Delia said softly and clasped her hands against her waist.

"You goin' over to the doings at the Davenports'?"

"Yes, ma'am."

Grandy nodded, her mouth set in a grim line. "I hear tell you got yourself a new beau. Is that so?"

"Yes," Delia whispered, dropping her eyes to the floor. With her breath held, she anticipated Grandy's next question.

"Anyone I know?"

"No, I don't b'lieve you've met." Delia glanced briefly at her grandmother, then fixed her gaze on the painting of a bowl of fruit that hung above the bed.

"Will he be takin' you to the Davenports' party this evenin'?"

Delia nodded. "He ought to be here any minute to fetch me," she lied, knowing full well she had agreed to meet Cord at the crossroads.

Agatha narrowed her eyes. "It's a shame I'm not feelin' well enough to go downstairs and meet him."

"A *real* shame," Delia muttered, then cleared her throat. "Well, Grandy, it's gettin' late. If you don't mind, I'd best be on my way."

"And you wouldn't want to kept your young man waitin'. You will bring him 'round soon to introduce him, won't you?"

"Of course." Delia smiled, bent over, and kissed her grandmother's forehead. "You rest now. I'll peek in on you when I get home."

Agatha returned a weak smile and patted Delia's cheek. "Have a good time, dear."

"I will," she replied, hurrying toward the door.

"Adelaide?"

Delia stopped and turned slowly. "Yes, Grandy?"

"You haven't forgotten about our agreement, have you?"

"No, Grandy. I haven't forgotten."

"Oh, Cord, there's Milly." Delia waved at the dainty, dark-haired beauty standing in the arched doorway on the other side of the ballroom. Turning to him, she squeezed his arm. "I simply must speak to her in private a moment. You won't mind bein' left alone for a few minutes, will you?"

Cord's gaze dipped briefly to the enticing view of Delia's low décolletage. "But of course not. You are paying me to do as you wish, are you not?"

Delia pursed her lips and lowered her brows, then quickly concealed her perturbed expression behind an ivory-and-silk fan. She moved so close to Cord, the scent of the orange blossoms in her hair overwhelmed him. "Do keep your voice down. *That* isn't exactly somethin' I'd like the whole town t' get wind of. Now, if you'll excuse me, I'll be back directly."

In a swirl of rose-colored satin, she turned and proceeded to sashay her way through the mob of Southern Louisiana upper crust. Cord watched the sway of the pink lace flounces overlaying her skirt as she adjusted the hooped hem to accommodate her progress. He let his eyes linger on the small of her back, appreciating the curve of her tiny waist, which he assumed had been laced into compliance.

Cord leaned stiffly against the wall between two of the many open French doors leading onto the veranda. He ran a finger around the inside of his highly starched bow-tied cravat and silently prayed for an evening breeze.

Considerably more uncomfortable than he'd been the day before at Faldene's, he observed the other Davenport guests with interest. Straight-backed gentlemen milled about in their swallow-tailed jackets, their chins set at arrogant angles. From an adjacent corner of the room a soprano voice, accompanied by a rosewood piano, war-bled "Greensleeves." The bittersweet tune min-gled with the endless chatter. Dressed in a rainbow of ruffles, the ladies spoke with animated gestures, making ostrich plumes attached to coif-fures bob and jewels sparkle beneath the chan-delier.

Cord ignored the sidelong glances cast in his direction and let his attention drift across the room. Delia and Milly were huddled in conver-sation behind Delia's fan, both young women peering at him above the brim. Disturbed by their obvious discussion of him, he swiftly lowered his eyes and studied the polished parquetry floor.

He had never imagined such opulence existed inside these grand plantation mansions. Mr. Grayson's town house had been large and com-fortable, and had appeared no less than a king's palace to Cord at the age of fourteen, but it wasn't on a scale with the Davenport house.

Cord closed his eyes in an attempt to shut off the commotion around him. Unexpectedly, one of the few memories he'd chosen not to discard of his time with Winston Grayson came to mind: the memory of going to sleep with the fresh smell of clean sheets beneath him. On the several occa-sions when he'd been confined in the prison hot-house, he had wandered backward through the years and reached for the comfort of those cool, crisp linens. Yet he'd never been able to mentally reproduce the exact sensation.

A drop of sweat trickled down his chest behind his cravat. He needed air. The huge ballroom was overcrowded and stifling. Everyone was watching him as if he might try to snatch the silver candle-sticks.

Halfway to the open French door, a tingling covered Cord's scalp. He halted his footsteps, turned, and his gaze collided with a pair of fa-miliar gray eyes.

Winston Grayson stared back at him. No more than a few feet apart, they both stood motionless as if somehow frozen in time. For a mere moment it was as though nothing had changed . . . as though the father-and-son relationship that had developed so long ago still remained intact.

Then the glow in the elderly gentleman's eyes diminished, and a pained expression altered his features. "Cord? My God . . . it is you, isn't it?"

"*Oui*, m'sieu," Cord managed, though his heart rose to his throat. "It is I."

"I heard you were back in town." Winston paused, fingering the brim of the stovepipe hat he held at his waist. "You . . . you've gotten taller. How you doin', son? You okay?"

"I am fine, sir," Cord answered, taking ac-count of the other man's appearance. The years had apparently been good to Mr. Grayson. He still had a full head of hair, though time had switched the color from gray to white. "And you, m'sieu? You are well?"

A small smile quivered at the corners of Win-ston's mouth. "As well as can be expected at my age, I s'pose."

An awkward silence hung heavily between them. They simply looked at each other, neither seeming to know what to say.

Try as he might, Cord had not ever succeeded in wiping Mr. Grayson's kindness to him from his memory. Standing there now, he remembered how, after his parents died, no respectable family in Boudreaux Parish had wanted to raise him alongside their own children except for Mr. Grayson, who took him in and treated him like a son.

Cord had guessed that the old banker's reason for offering him a home had had something to do with Grayson's young daughter running off with a shady gambler. Shortly after moving in, he had overheard the housekeeper telling one of the neighbors that Mr. Grayson had grieved for his daughter for over twenty years. The housekeeper had suspected the man of merely replacing one wayward child with another.

Whatever his reason, Grayson had been kind to Cord. Patiently, but persistently, the man had drawn Cord out of a place within himself where he'd forever hidden from the world. He had awakened dead emotions that Cord had never known he possessed. Little by little, he had gained Cord's trust.

Winston Grayson had given him much more than a home. He had given him his first taste of self-worth. Cord would never forget the significance of the moment when he had started looking up to Mr. Grayson. One stormy, gray morning, Winston had taken him to work with him. Before the bank had opened, the older gentleman had handed him a broom, lain a hand on his shoulder, and, smiling down at him, said, "Cord, my boy, if you want to become a teller, you'll have to work your way up from the bottom just like anyone else.''

The memory flickered and faded all too soon, and left Cord with a hollow feeling inside.

Winston shuffled his feet. ''I'm sorry, son. I'm truly sorry things had to turn out the way they did,'' he said in a hoarse voice, then turned and walked away.

''Me too, m'sieu,'' Cord whispered. He watched his former guardian move through the crowd toward the foyer, and his chest tightened with the urge to go after the man. He wanted to shout across the room, tell Winston Grayson that he *hadn't* betrayed him.

But he had no proof of his innocence. On the contrary, the evidence that had been presented in court had confirmed his guilt. The entire amount of money stolen had been found in his satchel. Witnesses had seen Cord enter and leave the bank after hours—during the alleged time the funds were taken. Cord had been the only employee of the bank, other than Mr. Grayson himself, who had known the combination to the safe. Had he been in Mr. Grayson's position, he wouldn't have been able to ignore the hard, cold facts, either.

''You havin' yourself a good time, boy?''

The question jarred Cord from his thoughts. Turning his head, he found a medium-built man with sideburns the size and shape of pork chops standing next to him.

''Cord . . . Cord Kibedeaux, isn't it? Surely you recollect all those Sunday dinners you had with us.'' He extended his hand. ''Herbert Bateman, remember? Winston's brother-in-law.''

''Of course. M'sieu Bateman.'' Cord firmly shook the hand offered, but his attention strayed to where Winston paused in the arched doorway. The old banker met Cord's gaze briefly before he disappeared into the corridor.

"Wasn't that Winston I just saw you talkin' to?" Mr. Bateman asked, looking from the doorway to Cord and back again. "Well, I hope the two of you got your differences settled. Winston was awfully fond of you, you know. After Mary Ann ran off, he was just miserable till you came along. Be good for y'all t' resume your friendship." Bateman brushed a piece of lint from his coat sleeve. "Don't s'pose it can ever be quite the same, though," he added.

Cord lowered his head, trying to get a grip on the annoyance that seized him. He clenched his jaw to keep from bluntly telling Herbert Bateman that the matter between himself and Mr. Grayson was private.

"Ah, well," Bateman drawled. "What happened, happened a long time ago. Let bygones be bygones, I always say. You certainly don't look any worse for the wear. Grown into a strappin' young buck, haven't you?"

Cord raised his gaze gradually, masking his inner turmoil with a slight curve of his lips—a smile he couldn't quite produce in his eyes. "You are still practicing law?" he asked with more interest than he actually felt.

"Oh my, yes. I'm far from retirin' yet." Lifting his chest, Mr. Bateman caught hold of his lapels and bounced twice on his heels. "Winston, as well as all my other clients 'round here, tend t' keep me rather busy these days."

"And Mrs. Bateman, she is well?" Cord made this inquiry with all sincerity. He'd held fond memories of Alicia Grayson Bateman. Winston's

younger sister had possessed a heart as tender as
her brother's.

Bateman's face fell and his eyes glazed. "We
lost Alicia to yellow fever in '49. She was visitin'
a friend in N'orlens when the epidemic broke
out."

Cord remained silent for a moment, absorbing
the news that the gentle, gracious lady was gone.
So many things had changed in his absence. "I
am truly sorry to hear that, m'sieu," he said quietly. "She was a fine woman."

"I do so miss her," the older man said in a
faraway voice. "But with the help of the Lord,
I've managed." He blinked, cleared his throat,
then smiled a little too brightly. "I was just fixin'
to step outside and have myself a smoke. Will
you join me?"

Sorely tempted to take the man up on his offer,
Cord looked over at Delia, hoping she might still
be preoccupied with her friend. Much to his disappointment, she was already weaving her way
through the crowd toward him.

Her eyes danced like a butterfly about the room,
then lit on his and held steady. She smiled, and
something moved inside Cord—something
strange and warm that made him want to return
the smile. Before he could stop himself, one corner of his mouth lifted. He was certain the other
side would have followed suit had Mr. Bateman
not elbowed him.

"Don't look now, boy," Herbert said with a
wide grin, "but 'ppears to me Miss Adelaide
Abernathy's makin' eyes at you. And damn if she
ain't cuttin' a path this way." He gave Cord a
knowing wink. "B'lieve I'd forget about the
smoke if I was you."

Cord smiled at the twinkle in Mr. Bateman's eyes. "Perhaps another time, m'sieu, *hein?*"

"Anytime, my boy, anytime." Herbert pulled a fine Cuban cigar from inside his jacket and, inhaling deeply, dragged the length of it beneath his nose. "I always carry an extra smoke." Sliding his gaze toward Delia, he pointed the cigar at her. "Have a care with that one, you hear me? She's as pretty as a hibiscus blossom, but word has it she's downright ruthless when it comes to shatterin' a young man's heart."

"I appreciate your concern," Cord replied, arching a brow. "But I can assure you, you need not worry on my account. My heart is a sturdy one and not so easily broken."

Mr. Bateman narrowed his eyes thoughtfully, his grin growing broader. "I'd wager Miss Adelaide is about to meet her match," he said with a chuckle. "And who knows? Might just be a match made in heaven."

Cord met that remark with a disbelieving laugh of his own.

"Well, my boy, if you'll excuse me, I'll just mosey on outside and leave you to do your courtin' on your own. I'm gettin' too old to even offer any aid in such matters." Bateman patted Cord's shoulder, said, "Good luck," and headed out the French doors.

Delia was no more than a stone's throw away from Cord when Cynthia Davenport caught her arm. "Why, Delia, aren't you even goin' to introduce me to your new beau?"

Before Delia could answer, the tall, willowy redhead tugged her in the Cajun's direction. Cynthia assessed Cord above her fluttering fan for the span of a few footsteps, then leaned close to Delia's ear. "My, he *is* well made, dear, isn't he? *I* certainly wouldn't have left him unattended so long."

Delia glanced at her friend askance. The sight of Cynthia lowering her lashes coyly as they stopped in front of Cord set Delia's chest on fire. The heat spread rapidly up her neck when Cynthia nudged her.

Delia caught herself in mid-frown before fixing a smile on her face. "Cord Kibedeaux, I'd like to introduce our hostess, Miss Cynthia Davenport— soon to be *Mrs*. Parker Haywood."

Cord inclined his head slightly in a fashion that made his midnight hair gleam beneath the chandelier. "It is a pleasure, Mademoiselle Davenport," he said in his low, throaty voice.

Hiding a giggle behind her fan, Cynthia blushed, then cocked her head to one side and placed a hand upon her heart. "Oh, the pleasure is all mine, I assure you."

Delia thought the woman might wilt to the floor at any given moment.

"May I congratulate you on your forthcoming marriage?" Cord asked, and Delia wondered if the spark that touched his amber eyes wasn't deliberate.

"Why, thank you, Mr. Kibedeaux," Cynthia replied in a breathy little voice that made Delia roll her eyes. "Tell me, do you dance?"

Delia thought she detected a slip in Cord's cool composure. He definitely hesitated before he opened his mouth to speak.

"Why, Cynthia," Delia said, taking advantage of the pause, "I do believe Parker is tryin' to get your attention."

When Cynthia turned to scan the room for her

fiancé, Delia gave her a subtle push forward. Cynthia glared at Delia over her shoulder, but Delia merely smiled sweetly. "Best not keep Parker waitin'," she remarked, then sidled next to Cord and hugged his arm.

Cynthia's pinched mouth turned soft and curved upward as she slid her gaze to Cord. "Mr. Kibedeaux," she said with a nod, then pinned Delia with one more hateful glance before she whirled and rustled off.

Delia watched her friend retreat, resisting the urge to make a face at the woman's back. She couldn't decide whom she was more disgusted with: Cord for encouraging Cynthia, or Cynthia for carrying on so.

Loosening her hold on Cord's arm, she looked up at him. His mouth was drawn tight at the corners in what Delia deemed a satisfied grin. She came to the swift conclusion that he rather enjoyed antagonizing her.

"Just what do you think you were doin' playin' up to Cynthia like that?" she whispered fiercely.

Cord tucked his chin. "I was merely being cordial, *chère*."

"Oh, you were bein' *more* than cordial, and you know it. Why, I could almost hear the pitter-patter of Cynthia's heart above the music."

Cord furrowed his brow. "You must forgive me, then." He pressed a hand to his chest. "Me, I would never give the woman such an impression intentionally."

Delia studied him suspiciously. "Well . . . the next time I introduce you to a lady, just don't go doin' that thing with your eyes."

"What thing with my eyes do you speak of?" Cord asked, then lowered his lids.

"That. Right there." Delia pointed her finger at his face. "*That* very expression is what made Cynthia nearly swoon. And you'd best not let me catch you doin' it again, or I'll surely—"

"Delia. There you are." Chauncy Bateman's fingers banded her elbow. "May I have this dance?"

Startled by Chauncy's sudden appearance, and concerned he might have overheard more than he should have, Delia was temporarily dumbstruck.

In the moment it took for her to regain speech, she watched him focus on Cord with a vicious gleam in his eyes. Cord met the man's gaze levelly, his features showing not a sliver of emotion. Yet Chauncy's hostility filled the space between the two, and settled over Delia like a dark shroud.

Fearing Chauncy might demonstrate his feelings with his fists instead of with his expression, she quickly found her voice. "Why, Chauncy, you silly, of course I'll dance with you." She placed a palm against his chest, urging him backward toward the dance floor.

With a parting glance in Cord's direction, she practically shoved her partner through the crowd just as the music began.

Delia could hardly wait for the dance to end. Chauncy held her too close, as usual. She followed his lead mindlessly, letting years of practice guide her graceful steps. She evaded most of his questions, answering a few only vaguely. Whenever the opportunity presented itself, she peered past her partner at Cord.

Just before the music stopped, she watched the Cajun slip out onto the veranda. She hoped that neither Cynthia nor any of the other ladies who'd been ogling the man all night had noticed. It simply wouldn't do for one of them to be caught on the veranda with him.

She left young Bateman's arms the moment the dance was over. But as she moved around him, he grabbed her wrist.

"Delia" he pleaded. "You have to tell me what all this is about."

She dipped her gaze to his fingers encircling her wrist. "I don't have to tell you anything," she remarked dispassionately, then wrenched free of his grasp. With swift strides, she crossed the room and swept through the French doors. Failing to find Cord on the veranda that enveloped the entire back of the house, she walked down the steps and headed for the rear gardens.

A balmy night breeze stirred the curls at Delia's temples and roused the mingled fragrance of magnolias and wisteria. Though bright with stars, the moonless sky lent little light to the path that led to the Davenports' reflections pool.

The music from the house grew softer as Delia made her way down the shrub-lined trail. Now and then she heard low, tender-laced voices on the other side of the hedge. Once in a while a shrill giggle coming from somewhere deeper in the garden reached her ears.

Delia knew what went on behind the bushes. She had been lured off the path by a gentleman or two in her day. Chauncy Bateman for one, she recalled with a grimace. Of course, her few ventures into the evening-shaded gardens had all ended in disaster. As it was, the young men involved hadn't been satisfied with a mere kiss. They had insistently wanted more than Delia had been willing to give.

"Do you grow tired of dancing so soon?"

Delia halted her footsteps at the sound of the deep voice in the darkness. She narrowed her eyes on the tree ahead that split the walkway, and a tall, shadowy form broke away from the wide trunk.

"Cord?" she whispered. "Is that you?"

"*Oui*," he answered, moving forward until his features were visible in the wan light. Stopping before her, he frowned down at her. "Is it wise for such a beautiful young woman to wander about in such a place unescorted?"

Delia pursed her lips and smoothed the bodice of her gown. "Well, I'm not exactly unescorted now that you're here, am I?"

Cord glanced from her to the house and back again. "You came out here looking for me?"

"Yes."

"But I could not have been gone for more than a single dance, no? Me, I figured you would be waltzing with M'sieu Bateman for at least two or three more tunes."

"Well, you figured wrong." Delia peered up at him. Faint music from the ballroom and the sweet scent of honeysuckle drifted on the air. "Tell me," she said, then wet her lips. "*Do* you dance?"

One corner of his mouth lifted into a grin, and he slipped his hands into his pants pockets. "I fear the prison guards neglected our training in such social graces."

"Would . . . would you like to learn how?" she asked, a little uncertain about why she suddenly wanted to teach him.

Cord arched one brow, then shrugged. "Why not? It appears to be a pleasant pastime, no?"

Delia's tentative smile broke loose. "Very well. Let me have your hand."

"Which one do you want, *chère?*" Dragging his hands from his trouser pockets, he spread his arms wide.

She reached out and caught his right hand. "You put this one here," she said, placing it in the curve of her waist. "And the other . . . the other . . ."

All talk of dance lessons abruptly left her mind. She stared at Cord's chin, her thoughts overpowered by the heat of his palm penetrating the thin satin of her gown . . . warming her skin.

Delia's heartbeat quickened, grew louder until it pounded in her ears. She lifted her face and encountered Cord's gaze. Both of them stood completely still for a long, endless moment.

Insane notions filled her brain, making her light-headed and dizzy. Without heeding the consequences of her actions, she caught his forearms. She'd only meant to steady herself until her senses ceased swimming.

But then his muscles tensed beneath her touch. His pulse began to thump hard against her fingertips . . . and with a will of their own, her hands slid up his arms, over his broad shoulders, and settled around his neck. Knowing all the while it was a wicked, brazen thing to do, she rose on her tiptoes and touched her lips to his.

Cord stood like a stone statue for the space of a heartbeat, not breathing, not responding. Then in one swift motion he gripped her waist and pulled her to him in an almost suffocating embrace.

Delia gasped as his mouth, firm and tightly drawn at first, melted against hers. Tilting his head, he leaned into the kiss, applying an urgent pressure.

A surge of fearful excitement seized Delia. Her knees buckled with the shifting of the ground beneath her. Chauncy and the few others she had allowed to kiss her had repulsed her with their awkward groping. But Cord's kiss . . . she couldn't find words to properly describe what he was doing to her.

Leaving her lips tingling in the sultry night air, Cord brushed his mouth across her cheek and nibbled her earlobe. She trembled inside as he slowly, slowly trailed feathery kisses down the side of her neck.

"Oh." The faint little sound escaped Delia's parted lips all by itself, yet brought her a fraction closer to her senses. "Oh . . . oh, my stars," she somehow managed to say. "I . . . oh . . . I don't think we ought to be doin' this."

Cord's mouth froze on her throat. *"Mon Dieu,"* he whispered, his warm breath grazing her skin. Straightening to his full height, he searched her face momentarily before stepping away from her. "Forgive me," he said, then dropped his gaze to the ground and raked a hand through his hair. "Holy Mother. Me, I must be going crazy. How could I have let such a thing happen?"

Delia pressed her fingertips to her mouth, waiting for the return of her equilibrium, groping for her composure. She focused on Cord's remorseful features, aware that he took the burden of blame upon himself. Shame rose above the mishmash of emotions that whirled in her head. She simply couldn't allow him to take responsibility for something she had clearly initiated.

"I s'pose I ought to be the one apologizin'," she murmured, then lowered her head. No words had ever been harder to say. She'd seldom been sincerely sorry about anything she'd done. And even on the rare occasions when she'd had regrets, she'd been too stubborn to admit it.

"Ah, *non, chère*," Cord said softly, his accent slipping through. "You are young. Impulsive, no? Me, I can claim no such excuse. I should have stopped—"

"Mr. Kibedeaux," Delia interrupted. She peered at him from beneath her brows. "How would you feel about just forgettin' anything ever happened out here tonight?"

Cord nodded. "I think that would be best."

Delia glanced around the garden, and the chirping of crickets amplified the uneasy silence. "I guess we ought to be joinin' the others," she suggested, then looked over her shoulder at the brightly lit house. "They'll be servin' the midnight supper soon. We wouldn't want to miss the final gallantries in honor of Cynthia and Parker."

Cord didn't take Delia's elbow as they walked back toward the Davenport mansion. Nor did she slip her hand in the crook of his arm. They didn't touch. And they didn't talk.

Chapter Eight

Delia peered out one of the tall, narrow windows that lined the double doors to the foyer. With a sigh, she released the lacy curtain, letting it fall back into place, then straightened her spine. Frowning, she toyed with the ruffled collar of her white linen blouse.

Of all the mornings for Cord to be late.

"Adelaide?"

Delia whirled at the sound of her grandmother's voice. With hands on hips, Grandy stood in the library doorway, wearing a perturbed expression. "What time did you say this young man was supposed to be here?"

"He didn't precisely give me a set time." Delia swallowed and clutched her hands against the waistband of her skirt. "We agreed he should come between ten o'clock and half-past ten."

Grandy reached into the pocket of her black skirt and withdrew Grandfather Abernathy's timepiece—a keepsake she'd carried with her for as long as Delia could remember. Flipping the gold lid open, she squinted at the face of the watch. "Well, it's nigh on ten-thirty now. I'm afraid I won't be able to see him this mornin' if he doesn't arrive soon." She narrowed her eyes on Delia. "I have accounts that need goin' over, you know."

Delia squeezed her clasped fingers tighter. "I'm sure he's just been delayed and will be here directly."

"Well, if he happens to come callin' within the next few minutes, you let me know. If not, I s'pose he'll just have to see me after supper." With that she snapped the pocket watch shut, whisked into the library, and closed the door.

Worrying her bottom lip, Delia returned to her post at the window.

Folks had definitely treated Delia differently since she'd taken up with Cord. Several acquaintances had gone so far as to ignore her whenever they'd passed her on the street.

Paying her former friends little heed, she'd paraded Cord in public two more times over the past week. They'd had supper in town one evening at the hotel restaurant, then met a few days later at Faldene's for coffee.

Neither she nor Cord had mentioned the incident in Cynthia Davenport's garden. Ever since that night, Cord had remained aloof, quiet, speaking only when spoken to. Delia had carried the bulk of the conversations, expelling bursts of nervous chatter and carefully avoiding the issue of the kiss.

But the issue of the kiss had never been far from her mind. She still trembled inside whenever she thought about it—which was entirely more often than she wished to.

Every single morning after she'd so foolishly pressed herself upon Cord, she'd awakened with the feel of his lips lingering on hers. The memory of the warmth and strength of his hands had popped into her head at the most inopportune moments, causing her to leave sentences dangling half finished in the midst of conversation. In truth, she had hardly been able to focus her attention on anything else.

Willfully pushing these unwanted thoughts from her mind once again, Delia concentrated on the horizon, seeking some sign of the Cajun's approach. She had told herself repeatedly over the past few days that her fascination for Cord Kibedeaux was nothing more than a passing fancy. Her bold nature, she'd deemed, was merely attracted to the danger and mystery that surrounded the man.

But she lost her grip on those rationales the moment she spied Cord walking across the fields. He moved with a casual swagger of his hips that she hadn't noticed before. Barely aware that she did so, she watched him almost obsessively until he had neared the house and come up the steps.

Quickly ducking away from the window, she smoothed her skirt and tucked a stray curl back into place. When he knocked, she waited an appropriate length of time before answering, not wanting him to think she'd been dawdling by the door.

Her first glimpse of him standing on the porch, holding his hat against his chest in one hand and a cluster of white jasmines in the other, caused Delia's heart to commence pumping harder.

Annoyed by the unwelcome quiver in her abdomen, she grabbed his arm and hauled him into the foyer. "Where on earth have you been?" she whispered fiercely, then glanced toward the library. "Grandy has asked me twice if you were still comin'."

Cord opened his mouth, but Delia gave him no chance to reply.

"Oh, never mind," she said, steering him in the direction of the library. "I b'lieve she may just suspect somethin'. She's had a funny little gleam in her eyes all mornin'. I swear, sometimes I honestly think that woman is part fox." Delia paused at the door of her grandmother's study and faced Cord, unable to meet his gaze directly. "Oh, everything's gonna be fine," she murmured, more to herself than to him. Absently reaching out, she straightened his bow-tied cravat. "You just remember to act like you're dyin' for my hand, you hear? Oh, and don't forget to—"

As Delia brushed a piece of lint from his frock coat, Cord caught her nervous fingers and gave them a gentle squeeze. "You must not worry so, *chère*. It shows on your face." He dipped his head until his eyes were level with hers. "If your *grand-mère* is as clever as you say, she will surely see this, will she not? You must smile, wear the happiness of a woman in love. Everything will go as we planned, you will see, *hein*?"

The corners of Delia's mouth lifted right along with her heart. Cord's confidence that all would go well fortified her own. Facing the door, she grasped the arm he offered. "I'd best warn you," she told him in a confidential tone. "Grandy's generally in a foul mood when she's been kept waitin'."

"This could be to our advantage, no?" he asked with an arch of one brow.

Delia could only hope he was right in that respect. She placed a hand on the doorknob, took a deep calming breath, then entered the library with her proposed choice of a husband in tow.

Agatha Abernathy looked up from her paperwork. She straightened her back, closed her ledger, then laid her palms flat on either side of the big black book. "So this is your young man," she stated rather than asked.

Cord met the silver-haired woman's cool gray stare and could easily understand why the whole of Boudreaux Parish regarded her with such high esteem. Despite her small-boned daintiness, she appeared utterly formidable as she sat regally in her thronelike chair, her mouth fixed in a hard, no-nonsense line. Cord was indeed impressed. But perhaps because his reason for being there held no true purpose, he was not in the least intimidated—despite an inner voice in the back of his mind that warned he probably should be.

Without further ado, he disengaged his arm from Delia's hold and stepped forward. "Allow me to introduce myself, Madame Abernathy." He bowed curtly from the waist. "My name is Cord Kibedeaux."

"Mr. Kibedeaux," Agatha replied with a slight inclination of her head. "Your reputation proceeds you, sir," she added, though her expression never wavered. "Do sit down. You too, Adelaide. You look a bit pale."

Cord politely waited until Delia settled into one of the high-backed chairs that faced the desk. He was in the process of taking the seat next to her when he remembered the bunch of jasmines he held. Leaning forward, he handed the bouquet across the desk to Grandy.

"I almost forgot, madame. These are for you,"

he said, then eased back into his chair, crossed his legs, and rested his hat on his knee.

A flicker of surprise passed over Agatha Abernathy's features. She stared blankly at the flowers for a moment. One corner of her mouth quirked slightly upward as she lifted the sweetly scented cluster to her nose.

Then she blinked, cleared her throat, and laid the flowers aside. "How kind of you," she remarked, her features transforming into stone once again. "It's been a good while since a gentleman's brought me flowers—which causes me t' believe you might have some particular motive for doin' so."

Cord's cheeks ached with the urge to smile. "You are very wise, madame."

"I'm old, Mr. Kibedeaux." Her tone rang cranky, but a twinkle touched her eyes. "Wisdom is one of the scant few benefits of agin'." Grandy slid her gaze from Cord to Delia and back again. "Unfortunately, one of the drawbacks of gettin' on in your years is realizin' you no longer have enough time to dillydally. So suppose we get on with this."

Clasping her hands together atop her ledger, Agatha focused on Delia. "Adelaide didn't go into any big rigamarole about why you two wanted to see me today, but I can fairly guess it has somethin' to do with a proposal of sorts. Is that correct?"

Cord lowered his eyes to shield himself from Agatha's piercing gaze. Slipping his hand to the arm of the chair next to him, he wrapped his fingers around Delia's. *La belle de Boudreaux Parish* looked at him, her eyes wide with vulnerability.

To play his part more convincingly, he fastened

his gaze on her lips and reached into the forbidden territory of his mind for the stowed-away memory of their first and last kiss. *"Oui,* madame, you are correct. I wish your permission to marry your granddaughter."

"Do you love her, Mr. Kibedeaux?"

The blunt question caught Cord off guard. He glanced askance at Agatha Abernathy before he could alter his expression.

"But of course, madame," he answered in a calm, even tone as soon as he was able. He held a vague hope that perhaps the woman had missed the fleeting frown that had been on his face. On second thought, he highly suspected hardly anything slipped past Agatha's keen observation.

"And you, Adelaide, do you love this young man?"

Delia, too, had recovered from her initial surprise at the question and smiled brightly at her grandmother. "Oh, I do, Grandy."

Delia's unique ability to arrange her features to suit the given situation amazed Cord once again.

"I love him more than anything else in this whole wide world," she proclaimed, and fixed an adoring gaze on Cord.

Agatha pressed her mouth into a tight line, eyeing one, then the other. "Mr. Kibedeaux, you've got a lot of gall walkin' in here today and askin' for Adelaide's hand. I've got to give you that much. Surely you didn't expect me to give my wholehearted approval."

"But, Grandy—" Delia puckered her lower lip, leaned closer to Cord, and hugged his arm. "I couldn't even think of marryin' anyone else. What Cord and I have together is special."

Agatha smirked. "Oh, I've heard all about how

special your relationship is, Adelaide, don't you think I haven't. I may not get out of the house as often as I used to, but I do have my sources for gossip, dear. And I ought to tell you, I'm not at all pleased with what I've been hearin' lately." She frowned pointedly at Cord. "The two of you sneakin' around behind my back."

"You know good and well you wouldn't have allowed us to see each other any other way," Delia remarked with a tilt of her chin.

"You're absolutely right, dear. I wouldn't have." Agatha leaned back, braced her elbows on the arms of her chair, and steepled her fingers against her lips. "I hate havin' to bring such a delicate matter up," she said, directing the statement to Cord, "but there is a distinct difference in upbringin' here."

"*Oui*, madame. I am aware of that." Cord ducked his head and peered at her from under his eyebrows, attempting to appear dutifully dejected.

"Adelaide does have an obligation, you know, to uphold the fine, upstandin' Abernathy name. Although she hasn't often done such a good job of it." Agatha paused long enough to glare at her granddaughter. "On the other hand, you and your family don't exactly have the best reputations around these parts."

"No, madame, we do not," Cord agreed.

Agatha sighed in an exasperated fashion, then spent a long, quiet moment glancing back and forth between the two.

Delia settled further back in her chair and clasped her hands together in her lap. Just before she bowed her head, she discreetly gave Cord a secret smile.

He assumed her subtle satisfaction indicated their scheme was working according to plan. He should have felt relieved that the game was almost over. Ending his association with Delia would give him more time to pursue his own business. But for some strange reason, a small twinge of disappointment tugged at him.

"You're not at all suited socially," Grandy uttered with a shake of her head. "Not at all suited socially. However, I like a man with backbone, Mr. Kibedeaux. I admire a man who is not easily intimidated. So many young fools are these days, you know." Agatha tapped her steepled fingers against her chin. "You look to be a strong, healthy young man, Mr. Kibedeaux. Strong, healthy . . . and virile, if you don't mind me sayin' so. I'm of a mind to believe you may just be exactly the sort of man my Adelaide needs."

Preoccupied with the thought of meeting her father in Europe, Delia had been only half listening, but Grandy's last words nudged her from her daydreaming. She raised her gaze by degrees to her grandmother.

"What?" she asked, certain she'd simply heard Grandy wrong.

Agatha granted her granddaughter a rare smile. "By heaven," she said, then slapped the desktop, "I think we could use some new blood in this family. It appears to me that this young man of yours could pass on some worthwhile qualities to my great-grandchildren."

Delia gripped the sides of her chair and felt the color drain from her face.

"Of course, the two of you marryin' isn't goin' to set too well with most in Boudreaux Parish," Grandy went on. She glanced to the side as if considering this. ''There's liable to be a ruckus to contend with at first, but sooner or later folks'll just have to get used to it. You know, Winston Grayson's wife, Leana, was Acadian, and eventually, everybody warmed up to her. Besides, I b'lieve it's high time things changed 'round here.''

Grandy rose and rounded her desk. Clutching her blue-veined hands to her waist, she smiled down at Delia, then stooped to kiss her granddaughter's forehead. ''You've no idea how happy all this makes me, Adelaide.''

Delia closed her eyes. *This can't truly be happening. I have to wake up from this nightmare,* she told herself. But when she lifted her lids, a sight more treacherous than any horrid vision that she could ever imagine greeted her.

Grandy held Cord's hand in both of hers and was viewing the man as if he'd sprouted wings and donned a halo. ''Welcome to the family, Mr. Kibedeaux,'' she said, then reached out, caught Delia's limp wrist, and wedged her numb fingers into Cord's damp palm.

Delia looked at Cord and noted he, too, had paled considerably. He opened his mouth, closed it, then opened it again, but nothing came out.

''Now, now. There's no need to say anything.'' Agatha released their hands, letting them fall and dangle loosely entwined between their chairs. ''I know you both must be overwhelmed.'' She sniffed and swiped at a tear rolling down her cheek. ''I'm sure the two of you will want to celebrate. Adelaide, why don't you ask Bess to fix you a bite to eat and have a picnic on the back lawn? It's a beautiful day.''

Unable to move a single muscle, Delia stared blankly at her grandmother.

"Well? What are you waitin' for, dear?" Agatha skirted her desk and took her chair. "I'd join you myself if I wasn't so far behind on my books." She opened her ledger, picked up her pen, and held it poised above the page as she regarded the newly betrothed. "Well, go on now. Off with you two. I've got work to do. Lord knows it's goin' t' be hard enough as is to keep weddin' plans from poppin' into my head all day."

Cord staggered awkwardly to his feet and took Delia's arm, practically lifting her from her seat. She would have swayed had he not grabbed her shoulders and steadied her as he steered her toward the door.

"Oh, and Adelaide," Grandy interjected, stopping them before they could leave. Delia turned her head mechanically, and was a bit surprised to find her grandmother struggling to maintain a strict expression. Especially when the stern set of Grandy's mouth had always seemed to come so naturally to the woman.

"Y'all make sure you have your little picnic in full view of the house, you hear? I'd best not catch you meetin' without a chaperone no more—leastways, not till after you're properly wed. Is that clear, Adelaide? Adelaide?"

"Yes, ma'am," Delia murmured absently and allowed Cord to lead her from the library.

They stepped into the foyer and closed the door behind them. Delia pressed her fingertips to her temples. "Lord Almighty," she said under her breath, then turned frantically toward Cord and grasped his lapels. "What in the blue blazes are we goin' to do now?"

He peered down at her as if she'd suddenly lost her mind. "We? What are *we* going to do?" A short, breathy, cynical laugh escaped him. "Oh, no. *Non, chère.*" He shook his head and pried her fingers from the front of his jacket. "*This* was not part of the bargain. I only agreed to *pose* as your fiancé. Nothing more."

Donning his hat, he strode toward the front door.

A suffocating pressure gripped Delia's chest. She hurried ahead of him and positioned herself at the door, blocking his exit. "Cord, please." She accentuated the plea with her eyes. "You have to help me."

Cord braced a palm against the doorjamb and brought his face menacingly close to hers. "My part in this is finished, Mademoiselle Abernathy. Me, I have done what you asked of me. Your troubles are your own, *chère*. They are not mine."

"Cord . . . please, wait. Just help me think of something. Maybe we can make Grandy—"

He clamped a hand over her mouth and glanced over his shoulder in the direction of the library. When he brought his eyes back to hers, they were filled with a soft, sad glow. "Do you have any idea how much your *grand-mère* cares for you?" he whispered. "Me, I would give anything to have someone care so much for me." The sorrow in his gaze turned to bitterness. "Your *grand-mère*, she is a fine woman. You, you are but a spoiled child who thinks she can stomp her foot and have her way. You think you can move people around like checkers on a game board, no?" He slipped his hand from her mouth and pointed a finger at her nose. "Well, not me, *chère*. Not me. Not anymore. I will no longer be a party to your conniving, *hein?*"

Pushing her easily out of the way, Cord opened the door. He paused just outside and, without a backward glance, added, "Good day, Mademoiselle Abernathy. *Adieu* and farewell."

Then he strode across the veranda and down the steps, leaving Delia weak and worried as she wilted against the doorjamb.

Chapter Nine

Banns were read aloud the following Sunday.
Delia closed her eyes and cringed at the
sound of Father Hopkins's booming voice echo-
ing throughout the church. Ever since the disastrous meeting with Cord and Grandy, she'd tried
to come up with a plan, *any plan*, to forestall this
dreadful moment. She had conjured up a dozen
sensible reasons for delaying the marriage, but her
grandmother wouldn't hear of postponing the
wedding. On the contrary, with each debate,
Delia had felt herself being dragged closer and
closer toward the jaws of matrimony. So far, she
had been helpless to prevent the inevitable pro-
cession of events.

Gasps, groans, and whispering rippled through
the congregation. Delia rolled her eyes behind her
lids. She didn't understand what all the fuss was
about. Most of the churchgoers already knew
about the upcoming marriage anyway, thanks to
Grandy and her gossipy friends.

Delia fidgeted to the edge of the pew, peered
around her beaming grandmother, and searched
the adjacent row of benches.

Millicent Mosely craned her neck forward from

the line of people and looked at Delia, her eyes appearing as if they might pop from their sockets.

Delia grimaced.

Milly pressed her lips into a tight line.

The exchange clearly indicated they would meet as soon as the service ended. With a full half hour of mass left, each woman settled back in her seat and focused straight ahead, neither one hearing a single word of the sermon.

As the organ played the last note of the closing hymn, Delia hurried Grandy down the aisle.

"Goodness gracious, Adelaide," Agatha complained, lifting her elbow from Delia's grasp. "Slow down a bit."

"Sorry, Grandy. I'm just a little anxious to talk to Milly, that's all."

Agatha tucked her chin and tried to look stern, but the twinkle in her eyes gave her good mood away. "Oh, go on," she said with a swipe of her hand, then chuckled. "I s'pose the two of you have lots to talk about. I'm assumin' you're goin' to ask her to be your maid of honor?"

Delia glanced to the side. "Um . . . yes. Why, yes, I am."

"Well, now, don't you worry none about me. You go on and chat with Milly as long as you want. I'll see myself home."

Delia helped Grandy to the carriage, bade her farewell, then scanned the crowded church grounds for Milly.

She spied her friend gesturing wildly beside the cemetery adjoining the church. Once Milly had caught Delia's attention, she turned and scurried through the wrought-iron gate of the graveyard, disappearing down a row of tombstones.

Attempting to move toward the cemetery unnoticed, Delia walked at a casual pace. Now and then a member of the congregation snidely congratulated her on her engagement. She merely smiled or nodded in passing, ignoring those who made nasty remarks.

She had almost reached the ornate gate when someone seized her arm from behind. She gasped as she was whirled around to face Chauncy Bateman.

"Tell me why, Delia," he demanded, his handsome features tinged with anger. "Tell me why on God's green earth you would do such a thing."

She looked past him at the thinning crowd lingering outside the church. "Chauncy, I really don't think this is the time or place—"

With one quick glance, he traced her gaze. Then, gripping her shoulders, he pushed her into the recess of bushes that edged the graveyard.

"Oh, it's time, all right," he whispered, leaning close to her ear. He brushed his thumbs along her collarbone. "I'd say it's *high* time you told me what the devil's goin' on. Tell me, Delia." He increased the pressure of his fingers on her skin. "You're goin' to tell me here and now why the hell you'd up and marry the likes of that stinkin' white trash."

Delia stared at him in numb disbelief for a long moment. She'd never seen Chauncy in such a blood rush. For as long as she'd known him, he'd been mischievous and always had a mean, teasing streak. But he'd never displayed the characteristics of a madman before. The rage glowing in his eyes frightened her.

In the space of her next breath, the fear rising in Delia's abdomen turned to fury. With one swift motion, she jerked out of his grasp and shoved him away.

"How dare you manhandle me in such a fashion, Chauncy Bateman!" She jabbed his chest and he staggered backward. "I don't have to explain anything to you, do you hear? What I do . . . who I see . . . who I marry . . . or who I don't marry is none of your damn business. Understand?"

Pure hate emanated from Chauncy's glare. He curled his hands into fists at his sides. "You led me to believe you cared for me," he said in a deathly quiet tone, "while all along you were only toyin' with my affection. And now . . . now you're goin' to make a fool of me over some damned, no-account Cajun." Chauncy swallowed hard, his eyes bright. Beads of sweat formed on his upper lip, and a pitiful agony mingled with the animosity in his expression. "I'll never forgive you for this, Delia. You mark my word," he warned, aiming a finger at her. "I'll get even with you and that swamp rat if it's the last thing I ever do."

A heaviness settled in Delia's breast. She'd imagined Chauncy might be a little miffed when he heard the news, but she hadn't expected the intensity of his reaction . . . hadn't known the depth of his feelings for her.

"Oh, Chauncy." She stretched a hand toward his cheek, but he flinched from her touch. "You and I grew up together. Of course I care about you. We had some good times. But I never told you that I loved you or anything, did I? And I never made you any promises."

"You made promises, Delia . . . with those big blue eyes of yours . . . and every time you smiled at me."

"Chauncy, please. Let's not fuss over somethin' like this. It's not worth it. Believe me, it's not what you think. Really. It's just—" On the verge of disclosing the whole story, Delia clamped her mouth shut. She rummaged through her brain, seeking some alternative solution for soothing Chauncy's hurt feelings. But before she could come up with a suitable answer, he walked off in a huff.

She closed her eyes and hugged her waist. Her head ached. The situation wasn't getting any better. *Damn it all to hell and back.* Everything was growing more complicated by the minute.

With a deep sigh, she reopened her eyes, left the bushes, and slipped through the cemetery entrance. No doubt Milly would be bursting with questions. Delia's tension eased at the thought of discussing the undistorted truth with her confidante. Together, perhaps they might think of some way out of this messy predicament.

Delia halted abruptly when she approached the stone angel in the center of the graveyard. The artfully chiseled features of the statue had been designed to provoke a sense of serenity, although she felt no such peacefulness. Her scalp prickled as the celestial being looked directly down at her.

This particular section of the cemetery was not one of her most favorite places. When she'd been nine, Chauncy and his friends had left her stranded in this very spot; then later the lot of them had sprung out from behind the angel's huge wings, making horrible noises.

Shuddering at the memory, Delia veered off the archangel's path. She turned down the row of headstones and searched for some sign of her friend. It was too quiet, she decided. Too tranquil for her taste.

"Milly," she whispered, carefully weaving around the neatly kept graves. "Milly? This isn't funny now. Where are you?"

She nearly jumped out of her skin when Milly walked up behind her and tapped her shoulder. Delia swung around, pressing a hand to her thrumming heart, then frowned threateningly at her friend. "Hell's bells, Milly, don't go sneakin' up on me like that. You know this place gives me the willies. What on earth possessed you to have me meet you *here* anyway?"

"Oh, dear." Milly clasped her hands to her chin and wrinkled her nose. "I'd forgotten this cemetery scares you. I'm terribly sorry. Really, I am. I just thought we could talk here without any of those nosy ol' gossips millin' about the churchyard closin' in on us."

Delia cocked her eyes heavenward, shook her head, then smiled. "Of course, you're right," she said, locking her arm through Milly's and guiding her to a nearby bench. "I s'pose it's plain silly of me to let a cemetery scare me so. Here, let's sit down."

They settled themselves on the marble slab seat and adjusted their hooped skirts.

Delia looked sideways at her dark-haired friend and sighed in an exasperated fashion. "Oh, Milly. Have I got an earful for you."

Three days later, Delia lay across her bed well into the afternoon, nibbling on her nails, no closer to solving her problems than she had been on Sunday.

Milly hadn't been able to offer any suggestions.

She had simply gasped after Delia's every sentence and murmured, "Oh, my."

Delia shifted her weight on the mattress at the sound of a knock on her door. "Come in," she muttered absently.

Grandy entered, carrying a silver serving tray. "Good afternoon, Adelaide," she said cheerfully and, walking over to the bed, placed the tray on the nightstand. "Bess just made a nice batch of molasses cookies. Still hot, straight from the oven. I thought I'd bring them up myself so we could have a little chat."

Delia rolled onto her stomach, glared at the glass of milk and plate of cookies, then buried her face in her pillow. "I'm not hungry," she mumbled into the fluffy mound of feathers.

"Oh, come now, dear. You've got to eat *something*." Agatha strode to the window and flung open the curtains, letting in a bright ray of sunshine. "You been holed up in here since the banns were read. And I think I know why."

Delia lifted her head and turned toward her grandmother, squinting into the glaring light that filled the room. "You do?"

"Well, of course I do, dear." Agatha settled herself on the edge of the mattress. "Oh, Adelaide," she said softly, brushing a lock of hair from Delia's forehead. "I s'pose we shoulda had this discussion long ago. But, you see, I've always looked upon you as a child. It was that incident about you steppin' out into the garden with Chauncy Bateman that finally opened my eyes . . . made me realize you were growin' up. Now that you're gettin' married, I *know* there are certain goings-on between a man and a woman I need to tell you about."

"Grandy, I don't wanna talk about *that*." With a groan, Delia pulled the pillow over her head.

"But, Adelaide, dear, we *have* to. It's high time you knew about these things."

"I'm not gonna listen," Delia replied in a muffled tone.

Grandy snatched up the pillow and tossed it to the end of the bed. "Oh, yes, you are, Adelaide. Now turn over so I can see your face. I wanna make sure you get the full meanin' of what I'm about t' say."

Reluctantly obeying, Delia rolled onto her back, crossed her arms over her chest, and stared at the ceiling.

"That's better. Now—" Agatha paused and took a deep breath. "Marriage carries a great responsibility for a woman, Adelaide. A wife is expected to . . . well, perform certain duties, shall we say . . . in bed. No matter what you've heard, dear, those particular duties don't always have to be unpleasant."

Delia squeezed her eyes shut, feeling the temperature of her cheeks rise.

"The first time your husband . . . well, when he . . . *consummates* the marriage, it might be a little . . . uncomfortable, but you'll get used to it. You'll even grow to enjoy the attentions of your husband. Land sakes, when your granddaddy and I—"

"Grannn-dy!" Delia wailed, covering her face with her hands. With tears of embarrassment stinging her eyes, she spread her fingers and peered at her grandmother. "Please . . . *please*, don't say any more. I can't bear it. I can't—"

"There, there, now, dear." Agatha tugged Delia's hands from her face and clasped them tightly in her own. "It's all right. I won't go any further. I've told you pert-near everything that's necessary, I s'pose. Anything else, you'll learn for yourself on your weddin' night."

Pursing her lips, Grandy ran her thumbs back and forth over Delia's knuckles. "I didn't mean to upset you. I just thought you ought to be prepared." She smiled sympathetically. "Why don't you try one of Bess's cookies?"

"I don't want a cookie," Delia replied in a voice drained of emotion.

Agatha cocked her head. "You need to get up, Adelaide. Proper ladies don't lie about in bed all day. Everyone's gonna think you're lazy."

"I don't care what anybody thinks." Delia dragged her hands from her grandmother's grasp and turned onto her side, pulling the covers to her chin.

"Would you like to go over the guest list with me? Might cheer you up a bit."

"No," Delia answered quietly. "I just want to be left alone."

"Very well." Agatha sighed, reached out and patted her granddaughter's hip, then stood. "I s'pose it's only natural for a bride-to-be to harbor a certain amount of moodiness. You go ahead and rest today, dear. Tomorrow, I'll expect you to come downstairs for breakfast. We can discuss some of the finer details of the weddin' then."

"Grandy?" Delia stopped her grandmother's progress toward the door.

"Yes, dear?"

"I want to see Daddy," Delia blurted out, latching onto Grandy's moment of compassion and hoping she might be moved to give in to her request. "Can't we *please* put all of this off till I've had a chance to talk to him?"

"I'm afraid not." Grandy firmly shook her head. "I've sent word to Wendell, notifyin' him of your plans to wed, but I doubt he'll be able to come all the way from Paris in time to attend the ceremony. I'm sorry, Adelaide, but the date is set, and most of the arrangements have done been made."

Delia's heart sank into her stomach. In desperation, she looked pleadingly at her grandmother. "Grandy . . . I'm not ready," she whispered in all sincerity. "I'm not ready to marry."

Agatha gave her a small, bittersweet smile. "None of us is ever quite ready, dear." She searched Delia's face for a long moment, then turned and disappeared into the hall.

Delia stared at the vacant doorway, and a hot tear trickled down her cheek. Her whole life was a mess. Even if she could muster up the courage to tell her grandmother the truth, at this point Grandy would probably make her go through with the wedding just for spite.

The way things were going, she'd never be able to join her father in Europe. If only she'd been wise enough to save some of her allowance now and then. But she hadn't. Not one penny. She had spent every single cent on hats and lace hankies and other such frivolous nonsense. She owned a few pieces of jewelry that might be worth something, but not nearly enough to pay her passage to Paris. She needed a lot more money than any of her baubles would bring if she intended to leave Boudreaux Parish for good. And she did intend to leave. It was just a matter of when and where she would find the funds to do so.

Weary from worrying, Delia felt her lids grow heavy. Her thoughts trailed off into nothingness for the extent of several deep, rhythmic breaths.

Then her eyes flew open.

Acquiring her inheritance was the only way to get what she wanted. Marrying was the only way to obtain her inheritance. Delia sat up in bed, and the answers to all her problems began to fall into place.

She *would* marry Cord Kibedeaux. She would marry him, live with him for the agreed term of six months, then collect her inheritance and sail for Europe.

It was such a simple solution, Delia couldn't believe she hadn't thought of it before now.

As she wilted back onto her pillow, a peaceful relief began to flow over her. When all was said and done, Grandy could never dispute the fact that her granddaughter had fulfilled the requirements of the contract.

Delia smiled and snuggled deeper into the soft coverlet. With a plan to ensure Cord's willing assistance already forming in her head, she let the exhaustion of the past few days consume her, and fell fast asleep.

Cord leaned a shoulder against the doorframe of the shanty, took a bite of gumbo from the bowl he held, and viewed the early evening's lavender light creeping upon the bayou. He lifted each spoonful mechanically. He chewed, he swallowed, but he hardly tasted the spicy dish.

What the hell was wrong with him? he wondered. He'd been listless, lifeless, since his visit with Agatha Abernathy. It was almost as if a large hollow chasm had formed in the very center of his soul.

He had tried to convince himself over the past few days that this emptiness inside stemmed from his blundering association with Delia Abernathy. His short venture into the realm of society had turned up little or nothing about whoever had framed him. He had wasted precious time—time that should have been spent trying to identify the person responsible for sending him to prison.

A bird squawked somewhere overhead, signaling an intruder. Cord set his bowl on the chair and strode to the edge of the porch, half expecting *Tante* Netha Bea to appear from nowhere in her usual mysterious manner.

But as he peered up the bayou, a flatboat rounded the bend. He recognized the black man, Samuel, and spied the flash of a pale green skirt behind him.

Cord was tempted to put on his shirt, but instead remained where he was. Leaning insolently back against the porch rail, he hooked his thumbs in the waistband of his breeches and watched the two approach.

Samuel steered the skiff alongside the shanty's porch. Delia stood, teetered, then regained her balance and stretched out a hand to Cord.

He made no move to help her. He merely looked at her, keeping his expression bland. "There is no need for you to get out of the boat, unless you have come to pay your debt."

Delia's smile faltered, and the corners of her mouth fell.

"You have brought what you owe me, no?"

She drew herself erect. "No," she said sharply, then softened her haughty tone. "I'm afraid I didn't come here to pay you for your services. I just desperately need to talk to you."

"Ah, but we have nothing more to talk about, *ma chérie*. I thought I made that clear. *Adieu*, Mademoiselle Abernathy." Turning away from her, he started into the house.

"Cord! Please, wait. This is important."

He halted in the doorway and glanced over his shoulder. "Important to you, maybe. Not to me."

Lifting her skirt, Delia attempted to climb out of the boat unaided. In the process, an indecent view of her ruffled pantaloons caught Cord off guard. Before he could stop to think, he had swiveled around and found himself watching her scramble onto the porch. Her stubbornness almost made him smile. Almost, but not quite.

Marching up to him, she straightened her bodice, then placed her hands on her hips. "Will you just listen to me a minute?"

"No," he said bluntly, then proceeded to enter the house.

Delia grabbed his arm and he froze. The touch of her fingers scalded his bare skin. He raised his gaze from her dainty, well-formed hand to her eyes—a grave mistake—for he was instantly hit with the sensation of being dragged, pulled against his will into the depths of those blue pools.

Dread pressed against his sternum as the true reasons for his recent lethargy struck him full force. He *felt* something . . . some ravenous demand for Delia's attention, a repressed craving that had been lurking in the shadows of his mind.

He had hungered for female companionship, but never for a particular woman. Always before, any halfway attractive woman could fulfill his needs. What he felt for Delia was different, though. This emotion wasn't the same. It was new and foreign and . . . most definitely *disastrous*, he decided.

Cord lowered his lids, blocking the effect that her presence was having on him. In the same way he used to escape the terror of his father's blows, he closed an inner door on the world, barricading himself in numbness.

Only when he'd reached that detached state did he dare look at Delia Abernathy again. He opened his eyes slowly, confident he had all sentiment safely locked away, but at the first glimpse of her features he was instantly, powerfully, drawn into the realm of her spell once more.

Damn the woman. Damn the hold she has on me. Where in God's name is my self-control?

Letting anger fill the gap in his wavering restraint, Cord jerked his arm free of Delia's grasp. He paced the length of the porch, then pivoted and shook a finger at her.

"What right do you have to come here and bother me all the time, *hein?* Tell me that. You come here unannounced when maybe I am busy. You drag this poor man from his family"—he gestured to Samuel, and the black man ducked his head—"to bring you to the bayou. And for what? All for nothing, that's what!"

Cord took a step forward, but stopped, opening and closing his fists at his sides. Then, just to test his weakened will, he moved in slow measures toward her. Halting mere inches away from Delia, he looked directly into her upturned face. Her cheeks were flushed. Her eyes were bright, her lips slightly parted. He was determined to feel nothing. *Nothing*, damn it. "You and I have finished our business," he said with a chill edging his words.

She stared up at him for a matter of moments, her heartbeat pulsating at the base of her throat. "I won't be able to pay you unless you help me," she whispered. "Please, just listen. That's all I ask. I've figured out a way for both of us to get our money."

Cord searched her imploring expression with no small amount of skepticism. He had witnessed her *performances* before. She could be very convincing. Certain she was about to try her dramatic ability on him, he steeled himself.

"All we have to do is go through with the marriage," she stated in a demure tone, as if she had simply asked for some meager favor.

Had she reached out and unfastened his trousers, Cord could not have been more stunned.

"*Non.*" He shook his head, stepped around her, and started for the door. "You leave my house now. Go. Go home. And do not come back here, *hein?*"

He walked into the shanty, giving the door a push behind him, and went straight to the cupboard. Grabbing the bottle of homemade wine, he filled a glass, swigged it down, then poured another.

Delia peeked through the crack in the partially closed door. It was highly improper to enter someone's living quarters uninvited. Then again, she couldn't recollect ever letting propriety get in her way before.

Nibbling at her bottom lip, she shoved the door open quietly and trod softly into the room. Cord stood with his back to her, and she couldn't help but notice the scars marring his otherwise smooth skin. Her heart ached at the sight of the pale stripes across his bronze shoulders. She could only imagine the pain he must have withstood while acquiring such reminders of his past.

Pushing the unpleasant thought from her mind, she shifted her gaze, assessing the dingy, dust-layered interior of the shack. A tattered blanket hung across what she assumed was a sleeping alcove. A rickety table and a chair that matched the one on the porch appeared to be the only furnishings.

Cord muttered a curse, bringing Delia's attention back to him. He turned, and the drink he held stilled midway to his mouth.

"Holy Mary, Jesus, and Joseph," he muttered, then slammed his glass on the table so hard that the wine sloshed over the rim. Raising his hands, he spoke to the ceiling. "God in heaven, what must I do to rid myself of this crazy woman, *hein*?"

Delia laced her fingers together at her waist. "We would only have to live together for six months. Of course, the church would never sanction a divorcement, but I see no reason why we couldn't simply go our separate ways when the time was up."

Cord let go of a short, cruel laugh. "I could not live with you, *ma chérie*, for half a day, much less six months."

"I'll pay you double what I offered."

"*Non*. I do not need money that bad."

"Triple?"

"You do not hear so good, no?" Cord picked up his drink and downed the contents, glaring at her above the brim of the glass. His dark eyes glittered as he dragged the back of his hand across his mouth. "I will tell you this only once more. I will not . . . *will not* participate in any more of your scheming. Not for money. Not for your sweet smile"—he gave her body a bold appraisal—"nor for anything else you may offer. Now go. You are not welcome here. And we have nothing more to say to each other."

Delia's cheeks burned. Her eyes stung. No one had ever dared speak to her in such a manner. A red haze covered her vision. Lifting her chin, she returned his obvious contempt ten times over.

"Oh, but I'd say we do have a bit more to discuss, Mr. Kibedeaux," she remarked in a deceivingly calm voice. She picked an imaginary piece of lint from her sleeve, then cocked her head and looked at him. "I had hoped we might go about this in a civilized fashion. You see, I do so dread havin' to go to Grandy and tell her I'm expectin' your child."

Chapter Ten

Cord stared at her in a dazed manner for a long, endless moment. Then he blinked, and his whiskey-colored eyes narrowed into slits.

"Surely, mademoiselle," he said icily, "even you could not do such a terribly wicked thing."

"Why, of course I could. And I will, if you leave me no other choice."

Delia stifled a smile. This sweet taste of triumph overshadowed the stab of his hateful remarks earlier. She had him right where she wanted him now: underneath her thumb.

With a powerful surge pushing her forward, she moved toward him in a gentle sway, stopping just short of his reach. "I do so regret havin' to press you for your answer." She touched the dusty table and, lifting the grit, rolled it between her fingertips for an idle inspection. "But I'm afraid I can't leave till you make some sort of decision here. You see, Grandy's done set the date for the weddin' and I—"

Before Delia could say another word, Cord grabbed her forearms and jerked her against him.

Cold, raw fear paralyzed her. Cord's eyes glimmered gold, bearing down on her with an unnatural, demonlike light. With every muscle in his face drawn tight, she could see his temples throbbing . . . feel his hot, short breaths grazing her skin. Her panic rising, she suddenly realized part of her terror stemmed from his unique ability to quicken her pulse whenever he touched her.

"You little she-devil," he hissed through clenched teeth. "You surely must be the spawn of the evil prince himself."

Delia shoved at his chest in a futile attempt to free herself, but he only tightened his grip. His fingers bit into her flesh until she winced and ceased all struggle.

Near tears, she focused on the pulse throbbing in his throat. "You let me go." The intended command came out more like a whimper, yet the pitiful sound of it spurred her pride. She looked the Cajun straight in the eye, her chin quivering with indignation. "Do you hear? You let me go this very instant, damn you. You're hurtin' me."

"You do not know the meaning of true pain, *ma chérie*. If you only knew what happiness it would bring me to give you a few lessons. It would be so easy, would it not, just to put my hands around your neck and—"

"Samuel's right outside," Delia reminded him. Her stomach trembled, but she met his wrathful gaze without flinching. She remained perfectly still, afraid if she dared to move he might make good his threat. While she watched the storm fade from his features, she came to the conclusion that he honestly *was* capable of all the awful, horrid things everyone in Boudreaux Parish had always accused him of.

He let go of her abruptly, leaving the indentation of his fingers on her arms. Then he pivoted, raked a hand through his thick dark hair, and moved like a man walking through waist-high water to the window at the rear of the tiny room. With both hands he grasped the upper casement and braced his weight against the frame.

Delia lowered her gaze from the slanted lash marks across his broad shoulders, following the hollow ridge of his spine to his tapered waist. His forlorn stance tugged at her conscience. Bringing Cord to heel by telling Grandy such a wild untruth was wrong. Delia hadn't been too comfortable with the idea, but she had certainly been prepared to use it if necessary.

Leastways, until now. Now she wasn't so sure she shouldn't just leave Cord Kibedeaux be.

"You would actually do this?" Cord asked, his voice low and crisp as he continued staring out the window. "You would hold a gun to my head, *hein?*"

"Well, I wouldn't go puttin' it that way." Delia grimaced, wishing she could make him understand the verity of the situation. "But fact is, neither of us has much of a choice anymore. After all's been said and done, if we confess to Grandy now, she'll have *me* horsewhipped and *you* shot for sure."

Cord half turned, leaned against the window frame, and crossed his arms over his chest. "Me, I have little to lose, regardless. But you have plenty, no? Have you not once considered what actually marrying me could do to your reputation?"

Delia shrugged lightly and tilted her head, letting a long curl drape over her shoulder. "I suspect my reputation's a little spotted already. Not that it matters much. As soon as we dissolve our blissful union and I collect my inheritance, I'm leavin' for Europe anyway.''

Cord closed his eyes and massaged the bridge of his nose, then sank into the chair. Joining his hands loosely between his knees, he studied them for a moment before looking up.

Deep lines of worry creased his forehead, enhancing his handsome features. His "Why me?" expression nipped sharply at Delia's heart.

"So tell me, *chérie.*" He paused and flexed his jaw. "When have you decided this mock wedding should take place, *hein?*"

Cord ran a finger around the inside of his starched collar. When he'd finally given up and accepted Delia's harebrained proposal, he hadn't expected the ceremony to be performed so soon.

Yet a week and two days later, here he was, standing at the altar of St. Augustine's, waiting for his bride to make her entrance.

The pews were filled with prestigious strangers. Dressed to the hilt, they ogled him as if he were on display in a museum. Wearing a carefully guarded expression, Cord returned their stares without really seeing them. He projected an outward calmness he didn't feel, reassuring himself that no one noticed the occasional trembling of his knees.

The pipe organ blared the first prominent notes of the wedding march. The double doors at the rear of the church swung wide. And Cord swallowed the knot in his throat.

Milly gave Delia a push to get her started. Aiming a quick scowl over her shoulder at her maid of honor, Delia stumbled from the vestibule into the sanctuary.

When she turned her head frontward again, a sea of faces greeted her. Grandy's prestige in the community had packed the church to its full capacity. It seemed no one had refused Agatha's invitation to join her in witnessing this blissful occasion. And if anyone present disapproved, none of them dared show it.

Pausing to collect her wits, Delia tightened her grip on the bouquet of white roses and calla lilies. Then she took a deep breath, pasted a presumedly serene smile on her lips, and inched forward in yards of white silk that hid her dragging feet.

Her head still buzzed from the last-minute preparations. Hectic activity had invaded the Abernathy household during the past week.

Grandy hadn't wasted any time making all the arrangements. Completely waving aside the usual waiting period of a proper betrothal, Agatha had reserved the church for the Saturday two weekends after the announcement of banns.

Somewhere in the midst of all the hustle and bustle of the past couple of days, Delia had reconciled herself to her predicament. She had reasoned that the sooner the ceremony was over, the sooner she'd be able to join her father abroad.

At present, though, reservations started jumping about inside her again, and within the space of her next step they grew to panic-sized proportions. The moral side of her nature balked loudly at her sinful purpose for this so-called holy union. Distorted thoughts bumped against one another in her brain.

She moved down the aisle in a dreamlike state, mechanically acknowledging those she passed with a slight inclination of her chin. Somehow she managed to keep her smile intact, but her gaze roved over the guests impassively, until it settled on Cord.

At the sight of him, she felt her breath leave her lungs in a rush.

He stood tall and straight, looking incredibly stunning in his gray silk swallow-tailed jacket. As she approached, he crooked his elbow and offered her his arm.

Delia took her place beside him and looked up into his brown, stony eyes. *It's a crying shame you don't love him,* a small voice whispered from the back of her mind, *a crying shame the ritual about to be performed can't be real.*

"Who gives this woman in holy matrimony?" the priest asked.

"I do." Grandy's voice reverberated through the cathedral, turning Delia's head to Agatha's seat of honor in the front row.

Meeting Delia's gaze levelly, she added, "And her father sends his blessing by proxy."

As if hit by a sudden strong wind, Delia swayed. *My father's given his consent? He's known of Grandy's wicked plan all along . . . and hasn't lifted a finger to prevent all this madness?*

Without thinking, she tightened her grasp on Cord's arm. His biceps constricted, squeezing her fingers against his ribs. The discreet display of concern on his part made her look up at him again.

For a split second his cool, vacant stare wavered, and she glimpsed a bit of tenderness in his eyes.

"We do not have to go through with this," he said in a voice barely above a whisper. "It is not too late to stop it, *chère.* We can simply walk away and—"

"Yes," Delia murmured absently, then blinked. "I mean . . . no! No, we can't stop it. It's the only way, don't you see?"

The priest cleared his throat in an exaggerated fashion. "Shall we begin now?" He peered beneath his brows at the couple before him. "Or not?"

"I'm ready." Delia glanced askance at Cord. *"We're* ready, Father."

"You're sure?"

"Oh, yes, Father, I'm sure. *We're* sure . . . aren't we, *dear?"* She nudged Cord with her elbow.

A blank expression passed over Cord's features; then he shrugged and bobbed his head without meeting the priest's eyes.

Father Hopkins pressed his thin lips together and viewed the couple long enough for Delia to fear he might refuse to perform the ceremony.

At last, with a sigh, he lifted the Good Book he already had opened to the appropriate page and bellowed out, "Dearly beloved . . ."

Delia lost track of what he was saying. She let her mind wander from the sermon on love and duty. Father Hopkins was clearly annoyed when he had to repeat himself while asking her to kneel. Yet she continued to slip in and out of reality, catching only snatches of the priest's droning words: *Do you, Adelaide Elizabeth Abernathy, take this man to be your lawfully wedded husband . . . By the power invested in me, I now pronounce you man and wife . . . You may kiss the bride . . . kiss the bride . . . kiss the bride . . .*

Father Hopkins's final statement echoed in Delia's head, bringing her to, as if a cold hand had been placed on her bare back.

"Well, young man?" The priest turned his head and smiled indulgently at Cord's reluctance. "Go ahead. For goodness' sake, kiss your wife. Everyone's waiting."

Hesitantly, Cord placed his hands gently on Delia's shoulders and twisted her toward him. He lowered his head in slow measures, his uncertain gaze searching hers.

Delia's heart beat wildly in her breast. She closed her eyes and tilted her face in anticipation, spurred by sweet memories of his last kiss. Cord brushed his mouth across hers ever so softly, making her tremble. She waited for him to gather her into his arms and produce the same spine-tingling magic he'd applied in the Davenports' garden.

But Delia's luscious expectation burst abruptly when Cord pulled away. She opened her eyes, seeing tiny little stars floating around his features as he withdrew.

On impulse, she tossed her bouquet in Milly's direction. Going up on her toes, she clutched Cord's neck and pressed her lips fiercely to his.

He stiffened as she leaned into him. His chest rose and fell rapidly against her own. Then he grasped her in a crushing embrace, and his mouth moved over hers . . . providing even more of that certain magic she'd yearned for.

"A-a-hem." Father Hopkins cleared his voice loudly again. "Here now, children," he said, prodding them apart with his Bible. "You'll have the rest of your lives for that sort of thing."

Blood rushed to Delia's cheeks the moment she stepped away from Cord. Her new husband's eyes mirrored her alarm. She wanted to say something that would diminish the impression

she'd just given him. Perhaps she should explain—tell him the truth. She merely liked kissing
him. That was all. She would just tell him—

The organ drowned out Delia's thoughts,
thrumming out Beethoven's "Ode to Joy."

Cord caught her arm and stooped to her ear.
"Me, I think we would have been better off jumping the broomstick, yeah."

Delia furrowed her brow. "Doing what?"

"It's an old Acadian custom for uniting couples
in wedlock. Much simpler than all this, do you
not agree?" Cord nodded toward the guests, inhaled deeply, then proceeded to usher Delia
down the aisle. "Come. We will finish this ordeal, *hein?*"

He hurried her through the gauntlet of well-
wishers. She ducked her head, shielding her face
from showers of rice, hiding her features from
prying eyes.

Once outside, he loped down the church steps,
gripping her waist when she paused to wrestle
with her long silk train. Nearly lifting her off her
feet, he headed straight for the waiting carriage
that had been elaborately decorated with purple
clusters of wisteria and white satin bows.

Cord hoisted Delia up and plunked her onto
the seat, then hastily rounded the horses and
climbed in beside her. She barely had time to put
on a smile and wave farewell before the buggy
jolted forth.

They left the churchyard at an accelerated
speed. Delia clutched the side of the rig and flattened a hand atop her head to keep her veil from
flying off. She glared at Cord, conveying her displeasure, but with his attention focused on the
road ahead, he paid her no heed.

By his handling of the horses, Delia could tell Cord was obviously upset. Had it not been for the hard set of his jaw, she would have pushed the issue of his reckless driving. As it was, she settled back in her seat, deciding she would tolerate his tantrum. But just this once.

A good three quarters of a mile from the church, Cord tugged the reins, slowing the buggy's pace.

Assessing his tightly controlled profile, Delia wondered if now might be a good time to account for her forwardness at the altar of St. Augustine's. Wedding guests would soon be following them to the reception at Grandy's. If she didn't take this opportunity to broach the subject, they might not have another second of privacy until they retired for the evening.

Putting a finger to her chin, Delia supposed discussing such intimacy so close to bedtime could be awkward. Especially considering they wouldn't be sleeping together.

"Cord, I'd like to talk to you . . . um, about something." She plucked at the skirt of her wedding gown. "I'd . . . I'd like to explain about the kiss."

Arching one black eyebrow, he slanted his gaze her way. "The kiss?"

Heat scalded Delia's cheeks. "Yes. Well, a little while ago at the altar . . . when I threw my arms around you and—"

"A kiss is but a kiss, *chérie.*" Cord straightened his spine and narrowed his eyes on something in the distance. "It means nothing."

Delia opened her mouth, then closed it and frowned. "Why, of course it didn't mean anything."

"Then why do you bring the matter up?"

Delia's scalp tightened. She raised her chest indignantly. "Because . . . because . . ." She paused, trying to think of a reply, but before a proper one came to mind, Cord looked at her point-blank.

"Let us not speak of it again," he said. "In fact, I would be most grateful if we did not talk at all for the rest of this little ride. Me, I would relish a moment of peace and quiet. Once we get to your *grand-mère*'s, I will be forced to be polite to your friends, and I do not like being *forced* into anything." With a meaningful glint touching his eyes, he turned and devoted all his effort to guiding the team.

Chapter Eleven

In spite of the cramp in her jaw, Delia held her smile in place while bidding the last few guests good-bye. The multitude of puckered lips expressing best wishes had left her cheeks chapped and red. Her back ached, and her feet hurt.

Grandy, still frisky for such a late hour, followed the handful of stragglers out the front door, chattering like a magpie.

Allowing the corners of her mouth to droop, Delia rolled her eyes at her grandmother's glee and settled her gaze on Cord. They were alone for the first time all evening. He stood next to her like a stone statue, his lids half closed, evidently lost in his own thoughts. Or perhaps he was just as dazed and exhausted as she was.

They had hardly spoken two words to each other since they'd reached the plantation. Their gaze had met briefly across the crowded room upon occasion, but the attention of one or the other had always been quickly diverted by a guest.

In Delia's opinion, what they both needed was a good night's rest.

"Cord," she said in a soft, weary tone, "let's

go on upstairs now. Cord?'' She laid a hand on his arm.

He turned his head slowly toward her and blinked as if just awakening.

''Did you hear me? I do b'lieve we ought to retire for the evenin', don't you?''

He stared at her for a long moment. ''But of course, if that is what you wish. I am, after all, at your beck and call, am I not?''

Delia regarded him coolly. ''Let's just get somethin' straight from the beginnin' here. There's no gettin' around the fact that we're gonna be in close proximity over the next few months. I see no earthly reason why we can't be gracious to one another.''

Cord placed a hand over his heart. ''Was I being ungracious?''

''You know damn good and well you were. So you can just quit makin' those puppy eyes.''

''Well, my, my, havin' a love spat already, Adelaide?'' Grandy asked from the doorway.

Delia swung around and the blood drained from her face.

Agatha strode forward, the hint of a smile curving her lips. ''Looks like the both of y'all got a little fire in you.''

Wedging herself between Delia and Cord, she looped her arms through theirs and steered them toward the wide, curving staircase.

''Well, now, there's nothin' wrong with sparks flyin' now and then,'' she added as she led them up the steps. Still clutching them tightly, she pivoted when they reached the mezzanine and walked them down the hall. ''Not one little thing. Just shows high passion, that's all. Why, me and old Granddaddy Abernathy used to have ourselves a spat or two weekly."

Agatha stopped before a bedroom door and turned her charges loose. She faced them with a lifted brow. "Makin' up proved to be quite entertainin'. Besides bein' a whole lot of fun, it's good for the circulation."

Delia slid her eyes closed and almost died from embarrassment. "Grandy, I really don't think—"

"No, Adelaide, you don't, do you? That's just the problem with you, dear. You so often jump into things without givin' the matter much thought."

Delia put her hands on her hips and cocked her head, viewing her grandmother suspiciously. The woman was twinkling a bit too brightly for her age. "Grandy, I truly fear you may have dipped into the punch bowl more times than you shoulda tonight."

"And what if I did? I was celebratin'." Agatha smiled, then curled a finger over her shoulder, signaling them to follow her. "Come on. I want to show you two your weddin' present."

She pushed the door of the adjacent bedroom open and swept inside.

Remaining in the hall, Delia and Cord exchanged glances.

"We should humor your *grand-mère*, no?" he asked.

Delia twisted her mouth to one side. "Probably so. You go first."

Not me, *chérie*. She is your *grand-mère*."

"And yours by marriage now, remember?" Delia flashed him a sarcastic smile. "We'll go together."

They entered the room cautiously.

"Well, what do you think?" Grandy turned a full circle, spreading her arms wide.

Delia scanned the lavishly redecorated suite that had once belonged to her parents, then looked at Cord. He was either overwhelmed or very impressed. She couldn't tell which, but she was neither.

Strolling further into the room, she ran a fingertip over the pale blue brocaded lounging chair. The color had once been a dark, rich gold. Delia remembered sitting in the chair when she was little. It had seemed much larger then. She hadn't set foot in this suite in years, yet in her childhood she had visited the chamber often. She used to come here and have pretend conversations with the mother she'd never known. There had been a time when she'd honestly believed her mother had answered her. Delia smiled inwardly at the absurd notion and lifted her gaze to the matching blue drapes. The room was lovely, but so different. She wasn't quite sure she liked the changes Grandy had made.

"Blue *is* your favorite color, isn't it, Adelaide? Don't you like what I've done in here?" Agatha asked.

Delia eyed her grandmother's hopeful expression and managed a small upward curve of her lips. "It's charmin', Grandy. Really. I s'pose I'm just tired."

"Well, of course you are. And here I stand on your weddin' night babblin' like an old fool when the two of you ought to be makin' me a great-grandbaby." Agatha crossed the room abruptly and cupped her hands around Delia's face. "Have I told you to be happy, Adelaide?"

"At least a hundred times today, Grandy."

"Well, you'll have to excuse me, dear. Memory fails me now and again these days, you know." She brushed a thumb over Delia's cheek, and a mistiness touched her steel-gray eyes. "Just believe me, that's all I've ever wanted for you, Adelaide—for you to be happy." Leaning forward, she kissed her granddaughter's forehead. "Good night, dear."

" 'Night, Grandy," Delia murmured.

Agatha marched toward the door, but stopped beside Cord and peered up at him. "Well, stoop down here and give me your cheek. I could jump, but I'm not as spry as I used to be."

Cord smiled slightly and bent obediently from the waist, receiving Grandy's peck on the cheek.

Something akin to lightning crackled in her eyes when he met the old woman's gaze again.

"You be gentle with her, now, you hear me?"

Satisfied with Cord's earnest nod, Agatha glanced over her shoulder at Delia once more, then left the room, closing the door behind her.

As soon as Grandy was gone, Delia sank into the lounge chair, sighed, then frowned at Cord.

"I s'pose I forgot to mention my grandmother has a bit to drink now and again," she commented, dragging the veil from her head. "She generally claims it's to ease her rheumatism, but whenever she's had a nip too many, she tends to get a little loose-tongued. I do hope you'll excuse—"

"You do not need to make excuses for your *grand-mère*. She is an extraordinary woman, *ma chérie*." One corner of his mouth slid into a grin. "Utterly delightful." Surveying the room once more, he shrugged out of his jacket, then walked over and hung it on the bedpost. "I am amazed you cannot see this for yourself. At first I thought she would be like all the others who think they are so much better than the rest of us, but she is not. And M'sieu Bateman? Chauncy's father? He was very cordial to me at the gathering at the Davenports'. Perhaps I have been too quick to judge you people, *hein?*''

Delia barely heard his last sentence. She was mesmerized by his long fingers untying his cravat. She watched in fascination as they moved down his white pleated shirt, working each button free. For several seconds she stared at the chest hair the gaping garment exposed before she realized she was doing so.

She dropped her eyes to the floor. ''What . . . what are you doin'?'' she asked.

''What am I doing?''

Delia glanced at his well-made chest once more, blushed, then directed her question toward the polished plank boards beneath her feet. ''Are you . . . takin' your . . . clothes off?''

''Yeah, well, you see, *chère,* we Cajuns have this very old custom of undressing before we go to bed.'' He paused shortly, then added, ''Ah-h-h. This bothers you, no?''

''No. No, not at all.'' Delia lifted her head in spite of her chagrin. She was careful, though, not to let her gaze linger on him. Instead, she feigned great interest in Grandy's embellishment of the bedroom. She studied the beautifully patterned rug, then looked momentarily at the big four-poster bed. She examined the painting of bluebirds in flight, then glanced briefly at the bed again. She admired the costly blue delft vase filled with white roses atop the carved dresser. But her mind remained on the bed.

Silence stretched on too long. A knot formed in Delia's stomach. From the corner of her vision, she saw Cord's hand move to the waistband of his trousers.

"Um, well," she blurted out. "Seems like this chair here will be real nice and comfortable to sleep on." She patted the seat beside her thigh. "Yessiree, just pull this footstool up here like this." She stood and shoved the matching piece against the chair. "There. Now. We can toss a pillow and one of the light blankets over here, and it'll work just fine."

Delia whirled in a flurry of white satin and, skirting around Cord, ducked behind the dressing screen, while he remained standing right where he was.

Surely he had understood her expressed desire. She didn't know how much plainer she could have said it. "Um . . . Cord, after you fix up that pallet on the chair, could you put out the lamps, please?"

"But of course, chérie. Will there be anything else?"

The touch of cynicism in his voice grated across Delia's tattered nerves. "No, no. That's all," she replied as calmly as she could.

Pressing her ear to the screen, she listened to the rustle of crisp linens being torn from the bed. She heard the apparent thump of a pillow hitting the lounge chair. Cord's footsteps moved briskly to the other side of the bedchamber. The room dimmed to a soft yellow glow, then went black.

Delia inhaled deeply and straightened her spine. The plunk of Cord's boots hit the floor. She fumbled in the darkness with the tiny buttons down her back, trying not to dwell on what he might take off next. No doubt Bess hadn't shown up to unfasten her because she'd assumed that Delia's new husband would perform the task.

Several silent curses later, Delia struggled out of the cumbersome wedding gown. Finally managing to remove her corset, she slipped into her nightdress.

Her limbs were limp by the time she stepped from behind the screen. She made her way blindly to the bed, feeling in front of her for fear of tripping over the rearranged furniture.

The tension stored between her shoulder blades vanished the moment she reclined on the soft down mattress. Her eyes closed automatically, and encountering the end of the hellacious day, she was lulled into blissfulness.

Then the mattress shifted slightly.

Delia's lids fluttered. She was dreaming . . . just dreaming, she assured herself.

But when the bed bounced harder and in one swift motion something bumped against her back, she yelped. In her scramble to flee the demon, the sheets ensnarled her legs. She fought like a madwoman for a matter of several frantic thumps of her heart.

Then, slowly, her rationality returned and she sat back on her heels. Peering through the darkness, she spotted a big lump in the center of the bed.

As her sight adjusted to the wan light, she focused on a thatch of dark hair. Leaning forward, she tugged the covers from Cord's shadowy profile.

"Cord!" she whispered ferociously, then hit his

shoulder. "Damnation! What are you doin' here? Cord!"

"Hmm-mm?" he groaned.

"I said, what are you doin' in this bed?"

Cord raised his head, lifted his lids to half-mast, and furrowed his brow, then collapsed against the mattress. "Sleeping," he mumbled groggily.

Delia refrained from striking him again, but doubled her fists and kept them at her sides. "You're s'pose to be over there on that chair."

Cord expelled a long sigh, flopped over onto his stomach, and turned his face away from her. "I thought it was you, who wanted to sleep in the chair," he muttered into his pillow.

"Well, you thought wrong." Delia crossed her arms over her breast, glowering at the back of his head. "Now get up. Go on. Get up this very instant and get on over there. Do you hear me?"

Cord raised himself up on his elbows, causing the sheet to slip down to his waist. With night shadows dipping into the contours of his back, he cocked his head toward Delia.

"Me, I am tired. It has been a long time since I have slept in such comfort. You can sleep in the chair yourself. You can sleep on the floor if you wish. Or you can sleep beside me. It makes me little difference. But I can tell you right now, you're going to play hell, yeah, trying to make me leave this bed."

Delia narrowed her eyes on him, but the cold, determined set of his mouth soon made her avert her gaze.

With a small nod, Cord settled into his former position.

Delia sat for a while glaring at him, watching him drift off to sleep. Her emotion changed from one breath to the next. She wanted to cry. She wanted to scream. Though the lounge chair across the room kept calling to her, she wouldn't budge. She couldn't let Cord think he could bully her.

At last, out of sheer stubbornness, she hesitantly stretched out as far away from him as she could get. Wide-eyed, she lay stiffly on her back, hugging the edge of the bed and damning Cord Kibedeaux's black soul to hell.

All the while she wondered how her simply perfect plan could have gone astray. Every time she'd thought all her troubles were behind her, another problem had cropped up.

Delia flung an arm over her eyes. She would have moaned had she not been afraid of waking the devil beside her. *Damn him, damn him, damn him.* What on earth had possessed her to pick a Cajun convict as her rescuer? How was she going to tolerate such high-handedness for six whole months? Why, she doubted if she could stand his—

Cord rolled over and his hand landed low on her abdomen.

A gasp lodged in Delia's throat. Other than the involuntary tightening of her stomach muscles, she remained stock-still. She held her breath, feeling all the heat in her body gather beneath his palm.

Slanting her gaze his way, she noted that his eyes were closed. Was he truly asleep? Or merely pretending to be?

The very idea that he might be playing possum and touching her in such a fashion made her blood rise to boil. If he thought he was going to chase her from her own bed, he was wrong. It would be a cold day in hell before she allowed him to—

Cord scooted closer, snuggling against her, and in the same motion his hand shifted upward to cup her breast.

Delia instantly grabbed his wrist and flung his arm away as she jumped out of bed.

Cord jerked to a sitting position with a deep, harsh groan. An expression of terror passed over his face before he focused on Delia.

"How dare you," she ground out, then perched her fists on her waist.

Cord blinked in a sleepy manner. "How dare I what?"

"How dare you you-know-what," Delia spat, then turned and padded over to the lounging chair. She snatched the blanket and, with a flick of her wrist, flared it out over her as she plopped into the chair.

She cast a hateful glance in Cord's direction and saw his shadowy form fall back onto his pillow. Reclining on the cushions, she shifted her weight, trying to find a halfway comfortable position.

"Pleasant dreams, my sweet-tempered wife," Cord mumbled through the darkness.

Delia made an ugly face, then pulled the covers over her head. She slammed her eyes shut, fully intending to drown herself in blessed slumber.

But for the next half hour or so, her mind raced on, labeling her new husband with every nasty name she'd ever heard.

* * *

Cord helped himself to another plateful of breakfast from the sideboard in the dining room.

Bess burst through the swinging door from the kitchen with a pot of hot coffee just as he was sitting down at the end of the long rosewood table.

"Why, Mista Kib-doe, what you be about now?" Bess bustled over and poured the steaming brew into his empty cup. "I coulda done fixed that second helpin' for you."

"*Merci*, Bess, but you need not wait on me." Cord tilted his head and grinned at the housekeeper. "You have enough to do, and me, I am perfectly able to fill my own plate."

From the other end of the table, Delia raised her eyebrows at the exchange, silently fuming. Bess had hovered over Cord like a mother hen all morning.

"Is dem eggs to your likin'?" Bess asked him.

"Ah, they are perfect," Cord replied, then rolled his eyes and kissed his fingertips. "Everything is perfect. I have never tasted better food in all my life."

Delia could have sworn Bess's round brown cheeks pinkened. Regardless of whether the woman actually blushed or not, the lift of her ample bosom indicated her pleasure in Cord's praise.

"Aw, Mista Kib-doe, you is teasin' me for sure." Bess rested her hands on her wide hips, shook her head, and giggled. "Ain't no man thinks anybody can cook as good as his mamma."

Cord's expression went flat. Dropping his gaze to his plate, he stabbed a piece of ham with his fork. "My mother, she never cooked for us," he commented dryly, then popped the meat into his mouth.

"What do you mean she dint cook for you? Why, Ah ain't nevah heard the likes of a mamma that dint feed her chilren."

Cord stared at his food for a long moment. "My mother, she was always very ill. Me, I made what meals we had."

Delia contemplated Cord's sudden change of mood. She didn't want to consider his unpleasant past. She wasn't about to let him spoil her breakfast after the way he'd kept her up all night. She took a bite of her biscuit and willfully chewed it, but the doughy glob grew bigger in her mouth and was extremely hard to swallow.

"Mmm, mmm, mmm," the housekeeper remarked indignantly. "Well, now, anytimes you want ol' Bess to fix you a lil' somethin' to tides you over till supper, you jus' lets me know, Mista Kib-doe, you heah?"

Picking up an empty platter off the sideboard, she headed for the kitchen. "Gots mo' grits in heah, too," she said over her broad shoulder. "You wants some, you jus' holler."

Bess had no sooner left when Grandy swept into the dining room.

"Well, well. Good mornin', children." She paused and held a hand to her heart, shifting her smile back and forth between Delia and Cord. "My, what a pleasant surprise. I kinda figured y'all might still be abed."

"Mornin', Grandy," Delia murmured. She lowered her eyes to her cold eggs, avoiding her grandmother's inquisitive gaze.

Cord dabbed his mouth with his napkin and

politely rose from his seat. "*Bonjour*, madame. It is a lovely day, is it not?"

"It is most certainly one of my better days." Agatha's smile grew broader. "Oh, do sit down and finish eatin'," she said with a wave of her hand, then went to the sideboard and began dishing up her breakfast. "And I'll have no more of that "madame" nonsense, you hear? Why, you're family now. You can call me Grandy—or Agatha, if you'd rather. Bess! I'd like a nice hot cup of coffee, if you please," she bellowed toward the kitchen.

Agatha brought her plate to the table and seated herself halfway between Cord and Delia. "Did I neglect to mention last night that I've re-established your good standin' with our creditors, Adelaide?" she asked nonchalantly, spreading her napkin on her lap.

Delia looked at her in surprise. "As a matter of fact, you did forget to mention that."

"Well, I have. And it's in both of y'all's names." Grandy winked at Cord, then regarded her granddaughter once more. "Of course, it *is* still only for the amount of your usual allowance, you understand. You won't be gettin' your inheritance money till y'all have lived together as man and wife for the full six months. You will recall, we agreed upon—"

"Oh, I recall the terms of your agreement very well, Grandy," Delia cut in with a grimace.

"Just wanted to make sure you understood, dear," Agatha commented with a lift of one shoulder. Turning her attention to her meal, she took a bite of ham, chewed thoughtfully, then pointed her fork at Delia. "You know, Adelaide, in truth, I'm a tad disappointed to see y'all up so early. I had honestly hoped you'd stay locked up there in your room for a few days, workin' on gettin' me a great-grandbaby.''

''Grandy!'' Delia slapped her palms down on either side of her plate. ''I can't believe you'd come waltzin' in here and say somethin' like that!''

Agatha shrugged, picked up her biscuit, and proceeded to butter it. ''Now, now, Adelaide. No need to go gettin' all riled. I'm merely lookin' out for the welfare of my great-grandbaby, that's all.''

Delia curled her fingers into fists against the linen tablecloth. She closed her eyes and counted to ten before reopening them.

''Grandy,'' she said in a tightly controlled voice that made her jaw ache, ''there *is* no great-grandbaby to worry about at this precise time.''

''Not yet, maybe.'' Agatha dipped her spoon into a bowl of honey and ladled a liberal amount on her biscuit. ''But you never can tell, Adelaide. It can happen right off, you know. And as I said before, Cord does appear to be a very virile—''

''Oh, stop it!'' Delia came to her feet, nearly knocking over her chair. ''I'm appalled you would bring up such a delicate matter at breakfast, just *appalled*.'' She glowered at Agatha and in a low whisper added, ''And I refuse to sit here another second and listen to such talk.'' Flinging her napkin on the table, she left the room.

Agatha arched her brow and looked at Cord. ''She's a bit high-strung, you know.''

''So I have gathered,'' he replied in agreement, glancing at the door his wife had just exited.

"Delia was even a mite moody when she was a little girl," Agatha commented, then took a bite of her biscuit and chewed it pensively. "I tried my best to make her happy, but . . . well, she missed havin' a mamma and daddy around like all the other children hereabouts. Her mamma passed away when she was a baby."

"But her father, he is still living, no?" Cord asked.

"Oh, land sakes, yes." Grandy dabbed at the corner of her mouth with her napkin. "In fact, Wendell—that's my son—lives a little too high on the hog, if you ask me." She pursed her lips. "He's in Paris, France, at the moment. Hardly ever comes home anymore. I have an inklin' that's why Delia acts up the way she does sometimes."

Cord frowned, considering this tidbit of information.

"She's always fancied herself goin' over there and livin' with him," Agatha went on. "But just between you and me, he doesn't want her. Oh, I know he loves her. She's his daughter, for cryin' out loud. But he couldn't be bothered with seein' to her welfare. And he certainly wouldn't want her underfoot, spoilin' his good times. I've just never had the heart to tell Delia the truth."

Cord focused on the platter of biscuits in the middle of the table. He had once thought that the people who lived in these fine mansions could not possibly have any worries. But it appeared both Delia and her grandmother had had their share of grief. At least where Wendell Abernathy was concerned.

"Cord, would you do somethin' for me?"

He slid his gaze to Agatha's and found her wearing a pained expression. "What is it you wish me to do?" he asked.

"Be good to Adelaide. Promise me you'll treat her well. Oh, I know I've spoiled her, and goodness knows that fact shows. You just got to look a tad deeper for her good side. It's in there somewhere."

Cord wet his lips, then nodded, but chose his words carefully. "I will try to make her as happy as possible throughout our marriage."

His answer seemed to satisfy Grandy, for she smiled at him lovingly for a long moment. Then she turned her attention toward the kitchen door. "Bess! Where the devil is that coffee I asked for?"

"Ah's comin'," Bess murmured as she scurried into the dining room. "Ah hads to brews some mo'." She tipped the coffeepot over Grandy's cup. "Mornin', Miz Abernathy. How be your rheumy-tism on dis fine day?"

Agatha smiled up at the housekeeper. "I feel absolutely wonderful this mornin', thank you."

"Uh-huh." Bess chuckled. "Ah knows what you mean. Feels goods havin' a man 'round here agin, don't it?"

"Why, indeed it does, Bess. Indeed it does."

Bobbing her head, the housekeeper returned to her duties in the kitchen.

Agatha's features softened as her gaze settled on Cord again. "Well. Do you and Adelaide have any special plans for the day, dear?"

"No, I do not believe so."

"Would you like me to have someone show you

around the plantation?" she asked, then took a sip of coffee.

"I would like that very much . . . but perhaps another time, *hein*? I had thought to look up an old friend of mine today."

"Oh? And who would that be, dear?"

Cord wiped his mouth on the white linen napkin, laid it beside his plate, then met Agatha's steely-blue gaze. "A gentleman I used to work with at the bank," he replied. "John Hart. Perhaps you know him?"

"Well, of course, dear. Everybody does." Grandy shook her head sadly. "Poor ol' John."

The way Agatha said "Poor ol' John" piqued Cord's curiosity. "M'sieu Hart is unwell, then?"

"He's a sufferin' soul if I ever saw one." Grandy braced her forearm on the table and leaned forward. "Came into quite a deal of money some years back—some sorta inheritance from a distant relative, as I recall. Anyway, when his wife took sick, he spent every cent takin' her back and forth to some fancy doctor in St. Louis." Agatha paused and picked up her coffee cup. "You know, John never was too social, but he always used t' speak when you passed him on the street. Now he hardly ever leaves that old, rickety house of his. After his missus passed on, he was a changed man, I tell you."

Cord remembered John Hart as also being a kind and cordial man, though not overly outgoing. He ran his knuckles along the underside of his chin. "You said a relative left him some money?" he asked thoughtfully. "This must have happened after I was . . . well, after I went away, no?"

"Well, let me see." Grandy puckered her brow. "I do b'lieve it *was* after all that business at the bank. Yes, I'm sure it was. Shortly afterward, if memory serves me."

Chapter Twelve

C ord walked alongside the picket fence with chipped paint, taking in the disrepair of the house. He stepped through the gate that had been left ajar and turned to close it, but the latch was missing.

"*Mon Dieu*," he murmured under his breath. "What could have happened here?" Striding down the overgrown walk, he noted tall weeds had replaced the red rose bushes that had once flourished beside the porch.

Although one could hardly believe it now, John Hart's home had formerly been a showplace with trimmed hedges and neatly planted rows of colorful flowers. At one time, couples on a Sunday-afternoon stroll had gone out of their way to admire the charming little cottage.

The steps groaned beneath Cord's weight as he made his way onto the porch. He carefully avoided the more obviously worm-eaten boards. At the door, he started to knock, but his fist paused in midair.

Mr. Hart had not exactly been overjoyed to see him at Faldene's Coffee Shoppe. The old teller might not be too pleased with this visit. But

something Cord couldn't name had compelled
him to speak with the man. And seeds of doubt
about John's knowledge of the bank burglary had
cropped up since Cord's conversation with Agatha earlier that morning.

Taking a deep breath, Cord straightened his lapels, combed a hand through his hair, then wet
his lips and pounded on the warped doorjamb.

He waited for several minutes. When no one
answered, he tried again, but had no better luck.
Moving across the porch, he attempted to peer in
a window. From the corner of his eye he saw the
curtain jiggle in a window farther down the porch.

"John?" he called out. "M'sieu Hart? It is I,
Cord Kibedeaux. You remember me, *hein*? We
worked together long ago, you and I. I would like
to talk to you, if I may. Please, m'sieu. I will not
take much of your time."

The only response Cord received was silence.
After a moment, he turned and walked slowly
down the steps. He paused by the broken gate,
shoved his hands into his pockets, and glanced
toward the window once more. He could have
sworn he saw the tattered curtain flutter again.

Cord was reluctant to make any speculations,
yet he stood outside the picket fence for a while
doing just that. Someone inside the house was
watching him. He could feel it. Was John Hart
evading him merely because everyone else in
Boudreaux Parish did? From what Cord recol-
lected about the man, John had never been one
to take a stand, but neither had he based his life
on the opinions of those who ruled Boudreaux
Parish.

Cord surveyed the run-down place one last
time, shook his head, then made his way down

the street. Perhaps, just as Delia had claimed, the death of Hart's wife truly had turned the retired teller into a recluse. Something desperate had most definitely occurred over the past ten years for John to neglect his property so badly.

Cord rounded the corner and, upon spying Faldene's, decided to stop in for a warmed sling before returning to the Abernathy Plantation. The thought of facing his dear wife warranted a good, stiff drink. Besides, Delia had mentioned that John Hart frequented the popular coffeehouse upon occasion. Perhaps Cord could make a few discreet inquiries as to whether John's visits were routine or not.

Just as he started to enter Faldene's, three frolicsome young men burst out the door. One of them slammed into Cord, causing him to stumble backward.

"Here, now, mistah, you'd best be watchin' where you're goin'," the man drawled. Swaying from side to side, he glanced over his shoulder at his two inebriated companions and chuckled.

As the young man swiveled back around, Cord boldly met Chauncy Bateman's gaze. The anxiety Cord had experienced in his youth whenever Chauncy had taunted him surfaced now only briefly, then died a quick death.

Chauncy's red-rimmed eyes narrowed, and one corner of his mouth lifted in a sinister grin. "Well, well, well. Lookie what we got here, gents. Appears a swamp rat's done slithered into town. You reckon we ought to do Boudreaux Parish a great service and get rid of this slimy critter before it stinks up the place?"

Cord stood perfectly still while the chorus of laughter dwindled. Without batting an eyelash, he fixed Chauncy with a stone-cold glare. "I have no quarrel with you, Bateman," he said in a bridled tone, then started around the trio.

"Where the hell's your manners, Kibedeaux?" Chauncy bumped Cord's shoulder with the heel of his hand. "You don't walk away from a gentleman when he's speakin' to you, boy. Why, somebody's liable to take a buggy whip to your back."

Chauncy pushed him again, and Cord retreated, allowing the three men to nudge and prod him into the alleyway. Once hidden from view, Chauncy raised his doubled fists.

In lightning-quick succession, Cord reached out, caught Chauncy's flying punch, and folded his fingers over the other man's knuckles in a crushing grip. With his free hand, he grabbed hold of Chauncy's throat and slung him against the wall.

Sensing a sudden movement from behind, Cord tightened his grasp on Chauncy's neck. "If you value M'sieu Bateman's friendship, you will keep your distance," he told the two others. He looked deeply into Chauncy's terrified eyes and added, "Ten years in prison will teach you a lot of tricks, yeah. Unless you would like me to demonstrate a few I learned there, you will advise your playmates to stand back."

"Do as he says," Chauncy choked out. "Do as he says!"

Cord curved his mouth into a bitter smile. "Now, you and I, we're going to get several things straight, *hein?* Is this all right with you, my friend?"

Chauncy bobbed his head frantically, and Cord relaxed his hold on him a little.

"Good," Cord said. "First off, you should know I will no longer back down from you as I did when we were children. Me, I will not cross to the other side of the street. You understand this, no?"

Chauncy gave him a jerky nod.

"Well, now, you see? Things are getting better already, *hein*? You and I, we should understand each other, my friend. Me, I know you don't like me. I don't like you neither. So I tell you what. You don't talk to me. And I won't talk to you." Turning loose of Bateman, Cord spread his arms wide and arched his brow. "Is simple solution to our problem, no?"

Chauncy eyed Cord warily. With measured moves, Bateman reached up and rubbed his throat, then wet his lips. "Sounds like a damn fine solution to me," he rasped in a serious tone. "A *damn* fine solution, Kibedeaux."

"Just where have you been?" Delia propped her hands on her hips and watched her husband drag his shirt off his broad shoulders and toss it on the bed. "Grandy's been waitin' supper on us."

"Forgive me, *chérie*. I was unavoidably delayed." Turning his back, Cord poured water from the large blue pitcher on the dresser into the matching basin.

Delia squeezed her lips together and traipsed across the room to stand beside him. "Unavoidably delayed? *Unavoidably delayed?*" She glared down her nose at his bent head while he stooped over the washbowl, continuing to splash his face. "Cord, we've only been married five days. Now, I realize we've hardly spoken in all that time, other than in polite conversation while Grandy was present, but for you to go mysteriously disappearin' for hours every day is just—''

Cord reached out, blindly groping along the dresser.

With a sigh, Delia snatched the towel and stuffed it into his hand. ''I mean, if you're slippin' off to meet a lover somewheres, Grandy's bound to find out about it.''

In the middle of drying off, Cord stilled his hands on the towel. He straightened slowly, peering at her above the wadded cloth he held to his face.

Shying away from his intense gaze, Delia focused on a drop of water that clung to a wayward strand of hair in the center of his forehead.

With a slight shake of his head, Cord flung the towel aside, then went to the wardrobe, removed a clean shirt, and slipped it on. As he buttoned the garment, he regarded Delia with the low-lidded expression that she was quickly becoming familiar with. ''I do not have a lover,'' he said flatly.

''Do tell,'' she countered. ''Then just where *do* you go every day?''

Cord shrugged, picked up his cravat, and looped it around his turned-up collar. ''I told you before, I have business of my own to attend to.''

Delia cocked her head and eyed him skeptically. ''You're not up to somethin' that's gonna get you into trouble with the law again, are you?''

He glanced at the ceiling, evidently taking a moment to consider the question. ''No. I do not think so.''

''Oh? Then why do you s'pose Sheriff Juilliard stopped by this afternoon wantin' to see you?''

"He came here to see me?"

"Mmm. While you were out."

Cord paused in the task of tying his cravat and curled his bottom lip. "I cannot imagine why."

"Seems Barnaby Holloway burst into his office the other day with some wild story." Delia dropped her attention to the dresser and ran a fingertip along the edge. "Barnaby claimed you cornered him, Marlin Eldridge, and Chauncy Bateman in the alleyway next to Faldene's. Sheriff said when he tried to verify Barnaby's statement, though, Marlin refused to talk to him, and Chauncy swore it never happened."

Delia lifted her gaze, studying Cord for some reaction. Apparently unconcerned, he tugged down his cuffs and reached for his jacket. She was of a mind to ask him a few more questions, but before she could think of a clever way to go about it, he took her elbow and steered her out of the room.

She glanced at him askance as he ushered her down the stairs. He merely gave her that charming smile of his and remarked, "We must not keep your *grand-mère* waiting, *hein?*"

Delia sulked throughout dinner. She'd hardly said a word. But then, of course, no one had seemed all that interested in her opinion anyway. Grandy and Cord had carried on their own little delightful conversation.

Agatha and Bess had doted on Cord all evening as if he were some supreme being. When Delia could stand no more, she scraped her chair back and stood, turning everyone's attention her way.

"Y'all will excuse me, won't you?" She picked up the fan lying beside her plate and snapped it open. "I b'lieve I'll just step out on the veranda and get some air. My blood's about to boil in here."

"Why, Adelaide, what a lovely idea. It's probably lots cooler outside." Grandy cocked her twinkling eyes toward Cord. "What do you say we join her, Cord, dear? I'll tell Bess to fetch us a little nip of anisette."

"Me, I would be honored to escort two such beautiful women out into the moonlight." He winked, then wiggled his brow. "I can only hope so much loveliness beneath the starry skies will not cause me to lose my head."

"Oh, Cord, you dear boy." Agatha pressed her fingertips to her mouth and giggled. "You do go on, don't you?"

Delia rolled her eyes at the exchange. Her grandmother was actually blushing.

Cord rose from his seat, walked over, pulled out Grandy's chair, and offered the woman his arm.

Agatha took his elbow only long enough to stand, then patted his hand and smiled up at him. "You two go on ahead," she said. "I'll be out directly. I'll just pop into the kitchen first and have Bess fix us our anisette."

Delia took in the scene and lifted her fan to conceal the frown that was quickly forming on her face. In her judgment, Grandy was becoming way too infatuated with her new grandson-in-law.

"Just do not deprive us of your sweet company too long, *hein?*" Cord replied, walking toward Delia.

Delia flinched when he placed his palm against the small of her back, and stiffened her spine as he guided her through the double French doors.

Stepping onto the tiled veranda, she peeked over her shoulder to check Grandy's whereabouts. Certain they were beyond Agatha's earshot, she lowered her fan, exposing her true disposition. "Cord, what do you think you're doin'?" she whispered.

He tilted his face toward the dark sky and inhaled deeply. "Taking in some fresh air. Just look at those stars. It is a fine night, is it not?"

Delia narrowed her eyes to thin slits. "Don't go tryin' to sway me, Cord. You know what I'm talkin' about. What do you mean by encouragin' Grandy like that?"

"What is wrong with you, *hein?* I can see no harm in being kind to your *grand-mère*."

"Well, I can most certainly see the harm. And I don't like it. Do you hear? I don't like it one teensy bit." Delia snapped her fan closed, tapping his chest with it as she spoke. Turning away from him, she took brisk steps to the edge of the banister, reopened her fan, and set it to fluttering beneath her chin. "You were oozin' charm in there just now, and don't you try to tell me you didn't know it. Grandy's old, Cord. She's well past the age of seein' through a silver-tongued devil like you. But I—"

Cord whirled her around. Her shoulders lifted as he caught her elbows and pulled her to him. "No woman is past the age of needing a little attention. If a word of flattery can brighten your *grand-mère*'s day, why should you begrudge her that? Has it never occurred to you that I am genuinely fond of her? That, perhaps, I honestly do enjoy her company? The woman, she is clever and quick-witted. She has a good sense of humor too, yeah. Maybe you would know this yourself if ever you would take the time to talk to her.''

Delia swallowed. Tears pricked her eyes. ''How dare you,'' she murmured, then bit her bottom lip hard to still its quivering. ''How dare you suggest I ill-treat my grandmother.''

Cord moved his head closer to hers, his gaze searching her face. ''Ah, now I see, *ma chérie*.'' A grin lifted one corner of his mouth. ''You are jealous.''

''Jealous?'' Delia whacked his chest and shoved him away. ''*Jealous?* Hah!'' A short, breathy sound meant to be a laugh escaped her. She leaned a hip casually against the banister and folded her arms at her waist. ''Now I'm convinced what they say about you people is true. All you Cajuns really are crazy.''

Cord sidled next to her, so close their sleeves touched, but Delia refused to budge. She had a hunch he expected her to bolt like a scared rabbit, which was precisely why she didn't.

''So I am crazy, *hein*? You think so?''

''Yes. Completely, utterly insane.''

''And you . . . you, *chère* . . .'' He reached out and ran a finger slowly, tantalizingly, down the side of her face, and she froze. ''You are totally unaffected by a man's attention, no?''

''No,'' Delia whispered, then added quickly, ''I mean, yes.'' Although at the moment she wasn't quite sure what she meant, she remained perfectly still. She wasn't about to lose this little game of dare he played.

''And are you equally unaffected by a man's touch, *ma chérie*? And by his kisses?'' He leaned over and pressed his lips against her cheek.

Delia closed her eyes. The balmy air was thick

with the sweet scent of magnolias. And this was a dangerous game. She didn't want to play anymore. She wanted to slap the fire out of Cord.

But she couldn't. She couldn't move. Her weak limbs rejected her brain's command. Her mind went blank as Cord's mouth moved down the side of her throat. In a most traitorous fashion, she tilted her head, allowing his succulent kisses access to her collarbone.

"I had an inklin' this moonlight might be good for the two of you."

Jumping to attention at the sound of Grandy's voice, Delia stood ramrod-straight.

"I had so hoped, though, that my great-grandbaby would be conceived in the old four-poster upstairs," Agatha remarked from the doorway, then strolled out onto the veranda carrying a tray with a decanter and three jiggers. "That bed's a family heirloom, you know. Belonged to my grandmother. It was passed down to my mamma and daddy. I'm certain I was conceived in it. And I highly suspect you were too, Adelaide."

Delia aimed a scowl at Cord. "Now, see what you've done?" she murmured out of the side of her mouth. "You got her started up with that great-grandbaby nonsense again."

Behind Cord's smile was the devil's own grin. With a slight twitch of his shoulders, he left Delia standing alone and walked over to Grandy.

"Here, let me take that for you," he said and lifted the tray from her hands. "Would you like me to pour?"

"Why, thank you, Cord, dear. It's awfully gentlemanly of you to offer."

Cord set the tray on a small table between two

wicker chairs and opened the decanter. After filling the glasses, he handed one to Grandy, then picked up his and Delia's anisette and stretched Delia's jigger toward her.

Delia snatched the drink from him. She raised the glass, intending to down the sweet liqueur, but Grandy stopped her.

"Ah-ah-ah, Adelaide," Agatha chimed. "I b'lieve we ought to have us a toast. Now, let's see, what can we toast to? Oh, I know. Why, of course, we'll toast to my gr—"

"Grandy." Delia glared pointedly at her grandmother. "So help me, if you mention a great-grandbaby just once more, I'll—"

A bloodcurdling cry came from somewhere inside the house. Delia's jigger slipped through her fingers and shattered against the terra-cotta floor.

Cord swerved around the two women and tore into the house.

Agatha and Delia looked at each other, blinked, then dashed off in the same direction, following close behind Cord.

A long, hideous howl led them to the foyer. Bess danced at the top of the stairs, alternately pulling at her ample bodice and waving her hands in the air.

"Oh, Lordy, oh, Lordy!" she wailed. "Dey be hoo-doo at work dis night." She covered her face, then fell to her knees and burst into tears.

Cord took the stairs two at a time. Reaching the housekeeper, he stooped beside her and grabbed her arms. "Bess? Bess! What is it, *hein*? What have you seen?"

The black woman shook her head frantically.

"Bess!" Cord gave her a shake. "You must tell me!"

Gasping for breath, Bess settled her round, roving eyes on his and started rocking back and forth.

"Oh, Lordy, Mista Kib-doe. God in heaven gottsta save us all now. Somebodys done went and put a hex on dis house." A stream of tears rolled down her full cheeks. "Ah was jus' turnin' down you and Missy Adelaide's bed . . . and dere it was."

Whimpering again, she raised her hands in the air and shrieked, "Oh, God Jesus, he'p us!"

Chapter Thirteen

Delia raised her skirt and raced up the staircase. She paused at the top of the landing. Trying to catch her breath and gather her wits all at once, she laid a hand upon her chest and looked from Bess to Cord. "Land sakes, what is it, Cord? What's got Bess so spooked?"

"She is mumbling something about a curse." Cord rose from his position on the floor beside the black woman and met Delia's concerned gaze.

"A curse?" Delia glanced at the ceiling and sighed. "Oh, for cryin' out loud." Kneeling beside the housekeeper, she patted her shoulder, then gently pulled Bess to her feet and peered into her face. "Shh, now, Bess. It's all right. No need to fret so over some silly old superstition." Delia folded her arms around Bess, pressing the woman's plump cheek against her breast. "Probably just your imagination."

"Ain't my 'magination," Bess sobbed with a wide-eyed, glassy stare.

"What's happened here?" Agatha asked, hobbling up the last few steps. "Is Bess hurt?"

"No, no, Grandy." Delia stroked the coarse black hair sprinkled with gray peeking from un-

184

der Bess's *tignon*. "She's fine. Just fine. Thought she saw somethin', that's all."

"Ah dint *think* Ah seen somethin', Miz Abernathy." The housekeeper pushed herself away from Delia and focused on Agatha. "Ah done seen what Ah seen. Ah tells you, dey is evil at work in dis house. You can sees it fo yo-sef. Right yonder." She gestured down the hall. "Right down dere in Missy Delia and Mista Kib-doe's bed."

Cord's gaze followed the direction of the black woman's finger. "Delia, you and your *grand-mère*, you stay here with Bess," he commanded, then strode down the hallway toward the bedroom.

The moment he walked through the door, he spied the tiny black coffin wedged between the pillows on the bed.

"Well, heavenly days." Delia slipped around him and headed for the bed. "Is that little ol' thing what's got Bess so upset?"

"Delia! Do not touch it." Cord moved up beside her and caught her elbow.

"What on earth is that inside it?" She leaned forward and peered into the box, wrinkling her nose.

"It is a dead frog."

"A . . . *dead frog?* You mean to tell me this household's been turned upside down because of a childish prank?"

"I can assure you, it is no prank." Cord slid his gaze to hers. "Someone *has* put a hex on us—you and me."

Delia's jaw dropped. She tucked her chin skeptically, a chuckle bubbling in her throat. "Why, that's . . . that's the most ridiculous thing I've ever heard of. A hex? On us?"

Cord grasped her shoulders and twisted her toward him. He bent his head close to hers, regarding her intensely. "Voodoo," he whispered. "*Gris gris*, black magic. I suppose you do not believe in such things, *hein*?

"Well, I certainly don't think the dead toad in that little box is goin' to jump up and get us."

Cord turned her loose so abruptly that she teetered on her heels. He walked a few feet away, pivoted, ran a hand through his hair, then spread his arms wide in appeal.

"You do not understand, *ma chérie.* The creature in the coffin is a symbol signifying someone wishes us great harm. The spell they have cast begets tragedy."

Delia was disturbed by Cord's pensive frown. She'd always viewed him as being quite invincible. Yet he was obviously shaken at the moment.

With a sudden desire to calm his fears, she went to him. Reaching up to take his face in her hands, she looked into his eyes. "Cord, you can't possibly hold any stock in all this mumbo jumbo. Why, it's nothin' more than frightenin' stories made up by some cruel plantation owner years ago, meant to keep the slaves in line. Surely you must know that."

"I know this mumbo jumbo, as you call it, *works.*" He pulled back, disengaging his face from her touch. "Me, I have seen the damage these *gris gris* can cause."

"And just who do you think has cast this terrible spell on us?" Delia pressed her lips into a tight line. "Huh?"

"I do not know, *chère.* Me, I can think of many who wish me bad luck. How about you, *hein*? Has anyone approached you in anger lately?"

Delia's gaze veered off to one side. She stared past Cord, recalling the threats Chauncy had hurled at her at the cemetery gate. She'd dismissed his warning as merely a means for him to vent his hurt pride. But his rantings came vividly to mind: *You mark my word . . . I'll get even with you and that swamp rat if it's the last thing I do.*

"Delia? What is it?" Cord asked urgently. "There was someone you argued with, *hein?*" He cocked his head into her line of vision, but she closed her eyes. "There was, wasn't there?"

When she didn't answer, his fingers banded her upper arms. "Tell me." He gave her a shake, causing her eyes to fly open. "You must tell me. Whoever cast the spell must be made to rescind it."

"He wouldn't have done somethin' like this," she murmured with a shake of her head.

"Who, Delia? Who do you speak of?"

"Chauncy couldn't have—"

Cord squeezed her arms, then let go and walked to the window. Bracing a hand on the top of the frame, he glared out at the night.

"But of course," he said as if speaking to himself. "Why did I not consider Chauncy Bateman to begin with, *hein?* He does hold a grudge against us both, does he not? He was not at all pleased to learn of our marriage."

"Cord, Chauncy's a prankster, all right, but he isn't capable of somethin' like this," Delia said quietly, locking her hands together at her waist.

Cord peered over his shoulder, his expression hard and cold. "Anyone's capable of anything, *chérie*. This much you should always remember."

He turned his face toward the window again,

and Delia stood staring at the back of his head for a long stretch of silence.

"You go downstairs now." His command startled Delia when he finally spoke. "You take your *grand-mère* and Bess into the kitchen. Stay there, you hear me? Stay there, and stay together till I get home."

"But where are you going?"

"To see *Tante* Netha Bea. She will know what needs to be done with that evil thing on the bed."

Cord guided the pirogue through the bayou, stilling the crickets he passed with the soft swish of water.

Though the hour was late, *Tante* Netha Bea stood on her porch, her bony arms crossed over her chest, as if she'd expected her visitor.

Cord wasn't surprised. The old woman had often foreseen company coming. Tying the small craft to the railing, he climbed onto the porch.

"Me, I had a dream," *Tante* Netha Bea said, staring blankly straight ahead. "Last night, yeah. You stood in muddy water. High, like to your neck." She slashed her hand across her throat, then focused her dark, glimmering eyes on him. "Is bad sign, T-boo. Me, I been waiting. Come. We will go inside. I will fix us some tea, and you will tell me what has happened, *hein?*"

Following her into the house, Cord ducked under the dried weeds, herbs, and other assorted charms hanging from the ceiling. Crude shelves along the walls held birds' nests, beehives, powders and potions, and a variety of jars containing small, unidentifiable, pickled creatures. Places of honor were reserved for numerous religious statues and crucifixes.

A white candle flickered on the table in the center of the one-room shack, producing an eerie yellow glow. As Cord settled into his seat, Netha Bea placed a chipped cup filled with a dark, steaming brew in front of him.

"Now you drink dat all gone, *T-boo*," she ordered. "Is elderberry tea. I jus' gather de bark dis mornin', yeah. Is gonna make you strong too. And you gonna need all de strength you can get, yeah. Me, I know dat." She placed a finger on her temple. "Is bad times ahead."

Cord sipped his tea, then grimaced. "I fear the bad times may have already arrived."

Tante Netha Bea nodded, slipped into the chair across from him, and clasped her hands together on the table. "You tell me now, *hein*? I already know is evil. I cannot see what happens, no. My head, she no want to give me visions dis time, but a cold wind blows tru my old bones."

Cord focused on a trickle of wax dripping down the side of the snuff jar that held the candle. "Tonight someone placed a frog in a black coffin on my bed."

"*Mon Dieu!*" Netha Bea sucked in her breath and made the sign of the cross. "Oh, *cher*, you did not handle dat *conjag*—dat evil object, no?"

Cord shook his head. "*Non*, but of course not."

"*Ça c'est bon*," she said, then leaned back in her chair and sighed. Narrowing her eyes pensively, the old woman glanced around the room. Suddenly she sat upright and braced her forearms on the table. "Hokay, *T-boo*. You no worry, *hein*? I will fix. But first you tell me who you t'ink does dis awful ting. I'm gonna fix him too, yeah."

Cord grinned and cocked his head. "Was it not

you, old woman, who taught me two wrongs do not make something right?''

''*Mais oui*, I say dat.'' *Tante* Netha Bea bobbed her head vigorously. ''But me, I'm not gonna let some weevil cause you harm, no. Whoever put a hex on you, we gonna put a hex on dem right back.''

''No.''

''Yeah,'' Netha Bea countered with a dip of her chin.

''No.'' Cord fixed his mouth in a grim line and placed his palms on the table. ''I did not come here to have you cast a spell on anyone.''

''*Oui*. I know dat, *cher*, but somebody, they got to look after you.''

''Me, I can look after myself.''

''Oh, yeah, *T-boo*.'' *Tante* Netha Bea puckered her lower lip, shrugged, and spread her hands. ''I can see how good you take care of yourself. Dis is why you are in such big trouble, *hein?*''

Cord glowered at her. She glared back, and he pushed himself up from his chair. Moving a short distance to one of the shelves, he picked up a bottle filled with some sort of potion and pretended to examine it. ''Just show me what I must do with the dead frog,'' he said.

Netha Bea jumped up from the table, scurried over, and snatched the potion away from him. ''How many times I got to tole you,'' she said, shaking the bottle in his face, ''you don't be playing wit' my tings, no. Dis holds very potent magic, *T-boo*.''

After giving him a scolding look, she carefully replaced the bottle and shifted her attention to other items gathered on the shelf. ''Hmm,'' she murmured, stroking her jaw. "Ah, here is what we need."

She tugged a piece of red cloth from the clutter and spread it out on the table. "*T-boo*, you get me dat jar of ashes, *hein*? Is too high for me to reach wit'out a chair, yeah."

Cord brought her the particular container she pointed at, then stepped back and watched as she opened the lid. Whispering something Cord couldn't understand, she dipped her finger into the ashes and made a cross with the gray powdery substance in the middle of the fabric. She closed her eyes, folded her hands against her breast in a prayerful fashion, then said out loud, "Dis we pray, in de name of de Father, and de Son, and de Holy Ghost."

Opening one eye, she peered at Cord. "Remember dis, *cher*. No magic works wit'out prayer."

She waited for Cord to nod before she folded the cloth and handed it to him. "You take dis and wrap de coffin in it," she said. "Mind you, do not to let dat evil object touch your skin, or even your clothes, *hein*?"

"I will keep a respectful distance, I assure you."

"*C'est bon*. Once you have bundled it up, troe de *gris gris* in the closest stream and let de current carry de bad luck where it will. You will do exactly as I say, will you not?"

"I will not forget anything," Cord said, then smiled and laid a hand on her shoulder. "*Merci, Tante* Netha Bea. I will visit you again soon. Perhaps next time we can talk of pleasant things."

The old woman didn't disagree, but neither did she return his smile. Instead, a concerned frown creased her brow.

"Beware, *T-boo*," she warned. Then her eyes glazed. "It is not over yet."

Delia rolled away from the bright sunshine that broke through the gap in the drapes and pierced her lids. Snuggling deeper into the soft mattress, she smiled and hugged her pillow. The prank someone had played last evening had accomplished at least one useful purpose. Since Cord had refused to sleep in the bed, Delia had gladly traded places with him.

Thoughts of her husband made her peek from beneath her lashes in the direction of the chair. At the sight of the blanket folded neatly on the footstool, she raised her head.

Cord was by the door, pulling his jacket over a clean white shirt and apparently getting ready to leave.

"Cord?"

"Hmm?" He whirled around, wide-eyed, then smiled a little too innocently. "Ah, good morning, *chére.*"

"Where on earth are you goin' at this hour?" She sat up, tugging the coverlet up over the bodice of her thin night shift.

"Where am I going?"

"That's precisely what I—" Delia's sleep-drugged mind cleared swiftly as she recalled their conversation of the night before. "You weren't possibly considerin' payin' a call on Chauncy Bateman, were you?" she asked with a frown.

"As a matter of fact—" Cord nonchalantly tugged down his cuffs. "I *had* planned on visiting M'sieu Bateman, yes."

Delia scrambled to her knees, holding the blanket securely across her breasts. "Cord, you can't just go burstin' into his house uninvited this early in the mornin'.''

"Actually, I had thought I might simply knock on his door and ask to see him.''

"Well, you're not gonna out-'n'-out accuse him of puttin' that silly frog in our bed, are you?''

"I am,'' Cord replied with an arrogant lift of his chin.

Delia pinched her lips together and stared at him, wishing he were old and ugly instead of so damnably handsome in the morning light. "And I s'pose there is nothin' I can say or do to make you change your mind.''

Cord's eyes took on a lusty gleam, and one corner of his mouth quirked slightly upward. His gaze moved over her face, her hair, and lingered on the unmentionable parts of her body, causing a fuzzy, most uncomfortable warmth low in Delia's abdomen.

"I am certain, *ma chérie*, there is something you could do, if you were but willing.'' He lifted his eyes to hers. "Perhaps you could try to dissuade me with some of those kisses you promised me. But there is undoubtedly nothing you can merely say to stop me. So unless—''

Delia hurled her pillow at him as hard as she could.

Cord artfully ducked into the hall, leaving the pillow to thump against the closing door and a shower of feathers floating about the room.

"Tell M'sieu I will wait, then,'' Cord replied to the tall black servant who had answered the Batemans' door.

The servant rubbed the back of his neck. "But, suh, Ah's done tole you already. Ah's ain't s'posed to 'nounce nobody who ain't been expected.''

"I will wait here on the veranda for M'sieu Bateman to finish his breakfast," Cord repeated for the third time. He kept his expression bland, but tightened his grip on the brim of the stovepipe hat he held against his chest. "You will tell M'sieu Bateman—"

"Heah, now, Jacob, what's all this fuss about?" Herbert Bateman asked, nudging the man aside.

At his first sight of Cord, Chauncy's father blinked. Then his mouth stretched into a wide smile, making his muttonchop whiskers appear even fuller.

"Jacob, you can go on about your business," Herbert said over his shoulder, then grabbed Cord's hand and pumped it hard. "Well, now, what a pleasant surprise. How you doin', boy?"

"Fine, m'sieu, thank you."

"Good, good. Tell me, what brings you 'round so early? Somethin' I can do for you? Not a legal matter, I hope. You haven't gone and got yourself into trouble again, have you?"

"No, nothing like that, I assure you. I would like to speak with Chauncy, if I may. But I do not wish to disturb your breakfast. I can wait here until he has finished his meal and can see me."

"Nonsense. Step on in heah, boy." Herbert tugged him into a highly polished foyer that smelled of lemon and beeswax. "We were just gettin' up from the table. Let me holler for Chauncy." Turning toward the arched doorway on his right, he yelled, "Son? You got yourself a visitor."

Within a few minutes, Chauncy poked his shaggy head around the doorframe.

"Who on earth would be callin' at this ungodly hour?" he asked with a frown. When he slid his gaze to Cord, his face flattened.

"Well, don't just stand there gawkin', Chauncy Allen." Herbert motioned his son forward. "You leave your manners abed this mornin', boy? Get on out heah and tend to your company."

Chauncy clutched his dressing robe tighter together and dragged his slippered feet as he entered the foyer. He eyed Cord warily. "Mornin' . . . Cord," he said, his voice lifting in pitch.

"Well, now, that's better." Herbert clapped his son on the back, then looked at Cord and winked. "You'll have to pardon Chauncy. Takes him a while to shake the sleep from his brain, that's all." Glancing between the two young men, Herbert smiled again. "Wish I could stay and chat myself, but I got some paperwork waitin' for me on my desk. Promised Winston I'd go over his accounts and have the books back to the bank by this afternoon. Good day, Mr. Kibedeaux," he said with a quick handshake. "Stop by again, anytime, you heah?"

Cord inclined his chin. "Thank you, m'sieu. You are most kind."

"Just good to see you boys gettin' along for a change, that's all." Herbert looked from Cord to Chauncy and back again. "Y'all have yourselves a nice visit now, ya hear?"

After Cord watched Herbert Bateman disappear up the wide staircase, his gaze collided with Chauncy's.

"Shall we step outside?" he asked, gesturing toward the front door.

Chauncy fixed his mouth in a hard line, then

swept out onto the veranda, leaving Cord to follow.

As Cord moved up behind him, Chauncy pivoted, cocked his head, and hooked his thumbs in the belt of his robe. "What the hell are you doin' here, Kibedeaux?"

"I would like to talk you," Cord replied, elevating his chin to an equal level.

"I thought we agreed to stay out of each other's way."

"*Oui*, but that was before you decided to sneak into my quarters at the Abernathy Plantation and leave Delia and me a . . . a little wedding gift, shall we say."

"A what?" Chauncy furrowed his brow. "I don't know what you're talkin' about."

"No?" Cord brushed an imaginary piece of lint from his coat sleeve. "You know nothing about *gris gris, hein*? Nothing about the significance of a dead frog in a black coffin placed in the home of a person you wish to be rid of?"

"No. Other than it's a bunch of hocus-pocus hogwash. But what else could I expect from the likes of you?" Chauncy narrowed his eyes and grinned. "Say . . . is that what this is all about? Huh? Somebody put a curse on you, Kibedeaux?"

Cord refused to give him the satisfaction of an answer. Instead, he studied Chauncy's face and mannerisms for some sign that he was lying.

Chauncy folded his arms across his chest and casually braced his shoulder against a large column that supported the porch roof.

"In case you ain't aware of it, boy, you got more than one enemy in Boudreaux Parish. Any number of people 'round here would like to see you vanish. Why don't you go ask some of them if they went and put a hex on you?" Pushing away from the post, Chauncy swerved around Cord and strode toward the door. "If you'll excuse me now, Kibedeaux, I got better things to do than stand out here jawin' with some crazy Cajun."

Cord made no attempt to stop him. He hadn't come here to threaten Bateman. He had merely wanted to assess the man's reaction.

He stared at the closed front door for a long moment, then walked down the steps of the Bateman mansion. He hadn't been able to detect a trace of crumbling composure in Chauncy—nothing that would prove his guilt beyond a doubt.

It occurred to Cord, however, as he climbed into the rig and took up the reins, that Chauncy had never actually denied casting the spell.

Chapter Fourteen

"**S**ee? I told you so," Delia commented. Snapping her fan open with a flick of her wrist, she gazed idly out of the carriage at the dusk-pinkened landscape rolling past. "You shouldn't have gone over there like that yesterday. I told you Chauncy wouldn't have done it."

Cord clicked his tongue, urging the horses onward, then peered sideways at his wife. "I am still not convinced he is not responsible."

"Tell me somethin', Cord. When we were children and Chauncy was houndin' you all the time, why didn't you ever just haul off and knock th' devil outta him?"

"Because it would have done no good," he answered, without the slightest show of being ruffled over the question. "Me, *I* was the troublemaker, or so they said. Had I fought Chauncy or one of his friends and won, they would have run off tattling, no doubt. And whose story do you think everyone would have believed, *hein?*"

"Well . . ." Delia smoothed her skirt over her knees. "I s'pose I never thought about it like that . . . but I guess you're right. Chauncy *was* an awful tattletale. But that was a long time ago, Cord. Y'all are grown men now. I still can't b'lieve he'd go and do somethin' as childish as puttin' a dead frog in our bed.''

''Your good friend Chauncy Bateman neither admitted nor denied the accusation.''

''My good friend?'' Delia sat back in her seat and touched her fan to her breast. ''Why, Cord, do I detect a note of jealousy in your tone?''

''Not a'tall.'' Cord frowned and fixed his eyes on the road ahead. He wasn't jealous. Was he? He had never once thought of himself as the jealous kind. But now that Delia had mentioned it . . .

Something angry *had* quivered inside him when she began defending Chauncy. He glanced at her . . . at the way the last of the day's sunlight played on her face. She lowered her lashes a bit and smiled a knowing little smile. And he looked away. Under the circumstances, he had no claim on Delia Abernathy.

Correction, Delia *Kibedeaux*. Mrs. Cord Kibedeaux.

Cord shifted his weight, feeling more uncomfortable than he'd ever been since the woman had first coerced him into this strange bargain.

Their marriage was a farce, he reminded himself. They had not consummated their vows, nor was it likely that they would. Cord closed his eyes, aware he should not think of such things— afraid Delia might read his mind.

The carriage suddenly grew too warm. In a spurt of restlessness, Cord scratched the itchy spot inside his high, starched collar. ''How long must we be at these people's house tonight, *hein?*''

"At the Willhites'? Not too late, I s'pose, It's just a dinner party. No dancin' or anything." Delia lowered her brow. "Why?"

"Oh, I don't know." Cord shrugged as he turned into the Willhites' drive. "Me, I am in no mood to be bored all evening, I guess."

"Well, do tell." Delia fixed her mouth in a perturbed fashion, then rearranged her hooped skirt. "So you think my dear acquaintances are borin', do you?"

"*Oui.*" Cord nodded and pulled back on the reins, stopping the buggy in front of the grand mansion. "They are boring."

Delia flounced out of the carriage before Cord could get around the rig to aid her. She lifted the hem of her dress and bustled up the steps.

Taking long strides, Cord easily caught up with her before she reached the door.

"Delia," he said, grasping her elbow, "forgive me. I should not have insulted your friends."

She gazed up into his dark, warm eyes, and her heart started pumping in her throat. That particularly tender part of her body, as well as others, had been doing all sorts of peculiar things lately whenever she looked at Cord. She simply couldn't understand how the man could irritate her so and fascinate her at the very same time.

"Just try to be cordial," she advised with a grimace, then allowed him to escort her into the house.

A servant took Cord's hat and frock coat and Delia's shawl. A young, pretty maid wearing a crisp white *tignon* showed them to the door of a large parlor where other guests milled about, chatting.

A half hour later, Cord and Delia had made the

rounds and politely spoken to everyone present. While they stood together, sipping their wine, Cord squeezed Delia's arm and bent to her ear.

"How would you like to go somewhere else tonight, *hein?* I know a place where we could have a much better time."

She slanted her eyes at him. "Perhaps the back room at Faldene's?"

"Oh, *non, chère.* Somewhere much better than Faldene's. A place filled with laughter, good food, and dancing. You like to dance, do you not? Me, I feel like dancing tonight."

Her lips curved into a smile. "You want to take me dancin'?" she asked with no small amount of skepticism.

"*Oui.*" Cord loosened his cravat and arched his brow. "We can go right now, yes."

Delia peered above the brim of her wineglass at the humdrum activity going on about the room. Assembled were the same prominent people who had attended the last social gathering in Boudreaux Parish. The buzz of conversation offered nothing new.

Bringing her gaze back to her husband, she suddenly felt very reckless.

"I b'lieve I've developed the most dreadful headache, Cord. Would you fetch my shawl, please? I'll make our excuses to Lydia and Tom."

After saying their hasty good-byes, they left. Delia walked out of the Willhites' door experiencing a sensation similar to the childhood thrill of ditching school to go fishing.

"You gonna tell me where we're goin'?" she asked as Cord helped her into the carriage.

"No," he said, then rounded the rig, climbed in beside her, and took up the reins.

Resisting the urge to question him further, Delia leaned back in her seat. The stars sparkled like diamonds on black velvet in the moonless sky. Though the night was balmy, a cool Gulf breeze blew through the marshland.

They drove along in companionable silence for a matter of a few miles. Delia pretended not to notice her husband's sidelong glances.

"Ah, Delia," Cord said, finally breaking the stillness. With a deep sigh, he shook his head. "You disappoint me, *ma chérie*. Are you not even going to try to badger me into disclosing our mysterious destination?"

"No." Delia could hardly keep from smiling. "To be quite honest, I'd rather you didn't tell me."

"You truly don't want to know?"

"No, I truly don't."

Cord curled his bottom lip. "Then I will not tell you."

"Good," Delia replied, but shifted in her seat. She watched his brow lower as he fixed his gaze on the road again.

Within a couple of turns of the carriage wheels, he angled another look her way. "How come? Why do you not want to know, *hein?*"

Mainly because you're just dyin' to tell me, Delia started to say, but changed her mind. She shrugged, toying with the tassel on the end of her fan. "I s'pose I have a fondness for surprises."

A twinkle touched Cord's eyes. His mouth lifted in a beautiful grin that handsomely displayed his white, even teeth.

Delia stared at him as if seeing him for the very first time. Indeed, he'd never shown her such a fetching expression. He looked years younger. All his other smiles had been overlaid with cynicism. But this smile . . . this smile went straight to her heart.

"So you like surprises, *hein?*" he asked in a teasing tone.

"Very much. Daddy always brings me a surprise when he comes home."

"What is he like, your father?"

"He's wonderful." Delia's gaze slid past Cord. The corners of her mouth rose automatically. "He's devilishly handsome. Witty. Charmin'. When he walks into the house, it's like Mardi Gras."

Cord's smile dissipated, and his eyes hinted at melancholia. Delia wondered if he might be thinking of his own father.

"He lives in Europe, I have heard," Cord commented.

"Yes, in Paris mostly, but he also has a villa on the Mediterranean. Then again, he stays with friends sometimes."

"Do you never visit him abroad?"

Cord hit upon a sore spot—unintentionally, Delia knew, but his question stung nonetheless. Her father had always discouraged her from traveling to Europe to see him.

"Um . . . no." She twisted her hands in her lap. "No, I don't. My father has . . . very important affairs to tend to there. Why, I wouldn't possibly think of pesterin' him. He'd probably feel like he had to entertain me, and all."

"But did you not say you planned to visit Europe once our business was finished?"

"Well, yes. But that's a different matter entirely." Delia dropped her lashes and bit her bottom lip, searching her brain for a quick change of subject. "I wonder why Milly wasn't at the Will-hites' tonight," she remarked, saying the first thing that popped into her head.

"Perhaps her *mère* would not allow her to attend."

"You're more than likely right about—" Delia narrowed her eyes on the lights shining from the large house on the horizon. "Cord, that's our plantation ahead. Why are you taking me home? I thought you said we were going somewhere to dance."

"We are. But first we need to change our clothes."

"Change our clothes?" She scrunched her nose. "Whatever for?"

"You will see."

"All right," she said, folding her arms over her chest. Her curiosity finally piqued. "S'pose you tell me just where it is we're goin' now."

"Oh, *non, chère*. I cannot possibly tell you that. Not after I know how much you love surprises."

Delia took Cord's extended hand and stepped into the skiff. She sat down, tucking the full calico skirt around her knees that he'd "borrowed" from the clothesline behind the servants' quarters.

Dressed in clean work clothes, Cord stood, his feet planted wide, at the front of the small craft. With the long pole he held, he pushed them away from the grassy bank.

"The bayou," Delia stated rather than asked, as Cord guided them through the murky waterway. "We goin' to the bayou at this time of night?"

"Oui." He looked over his shoulder. "You are afraid, no?"

She took in the dark canopy of Spanish moss overhead. Shadows played on the silhouettes of twisted cypress trees along the shore. Some animal shrieked in the distance, and Delia folded her arms around her waist.

"I am *not* afraid," she said with a lift of her chin. "Just curious, that's all. Is . . . is there really . . . I mean, people say wolflike creatures roam around these parts after dark. You ever saw one?"

"Loups-garous," Cord whispered hoarsely, then turned away from her. *"Oui,* I have seen them many times. But only in my head."

"Only in your head?" Delia watched the muscles in his back expand as he shoved the pole in the water again and the skiff surged forward.

"My mother, she used to tell me stories of *loups-garous.* She used to say, '*The loups-garous* are coming to get you, boy.' "

"How horrible," Delia said with a shiver.

"Oui. I used to be terrified to close my eyes at night."

Delia pressed a hand to her throat, recalling the rumors about Cord's mother. Gossips had claimed she'd been prone to fits of madness. Delia felt obliged to say something, but could think of nothing potent enough to break the barriers of time—nothing that could reach and comfort a frightened child of long ago.

A stretch of quietness passed; then Cord chuckled unexpectedly. "You need not fear *loups-garous* while you are with me, *chère.* Me, I know how to fix them now. *Tante* Netha Bea, she taught me, yeah."

"How?"

"You sprinkle them with salt or throw a toad at them. They are scared of toads, you know." Cord glanced at her and winked. "But let us talk no more of *loups-garous*. Tonight we go dancing, *hein?*"

Delia sighed and tipped her head. "Hey . . . wait a minute. You told me at Cynthia's engagement party that you'd never learned to dance."

"I lied," Cord replied.

Delia eyed him skeptically. She was beginning to think she'd been duped into this after-dark boat ride for alternative reasons.

"Cord, admit it. There is no dance, is there? You were just bored at the Willhites', right? Then you came up with the idea of whiskin' me off to the bayou and givin' me a good case of the willies. I trust I'm s'posed to fall tremblin' into your arms about now. Well, it's not gonna work. So you can just—"

"Shh. Listen." Cord cupped one of his ears. "Do you not hear the music?"

Delia started to roll her eyes. Then the faint sound of an accordion drifted through the air. The slow, sweet ballad grew steadily louder with the accompaniment of a nasal crooning. Delia couldn't understand the words, but the male tenor surely sang of some lost love.

When Cord steered the skiff around the next bend, she saw the lights. Numerous lanterns dangled from the edge of the porch roof hanging over the bayou, reflecting brightly off the water. Laughter mingled with the music and floated out the open door.

"Oh, Cord." Delia hid a wide smile behind her hands. "It's a *fais-do-do*, isn't it? I've heard about them since I was a child. But . . . I didn't think outsiders were allowed."

"You will be accepted as my wife," Cord said. Pulling the boat up next to the shack, he turned and helped her climb out.

"Hey, Kibedeaux, what you got dere?" an old man with a long white beard hollered, moving forward from the shadows on the far end of the porch. "Is dis dat Ameri-kawn wife I hear about?"

"*Bonsoir*, Artelus." Cord smiled and slipped an arm around Delia's waist. "*Oui*, this is my wife. She is a pretty one, no?"

"Hooyie! Is she ever, *mon ami!*" Artelus lifted his jug in tribute. Two more old-timers poked their heads over his shoulders and nodded. Artelus grinned, exhibiting several missing teeth, then made a shooing motion with his hands. "Y'all go on in dere wit' the young peoples. Get y'all somet'ing to eat. My Philomine, she make de bes' gumbo in all Boudreaux Parish, yeah."

"*Merci*, Artelus," Cord said, then winked. "Don't drink too much of that wine, now, you hear?"

"We done did," Artelus replied with a shrug. "But is hokay. Wine, she is good to circulate de blood, no?"

Cord laughed—a deep, warm, mirthful sound Delia had never heard from him.

Men, women, and numerous children crowded around the Kibedeauxs the moment they stepped through the door. Delia was passed around, hugged, kissed on the cheek, and congratulated. Cord was clapped on the back and showered with wishes for many strong sons and daughters. Plates piled high with boiled crawfish, jambalaya, and a bowl of gumbo were then pushed into their hands.

The fiddler struck up a lively tune and the squeeze-box player joined in, diverting everyone's attention. With a tip of his head, Cord indicated a vacant bench along the wall. Delia trailed after him, dodging the dancers who jigged their way to the middle of the room.

She settled beside her husband and, following his example, balanced her dishes on her knees. Enthralled by the jovial goings-on, she lifted a spoonful of spicy rice to her mouth. Cajuns of all ages reeled about as if they hadn't a care in the world—some with partners, some without.

The energy of the merriment surrounding Delia began to pulsate in her veins. Before she took her second bite, her toe was tapping against the wooden floor.

"See?" Cord nudged her with his elbow. "Is this not much more interesting than dining quietly with the Willhites?"

"I must admit it is." Delia smiled and watched him shell a crawfish and pop it into his mouth.

His eyes met hers, and his jaw slowed in the task of chewing. Something very special passed between them in that moment, though Delia couldn't say exactly what it was. His gaze held her, pulled her . . . in a direction she wasn't certain she wanted to go.

A worrisome thought that her own eyes might reveal feelings more properly kept hidden made her lower her lashes abruptly.

"Thank you for bringin' me here tonight, Cord," she said, groping for a subject that could ease her sudden discomfort. For several minutes, she turned her attention on enjoying her meal.

Then, she lifted her head and nodded toward the high-steppers whirling around the room. "I've never seen such a spirited bunch. My, these people do know how to have a good time, don't they?"

"Cajuns have a zest for life, *ma petite*." Cord cocked his head and observed the dancers, lifting a corner of his mouth. "They love to celebrate and seize any opportunity to do so."

"Oh? And what's the occasion tonight?"

"There is no occasion this evening." Cord looked at her blankly. "This is Saturday night. There is always a *fais-do-do* every Saturday night."

"What does it mean, *fais-do-do*?"

"*Fais-do-do* comes from *fête de Dieu*, or festival of God," Cord replied, viewing her plate. "Are you through eating?"

"Gracious, yes. I'm full as a tick."

"Ah, good." Cord took her dishes, stacked his on top, set them next to him on the bench, then turned to her and wiggled his brow. "I promised you dancing, did I not?"

"Why, I b'lieve you did mention somethin' of the sort."

Grasping her hand, he rose and tugged her into the center of the room. He caught her waist. She laid her hands on his shoulders. And they were off, blending in with the rest of the merrymakers.

Cord swept Delia across the floor with graceful moves. They kept time to the frolicsome tunes at a breathless pace. The fun-loving mood encircling Delia quickly drew her in. She laughed freely, and often, while Cord attempted to teach her the words to the songs.

Hours passed and the music never stopped, but Delia's side started to ache. Uncertain whether

her ailment stemmed from dancing or an overdose of Cord's humor, she begged her husband for a rest.

"Ah, *non, chère*," Cord teased with a mocking grin. "You mean to tell me I got myself a wife who can't keep up with me?"

"I just want to sit out one song." She ran a hand down her damp bodice. "Just long enough to catch my breath."

He led her to the punch bowl and dipped her a cup as he glanced around the room. "Well, I guess I'll just have to find another partner for the mazurka they are playing, *hein*?"

A hopeful little twinkle touched his eyes, and Delia suspected him of trying to make her jealous. She took a sip of the cool drink, then motioned toward the dance floor with her glass. "Oh, by all means," she said. "You go right ahead. I'll just wait here for you."

Cord looked at her for a second or two. Then he reached out and stopped the first woman who passed. "Hey, Lena, how are you?"

"Cord!" The dark-eyed beauty shifted the toddler she held to her other arm and smiled. "*Sacrebleu*, where have you been? Me, I was jus' telling Ovide the other day we need to have you over for supper."

"I have been around," Cord answered. "Come. You dance with me, and catch me up on all the gossip, *hein*?"

"Oh, *non*." Lena laughed and lowered her lids. "I cannot. The *bébé* here, she is sleepy, and Ovide, he will—"

"My wife will tend the little one." Cord took the baby and handed her to Delia. "And I will tell

Ovide you looked so pretty tonight that I could not resist."

Cord caught the woman's elbow and led her off before Delia could find her voice. Holding the child awkwardly—an arm's length away from her—Delia glared at Cord's retreating form.

A soft gurgling sound brought her gaze back to the baby. Dark ringlets framed the little girl's cherublike features. With a wide-eyed and wary expression, the child chewed a chubby finger and stared at Delia.

Delia glanced around, noting how the other mothers propped their children on their hips. Copying their stance, she stood and positioned the baby likewise, then checked the little girl's face to make sure she'd done the proper thing. The tot smiled at her before laying her curly head against Delia's breast.

A wonderful warmth filled Delia to the brim. With her lips curved upward at a serene angle, she watched the child's long dark lashes flutter shut.

Lena's laugh drew Delia's attention as the woman and Cord approached.

"Hooyie! Your man can dance, yeah," Lena remarked, reaching for the baby. "Oh, *merci*, madame," she added in a whisper. "You got her to sleep. *Merci*. I am grateful."

"My pleasure," Delia replied, unable to take her eyes off the baby girl Lena cradled in her arms. "She's beautiful. What's her name?"

"Bré. It is my maiden name."

"Bré," Delia repeated, then looked at Cord. "If you two want to dance again, I'd be happy to hold her a while longer."

"Oh, no, no. *Merci*, but my Ovide, he is waiting. It is late, and we must get the children home." With a wave, Lena hustled off.

"We should be leaving soon too, no?" Cord asked.

"Just one more dance?" Delia suggested.

The accordion began a slow, bittersweet song, and Cord took her in his arms. Pressing her cheek to his chest while they waltzed, Delia closed her eyes and sighed. It was the perfect end to a perfect evening.

Chapter Fifteen

The night had stretched into the wee hours of the morning by the time Cord and Delia tiptoed up the stairs of the Abernathy mansion.

Cord lit their bedroom lamp and turned to find his wife's pleasant mood still intact. Leaning a hip against the dresser, he folded his arms over his chest and watched Delia sway from side to side, softly humming the last tune they'd heard at the *fais do-do*.

"Oh, Cord, thank you so much for taking me to the bayou this evenin'." She caught the sides of her skirt and swirled in a circle toward the dressing screen. "I had a simply glorious time." Her hands went to the buttons at the small of her back, and she started to step behind the partition.

"Here," Cord said, crossing the room, "let me help you with that."

"Oh . . . well." She glanced over her shoulder at him as he pushed her hands aside. "I do have the most awful trouble . . . I mean, since Bess stopped helpin' me . . . I mean, it's so hard to do by myself."

"Shh, *chère*. There is nothing wrong with a man aiding his wife in these things." Cord's nimble

213

fingers moved skillfully down her spine, unfastening the tiny buttons.

"I . . . I s'pose not," Delia murmured. As exhausted as she was, she stood rigid while he performed his task. He was tired too, she assured herself. Surely much too weary to try anything frisky.

"There. Now, slip off your dress and I will untie your crinoline and corset for you, *hein?*"

Other than biting her bottom lip, Delia didn't move.

"Come, come, *ma petite*. It would take you twice as long to remove your underthings yourself, would it not? I don't know about you, but me, I would like to get some sleep before the sun comes up."

Delia hesitantly stooped down, caught the hem of her skirt, and tugged the dress over her head.

When Cord unfastened her crinoline without a single fishy move, Delia's apprehension thawed. He immediately went to work on the strings of her corset. At some point during the time-consuming process, her head lolled to one side. Glad she didn't have to struggle with the stays all by herself, she closed her eyes and wondered how he knew so much about ladies' undergarments.

In her fatigued state, she let her arms dangle. At last, cool air met the damp part of her shift where the fabric stuck to her ribs. She took a deep breath—but the breath caught in her throat as Cord's warm palms rested against her shoulders from behind.

"Ah, your skin is so soft," he whispered, his hands gliding up and down her arms.

Despite her urge to bolt, Delia stood motionless

while he brushed her hair aside and pressed his lips to the back of her neck.

"So soft," he said, then trailed feathery kisses along her shoulder blade. "So sweet."

Delia shuddered. Her heart pounded hard against her sternum. Somewhere in the back of her mind, a fast-fading voice echoed that she should push him away, but all thought was overshadowed by the magic of his touch.

Cord turned her around, tucked a finger beneath her chin, and tilted her face to his. Streaks of golden fire glimmered in his heavy-lidded eyes, laying bare his desire. Yet uncertainty also lingered in the depth of his gaze.

Delia knew he awaited her response. She knew a word, a look, a single motion would determine his course of action. She could end it all here and now. She could stop whatever was about to happen.

But she didn't.

Instead, she slid her hands up over his chest, feeling the crisp, coarse hair prick her palms through his linen shirt . . . feeling his heart pulsate with the same erratic rhythm as her own.

Cord needed no further prompting. His mouth met Delia's, emitting a force that gave her no choice but to return his kiss. Embracing her with an urgent tenderness, he molded her against the muscled plane of his body.

Delia's mind went numb while the rest of her awakened to new sensations simmering in her veins. She was only barely aware of losing a grip on her emotions—and completely indifferent to the notion that she was no longer master of the game.

"Delia, Delia," Cord whispered, brushing his

lips back and forth across her cheek. "Let me love you, *chérie*. Let me show you what pleasure is. We are married, yes? Let me be a real husband." He slid his hand over her shoulder and cupped her breast. "Let me make you my wife."

Delia hesitantly covered his hand with hers and stood paralyzed in a moment of indecision. A warm tingling sensation flowed from his palm, penetrating her skin. Her common sense waged war with the feelings Cord evoked deep inside her chest.

When she weighed the consequences of giving in to her heart, rationality only barely won out.

With no small amount of effort, she squirmed free of Cord's grasp before his tantalizing touch could change her mind again. Stumbling away from him, she hugged her rib cage, and a slow shake of her head became progressively stronger.

"No," she said firmly. "We can't do this. I've already taken too many steps in the wrong direction. I can't afford to make another mistake. I can't take the chance of you gettin' me with child."

Rubbing her upper arms, she turned away from him and walked to the window. She inhaled deeply, staring unseeingly at the dark prelude of dawn.

"I *am* goin' to join my father in Europe, Cord. The trip will surely be tedious enough without the added burden of bein' heavy-bellied with your baby. I won't allow that to happen. Land sakes, what would Daddy think if I walked into his house that way?" Angling her chin over her shoulder, she met his gaze. "You understand me,

Cord? Nothin's going to keep me from goin' to Paris.''

Purple shadows accented Cord's chiseled features. "Tell me, do you not like the way I kiss you?" He arched an eyebrow. "You quivered when I held you, not because of fear, no. You felt something else, did you not? Perhaps a warmth here—" He thumped a fist against his chest. "And here?" He dropped a hand to his stomach.

Delia's throat tightened. With an iron will, she swiveled her head and looked out the window again. "It doesn't matter what I felt. We can't just go settin' off sparks that might beget a baby. It wouldn't be fair to you, or me, or the child.''

His footsteps fell softly on the floor. Delia closed her eyes as he moved up behind her. "I mean it, Cord. We can't . . . can't . . .''

Her sentence dangled as his palms grazed her hips. On a downward course, his fingers made sensuous circles over her thighs, dipping teasingly beneath the hem of her shift. "There are other ways, sweet Delia." His breath stirred the wisps of hair behind her ear. "There are many ways for men and women to make love. I can show you, *ma petite.*''

"Stop that," she said, though her voice lacked her usual commanding tone.

"Stop what? That? Ah, *chère*, you don't like that?''

"No." She cleared her throat. "No, I definitely—''

"Perhaps you will like this better.''

Delia clamped both hands on Cord's wrist as he hooked his thumb in the waistband of her pantaloons. With one swift motion, she flung his arm aside and unintentionally gouged him in the stomach with her elbow.

Cord's shoulders sagged forward from the impact of the blow. He widened his eyes on Delia, appearing more surprised than in pain. "What the hell . . . did you do that for, *hein?*"

Taking advantage of his short-winded condition, Delia scampered out of his reach. Once assured she hadn't seriously injured him, she lifted her chin. The unfortunate incident had had a sobering effect on both of them, she reasoned.

"I told you to stop," she said, then took a giant step farther away from him. "I made it plain as day I didn't care for none of your horseplay."

Cord straightened and flexed his jaw.

Delia retreated when he started toward her. She bumped into the bed. Climbing onto the mattress, she scrambled to the headboard and clutched a pillow to her breast.

Without breaking his stride, Cord crawled across the bed after her. Delia's heartbeat pounded in her throat and between her ears as he approached. He pushed her backward against the mattress and braced his hands on either side of her head. Then he lowered his face so close she could see her reflection in his eyes.

"Did you not promise me that I could kiss you anytime I wanted?" he inquired harshly. "This was part of our bargain, was it not? Answer me, sweet Delia. Yes or no?"

"Yes," she whispered, wide-eyed. "I said you could kiss me . . . but I offered nothin' mo—"

Cord's mouth took hers swift and hard. His tongue, hot and sweetened with wine, delved urgently between her lips. Delia trembled, responding involuntarily to the kiss. But in the moment that her resistance melted, Cord pulled back. His face hovered above hers, and a dark glint filled his eyes.

"So, *ma chérie*. You do not care for my 'horseplay,' *hein*?" He gave her a malicious smile that made her spine tingle. "On top of all your other disreputable traits . . . you lie like the devil too."

Cord bounced off the bed and walked to the door.

"Just where do you think you're goin' at this hour?" Delia asked, gaining a bit of bravado with him clear across the room.

"Outside to cool off," Cord replied, then grasped the doorknob. "Which is what I should have done two minutes after I entered this bedroom tonight, no?"

A light wind whispered through the garden, ruffling Cord's hair. He shoved his hands into his pockets and inhaled the mixed fragrance of orange blossoms and wisteria.

He couldn't quite grasp what had just happened between him and Delia. Staring at their bedroom window, he noted that she'd put out the lamps. He wondered if she'd fallen asleep.

He hoped not.

If there was any justice in the world, she would be lying awake in anguish. *Non*, he would not wish her sweet dreams. He wanted her to ache as badly as he did.

Cord dropped his gaze. He tugged his shirt out of his trousers and unfastened the buttons. Delia was surely dozing peacefully, he decided, for as far as he knew, there was no justice. Not for him.

He looked at their window again. The breeze flapped his shirttail against his sides. For the past several hours he'd forgotten who he was . . . and what he was. He'd forgotten how life had betrayed him.

For a short space in time he'd merely been a man. And Delia had been his woman. But the few hours of happiness God had granted him were over now. Gone with the break of dawn.

Cord searched the lavender-tinted sky, his head clearing with the fresh, early morning air. Delia's charms had steered him from his purpose. He had returned to this place to prove his innocence—not to court *la belle de Boudreaux Parish*.

He had dallied far too long making polite inquiries that had led him nowhere. He would not waste any more time being courteous. John Hart would speak with him today—if Cord had to break down the man's door.

The tension between his shoulder blades eased. He reached into his shirt pocket, pulled out a cheroot, and stuck it between his teeth. He made a silent affirmation to keep his distance from his wife. He vowed John Hart would escape him no more. Lighting his cheroot, Cord drew the smoke deep into his lungs and watched the sun rise.

"Adelaide, dear, you feelin' poorly this mornin'?" Grandy squinted at her granddaughter across the breakfast table. Straightening in her chair, Agatha clasped her hands to her chin. Her eyes twinkled and a suspicious smile curved her lips. "Not nauseous, are you? You've hardly eaten a bite."

"I'm fine," Delia replied, then stabbed her egg with her fork. Unfurling her brow, she gave Grandy a poor attempt at a smile. In her present mood, it was the best she could do. "Why do you ask?"

"You look a little peaked. Dark circles under your eyes, and all. Didn't you sleep well?"

"No. I didn't." Delia slid her gaze to Cord, who dove into his food without the slightest sign of a bothered appetite. She tried hard to keep from frowning again. "Cord and I were out dancin' all night, weren't we, Cord?"

"Hmm?" A biscuit dripping with honey paused halfway to his mouth. "Forgive me, *ma petite*. What did you say? My thoughts were elsewhere."

"Obviously." Delia conveyed her disgust to him with a pointed look, then smiled as sweetly as her temper would permit. "I was tellin' Grandy you took me dancin' last night."

"Oh, *mais oui*." Cord's expression brightened as he turned to Agatha. "Your granddaughter, she is very light on her feet." He cocked his head Delia's way. "Surprisingly agile."

Delia caught the double meaning of his words and openly sneered at him.

Grandy studied the couple at her breakfast table. Picking up her cup, she took a sip of her coffee. "Are the two of you gettin' along all right?"

"But of course," Cord said, putting on the certain smile that never failed to charm Agatha. "Delia and me, we are like a pair of sweetheart doves, yeah." Rising from his chair, he dabbed his mouth with a napkin, then rounded the table and laid his hands on Delia's shoulders. "Is that not so, *ma chérie*?"

Delia reserved her comment, but cast a narrowed gaze up at him.

"You know I hate to leave your side, my love, but I have some things to attend to in town this morning." Paying little heed to her scowl, Cord kissed her swiftly but thoroughly on the mouth, then moved to Grandy and pecked the older woman's cheek. "As usual, Agatha, breakfast with you was a delight that will brighten my whole day."

He paused in the doorway and curled his bottom lip. "Ah, Delia, do not pout so. I promise I will be home soon, *hein?*"

Squelching the urge to throw her plate at him, Delia gripped the arms of her chair and glared at the empty space he left as he disappeared into the hall.

"That boy is such a treasure," Grandy murmured.

"Oh, he's somethin', all right," Delia commented dryly.

Cord lounged against the clapboard building in the alley across from Faldene's. For the first time in his life, he regretted not owning a watch.

It seemed as if John Hart had been in the coffeehouse for hours, but from the position of the sun, Cord calculated a passing of no more than thirty to forty-five minutes.

The door of the coffeehouse opened and Cord pushed away from the building, only to slump back against the wall when a middle-aged couple stepped onto the sidewalk. But before the door had closed completely, John Hart slipped out behind them.

Hart made a quick survey of the area, then

tugged down the brim of his hat and walked briskly in the direction of his house.

Cord followed, ducking from sight whenever John stopped and looked around. Rather than taking the main streets, he led Cord through alleyways and neighborhood yards.

John stayed close to the tall hedge that lined his property. He avoided the front door. Instead, he went to the rear of the house and swiftly climbed the steps of the back stoop.

Cord appeared behind him just as John inserted his key in the lock. "*Bonjour*, M'sieu Hart," he said.

The elderly man jerked around. Flattening himself against the door, he clutched at his heart.

"Easy, m'sieu." Cord's eyes narrowed with concern, and he raised his hands slowly to assure Hart he meant no harm. "I only wish to talk to you."

A little color seeped back into John's pale features. Apparently attempting to compose himself, he frowned. "You . . . you leave me be," he said in a shaky voice.

"A few moments of your time, this is all I ask."

"Won't do you any good. I told everything I knew at the trial." Dropping his gaze, Hart wet his thin lips. He gave his lapels a tug, then turned and started jiggling the key in the door.

As the lock clicked, Cord reached around John and caught the doorknob. "I need answers, m'sieu. I must know the truth."

Hart looked up at him, his bloodshot eyes wide and terror-filled. "I can't," he whispered. "If I say anything—" He pinched his mouth shut, then hung his head. "Come inside," he muttered, pushing the creaky door open.

Cord stepped into the house behind John. Tightly drawn shades darkened the kitchen but couldn't hide the clutter. Cord watched Hart cross the room. John lifted the globe from a lamp on the table, then opened a cupboard and rummaged through the contents.

The kitchen took on a soft gold glow as Hart lit the lamp. When he turned back to Cord, the light glinted off the barrel of a pistol he held.

"Take my advice, boy. Quit snoopin' around. What's done is done and can't be changed. Lord knows it's caused us all enough misery." Hart's eyes drifted off to one side. For a moment he seemed lost in some painful memory, but he quickly focused on Cord again. "You go askin' too many questions, Kibedeaux, and you and I both are liable to end up floatin' dead in the bayou. Now, you get. Go on," he said, waving his gun toward the door. "You come botherin' me any more and I'm goin' to the sheriff and filin' a complaint. Don't reckon that'd set too well, would it? You bein' straight outta prison, and all."

"No, m'sieu, you are quite right." Cord eased toward the door, glancing from Hart's disturbed expression to the quivering pistol in his hand. "Me, I don't want no trouble."

Cord backed out onto the stoop and went cautiously down the steps. The door slammed before his feet touched the ground. He expelled the breath he'd held, then wasted no time in leaving the premises.

As he drove the buggy along the cypress-lined road that led to the Abernathy Plantation, Cord viewed his visit with John Hart as having been very informative after all. Though John had been reluctant to provide any answers, the old teller's actions had told Cord plenty. Hart was afraid, not just of Cord, but of someone else.

Chapter Sixteen

ord stood stiffly to one side of the crowded Abernathy parlor, a little perturbed that Delia's birthday soiree had interrupted his increased surveillance of John Hart.

In the week that had passed since Cord's confrontation with Hart, John had hardly left his rickety old house. Sooner or later, though, Cord figured John would lead him to something, or *someone*, of vital importance—possibly a link to what had really happened at Winston Grayson's bank.

Delia's laughter grated across Cord's nerves *again*. Before he could stop himself, he glanced in her direction *again*—just in time to see her change partners *again*.

For the past week, Cord and his wife had exchanged no more than forced politeness. They had spoken only when it was unavoidable. Other than his brief appearances at meals for Agatha's sake, Cord had steered clear of Delia. Every night after the household was abed, he had slipped quietly off into the darkness and stood in John Hart's overgrown garden.

Resisting the impulse to unfasten his high,

starched collar, Cord locked his hands behind
his back, pushed his thoughts from Delia, and
resumed his study of the guests. His eyes
rested on Mr. and Mrs. Petty across the way, a
distinguished couple Cord guessed to be in
their late forties or early fifties. He'd been
briefly introduced to them at the Davenports'.

While Arthur Petty conversed with another
gentleman, his wife glanced idly about the room.
Lucile Petty, still strikingly attractive for her age,
met Cord's gaze. Fingering her pearl-and-jasper
necklace, she smiled ever so slightly, transmitting
a silent message Cord couldn't quite accept.
Surely he misconstrued the intention of the woman's bold stare. A lady would not stand beside
her husband making the suggestions Lucile's sultry eyes brought to mind.

The sudden change of Mrs. Petty's expression
when Arthur bent to her ear, the quick drop of
her lashes, made Cord wonder just the same.
Uncomfortable with the notion that she was
sending him some sort of invitation, he diverted
his attention elsewhere. If Lucile Petty was in
the habit of straying, that was Mr. Petty's problem.

Cord had troubles of his own to consider.
Clutching his jacket lapels, he observed the colorful swirl of ladies' skirts moving gracefully
about the floor. His gaze lit on Delia once more.
She certainly appeared to be enjoying herself, he
thought dryly. She hadn't missed a single dance,
accepting offers from all the eligible gentlemen.
Her cheeks were flushed, her eyes bright, and her
smile never-ending.

Cord bristled at his wife's pleasant mood,
though he didn't know why. He wasn't jealous.

Not at all. It was merely a coincidence, he reasoned, that an attack of indigestion flared up whenever he caught sight of a young man holding Delia a trifle too close. He had simply eaten something that didn't agree with him, he suspected.

"My, my, don't we look grim," Milly commented, sidling up to him.

Cord regarded the petite brunette peering at him from above her wavering fan.

"Why, anybody'd think you were at a funeral, Cord Kibedeaux, 'stead of a party. Mind if I ask how come you're not dancin'? Delia tells me you waltz like an angel."

"She said that about me, *hein?*" One corner of Cord's mouth pulled into a grin. He glanced from Milly to his wife and back again.

"She most certainly did." Milly raised her eyebrows and leaned a tad closer. "But now, you didn't hear that from me, you understand."

"Ah, *non.* Of course not." Cord sobered his expression. "I would never reveal the source of such a confidence, mademoiselle."

"Well, I knew you wouldn't." Milly lowered her fan to her chin. "Actually, I never would have brought the matter up, except . . . well, you looked so lonely standin' here by yourself, and I thought maybe, since Delia is otherwise occupied with her guests, and all . . . Well . . . they *are* playin' a waltz, you know, and—"

"Milly!" Delia called as she rustled forward in yards of green taffeta. Squeezing in between Cord and her friend, Delia looped an arm through each of theirs. "How kind of you to tend my husband for me, Milly." She gave the smaller woman a tight smile. "I have been neglectin' him, haven't I?"

"Why, yes, I do b'lieve you have," Milly answered honestly, then turned her head the other way. "Oh, look, there's Harley Beasley standin' all by himself. I think I'll mosey on over and visit with him a spell. See y'all later," she said with a little wave of her fan.

Delia watched her friend walk off, then glanced at Cord. "You and Milly have a nice chat?" she asked, attempting to sound only casually interested.

"*Oui*. Mademoiselle Mosely is quite a talker, is she not?"

Tightening her grip on Cord's arm, Delia lost her nonchalance. "What did she tell you?"

Cord curled his bottom lip and shrugged. "Nothing I could repeat."

"What did she say, Cord?" Delia ducked her head and peered at him from beneath her furrowed brow.

"I promised I would not tell. Would you care to dance."

"No."

"But of course, you are tired of dancing, *hein*? Perhaps a walk in the garden, then?"

Delia twisted her mouth in a perturbed fashion. "What I want, Cord, is—"

"Your birthday present, *oui*?"

Delia blinked. "My birthday present?"

Cord patted his breast pocket. "I have it right here. Are you not curious? You once told me you liked surprises, did you not?"

"Yes, but—" Delia completely forgot what she'd been about to say as she focused on the hand he held over his pocket. Lifting her gaze to his, she bit back a smile. "What is it?"

"Come." He tilted his head toward the doors that led to the veranda. "Come outside with me. Ah, *chère*, do not look so skeptical. I only wish to give you my gift in private. You have my word I will conduct myself as a gentleman."

Delia allowed him to steer her out the door, down the steps of the veranda, and into the garden. Her heart beat faster with each step she took. What worried her was that she knew her erratic pulse had nothing at all to do with the promise of a birthday surprise. She was fully aware that the flutter inside her chest was caused by the prospect of being alone with her husband.

"This should be far enough," Cord said, stopping in a secluded spot beside a large willow tree. "Close your eyes, Delia."

She did as she was instructed, but couldn't keep from squinting when he reached into his pocket.

Cord stifled a chuckle. "No peeking."

Delia squeezed her eyes shut and shifted her weight.

"It isn't much." Cord reached out and caught her hand, folding her fingers over something cold and hard. "It belonged to my mother."

Delia opened her eyes. Moonlight reflected off the gold, heart-shaped locket lying in her palm. Intricately etched flowers trailed the outer edge of the heart. In the center was a tiny wishing well.

"Oh, Cord," she murmured. "This is beautiful. It was your mother's?"

"*Oui*. Her initials are inside. The inscription indicates it was a gift from her father, though for what occasion I do not know. She never spoke of her family.''

Delia dragged her gaze from the locket and looked up at him. ''Gracious, Cord, I couldn't possibly accept such a keepsake. It's a very valuable piece, and the sentimental attachment—''

''Let me help you put it on.'' He took the locket and turned her around before she could protest any further. ''I harbor no sentimental feelings for my parents,'' he commented.

His last words were cold, but his fingers were warm as he brushed Delia's hair aside and fastened the necklace at her nape.

Pivoting slowly, she searched his unreadable features. ''Are you sure?'' she asked.

His lids lowered a fraction of an inch. ''I want you to have it.''

''Thank you,'' she whispered and touched the gold heart, which hung just above her cleavage. I'll surely cherish this forever.''

Cord's eyes skittered from hers, falling first to her lips, then to the locket. He stared so long and intensely at the pendant that Delia began to wonder if he'd forgotten his promise to be a gentleman.

''What was she like?'' Delia asked off the top of her head, hoping to divert his attention from her low neckline.

Cord raised his gaze by gradual degrees and frowned. ''Who, *chère?*''

''Why, your mother, of course.''

''She was a madwoman,'' he replied without an ounce of emotion in his voice or on his face. ''The rumors you must surely have heard, they are all true, yeah.''

Delia folded her arms at her waist, uncomfortable with the subject, but nevertheless intrigued. "No, I didn't mean . . . I meant . . . was she pretty?"

Cord snickered. Stuffing his hands in his pants pockets, he looked up at the sky. "She used to rant about wearing fancy dresses, going to parties, and being a beauty when she was young—before she married my father." With a shrug, he glanced at the ground. "Me, I don't remember her being anything but haggardly. And I don't recall her ever going anywhere. She had a terrible fear of leaving the house."

"What about your father?" Delia blurted out, then bit her lip, ashamed for prying but unable to stop herself.

"My father?" Cord angled a bitter grin her way. "You really want to know about my father, *hein*? I will tell you, then." Cord stepped closer to her and cocked his head to one side. "He was a roving, no-good bastard. He would lie, cheat, or steal for the means to play poker. He would have sold the locket you wear for a shot of whiskey had my mother not hidden it." Raking his fingers through his hair, Cord stared past Delia. "He was always in trouble with the law. Always. We moved so often, used so many last names—Giffault, Abadie, Blouin—I don't even know whether Kibedeaux was his real name or not."

A knot formed in Delia's throat. Hesitantly, she laid a hand against Cord's cheek, bringing his gaze back to hers. "I'm sorry," she whispered. "I . . . I'm sorry," was all she could say.

Cord's jaw flexed beneath her palm, then he stepped away from her.

"I do not want your pity," he said in a chilly tone that made goose bumps rise on Delia's arms. "Me, I don't need anybody's pity."

She opened her mouth, then closed it, then tilted her chin up indignantly. "I . . . maybe I wasn't offerin' my pity. Maybe . . . just maybe . . . I was workin' up to kissin' you. Did you ever once think of that, Mr. Know-It-All?"

The anger clouding Cord's features dissipated. He eyed her suspiciously. "Oh, yeah, *chère*, I'm supposed to believe that?"

"I don't really give a hoot whether you believe it or not. It's the truth." Delia spun on her heel, intending to leave.

Cord caught her shoulder and twisted her back around before she got out of his reach. Wrapping his arms around her waist, he peered deeply into her eyes.

"And why would you want to kiss me?" he asked in a hoarse whisper. "Tell me that, *hein?*"

Delia focused on his mouth. "Maybe I wanted to thank you properly for the locket."

"Let me see your eyes. Look at me, Delia."

His commanding tone raised her lashes, but she had a hard time keeping her gaze steady on his.

"It is very dangerous to tease a man so."

"But I didn't . . . I wasn't . . ."

"Shh," Cord said softly, touching a finger to her lips. "No more lies. Just listen. I'm going to tell you something for your own good, *hein?*"

Delia closed her eyes, unable to bear his scrutiny any longer. She couldn't move. She couldn't think. He was too close. The strong scent of honeysuckle drifting on the air was too sweet.

He kissed her cheek, then slid his lips to her

ear. "Little girls who play with fire, sooner or later they get burned, yes."

Gliding his hands downward swiftly from her waist, he cupped her bottom and fit her snugly against him.

Delia gasped, but didn't struggle. She kept her eyes tightly shut, waiting for . . . whatever came next. Cord's warm breath skimmed her skin, stirring closer and closer to her mouth.

A loud, warbling voice turned Delia's and Cord's head simultaneously toward the garden walk. Two plump old women strolled down the path in their direction.

Ducking quickly through the low-hanging branches of the willow, Cord tugged Delia along and hugged her against the tree trunk.

"Did you ever hear of such in all your born days? Why, I like to've died when Mertle Jackson told me." The heavier of the two ladies paused beside the draping willow limbs that hid Cord and Delia from view. In a sharp pivot, she pointed her fan at her companion. "And did you see that Lucile Petty tonight? Can you imagine? Makin' eyes at Adelaide's young Cajun husband the way she did? Why, she's twice that boy's age—and then some, I'd wager."

"Mmm, mmm, mmm. It *is* just awful," the smaller woman commented with a wave of her hand. " 'Course, Lucile always has carried on so. Surely you recollect that altercation poor Arthur had with that Kibedeaux boy's daddy? Musta been . . . what? Twenty-some-odd years ago, I s'pose. Anyways, Lucile never made no bones about lustin' after *that* Cajun devil neither, you know."

Both ladies sighed deeply, shook their gray heads, then locked arms and started down the path. "I s'pose you heard 'bout that doctor in N'orlens wantin' to pull out all Amos Dimpsy's teeth," one said to the other.

As the women's chatter faded into the distance, Delia felt Cord's arms slacken around her. She peered at him, seeking his reaction, but the shadows concealed his face.

"Cord?" she whispered softly, tenderly.

He stood motionless, leaning against the tree trunk, and neglected to respond.

"Cord, don't pay those biddies no mind. They're just a couple of old gossips. Probably half of what they said is made up."

"*Non*. My father was not discreet." Cord's voice was low and laced with cool indifference. "I knew he took many lovers. Everywhere we went, there was a new woman—sometimes more than one.

"Come." Catching hold of Delia's wrist, he pushed away from the willow and guided her through the curtain of leafy sprigs. "We should go back to the party. Your guests will be wondering where you are, no?"

While they walked toward the house in silence, Delia weighed Cord's childhood against her own.

Her father's absence had been a source of grief in her life. Every time he had left again for Paris, she had run to her room, fallen across the bed, and spent the entire afternoon wallowing in self-pity. Her bouts with sorrow, however, had been few and far between.

Cord's pain, she surmised, had been continuous—a daily substance he'd accepted as routine. Whereas Grandy had always pampered her, it seemed Cord's parents had given him nothing but misery.

Delia slanted her gaze and studied her husband's moonlit profile. The reasons for his arrogance were clear now. She understood what prompted his distance. She knew why he cloaked his emotions—why his eyes were often aloof, why his mouth remained fixed in a hard line most of the time. *Most of the time.* But not always.

She had glimpsed a softer side of Cord Kibedeaux. A side she suspected he didn't show often. Climbing the steps of the veranda, Delia fingered the heart-shaped locket. On impulse, she tightened her grip on Cord's elbow, stopping him just short of the door.

When he halted in mid-stride and looked at her, she raised up on her toes and kissed his cheek. "Thank you again for the lovely gift," she whispered.

Unexpectedly flustered, she lowered her head and clasped her hands at her waist.

An endless moment passed before Cord curled a finger beneath her chin and lifted her gaze to his. He smiled ever so slightly.

"You are most welcome, *chère*," he murmured, then pressed his lips to hers in a slow, tender way that made Delia shiver.

"Well, there you two are," Grandy called, pushing the veranda doors wide and causing Cord and Delia to spring apart. "I'll swan. Don't y'all get enough of smoochin' in the dark?" She put her hands on her hips and wrinkled her nose in a disgusted fashion. "Well, don't just stand there lookin' guilty. Get on in here. We're all waitin' to cut the cake."

Delia glanced at Cord. He winked, then bent to her ear.

"I think we should do as she says," he advised, "before she starts in about the great-grandchild again, *hein?*"

In total agreement, Delia nodded, grabbed his hand, and hauled him inside.

Chapter Seventeen

Delia leaned closer to the dresser mirror and tugged a curl at her temple. She fixed her gaze on Cord's reflection as he stepped behind her to tie his cravat. "Why do you s'pose the Pettys asked us to dinner tonight?"

"For any number of reasons, I would guess." Cord turned and reached for his frock coat hanging on the bedpost. "Perhaps they merely enjoy our company and would like to get to know us better."

Delia swiveled on her dresser stool and crossed her arms over her chest. "Perhaps *Lucile* wants to get to know *you* better, you mean."

Cord paused in the task of shrugging on his jacket and cocked his head to one side. "She *is* attractive, is she not?"

Delia frowned. "Not that attractive. Her face is too thin. Her mouth is too wide. And her nose is way too—"

"Delia, are you jealous?"

"Absolutely not." Spinning back around, she faced the mirror, picked up her bottle of lilac water, and began dabbing liberal amounts behind each ear. "Why on earth should I be? I can't b'lieve you could even suggest such a silly—"

"Delia, Delia." Cord moved up behind her and grasped her shoulders. "I have no romantic interest in Lucile Petty," he said with a scant grin, then placed a chaste kiss on top of her head.

She met his gaze in the looking glass. "Cord, I know you claimed that the gossip we overheard about your father and Lucile Petty at my birthday party didn't bother you, but that was over a week ago, and you've been actin' strange ever since."

The teasing twinkle in his eyes abruptly faded, replaced by a sudden remoteness. Stepping away from her, he brushed a piece of lint from his coat sleeve. "I told you then, and I will tell you again, news of my father's escapades has never affected me one way or the other."

Delia watched Cord move across the room to the wardrobe and thumb through the expensive new clothes Grandy had bought for him. He hadn't been too enthralled with the purchases and had accepted them only upon Agatha's ardent insistence. Now he appeared to take great interest in his ties, and suddenly changed his cravat for no apparent reason.

Delia realized she had lost him again.

An overpowering urge to reach out to him struck her hard. She had experienced the stirrings of such notions ever since the night of her birthday party, only this time the craving to touch him was much stronger.

Something was dreadfully wrong. Despite Cord's assurances otherwise, he was deeply troubled. He had been disappearing for hours during the past several days. Every night, when he'd assumed she was asleep, he had crept quietly out the door and not returned until dawn.

Some catastrophe was about to happen. Delia couldn't say what or when. She simply sensed it—in the room—in the balmy air blowing through the curtains . . .

"Cord, why are you here?" she asked, unable to stop the question from popping out of her mouth when it came to mind.

Cord turned slowly with a forced smile, then shrugged. "You made me a generous offer, did you not?"

"That's not what I mean, and you know it." Delia rose from the stool and laced her hands together at her waist. "Why did you come back to Boudreaux Parish?"

Cord stared at her with a blank expression for a long moment. "We should go now," he said. "I do not wish to keep the Pettys waiting."

Imprudently, Delia took a step forward. "Where do you go at night?"

The brief delay in his reaction worried her. She was even more disturbed, though, when he walked toward her exhibiting the sensuous, low-lidded gaze that never failed to sway her train of thought. The charming smile he added as he stopped before her didn't help matters.

"Why so many questions, *chère? Hein?*" Cord ran his fingertip down her nose and gently tapped her chin. "I do nothing that would shame you. I am a man. You are a beautiful woman. Me, I cannot lie in the same room with you night after night and not want to hold you in my arms. So I go for a walk."

"Every night?" Delia searched his face.

"Sometimes I sleep in the carriage house."

She was torn between believing and disbelieving him. Every rational bone in her body screamed
he was lying through his teeth. Yet, with his
handsome features fixed as they were, he was
powerfully persuasive.

"You see, you fret needlessly, *ma chérie*. Now,
come. Jedidiah is probably already waiting with
the carriage out front."

Delia allowed him to lead her from their room.
They were halfway down the stairs before Cord's
charisma wore off and foreboding seized her once
more.

She focused on the young black boy in the driv-
er's seat of the carriage, then gazed past Jedidiah
at the dark clouds gathering in the evening sky.
Stopping just short of the rig, she lifted her elbow
from Cord's grasp.

"Delia?" Cord looked from her to the sky and
back again, then tugged at the brim of his hat and
frowned. "What is it?"

"Let's not go, Cord. There's a storm brew-
in'," she murmured, still staring at the clouds.
"We could stay home and play brag with Grandy
and—"

"What are you afraid of?" He turned her to
face him. "*Hein*? Tell me."

"I don't know," she whispered. Her eyes
misted as they met his. "I just have this awful
feelin' somethin' bad will happen if we go to the
Pettys tonight."

"*Now* who is being superstitious?" He arched
a brow.

Delia closed her eyes for a moment and took a
deep breath, trying to clear her head. Cord was
right. She was being ridiculous. "I s'pose it *is* a

silly notion," she conceded, forcing the corners of her mouth upward.

"But of course it is." Cord slipped an arm around her and gave her a squeeze. "What could possibly go wrong? "Wine, dinner, and a little conversation. We will come home early, if you wish. Now, up you go."

As he swung her into the carriage, his cuff snagged a bolt on the side of the rig.

"Ah, damn," he mumbled, examining the small tear in the linen at his wrist. He compressed his lips, then brought his attention back to his wife. "I will change and catch up to you on horseback, no?"

"Don't be long, hear?" Delia urged.

"I will hurry," he said with a wink, then squinted at Jedidiah. "Take your mistress on ahead."

The young black man nodded and picked up the reins.

Jarred forward as the buggy was set in motion, Delia peered under the fringed top and watched Cord disappear into the house. Her uneasiness returned, and she settled back in her seat, rubbing the goose bumps that rose on her arms.

She absently viewed the purple shadows slipping between the trees they passed. She disregarded the eerie Spanish moss that dangled from the branches, seemingly changing shape as the carriage rolled by. Her thoughts were focused inward, on the ache that accompanied her restlessness.

This ailment that cinched her heart had been plaguing her on a regular basis for the past week or so, particularly during Cord's frequent absences. Perhaps she should see a physician.

Then again, something deep inside told her that these little spells had nothing at all to do with poor health. Cord Kibedeaux was the cause of her affliction.

Delia shifted in her seat, wanting desperately to deny the notion that Cord possessed the ability to arouse such distress. But in all honesty, she had to admit the Cajun had grown important to her. No matter how hard she'd fought to suppress him, to exclude him from her thoughts, he had remained steadfastly on her mind.

Delia worried her bottom lip and frowned, trying to convince herself that he was unworthy of occupying such a large space in her heart. He was all wrong for her. They belonged to two entirely different worlds. It was precisely for that very reason she had chosen him for this venture.

Refuting the suggestion that Cord could possibly mean more to her than he should, Delia closed her eyes. Behind her lids, though, a vision of Cord appeared. His presence overshadowed all other reflections and completely destroyed her resolve not to think of him. She watched him move gracefully across the dance floor . . . heard his deep-timbred laughter . . . saw his teasing smile and the rare twinkle in his whiskey-hued eyes. His tall, dignified image left her with the breathless impression that Cord Kibedeaux was more a gentleman than any of her past callers.

A sudden jolt of the carriage tossed Delia sideways. Her eyes flew open.

"Slow down, Jedidiah! For goodness' sake! What are you—" One look at the young man's frightened face cut her sentence short.

"Holds tight, missy!" he hollered, struggling

for control of the rig. "Oh, Lordy, I thinks we's gonna lose a wheel!"

Before Delia could clutch the seat securely, the buggy tilted. The horses reared. She heard a scream, then recognized, with horror, the terrified shriek of her own voice.

In slow motion, the carriage toppled endlessly as the ground traded places with the sky . . . over and over again.

Cord posted himself in a chair beside the bed, his long legs stretched out in front of him, his fingers steepled against his lips. He watched Delia's motionless form for a sign—the flutter of her lashes, the twitch of a muscle—anything that could confirm the doctor's assurances that she would be all right.

Grandy had long since retired. The sun was coming up. Cord was weary with worry, but alert. He hadn't been able to take his eyes from Delia's still features throughout the night.

Cord had known fear in his lifetime. He had tasted it, inhaled it. But he had never experienced the terror that had gripped him at the sight of the overturned carriage. Even now traces of the panic lingered inside him, along with anger, grief, regretfulness . . .

Delia had tried to warn him. Why hadn't he listened? No amount of information he could have gotten from the Pettys' guests could justify Delia's getting hurt. True, she had survived the accident with only a few bruises and a nasty bump on the head. Jedidiah hadn't been so fortunate. The boy's legs had been pinned beneath the wheel. The doctor couldn't be sure whether the young man would ever walk again.

Cord ran a hand through his hair, his gaze never wavering from his wife. Delia could just as easily have been injured more seriously.

A soft moan came from her, though her lips didn't move. Cord leaned forward and clasped her hand in both of his. Her eyes rolled behind her lids, then fluttered partially open. With difficulty, she focused on Cord's face.

"Where . . . what . . ." She paused, licked her lips, and frowned. "Mmm . . . my head . . . what happened?"

"The carriage lost a wheel, *chère*." Cord tenderly brushed a stray hair from her forehead.

"I don't remember . . . I can't remember—"

"Shh. Don't try to talk. The doctor, he says you will be fine in a couple of days. Just rest, *hein?*"

Delia's eyes drifted closed, then quickly reopened on him. "Stay with me, Cord," she murmured.

"*Oui.* I will be here watching over you until you wake, *ma chérie.*"

"Hold me," she said barely above a whisper. "Please? Just . . . hold me."

He slipped, fully dressed, into bed beside her and folded his arms around her. She nestled her cheek against his chest, and he laid his head against the pillow of her hair.

Cord had no idea how long they slept. He awakened when Delia stirred against him. Looking up, she gave him a sleepy smile.

"Mornin'," she uttered, then covered a yawn with her hand.

Cord positioned himself a little higher on the pillows and peered toward the window. "I believe it is more like the afternoon, if I am not mistaken.''

Delia started to rise on her elbows, then grimaced, easing back down on the bed.

"The doctor said you would be sore for a few days.'' Cord caught her shoulders and stuffed an extra pillow behind her head. "There, that is better, no?''

"Mmm.'' She gave him a pinched smile. " 'Sore' isn't the word for it. I feel more like I've been trampled by old man Jenkins's prize bull.''

Cord traced her jawline with his knuckles, trying to memorize the way she looked when she'd awakened. No matter what happened in the future, whenever he thought of her he wanted to remember how her tousled golden hair picked up the sunshine spilling through the window. He wanted to recall the drowsy-lidded beauty of her blue eyes.

But what he wanted most of all was to never see her hurt again.

He rolled off the bed and came to his feet. He could no longer delay leaving. With a deep breath, he strode to the wardrobe and pulled out his old work clothes.

"Cord? What . . . what are you doin'?''

"I cannot stay here, Delia.'' Keeping his back to her, he fumbled with the buttons of his shirt. "Not after what has happened. I do not wish to see you harmed because of me.''

"What?'' Delia struggled onto her side, bracing herself on her elbow. "What on earth are you talkin' about?''

Cord jerked off his linen dress shirt, then replaced it with one commonly worn by field hands.

"Damn you, look at me," she demanded. "Answer me!"

He turned around slowly, but couldn't meet her gaze. "Delia, when the carriage overturned . . . it was no accident."

"Of course it was an accident. What else—"

"*Non.*" Cord shook his head. He glanced around the room, his eyes finally settling on her. "When I pulled you and Jedidiah from the wreckage, I found these." Dipping into his pants pocket, he produced two bolts in the palm of his hand.

"So?" Delia shrugged. "The gadgets that held the wheel on came loose."

"Take a closer look, *chère.*" He crossed the room and held the bolts up for her inspection. "They were sawed halfway through."

Delia pressed her fingertips to her mouth. "Why would someone want to harm us?"

"Not us, *ma petite.* Me. Whoever did this believed I would be riding in that carriage."

She stared unseeingly in front of her. "I knew it," she whispered. "Slippin' off at night like that. You were bound to end up in trouble." She pinned him with a glare that would have frozen the Louisiana sun in July. "Damn you, Cord, you're not just gonna waltz out of here without tellin' me what you've gotten yourself into. You hear me?"

"You would be better off not knowing," he said, moving to the dresser to gather his few belongings. "It does not concern you."

"It damn sure does concern me. Have you forgotten *I* was ridin' in the rig that was tampered with? Why, I coulda been killed or lamed or—"

"I know!" Cord spun around, dragging both

hands through his hair. "I know that," he said in a calmer, more controlled voice. His gaze darted about the room, seeking refuse from Delia's scowl. He finally let it rest at the foot of the bed. "That is why I must leave. I cannot bear the thought of anything happening to you."

There was so much more he wanted to say. He yearned to expose his innermost feelings. But to tell her he truly cared for her would be ludicrous. Absurd, under the circumstances. She had made the terms of their farce marriage clear from the beginning. He was, after all, who he was. She was who she was. No matter what he felt, or how strongly he felt it, he would never be good enough for her.

Non. He would hold his tongue. He would not open himself up, only to be stabbed in the heart. He had had enough pain in his life. He would not go begging for any more.

"I must leave now." Tightening his jaw, Cord resumed bundling his scant possessions. "And you . . . you must rest. Rest, and get well. You will feel better in a couple of days. And you will see, what I do, it is best for everyone. No one else will be hurt, *hein?*" He knew he was rambling, but he couldn't stop himself. "I will explain to your *grand-mère.* She will understand. She is a good woman. She will—"

"You can't!" Delia pushed herself up from the bed and stood unsteadily. Staggering forward, she clung to the tall, ornate post at the foot of the bed. "You can't just walk out like this. We have an agreement."

"Ah, *ma petite,* you should not be up." Cord stretched out his hands and moved toward her. Her complexion was even paler than before, and she quivered with the effort it took to stand. ''The doctor says—''

''Damn the doctor! Damn you!'' She took a swing at him as he neared, stumbled into his arms, then burst into tears. ''Damn . . . Grandy,'' she sobbed. ''Damn her for causin' all this trouble in the first place.''

Ignoring her feeble struggle, Cord guided her back to bed. As she collapsed onto the pillows, she slapped at his chest before flinging an arm over her eyes.

Her soft weeping clawed at Cord's heart. At odds about what to do, he knelt beside the bed. He had no idea how to comfort her. Instinct urged him to wrap himself around her—to shield her from all sorrow. But what if she shrank from his touch? Any gesture he offered might only distress her more. He had done so many things wrong in the past.

Would one more mistake make any difference?

''Delia?'' With slow measures he reached out and gently stroked the side of her face.

She sniffled. Then she took a deep, shuddering breath, dragged her arm up her forehead, and cocked bright, red-rimmed eyes at him. ''What?''

''I'm sorry, *chère*. I'm so . . . *sorry*.''

''You certainly are. You ought to be horse-whipped,'' she said, shoving his hand away. She fixed her gaze on the ceiling and sighed. ''What does Lucile Petty have to do with all of this?''

''Nothing. I swear.''

''Then why were you so anxious to go to her little dinner party?'' Delia turned her head sharply and scanned his face. ''You'd best go ahead and tell me, because I fully intend to hound you day and night till I find out what you're up to. You hear me? I'll follow you wherever you go."

Cord lowered his head and massaged the bridge of his nose. He couldn't decide which was worse: watching her cry or listening to her nag.

"You said you were sorry," she added, curbing her harsh tone. "If you truly have regrets, the least you could do is give me an explanation."

Cord lifted his gaze to hers. He had no choice but to confide in her. Satisfying her curiosity seemed to be the only way to keep her from interfering.

Seating himself on the edge of the bed, he rubbed the nape of his neck and peered at her from under his brow. "I can trust you, no?"

"If you can't trust me, Cord, who can you trust? I'm your wife, remember?"

"*Oui*. You are right." He nodded, eyeing her thoughtfully. "I suppose I do owe you some sort of explanation." He paused for a moment before continuing. "I . . . I want to prove to Winston Grayson that I did not betray him. I have been trying to clear my name."

"Clear your name?" Delia looked puzzled. "That's the reason you came back to Boudreaux Parish?"

"*Oui*. I did not steal the funds from m'sieu Grayson's bank."

Cord waited for Delia's reaction, not really expecting her to believe him. She toyed with the border of the coverlet, appearing to weigh his words, then observed him with an expression that held no skepticism at all.

"Well, if you didn't take the money, who did?" she asked, wrinkling her nose.

"I cannot say. Not yet. I do not wish to accuse

someone wrongly. But I do have my suspicions.''
Cord leaned a little closer and raised a finger.
''You see, I came to the conclusion that the thief
had to be someone prominent enough to move
freely about the bank, which is why I took your
offer of marriage. Me, I thought perhaps, within
the circle of your wealthy acquaintances, I could
learn—''

''Cord!'' Delia slanted her narrowed eyes at
him. ''Are you tellin' me . . . you married me just
to spy on my friends?''

''*Oui*.'' Cord curled his bottom lip. ''But it
worked, did it not? My appearance at such social
functions has forced the true thief to play his
hand, no? Perhaps he is worried I am getting too
close, *hein*? Do you not think so?''

Apparently lost in her own thoughts, Delia
stared at the ceiling again with her arms crossed
over her breasts and her mouth fixed in a perturbed line.

''Delia? Do you not think the real thief is worried?''

''I think I'm gonna scream, that's what I
think,'' she answered, continuing to stare at the
ceiling. ''If you aren't off this bed and out that
door by the count of ten, I'm gonna scream so
loud it'll rattle the pans in the kitchen.''

''What?'' Cord was completely baffled by her
sudden change of mood. ''Delia, why—''

''Out!'' She flounced over onto her side, presenting her back, then murmured into her pillow,
''I can't b'lieve you've been usin' me all this
time.''

''Ah, *non, chère. Non*, it wasn't like that . . .
well, maybe in the beginning—'' He reached for
her, but she scooted to the far side of the bed.

''Go!'' she shouted over her shoulder. ''Get out! Go on back to the bayou, where you belong. I don't ever want to see you again, you hear? Not ever again!''

Chapter Eighteen

"**M**illy!" Delia lifted the hem of her hooped skirt and rushed across the Moselys' lawn toward the gazebo.

Laying her book aside, Milly stood and moved to the edge of the summerhouse, meeting her friend halfway.

"Oh, Milly, I had to see you!" Delia gripped the delicate brunette's forearms. "Somethin' just awful has happened."

"Again?" Milly grimaced. "Gracious sakes, what is it now? No, no, don't answer yet. Come on over here and sit yourself down." Tugging Delia onto a bench beside her, she picked up her book and fanned Delia's face. "Oh, my, you look all flustered."

"Will you stop wavin' that thing around?" Delia snatched the book and tossed it on a nearby wicker chair. "I'm upset, Milly. I am not goin' to collapse."

Milly tipped her head apologetically and clasped both of her friend's hands. "Why don't you tell me all about it? Start from the beginnin'."

Delia opened her mouth, but she didn't know

where to begin. How could she express the turbulence that had raged inside her since Cord had walked out the door? She'd experienced every possible emotion over the past two days. Now she simply felt numb . . . empty . . . drained.

A familiar pain stung her eyes. She dropped her gaze to her lap and tightened her hold on Milly's hands. "He's gone, Milly."

"Who's . . . Cord? Cord's . . . Oh, my. Delia, are you sayin' he's left you?"

She nodded, afraid if she attempted to utter a sound she'd start crying again.

"Oh, dear. Oh, my stars," Milly muttered. "What did Grandy do?"

"I couldn't very well tell her the truth." Delia shook her head, the motion making a tear fall and spot her skirt. She swiped at her cheek. "I told her we'd simply had a terrible quarrel . . . that we just needed a couple of days apart to settle our differences."

"Delia, you didn't! You can't keep on lyin' like this. It isn't right. One lie leads to another, you know. And sooner or later you're gonna get caught."

"I know, I know." Rising swiftly from the bench, Delia paced to the other side of the gazebo, then turned in a sharp pivot. "Seems I just keep diggin' my own grave deeper and deeper."

Milly frowned disapprovingly. "Delia, what did you do to him to make him leave?"

"Do? What did I do?" She glanced around the gazebo, disbelieving her friend's audacity. "I didn't *do* anything."

"Are you certain?" Milly arched an eyebrow. "I mean, you must have said somethin' or—"

"But I didn't!" Delia took a step forward, then stopped and clenched her fists. She felt her lower lip quiver. "Oh, all right, I did. I told him to get out. Or somethin' along those lines. I don't know . . . maybe . . . oh, Milly, I can't be sure of anything anymore."

"There, there, now." Milly rushed over and threw her arms around her, and Delia broke down, weeping against her friend's shoulder. "Shh, now," Milly said, stroking her hair. "Everything's gonna work out. Hush. We'll think of somethin', you hear?"

"I love him," Delia sobbed. "I know it's wrong, but I . . . just can't help it."

"I s'pose I ought to be surprised to hear that," Milly replied calmly, then patted Delia's back. "But I suspected as much."

"But he's been usin' me all this time, Milly."

"Do tell." She set Delia an arm's length away and lowered her chin in a scolding fashion. "Of course, you yourself are beyond toyin' with other people's lives to further your cause."

Delia stared at her, digesting the verity of the woman's words, allowing the significance to settle in her brain . . . seep into her heart. She swallowed hard. "What am I goin' to do now, Milly?" she whispered. "What am I goin' to do without him?"

Milly lifted one dainty shoulder, and the corners of her mouth tipped upward. "If Grandy has already accepted him as your husband, why can't you?"

Delia pressed a hand to her breast, feeling her heart rapidly pick up pace. "You mean—"

"Precisely," Milly remarked, then brightened her smile. "If you want him back, Delia, go after him."

Cord answered the knock at the shanty door and froze. An apparition stood outlined against the violet evening sky.

He closed his eyes. *She wasn't here. She wasn't,* he reassured himself. If he stayed very still, very quiet, she would vanish as she had before. His mind played tricks on him, no?

Cord squinted one eye open. *Non.* No tricks this time. No visions of his mind. It was Delia, in the flesh, on his porch . . . clutching a valise to her waist?

Shifting his gaze, he caught sight of the tail end of Samuel's skiff rounding the bend. He furrowed his brow. The situation could not possibly be as it seemed. His thoughts raced, sorting, gathering, then discarding all logical explanations. Before he could arrive at a solid reason for Delia's unexpected appearance, she skirted around him and walked into the house.

"Goodness, Cord, why do you have it so dark in here?"

A little dazed, he rotated and found her turning up the wick of the lamp on the table.

"There, that's better. Lots more cheery, don't you think?" She gave him a small smile, then moved to the window. "And if you opened these shutters, you might get a breeze in here."

Delia flung the hinged boards wide and pivoted. Her features wavered slightly, disconcertingly, but only for a second. Recovering her composure quickly, she dropped into the chair by the table, bent forward, lifted her hem, and started untying the bow at her ankle. "Land sakes, I don't know how you can stand it, Cord," she commented as she slipped off her shoes. "Why, it's downright sultry in here."

Cord stood immobile, watching while she hiked her skirt to her knees and began rolling down her stockings. His eyes followed the path of her hands over the curve of each shapely calf.

Once the task was finished, she stood, straightened her skirt, and draped her stockings over the back of the chair. She took a step in Cord's direction, then stopped and lowered her gaze to the table. Running a fingertip across the top, she made a trail in the dust. "I can see I have my work cut out for me," she said and looked up with an uncertain smile.

"Delia, what are you doing here, *hein*?" Cord asked, finally finding his voice.

"I'm your wife, aren't I? Isn't a wife s'posed to be with her husband?" Delia hoped that would be enough. She absently focused on his shirtless chest, licked her lips, and locked her fingers together in front of her.

She'd had a whole slew of pretty words planned, a bushelful of vows and testaments to make once she'd arrived. Now the phrases she'd so carefully chosen blended in her brain, over-riding one another until none of them made sense.

Cord crossed his arms and lounged against the doorframe.

"Forgive me, *chère*. I am a man, and therefore a fool who often makes mistakes where women are concerned." Cocking his head, he glanced at the ceiling. "But did you, or did you not, tell me the last time we spoke that you wished never to see me again?"

"Well . . . I did. But I changed my mind," she hastily added. "You know they do claim women are fickle."

"*Oui*. This I know." He flashed a quick smile that was there one moment and gone the next. His dark eyes glimmered in the soft yellow glow filling the room. "Now tell me true, why have you come here?"

"I—" Delia reached for the voice within her heart, but pride stiffened her spine. "Grandy's contract clearly states we must live together as man and wife," she said, latching onto the first reason she thought might prevent him from sending her home. "Otherwise, I can't collect my inheritance. And if I don't get my inheritance, I won't be able to pay you, and—"

"*C'est assez!*" Cord bellowed, raising his hands. "Enough! I will listen to no more of your nonsense." He emerged on her and shook a finger in her face. "I have told you before, I care nothing for the money. You cannot stay here. I will take you myself to your *grand-mère* in the morning. I will instruct her to tie you up and lock you in your room if necessary."

Swerving around her, he strode to the open window and braced his hands against the top frame. The flickering lamplight cast gold hues across his broad, scarred shoulders, defining the muscles in his back.

Delia quaked inside. What on earth had induced her to mention the inheritance? Even if she could suddenly summon the nerve to tell him how she felt, he would never believe her now.

Some source of strength beyond her moved her toward him. "Cord? Please . . . don't make me go," she pleaded.

Though he made no response, as Delia approached him, she watched his ribs expand and contract with labored breaths.

"Cord? *Please*," she whispered, then lifted a trembling hand and hesitantly touched the hollow ridge of his spine.

He flinched as if her fingers were daggers.

"*Sacrebleu.* What do you want from me, Delia?" he asked, sounding raw and broken. "What more do you want? *Mon Dieu*, you have stolen my soul. Haunted me day and night, possessed me, when all the ghosts of this place could never do so. Is that not enough? *Hein?*"

Without warning, he spun and seized her by the forearms.

"Answer me!" he shouted, tightening his grip. "What more do you want from me?"

His eyes bored into hers, vacillating between an angry amber and a deep, dark, torturous brown. Delia stared up at him, frightened and fascinated, and completely transfixed. "I . . . want your . . . love," she stammered softly.

Cord's features tensed, becoming impassioned. "So now you want my love," he sneered. "You want me to lust for you, *ma chérie?*" A cold, sardonic grin creased his lips. In one swift motion he swung her around, seated her roughly on the window ledge, then jerked up her skirt. He pushed her knees apart and bumped the lower half of his torso against her.

"This is what you want, *hein?*" he asked

harshly. Locking an arm around her waist, he wedged himself even closer and began moving his lips bruisingly along the side of her neck. He paused after a few brutal kisses to murmur breathlessly, "Love and lust, they are the same thing, no?"

For a matter of heartbeats, Delia was too stunned to react. The heat of him, the hardness of his body pressing against her abdomen, made her head swim. But as his fingers crawled up her thighs, slowly climbing higher and higher, her senses flooded back.

"No! Stop it!" she cried, pounding his shoulders and chest. "Not this way . . . this isn't what I wanted. It isn't!"

Cord stilled instantly, then eased away, but remained within the reach of her fists. He allowed her to deal him several more blows before he reached up and caught both of her wrists in one hand. Keeping his eyes cast downward, he tugged her dress over her knees, then lifted her gently from the windowsill and set her on her feet.

Delia propped herself against the wall. From the corner of her eye she watched him stalk toward the open door.

"Cord?" His name grated past her throat, hardly audible. She tried again. "Cord?" Her voice, only slightly louder, stopped him in the doorway.

He slumped his shoulders and massaged the back of his neck. "God forgive me," he uttered, then exhaled deeply. "Delia . . . sweet Delia, forgive me. You make me crazy, *chère* . . . so crazy." He half turned and glanced briefly in her direction. "But what I have just done . . . is inexcusable. I shamed you. I . . . shamed myself.''

Delia's heart moved her forward until she stood before him. She tried to catch his gaze, but he slammed his eyes closed. Despite his attempt to shut her out, or perhaps because of it, she persisted along her dangerous course.

''Cord, you're wrong,'' she stated boldly, then continued in a quieter, gentler tone. ''About love and lust bein' the same? They're not.'' Delia frowned and considered the source of such information for a moment. ''I'm not exactly sure how I know that, but I just do.''

The harmony of crickets and katydids grew more distinct in the silence. Delia watched Cord carefully, waiting for a flicker of emotion on his face—some sign that he'd heard her.

He stood motionless, his broad shoulders rising and falling with each breath. Moonlight slanted through the door, across his stone-cold features. The only response Delia could detect was a tightening of the muscles in his cheeks.

Don't close the door on me again, she yearned to say. *Not again. Let me soothe the ache inside you. Let me help you forget the past.*

The words she couldn't quite bring herself to verbalize, she expressed with her hands as she cupped his face. His eyes opened a fraction of an inch, and he flexed his jaw beneath her palm. In all other respects, he didn't move.

Delia saw a challenge in his cautious, narrowed gaze. He would not give his affection easily, and his trust could not be won without effort. He seemed so confident, so sure his apathetic glare would put her off.

Wrong again, Cord. Rising up on her toes, she

pressed her mouth to his. Though his lips remained stiff and unresponsive, she proceeded to kiss him. She slid her hands through his hair, down the sides of his neck, over his broad shoulders and chest. He was breaking. She could tell that by his sharp intakes of breath, by the way his muscles jumped beneath her fingertips.

"See?" she whispered against his lips. "Lust and love are two entirely different things."

A low, rumbling groan came from deep within Cord's chest. Burrowing his hands in her hair, he tilted her face up.

"For you, perhaps, *chère*," he grated out between his teeth, his eyes blazing with a savage inner fire. "For you, there may be a difference. For me, there is not."

A surge of excitement and danger mingled in Delia's blood. Risking all, she lifted her chin a notch higher and smiled. "Would you care to place a wager on that?"

Cord's harsh expression wavered, and he looked away, but not before Delia saw a wave of tenderness seize his features. She laid her cheek on his chest, and, hesitantly, his arms folded around her. His heart thumped hard against her ear.

"Ah, Delia, Delia," he murmured, nuzzling the top of her head with his chin. While he stroked her hair with one hand, he rubbed her spine with the other. "You are playing too close to the fire, *ma chérie* . . . much too close."

"I'll take the blame if I get burned," she replied softly, then turned her face into his chest. She inhaled the sultry, musklike scent of him, kissed the salty-sweet skin below his breast.

Sweat beaded on Cord's forehead and upper lip. Delia's mouth seared his flesh. Her kisses, like flaming arrows, penetrated his chest, shattering what remained of his resistance.

He sank to the floor, taking her with him. Pressing her backward onto the hard board planking, he unleashed the indispensable need blazing within him.

The fierce pressure of Cord's mouth meeting Delia's made her gasp. Heat from his tongue flowed into her, setting her insides on fire.

Cord's hand glided over the sheen of perspiration misting Delia's skin, slid down her throat, dipped into her bodice. He kneaded the mound beneath the damp fabric with an urgency that arched Delia's spine.

In a smooth but swift motion, Cord rolled on top of her, locking his hips to hers, moving them, rocking them. Delia clutched her fists in his hair and quivered. His hands roved everywhere, over her breasts, down her ribs, up the insides of her thighs beneath her skirt. His urgency pushed him on, past caring.

Sparks popped like tiny bubbles inside Delia's abdomen as he caught the waistband of her pantaloons and tugged them down over her hips, working until he'd completely removed them. Then, slipping his hand between their bodies, he unfastened his breeches.

Delia froze with the feel of his velvety hardness poised against her most private part . . . the part of her that, until tonight, had remained untouched.

Thunder cracked overhead. Lightning flashed

outside, illuminating the cramped interior of the shack for a split second. In that moment, Delia saw raging passion in the depths of Cord's eyes. Yet other, more disturbing etchings flickered across his features. Wariness. Anguish. Fear. Anger.

Cord's stifled feelings broke loose with a vengeance, pumping his heart hard, pounding in his head, in his veins, until he couldn't separate one emotion from another. Through a red haze he stared into Delia's wide, brilliant blue eyes. She was solely responsible for the uprising inside him—the unwelcome revolt assaulting him with the force of the heavy rain beating down on the roof.

Delia symbolized everything he'd been denied in the past, all he could never hope for in the future. She was everything he had always longed for. Everything he'd never dared to touch. Delia was forbidden.

But tonight, she would be his.

A howling wind blasted through the window, flapping the shutters and banging the door against the wall. A crash of thunder rumbled the floor beneath Delia. Lightning turned the room bright white, and Cord drove into her.

Delia's entire body stiffened at the sharp, piercing intrusion. Unprepared for the reality of him, she dug her fingernails into his shoulders and futiley shoved at him.

"Shh, *chère*. No, no, do not push me away," he whispered, brushing his lips against her cheek. "I will kiss away the hurt. You will see, it gets much better."

His mouth covered hers, drowning the whimper in her throat. He started to move within her again, his rhythm slow and lazy like a hot summer afternoon. Each stroke lessened the discomfort a little more . . . and a little more.

And a bright, luminous sensation took over, spreading outward from the point that bonded them together as one, filling Delia completely. She wrapped her arms securely around Cord's neck and lifted her hips.

Upon her ardent invitation, Cord braced his hands on the floor and, arching his back, wedged deeper within her. He picked up his pace, driving Delia to do the same.

Sweat trickled down his temples and settled in the corners of his tightly drawn mouth. Closing his eyes, he attempted to block her face from his mind, tried to pretend she was just another woman. He launched himself more powerfully, but her features remained in the darkness behind his lids. Her passion-drowsy gaze and her sweetly parted lips haunted him. And in the recess of his mind and in his heart, Cord knew his feelings for Delia went far beyond mere lust.

Delia moved to the tune of Cord's body, floating as if she levitated above ground level. A flurry of rain blew through the open door and window, drenching their clothes, but not their urgent need of each other—cooling their fevered skin, but not their passion.

With a sudden desperation, Delia gripped Cord's arms. His muscles flexed beneath her fingers, and she soared higher. Her intense bliss grew and grew until it burst inside her, leaving a warm, pulsating glow that slowly spread into her limbs.

Cord plunged forward one last time and cried out with the final force. For an endless moment, he shuddered. Then, past the point of exhaustion, he collapsed against Delia, nestling his head between the soft mounds of her breasts.

Chapter Nineteen

The stormy thunderclouds rumbled off into the distance, leaving behind a steady shower hammering the roof. The roaring wind had calmed, and now breezed through the shanty window, cooling the muggy room.

Delia lay quietly on the wet floor, unmindful of her soaked clothes or her petticoats bunched beneath her. She focused on Cord's head resting on her chest and stroked the damp, dark curls behind his ear.

While she listened to the rain and waited for her heartbeat to slow to a normal tempo, a wondrous notion awakened inside her. Though Cord would probably never admit it, he needed her. He needed her love and trust and understanding. He needed her to show him the difference between love and lust.

Delia rubbed a silky strand of his hair between her fingers. She could give him all he needed, if he would only let her. Cord would no doubt have trouble accepting her attentions. Since his family had neglected to raise him with love, he more than likely considered himself unlovable. But Delia knew in her heart that he was just as lovable, if not more so, as anybody else. He wasn't nearly as callous as he would like everyone to think.

Tonight, she had infiltrated the fortress walls within her husband. For a brief and blissful time, Cord's soul had shone brightly into hers. She'd glimpsed no ugliness or wickedness in his spirit, only a spark of mournful yearning to belong—some essence that reached out for a place to exist peacefully in this world.

Marveling at the leather-smooth texture of his skin, Delia ran her hand down the tendons of his neck, across his water-misted shoulders, over the ridge of muscles in his scarred back. *I love you*, she wanted so desperately to say aloud.

But she didn't.

Drained and drowsy, Cord closed his eyes, completely intoxicated by the magic of Delia's hands roving over him. In all his life, no one had ever touched him with such tenderness. He remained perfectly still and kept his breathing shallow, afraid any sudden move might break the spell. Slowly, hesitantly, he absorbed her soft caress and her sweet lilac scent, trying not to take in too much too quickly.

I love you, Delia, he almost blurted out. But before the thought finished forming in his head, he discarded the foolish idea. He wasn't even sure he knew what the word "love" meant. He merely cared for Delia more than he'd ever cared for anyone. He enjoyed the feel of her hands on him, enjoyed being with her. Love, he suspected, was a different matter entirely.

Besides, women of Delia's class didn't fall in love with men like him. They only used them for their own selfish purposes.

Delia was no exception. She had the reputation of swaying young men to do her bidding. Cord had fallen right into her clutches along with so many others. He was no more to her than a hired hand, rendering his services. When she was through with him, she would cast him aside, with little or no damage to her reputation. After all, Boudreaux Parish would eventually forgive *her* transgressions.

The fantasy Delia had temporarily woven around Cord faded gradually. Reality seeped into him like a knife sinking into his sternum. Pushing the pain aside, he called forth his old friend, indifference. He basked in the numbness that flowed over him and prayed that all traces of his emotion would soon be gone.

Delia's breast quivered slightly beneath his head. Cord was neither surprised nor disturbed by the tightening of his traitorous loins. This was merely the stirrings of lust, he assured himself. It mattered not *why* Delia had offered him her most precious possession. The fact remained, he had stolen the one thing she could never give another. Tonight, Delia was his. He would take her to satisfy his own needs—as many times as she was willing. It was not imperative that he give his heart and soul in the process.

"Cord?" Delia's soft voice broke into the tranquil pitter-patter of rain. "Can I stay?" she asked, tracing his ear with her fingertip.

Cord lifted his head and met her sparkling gaze. *God, she is so beautiful.* He almost lost his train of thought. Almost.

"Do you not fear getting burned again, *chère?*" he inquired.

Delia smiled, cast her lashes down, and shook her head.

"No?" Cord reached out and brushed a damp curl from her cheek, letting his hand linger on the side of her face. "Then perhaps we should think of getting out of these wet clothes, *hein?*"

He tugged her to her feet, and she made no attempt to stop him when he turned her around and began unfastening her dress. Heat flickered inside her stomach again. She shut her eyes and tried to set her mind on something else for the moment.

"Where did you learn to do that so fast?" she asked conversationally.

Cord undid the last button at the base of her spine, then lifted her skirt over her head. "Do what, *chère?*"

Delia wriggled the rest of the way out of her dress and tossed it aside, then slipped off her petticoat. Clad only in her chemise and corset, she peered shyly over her shoulder. "Well, it seems you have a vast knowledge of women's garments . . . especially about how to take them off."

"I used to be a lady's maid," he said with a devilish grin.

"Oh, you were not!"

"Ah, you are not so easily fooled, *hein?* Hold still so I can loosen your stays," he said, furrowing his brow and concentrating on his task.

Delia turned her gaze forward and pushed her lower lip out. "Tell me the truth. Where'd a convict learn so much about women's unmentionables?"

"I have had a lot of women since I was released from prison," he replied, but with the teasing tone eliminated from his voice. "That is the truth."

Delia felt her stays give way. Cord's warm palms slithered beneath the fabric and glided around her ribs to her midriff, prying the sticky corset from her skin. As the lacy foundation fell to the floor, he massaged her breasts. Then one of his hands slid down her stomach, and his fingertips grazed the inside of her thigh.

The fire started again, low in Delia's abdomen the way it had done before, and she wilted back against him.

"You want to know the truth?" he murmured, nuzzling and kissing the hollow between her neck and shoulder. "You are the sweetest, *chérie* . . . the most beautiful of them all."

Delia rested on her side on the pallet and silently watched the muted morning light creep over Cord's sleep-filled features.

She knew now what desire was. She'd felt passion throbbing in her veins with all the turbulent severity of the previous night's stormy weather.

Yet, upon awakening, she'd immediately realized something even more powerful was monopolizing her senses this morning. She had barely opened her eyes and focused on Cord's lean form stretched out beside her when a warm, radiant glow rushed through her . . . hovered around her . . . filled her insides to near bursting. And her heart, it seemed, had swelled overnight.

This was surely love, she decided, her gaze never wavering from her husband's beautiful face. Delia curled her fingers against her breast

to keep from touching him. He looked so peaceful . . . so different from the way he looked
when they'd made love. He had tried so hard
not to give himself completely—had striven com-
mendably to stay beyond the boundaries of her
reach. But each time she'd seen him fix his
mouth in a determined line and sensed him pulling away, she'd locked her arms around his neck
and kissed him senseless until he was hopelessly
lost.

Such thoughts made Delia want to snuggle
against Cord, run her hand over the contour of
his bare hip, and roust him from his deep slumber. Knowing the extent of his exhaustion,
though, she was loath to disturb him. To avoid
any further temptation, she rose.

Delia donned a clean camisole and petticoat
from her valise, but decreed it was just too hot in
the small, stuffy quarters to put on anything else.
Idly, she strolled out onto the porch. Settling on
the rickety chair by the railing, she propped her
heels on the seat and hugged her knees to her
chest.

Sparse streams of sunlight peeked through the
overhead growth and Spanish moss. A layer of
fog hovered above the dark water. Frogs croaked,
joining the symphony of birds and other unidentifiable animals and insects. Delia inhaled the
lingering scent of rain and contemplated the eerie beauty surrounding her. Mornings in the
bayou, she discerned, held a magical, mystical
quality. Then again, perhaps this particular
morning was merely enchanted. Maybe it was
her mood that painted everything with lovely il-
lusions.

"Good morning, *chère*." Dressed in nothing but

his breeches, Cord strode across the porch, stretching his arms above his head. "You are up early, are you not?"

Delia smiled, her heart pumping a little harder at the sight of him. "I'd scarcely call it early. The sun is halfway to heaven."

One corner of Cord's mouth lifted, and the grin on his lips shone brightly in his warm gold-brown eyes. He swaggered forward and clasped Delia's hands, pulling her from the chair. Then he seated himself and tugged her down on his lap. Wrapping his arms around her, he laid his head on her shoulder.

Delia combed her fingers through the dark hair that tumbled over his brow. "I never imagined it could be so peaceful here," she commented.

"Me, I've never considered this place peaceful."

"No?"

"*Non.*"

"But it's beautiful. Just look at that." She pointed to a dragonfly skipping over the water.

The large iridescent-winged creature fluttered in their direction, encircled them twice, then darted through the open door of the shanty.

"*Tante* Netha Bea claims it is good luck for a dragonfly to enter the house," Cord remarked.

"Hmm. Is that so?" Delia looped her arms around his neck and lowered her lashes a fraction. "I s'pose that means you're bound to get lucky today."

Cord's gaze turned smoky. All but a hint of his smile faded. He traced the edge of her camisole with a fingertip. "Perhaps," he murmured, then leaned forward and kissed the mound of flesh above the lace-trimmed fabric.

Delia tilted her head back, preparing for the ecstasy she was sure would follow. But a distinct movement in the line of twisted trees to the right of the porch caught her eye.

"Cord," she whispered fiercely, gripping his neck, "there's somebody watchin' us."

He looked up, frowning at the intrusion. "Where?" he asked in a low voice.

"Over there." She gestured with a discreet nod.

Cord scanned the line of cypress and black willows. Narrowing his eyes on a particular spot, he muttered an oath under his breath. Then he straightened, sighed, and ran a hand through his hair.

"*Mon Dieu*, old woman," he shouted, "must you always sneak up on me? *Hein?* How come you can't come to the door and knock like everyone else?"

Delia watched as a darkly shrouded figure moved forward from the cover of shrubbery and low-hanging vines.

"Because you probably don't answer, dat's how come, *T-boo.*" Clutching her shawl around her throat, *Tante* Netha Bea set her beady black eyes on Delia. "Is dat your Ameri-kawn wife dere?"

With a shiver, Delia leaned closer to Cord, and he gave her a squeeze.

"*Oui.* She is pretty, *hein?*"

"Oh, *mais oui*," Netha Bea replied, bobbing her head. "She is too pretty for you, yeah."

"You are just jealous I did not up and marry you," Cord teased.

"Pooh! I would not have you! You'd be too much trouble, dat's what." The old woman braced her weight on her crooked cane and jutted her chin toward Delia. "He gives you any heartache, *chérie*, you come tell *Tante* Netha Bea. Me, I will fix him good, yeah."

Delia curved her lips timidly, quickly drawing the conclusion that the fearsome witch of Blue Moon Bayou couldn't be all that bad. Though Netha Bea hadn't once come close to smiling, her sense of humor twinkled in her ancient eyes.

"Why, thank you kindly," Delia replied, ignoring Cord's mock indignation. "I'll remember that."

"Oh, *merci*." Cord tossed his arms up in the air. "So now you are both going to curse me. Perhaps I should cook us all some breakfast, no? Maybe then you would at least spare me for the rest of the day." He winked at Delia, then directed a lazy grin at *Tante* Netha Bea. "Come join us, old woman. I will brew some chickory. Good and strong, *hein?* The way you like it."

"*Non, non.* I cannot stay." Netha Bea shook her head vigorously. "Me, I got work to do. Leontine Sabadi, her oldest daughter found a yellow tinge on her heels las' night. I got to make a *poudre de Perlainpainpain* for dat poor girl or she ain't never gonna marry, no. I jus' stop by to tell you I got a mess of crawfish dis mornin', yeah, and I'm gonna come for supper tonight." With that *Tante* Netha Bea turned and started to hobble off, adding, "You cook de rice, *T-boo.* I'm gonna fix some *étouffée.*"

Tante Netha Bea disappeared, blending into the bayou foliage until she seemingly vanished.

Cocking her eyes sideways at Cord, Delia furrowed her brow. "What did she say about somebody's heels bein' tinged with yellow?"

"A sure sign of spinsterhood," Cord explained.

"What was that stuff she said she had to make?"

"A powder of sorts, made from thistle seeds, and white beans, and who knows what else." Lowering his lids to half-mast, he focused on Delia's bodice. "But why do we talk of lovers' potions?" he asked, then leaned forward and nuzzled his face between her breasts. "The conversation we were having before we were interrupted was much more interesting," he whispered into her camisole.

His heated breath seeped through the fabric, scorching Delia's skin. She burrowed her fingers in his hair and clutched his scalp. "Let's go inside," she suggested in a husky voice filled with desire.

"It is too hot in there," Cord mumbled, gliding his hands down her back, over her hips, up her thighs.

Reluctantly, Delia broke away from him. Climbing off his lap, she grabbed his arm and pulled him to his feet. "It's too hot anywhere within ten feet of you, Cord," she remarked as she led him toward the shanty door.

Tante Netha Bea returned that evening as promised.

Cord took the huge kettle she toted and helped the old woman onto the porch.

Delia had suggested they dine outside on the porch. Cord had obliged by moving the table and chairs to a spot she'd selected next to the railing.

"Ah, now jus' look at dat," Netha Bea commented, gesturing toward the flickering white candle gleaming off the scratched but polished tabletop. Plates, silverware, and filled wineglasses had been arranged in perfect order. "Ain't dat nice?" she asked, then shook a finger at Cord. "See? I done tole you, you been needin' a wife for a long time. You would never think to do something like dis."

"I thought of it," he contradicted her with a lift of his chin. Then he glanced at Delia and shrugged. "Well, I helped."

"Yeah, but did you cook de rice?" *Tante* Netha Bea inquired as she settled herself in one of the chairs.

"*Oui*, but of course I—"

"Good. Den sit down, and le's eat before all of dis gets cold."

Exchanging a smile, Cord and Delia took their places. After *Tante* Netha Bea said a hasty blessing, they all filled their plates.

The evening proved to be more entertaining than any Delia could recall. The *étouffée* was delicious, the wine sweet and heady. The repartee between her dinner companions kept a smile on her face. *Tante* Netha Bea's dry wit and uncanny wisdom were amazing. By the time the woman rose to leave, she'd completely won Delia over.

"*Bonsoir*, T-boo. De rice coulda been taken from the stove a little sooner, but it was good, yeah." Netha Bea patted Cord's cheek, then turned and grasped Delia's hands. "I'm gonna fix something for your *grand-mère*'s rheumatis', *chère*. I like you. You're not jus' pretty, no, you're smart too. And Cord, he's gonna be a good man for you, you wait and see, *hein?*"

"I will walk you home," Cord said, handing Netha Bea her cane.

"*Non.* Me, I know de way." The old woman waved him aside. "You go fumblin' 'round in de dark, you gonna get me lost for sure, yeah."

"At least take this light with you, then." He held out the lantern he'd just lit.

Netha Bea's face paled and she backed up against the railing. Her eyes glazed as she stared at the red-gold flame. "*Non!*" she whispered, then covered her face with her hands. "Holy Mother Mary . . . *non, non.* I don't want to see dis, no!"

"*Tante* Netha Bea, are you all right?" Delia asked, taking a hesitant step forward.

Cord stopped her with a lift of his hand and a shake of his head.

Netha Bea dragged her hands down her cheeks and clasped them to her heart, then gazed unseeingly at the burning wick again.

"Oh, *T-boo*, is bad . . . *mauvais*, very evil." As she focused on Cord, she reached out and twisted her fingers in the front of his shirt. "You must not stay here, *cher.* You must promise you will leave! Promise me—promise!"

"Tell me what you saw, old woman." Cord caught her shoulders and searched her haggard features.

"*Non*, I cannot." She dropped her forehead against his chest. "Is too horrible to say."

Delia traded a concerned glance with Cord above Netha Bea's bent head.

"Come, *Tante* Netha Bea," he said soothingly. "I will walk with you to your house, *hein*?"

Lifting her elbow out of his reach, the woman blocked his way, brandishing her cane as she climbed off the porch. "It is not me the evil one wants. I'm gonna go home by myself and pray, yeah. You got to get your t'ings gathered. You must go from dis place. You promise me dat, *T-boo*."

Cord sighed, then said, "I promise," and shoved his fists in his pockets.

Delia moved up next to him, hugging her ribs, and he slipped an arm around her. Together they watched *Tante* Netha Bea melt into the darkness.

"What was that all about?" Delia asked with a frown.

"One can never be sure with that crazy old witch. But to be on the safe side, I am taking you back to your *grand-mère* in the morning."

Turning toward him, Delia flattened her palms against his chest. She opened her mouth to protest, but he touched a finger to her lips.

"No arguments, *chère*." He clasped her waist and gave her a tired smile. "You have already distracted me far too long. As I have told you before, I have certain matters to attend to."

"But I could help you," she suggested with a lift of her brow.

"*Oui*. You could help me by not distracting me so much."

Delia fixed her gaze steadily on his, although her insides quivered while she unbuttoned his shirt.

''You don't s'pose you might be persuaded to let me *distract* you just once more?'' she asked, then fluttered her lashes and slid her hands along his bare ribs. She felt him tense, saw the pulse at the base of his throat beat harder.

''Perhaps,'' he replied in a low, throaty voice, then swept her into his arms and carried her into the house.

Chapter Twenty

C ord teetered restlessly on the brink of consciousness, dipping in and out of the realm
of dreams, unable to sink into the painless, deep
sleep he needed.

He was ever aware of the soft, warm body encircled in his arms and the pillow of sweet-
smelling hair beneath his cheek. For a heartbeat
or two, once more, a blanket of false security
wrapped around him, and he relaxed.

Then the nightmares attacked again.

Iron manacles rubbed his wrists and ankles raw,
holding him down in the pits of hell. He couldn't
move, couldn't escape the sights and sounds that
ran rampant through his mind.

He heard his mother scratching the wall. Her
grating, singsong voice relayed the gruesome details of how *loups-garous* dealt with children.
Overlaying her words, Cord's father's face floated
into view, red with rage, teeth bared and fists
raised. Amidst the confusion, *Tante* Netha Bea's
warning kept surfacing: *You must leave this place
. . . leave this place . . . leave this place . . .*

Cord felt the heat in his head, the familiar pressure in his chest. His lungs constricted. He

couldn't breathe. Clutching at the ghostly fingers that closed around his throat, he bolted upright—only to find himself in a hazy black cloud . . . and still trapped in the terror of his dream.

Or so he thought, until real smoke pierced his nostrils and stung his eyes. Then he heard the crackle, saw the bright yellow flames.

A spasm of coughing jarred his body as he reached out blindly and shook Delia. Panic seized him when she didn't move. Grabbing the blanket, he hoisted her limp form over his shoulder and rose to a crouched position.

The porch and side walls were ablaze, blocking escape from the front of the house. Tongues of fire danced in the rear of the shack as well. Cord quickly determined that their only route to safety was through the burning window. He tossed the blanket over Delia, then covered his own mouth, nose, and head with one corner. Tightening his hold on her, he dove through the opening.

He hit the soft marshy ground outside and rolled from side to side, hugging Delia. When a choking sound came from her throat, he ceased all movement. Coughing, she braced herself on his shoulder, while he lay flat on his back and took great gulps of air into his parched lungs.

Delia opened her eyes on the blue brocade coverlet still neatly tucked over her husband's pillow. For three days in a row, she'd slept alone in the big four-poster at the Abernathy Plantation. Since the fire, Cord had barely touched her.

Reaching out, she smoothed the unwrinkled place next to her, and her heart split a little more. Cord's brooding mood was increasingly getting worse. He spent his nights pacing back and forth.

His daylight hours were devoted to some secret mission which he refused to discuss. And he dodged any effort Delia made to comfort him.

He had blamed himself for the fire, just as he had for the carriage accident. His insane notion that he could somehow shield Delia from danger by avoiding her in all respects was driving her mad.

She was losing him. Gradually. But most assuredly. Every day he pushed her farther away . . . sealed another crack, it seemed, in the wall that separated them. Nothing she said or did could penetrate the cool, apathetic glint that had settled in his eyes.

"Missy?" Bess called from the hall. "Is you awake?" she asked, then rapped on the door.

"Come in, Bess," Delia answered, and half-heartedly propped herself up against the head-board.

The housekeeper stepped into the room, carrying a tray. "Ho, now, chile," she said, her ready smile turning into a frown, "wha's dat long face all about?" Bustling forward, she set the tray on the end of the bed, bent forward, and pressed her palm to Delia's forehead. "Is you still feelin' poorly?"

"Now, don't you go frettin' over me." Delia attempted to smile, then slid Bess's hand from her forehead and gave it an affectionate squeeze. "I'm fine."

"Mmm-hmm." Bess tucked her chin and squinted. "You ain't nowheres near fine."

Delia's shoulders slumped by their own accord. Dropping all pretenses, she twisted her mouth to one side. "I never could fool you, could I, Bess?"

"No, Missy Adelaide. Ah knows you. They's a

gleam missin' from those purty blue eyes when things ain't right wit' you.''

Delia sighed and toyed with the edge of the coverlet. "I'm in love with my husband, Bess,'' she admitted in a quiet voice.

"Well, bless my soul, dat ain't nothin' nobody don't already know.'' The housekeeper placed her hands on her broad hips, shook her head, and laughed. "Land sakes, chile, you *is* in a heap o' trouble, then, ain't ya?''

"I'm certainly glad you find it so amusin'.'' Delia made a face and crossed her arms over her chest.

"Now, don't go gettin' your dander up, gal. What you worryin' 'bout anyhows? Ah done seen the way Mista Kib-doe looks at you. Hoo-ee!'' Bess rocked forward, clapped her knees, then chuckled again. "He's as lovesick as a puppy, that boy is.''

"Oh, he is not.''

"He sho' nuff is. You seen that limpid-lid look he gets? Well, tha's it. Tha's the look a man gets when he's done gone and los' his heart.''

Delia scrunched her nose. "Really?''

"Mmm-hmm.'' Bess bobbed her head, then picked up the tray and set it on Delia's lap. "Now, Ah knows you ain't gots much of an appetite— love'll do that to you, all right—but you bes' try to eat somethin'. You gots to keep up your strength. Cain't let no man go wearin' you down.''

Delia's stomach grumbled at the sight and aroma of the biscuits and gravy. She couldn't recall the last time she'd eaten. Lifting her fork, she gave the housekeeper a genuine smile. "Thank you, Bess.''

The black woman waved Delia's gratitude aside, but shook her head and giggled again as she started for the door.

"Bess, what's this?" Delia held up a sealed envelope with her name written on it that had been lying beside her plate.

The housekeeper stopped, looked back, and shrugged. "Somthin' somebody brought for you this mornin'."

"Who?"

"Ah ain't got the slightest inklin'. They slipped it under the front door. Somethin' wrong, missy?"

"No. No, I was just curious."

"Oh, my, Ah almost forgot," Bess said, raising a finger. "Your grandmamma axed me to tells you she be expectin' you downstairs for the noonday meal."

"I'll be there," Delia replied distractedly, turning the envelope over in her hands.

As soon as Bess closed the door, Delia opened the letter with her butter knife. She unfolded the plain white stationery and read the printed, child-like scrawl.

I KNOW WHO STARTED THE FIRE. MEET ME TO-NIGHT AT TEN O'CLOCK BY THE ANGEL IN THE CHURCH CEMETERY. COME ALONE!

A FRIEND

Delia frowned, then checked to make sure the message hadn't been addressed to Cord. But hers was the sole name on the envelope.

Putting her tray aside, she stretched out across the bed and read the note again. She didn't recognize the handwriting—of course, whoever had penned the message obviously hadn't meant for her to.

Cord had insisted the fire was no accident. She hadn't been so sure. She still couldn't recall whether either of them had bothered to snuff the candle on the table.

Closing her eyes, Delia held the paper against her forehead. News about the shanty burning had spread throughout Boudreaux Parish by noon the day afterward. Delia and Cord had been the topic of conversation for the past three days. People were still stopping by to ask after their welfare.

But who could possibly know how the fire had started?

Not Milly. Milly could be a bit overdramatic now and then, but she would never set up a secret meeting after dark in the graveyard—especially since she knew how much Delia detested the place.

Delia rolled over onto her back and frowned at the note again. Plain white paper. Black ink. She didn't have a single clue who could've written it. Anybody, she supposed. Almost anybody in town.

Pushing herself off the bed, she rose and started to pace, slapping the mysterious note against her open palm. She had to tell Cord. Despite the explicit instructions of the sender to do otherwise, she would be foolish to go to the cemetery alone. She shivered involuntarily at the very thought.

Delia halted her footsteps and stared at the door, willing Cord to walk through it soon. If he followed his pattern of the past few days, he wouldn't be home till after midnight.

Swiveling slowly, Delia met her reflection in the mirror.

With or without Cord, she would be in the graveyard at ten o'clock tonight. No matter how much she loathed the idea, she couldn't miss this opportunity to prove her love and loyalty. Cord would have to trust her if she brought him some sort of valuable information. He would have to let her help him.

The creaking of the cemetery gate made Delia grit her teeth. After closing it behind her, she clasped the cold wrought-iron bars tightly for an endless moment and took several deep breaths.

An owl hooted, making her jerk around and press back against the arched rock entrance. Then she almost giggled at the absurdity of being frightened by a bird. Forcing herself forward, she crept silently down the path toward the tall stone angel.

Moonlight played off the tombstones, causing shadows to change shape and direction as she passed by. Her heart thumped harder and harder with each step she took. Her palms grew moist and sticky. She told herself the heat of the night made her upper lip perspire . . . assured herself she only imagined the soft moans that blended with the wind rustling through the trees.

When Delia turned down the row of graves where the statue of the archangel came into view, her feet dragged to a halt. At the sight of the huge winged creature, she froze with fear.

No one else was there. No one but the angel. The tall stone guardian stared straight at Delia, its granite eyes boring into her soul. Panic spiraled upward from her stomach. Still, she couldn't move . . . couldn't utter a sound . . . not until the angel began to spread one wing.

Then the scream lodged in her throat broke loose.

Someone caught her from behind, clamping a hand over her mouth. As she was hauled backward, she widened her eyes on a dark figure fleeing from behind the statue . . . heard footsteps padding off into the distance.

In a half-crazed state, she clawed at the hand covering her mouth and swung her elbow viciously into her assailant's rib.

"Ahh! Delia, stop it! Stop fighting, *chère*. It's me."

The deep, familiar accent registered sharply in Delia's brain. Ceasing her struggle abruptly, she turned in her captor's embrace. She assessed his moonlit features briefly, then hugged his waist. "Cord, you came. You got my note."

"Your note?"

"The one I left on the bed along with the message someone sent this mornin'."

Cord grasped her shoulders and set her away from him. "Perhaps we should start again. I received no note. I have not yet returned to the plantation this evening."

"You haven't?"

"No."

She frowned. "Then what are you doin' here?"

"I followed Chauncy Bateman here. And I might have found out who he was meeting had you not shown up to frighten him away. Delia, you cannot interfere—"

"Cord, wait . . . wait a minute." She pressed her fingertips to her temples. "You mean that was Chauncy hidin' behind the angel?"

"*Oui*, but that is beside the point. You must not tag after me again like this. Do you understand?"

"I wasn't taggin' after you, you big arrogant oaf." Delia shrugged out of his grasp. "Don't you see? I think—I think maybe *I* was the one Chauncy was waitin' for."

"You?" Cord's face flattened. "Meeting Chauncy? But . . . why?"

"That's what I was just tryin' to tell you before you started jumpin' to conclusions. I got an anonymous note this mornin' from someone who claims to know who started the fire."

"And they told you to meet them here?"

"Yes." Delia looped her arm through his, glanced around the graveyard, and shivered. "Can we go home now?"

Cord nodded in response and started walking her toward the gate. Delia observed his thoughtful profile in silence for as long as she could; then curiosity got the better of her.

"Cord, you mind tellin' me why you were tailin' Chauncy?"

Cord blinked his pensiveness away. "Two days ago, Chauncy delivered a package to John Hart. They only exchanged a few words, but John is missing now."

"But what does all this mean?" Delia furrowed her brow. "You think Chauncy stole the money and framed you?"

"I do not know this for certain yet," Cord replied, slanting his gaze to hers. "But I think it is time Chauncy and I had a little heart-to-heart talk, no? I am tired of playing games."

Delia caught his coat sleeve as he stretched out his hand and pushed open the wrought-iron gate. "Cord, you can't just go burstin' in on the Batemans again. Chauncy was more than likely just prankin' me tonight. You can't go accusin' him of thievery. Not without proof."

Cord pried her fingers from his jacket, then gripped her upper arm, steering her through the rock archway.

"I will find the proof I need soon enough," he grumbled out of the side of his mouth. "If you will stay home where you belong, and stop interfering in my affairs."

Intense fury caught Cord off guard the next morning when he went to inspect the charred remains of the shanty. He'd always hated the shack, despised the memories it provoked. God forgive him, he had even wished once or twice that the place *would* burn to the ground. But as he walked among the debris, viewing the damage in broad daylight, the raging reality of what could have happened rose within him. Had he not awakened when he did—

Cord kicked a blackened board from his path, savoring the idea of snapping Chauncy Bateman's neck. The man had purposely, maliciously, started the fire. Cord harbored no doubts whatsoever now. Who else hated him enough to burn him out? *Oui.* He would like to strangle Chauncy with his bare hands. But death would be too easy for Bateman. Cord wanted justice. He demanded satisfaction. Chauncy's life could not sufficiently pay for all his crimes. *Non.* Cord relished the thought of the man rotting away in prison.

He surveyed the scorched rubble once more, seeking a piece of evidence that might prompt a lawful investigation. Perhaps Chauncy had left some sign of his involvement behind . . . a footprint, a button . . . something.

Cord crouched, scooped up a handful of ashes, and let the gray, powdery substance sift through his fingers. If a clue existed, he would find it. Taking off his jacket, he hung it on a tree limb and rolled up his sleeves.

For the next several hours, he rummaged through the incinerated shanty, clearing fire-chewed boards from what was left of the foundation. He had examined every tiny article he had come across, and had discovered nothing he couldn't eventually recognize.

Well past noon, he gave in to a moment of disgust and fatigue and settled down on the sturdiest part of the charred floor. He studied his hands, clasped loosely between his knees. Common sense urged him to give up, but another, stronger source, one beyond his understanding, prodded him to keep searching. There was something here. He knew it. He felt it.

Cord's gaze fell on the half-burned floorboard beneath his feet, and a shadowy object in the dark crevice below caught his eye. He jerked the rotted plank loose. Sparse sunlight flooded the hole, revealing a loaf-sized, battered tin box, which he recognized as once having belonged to Anna Kibedeaux.

His mother, Cord recalled, had clutched the small box to her breast each time they'd left one town for another. Upon arriving at the next shabby hovel they'd rent, she would frantically hunt for a hiding place for her treasure, never allowing anyone a peek inside.

Cord lifted the small chest from concealment and simply stared at it for a long moment. He turned the box over and over in his hands, wondering what a madwoman would guard so dearly.

He doubted his mother had ever possessed anything of great value.

Carefully prying the rusty lid open, he found very little for Anna to have fretted over: the dried remains of a magnolia blossom, an old hair ribbon, a folded piece of paper, and a photograph.

Picking up the portrait of a woman, he was amazed to see the likeness of his mother in the fresh, youthful face. When Anna's rantings had been at their worst, she'd often whimpered about having been beautiful, but Cord had never witnessed on her lips the lovely smile that was in the picture.

The flower crumbled when he brushed it aside and took out the yellowed, age-stained paper, which he unfolded. Since his parents had neglected to attend Mass, Cord had merely assumed they'd never bothered being married in the church. The certificate he held proved otherwise.

Cord rubbed his neck, thinking he ought be pleased to learn of his legitimacy. As it turned out, he was more intrigued by the peculiar familiarity of his mother's maiden name.

"What you sittin' dere like dat for, *T-boo?*" *Tante* Netha Bea called out, hobbling toward him.

Cord turned his head and stared blankly at the old woman. Then, for some reason, he quickly stuffed his mother's sole possessions back in the box and closed the lid.

Netha Bea stopped at the edge of the burned ruins and braced her weight on her cane. "There is no more for you here, *cher,*" she said, eyeing him curiously. "Can you not see dat?"

"*Oui.* Nothing," Cord murmured, still absorbed by his thoughts.

"You come here, *T-boo*, seekin' answers, *hein?* Me, I come to help you, yeah."

Riveting his attention on her, he rose, tucked his mother's box of treasures under his arm, and walked forward. "What have you seen, old woman?"

"I saw him, the man who did this. But it was too dark, *cher*, to see his face."

"*Sacrebleu!*" Cord muttered under his breath, then lowered his head. "The vision, it was not clear?"

"*Non.*" *Tante* Netha Bea cupped his jaw and lifted his gaze to hers. "You do not understand. I did not see him in my dreams. Dese old eyes, dey see him. He pass my house, movin' down the bayou in a pirogue, yeah, the night of the fire. Me, I couldn't tell who it was from my porch, but he flipped dis orange spark out of the boat. When I go down to see what dat was—" Snatching Cord's hand, she pressed something she apparently considered precious into his palm and folded his fingers over it. "—I find dis."

Chapter Twenty-One

C ord unfurled his fingers, blinked twice, then frowned at the cigar butt the crazy old witch had crammed into his hand.

"Look closer," *Tante* Netha Bea chanted, as if she read his thoughts. "Remember."

As Cord lifted the half-smoked cigar to his nose, determining the tobacco to be of an expensive Cuban variety, a recent memory flickered of someone else performing a similar action.

I always carry an extra smoke, my boy. Herbert Bateman's voice echoed in the back of Cord's brain.

Herbert Bateman. Chauncy's father had offered Cord a costly Cuban cigar the night of Cynthia Davenport's engagement party.

Groping for some significance of the implication, Cord peered into Netha Bea's wise black eyes. "What does this mean?" he asked.

The old woman shrugged. "The man who smoke dat cee-gar, he is the one you have sought all along, *cher*. This is all I know."

Cord's gaze drifted beyond *Tante* Netha Bea. Sight and sound closed off around him. He couldn't quite grasp the notion that Herbert Bateman was involved in any way. More likely, Chauncy probably smoked the same brand of cigars. Regardless, rather than waiting for the next accident to occur, Cord fully intended to pay both Batemans a visit.

Delia observed Cord carefully throughout the evening meal. He had carried on as usual, charming Grandy with witty conversation and complimenting Bess's cooking—though he'd hardly touched his food.

Delia wasn't fooled by his act. She had noted his preoccupation the moment he'd taken his place at the table, making apologies for being late. All through supper a dark, brooding mood had hovered just beyond the surface of his teasing grin.

Something was amiss.

Clasping her hands tightly in her lap, Delia studied her husband from beneath her lowered lashes. She had sincerely tried not to meddle. Instead of asking any questions, she had merely helped him out of his jacket when he'd come home late at night.

But her lip was nearly blue from biting it. Docility went against her nature, and patience fell low on her list of virtues.

"Why, Cord, dear," Grandy interjected affectionately, "how can you go runnin' off without finishin' your cobbler? You know Bess made it 'specially for you."

In the middle of rising from his chair, Cord leaned forward and scooped a big spoonful of dessert into his mouth. Through the chore of chewing the doughy cobbler, he gave Grandy a tight-lipped smile. Then he quickly dabbed the blackberry juice from his lips with his napkin, walked over to Agatha, and kissed her forehead.

"I will not be so late tonight," he told her. "Perhaps when I come home we can all have a glass of anisette on the veranda, *hein?*"

Agatha grabbed his hand as he started around the table to bid his wife farewell. "Cord, you're not frequentin' the gamin' tables, are you, son?"

"*Non.* You may rest assured I am not. It is strictly business." He patted her hand, then continued on his way to deliver his usual parting peck on Delia's cheek.

Sliding back her chair, Delia rose as he approached her, and when he bent toward her, she ducked his kiss. "I'd like a word with you," she said in a crisp, polite manner.

"Of course, *chérie,* as soon as I return—"

"*Now.*" She emphasized the request with a narrowing of her eyes, then looped her arm through his. "You'll oblige me with a walk in the garden . . . *dear.*"

Ignoring Grandy's inquisitive expression, Delia swiftly led her husband out the French doors, across the veranda, and down the path.

"Delia, I have no time to waste tonight strolling through the garden," Cord protested as she dragged him along.

"Whatever you have to do can surely wait till mornin'," Delia replied without slowing her steps. "We have to talk."

She stopped just inside the maze of tall hedges and released him. He shoved his hands in his pockets and looked down at her impassively.

"Well, what is it?" he inquired coolly. "What do you have to say to me that is so important, *hein?*"

Delia's heart rose to her throat. There were a million things she wanted to tell him, but she didn't know where or how to begin.

Cord moved closer, his features rapidly registering concern. Clasping her face between his hands, he tilted her gaze to his. *"Mon Dieu,"* he whispered. "Delia . . . you . . . you are with child, no?"

"No, of course not. Why, that's the silliest—" Delia sighed and compressed her lips. She tugged his hands from her face and held them loosely, rubbing her thumbs over his knuckles. "Cord, I . . . I was just wonderin' . . . well, are you aware that the day after tomorrow will be our six-month anniversary?"

Cord diverted his eyes from hers. *"Non,* I . . . I did not."

"I figured you'd probably forgotten." She dropped his hands and turned away from him, hugging her waist.

"In prison, *ma chérie,* I learned not to dwell on dates, years, or time too much. Old habits, I am told, die hard."

Cord, I don't want to end the marriage, Delia suddenly ached to say, but pride formed a hard knot in her throat. Cord had given her no indication he wanted to stay with her. On the contrary, with the way he had distanced himself from her in the past few days, he had implied just the opposite. She swiveled slowly and searched his face for encouragement.

With an unreadable expression, he stared at her for a long, agonizing moment. Then he shifted his weight and reached up and rubbed the back of his neck.

"So. I suppose you will be leaving for Europe soon to join your father, *hein?*"

It was an important question. One that had played over and over and over in Delia's mind lately. She phrased her answer carefully. "I . . . well, I s'pose there's nothing left for me here." She lifted her gaze to his, hoping to convey her heart's greatest wish through her eyes. "Is there?"

Cord licked his lips and shoved his hands back into his pockets. "*Non,*" he replied quietly, then shook his head. "I suppose once I finish my business here, there will be no reason for me to stay in Boudreaux Parish, either."

A crushing pressure cinched Delia's chest. Tremors of emotion flickered in Cord's dark eyes, but she couldn't decipher their meaning. If he could only show her . . . give her some sign that he cared.

Ask him. Ask him if he cares, a voice in the back of her brain whispered. She tried to obey, but when she opened her mouth, all that came out was "Where will you go?"

"I do not know." Although his voice quivered, Cord answered with a casual shrug of his shoulder. "Some place where no one knows me."

Stay with me, was on the tip of Delia's tongue. "I'll miss you," was what she said. And since she was no longer able to ignore the sting behind her eyes, a stream of tears rolled down her cheeks.

Cord hesitantly reached out and enfolded her in his arms.

"Shh, *chère,*" he whispered, stroking her hair soothingly. "I will miss you too. But neither of us can change what is to be. We both have our own paths we must follow, no?"

Delia closed her eyes, oblivious of everything but the warmth of his body. She inhaled deeply, filling her senses with his essence, absorbing the closeness he'd denied her for the past several days.

"I love you," she murmured ever so softly into the front of his shirt. The words were so muffled and sob-ridden that Cord couldn't possibly have heard the confession, but Delia couldn't bring herself to say them any louder. She couldn't risk the humiliation of his rejection.

Cord tightened his embrace, holding her as if he might never let her go. For an undeterminable length of time, they stood clutching each other in a blissful silence.

The peaceful evening was shattered by a dog barking in the distance. Cord released his breath sharply and looked down at Delia. His eyes held the lingering impression that he'd returned from somewhere far away.

"Come," he said with a forced smile and turned Delia toward the house. "We waste precious time here discussing matters that cannot be changed. Let us go to our room."

Slipping an arm around her, he guided her along the garden path. "I will kiss you senseless," he whispered against her temple. "I will love you till the sun comes up. And we will both forget who we are for a while, *hein*?"

Cord reined his horse on the edge of the Bateman estate, watching the bright orange sun crest the horizon.

What the hell had happened to him? To his objective? He should have been calculating his next move. He should have been anticipating the Batemans' reaction to what he had come to say this morning.

But his thoughts had remained in the big four-poster at the Abernathy Plantation. He kept envisioning Delia as he'd left her this morning: peacefully stretched out on the bed, her hair wild and wavy across the pillow, one tempting, slender thigh escaping the twisted sheets.

She'd been warm and willing in his arms all night long. Once again she had touched the deepest part of him, forcing him to give back just as much as she gave. Dawn's purple shadows had tinted the room before she'd finally fallen asleep.

Despite his weariness, tremulous emotions had held him from rest. He couldn't say how long he had lain beside Delia and watched her breast rise and fall with each sweet breath. But for a short, lax while, he had allowed himself the luxury of truly viewing her as his wife.

In the garden, she had said she loved him. She had murmured the words so quietly that they had only barely reached his ears, but they had sounded loud and clear in his heart. *She loved him.* It was an amazing notion that made him glow deep inside. How could *la belle de Boudreaux Parish* love someone like him? For an hour or two this morning, he'd actually imagined waking up next to Delia for the rest of his life.

Then reality had reared its ugly head. True, perhaps they could've found happiness together. But for how long? How long would it take for pride and poverty to push them apart? How long would it be before Delia started hating him because of his inability to care for her properly? She was accustomed to finer things than he could afford to provide. And his own pride would not allow him to live off her wealth.

Bright sunlight pierced Cord's eyes, penetrating his thoughts. He tugged down the brim of his hat resolutely.

If what he felt for Delia wasn't love, surely no such thing existed. In his heart she would always be his wife. But he could never tell her so.

Nor could he keep up the pretense of this marriage any longer. He should be glad it was almost over. He couldn't control his emotions anymore. He couldn't stop the rapid beating of his heart whenever Delia ventured near. But he could not change the fact that he was poor white trash—no more than Delia could change the fact that she was Agatha Abernathy's granddaughter. And neither of them could fight society.

Cord turned his horse, and his thoughts, toward the Bateman mansion. He urged his steed into a hard-paced gallop that suited his own restless mood. Pulling up short in front of the grand house, he dismounted, tied his horse to one of the ornate iron hitching posts, then strode deliberately up the wide steps.

The tall black servant Cord remembered from before answered his knock with a frown.

"Ah's done tole you once, suh," he said. "Master Chauncy don't take no un'nounced visitors.'Specially dis early in de day."

Cord wedged his foot against the bottom of the closing door. "Is M'sieu Bateman—Herbert Bateman—still abed as well?"

The black man tucked his chin, his dark gaze dancing between Cord's boot braced across the threshold and the riding crop Cord held. Opening the door wider, he motioned Cord into the foyer.

"You waits heah," he commanded with an air of authority. "I'll go ax him will he see you."

Cord barely had time to remove his hat and glance around the highly polished entry before the servant returned and showed him to the library.

When he entered the large study with bookcase-lined walls, Herbert Bateman came to his feet behind a large rosewood desk.

"Good mornin', my boy," he said with a smile that inflated his wide sideburns. Stepping forward, he took Cord's hand and shook it vigorously. "My, you are an early riser, aren't you? Here, sit down, sit down," he said, gesturing to a leather wing chair across the desk from his.

"*Merci,* m'sieu." Cord remained standing until Bateman rounded the desk and sat down. Then he seated himself in the leather chair and laid his hat on his knee. "I am most grateful you have seen fit to admit me without previous notice."

"Nonsense," Herbert contended with a wave of his beefy hand. "I b'lieve I told you you were welcome here anytime. Now, what can I do for you?"

"I regret I have come with some disturbing news, m'sieu." Cord looked past Bateman at the endless rows of law books and carefully weighed the wisdom of making any blatant accusations.

"Oh?" Herbert furrowed his brow, braced a forearm on his desk, and leaned forward. "And what disturbin' news might that be?"

"It concerns your son." Cord lowered his gaze

and gripped the brim of his hat. This was not as easy as he'd thought it would be.

"Chauncy?" Herbert sat back in his chair, locked his hands across his middle, frowned, then shook his head. "That boy's always had him a mischievous streak, but ever since his mamma passed away, he's been downright malicious. What's he done now?"

Cord pulled the cigar butt from his coat pocket and placed it on the desk. "Is this the same brand of tobacco as the one you smoke, m'sieu?"

Herbert picked up the partially smoked cigar and rolled it between his thumb and forefinger, closely examining the stub. "Seems to be."

"Does Chauncy not smoke the same brand?"

"Sometimes." Mr. Bateman looked puzzled. "Why?"

"That cigar butt was found in the bayou not far from my place the night my cabin burned down." Cord searched the older gentleman's expression intently. "Someone told me they saw a man in a pirogue throw it into the water just after the fire started."

Herbert narrowed his eyes. "Just what are you gettin' at, boy?"

"M'sieu, the people who live in the bayou, they cannot afford such a fine variety of cigars. They smoke cheroots." Cord's gaze returned to his hat, and he fiddled with the brim again. "I believe this cigar butt was dropped by the man who set fire to my house."

"You sayin' you think Chauncy had somethin' t' do with your place burnin' down?" Mr. Bateman sat upright in his chair. His face turning red with anger and indignation, he tossed the stale cigar stub across his desk. "You're makin' some mighty serious charges based on awfully flimsy evidence."

Cord squared his shoulders. "I have other reasons as well to suspect Chauncy."

"What other reasons?" Bateman asked skeptically.

Cord shrugged. "A secret meeting between Chauncy and John Hart. Your son gives John a package, and poof, he disappears."

"What's that got to do with anything?" Bateman asked harshly.

"Perhaps there is some connection," Cord answered.

Herbert dragged a hand over his face, his fury quickly changing to worry.

"Chauncy also lured Delia to the cemetery the other night," Cord went on. "For what reason, I do not know."

"The cemetery?" Bateman appeared bewildered. "Why in God's name would he do somethin' like that?"

"That is one thing I want to find out myself, m'sieu." Cord paused, watching the man's expression turn thoughtful. "With your permission, I would like to ask Chauncy a few questions. In your presence, of course," he added.

"Absolutely not," Herbert bellowed, then stood and grabbed a decanter of brandy off the shelf behind him and poured himself a jigger. "I will not have my son subjected to an interrogation." Facing Cord again, he downed the drink and dragged his hand across his mouth. "Not by the likes of you, I won't."

Cord arched an eyebrow. "Perhaps you would rather have the sheriff question your son?"

"Question me about what?" Chauncy's voice turned Cord's and Herbert's eyes to the open doorway. "What's goin' on here, Kibedeaux?" he asked, strolling into the room.

Chapter Twenty-Two

"**N**othin' for you to worry your head about, son." Herbert set his empty glass on the desk and stepped forward. "Cord was just leavin'." The older Bateman directed a pointed look at Cord. "Weren't you?"

"No, actually, I hadn't planned on leaving just yet." Cord met the man's gaze levelly and made no move to get up from his chair. "Not until I have spoken to Chauncy, m'sieu."

"Just what do you figure you and me have to talk about, Kibedeaux?" Chauncy asked, folding his arms across his chest.

"A bunch of nonsense," Herbert grumbled before Cord could answer. "Seems Cord here has some wild idea you started the fire out at his place the other night." Herbert stalked to the decanter and filled his glass again. "Can you believe he would come up with such a ridiculous notion?"

Chauncy's eyes widened as they shifted from his father to Cord. "No matter what you think of me, Cord," he said in a low, trembling voice, "I would never do anything to hurt Delia. I swear I wouldn't."

Cord checked his emotions, keeping his face bland. "Perhaps you could explain why you asked her to meet you in the cemetery the other night, then, *hein?*"

"The cemetery?" Chauncy let go of a nervous little laugh. "I never asked Delia to meet—"

"I saw you that night in the graveyard. And you saw me, I think. Remember?"

"You must be mistaken, Kibedeaux. I never—"

"You delivered the note yourself. One of the stableboys at the Abernathy Plantation saw you slip it under the door."

Chauncy's face paled. Twisting his hands at his waist, he turned and walked across the room. "I wanted to warn . . . to *talk* to her, that's all. I just wanted to see her."

"That'll do, Kibedeaux," Herbert snapped. "You got no call t' go tormentin' my boy this way."

"No, m'sieu, I'm afraid that will *not* do." Cord brushed a piece of lint from his trousers. "I have a few more questions for your son."

"Look, Cord." Chauncy pivoted on his heel and spread his arms wide. "I don't know what this is all about, but—"

"What was in the package you delivered to M'sieu Hart?"

Chauncy's gaze oscillated between Cord and his father. "I—I think you'd best g-go now, Cord," he stammered.

"Very well." Cord rose from his chair and tugged at his lapels, regarding both men coolly. "I will go. But I will be back shortly with the sheriff. Good day, gentlemen," he said, then headed for the door.

"Hold it right there, Cord," Herbert demanded.

Cord glanced over his shoulder to find Herbert Bateman pointing a pistol at him. In slow, measured moves, he faced the man.

"Daddy, for God's sake, put that thing back in your drawer." Chauncy started toward his father. "What're you—"

"You just stay put, Chauncy." Herbert's command stopped his son's advance. "Don't go interferin' here."

"But, Daddy, you can't just shoot a man in cold blood for no reason. Cord hasn't done nothin' to warrant—"

"He's done plenty," Herbert interrupted, giving Cord a deadly glare. He licked his lips and looked at Chauncy pleadingly. "Don't you see, son? I can't just let him go waltzin' outta here after the sheriff."

In the length it took for the clock on the wall to chime ten times, Chauncy stared at his father as if he'd never seen him before. Then he stretched out his hand and moved across the room with careful steps.

"Give me the gun, Daddy. Shootin' Cord ain't gonna settle nothin'. Just get you in t' trouble. Please . . . just put down the gun, and we'll all sit down and discuss this like gentlemen."

"You should do as your son says, m'sieu," Cord suggested. He studied both of the Batemans with mixed thoughts. "Chauncy is right. Lay down the pistol and we will talk, *hein?*"

"You shut up!" Herbert's full attention swiftly returned to Cord. "You just shut the hell up, you hear?"

In that one moment of distraction, Chauncy

bounded forward, caught his father's wrist, and wrestled the gun from his hand.

Herbert's face registered shock, then despair. Cord expelled a long-held breath, but remained where he was.

"Damn it, boy, why'd you have to stop me for?" Herbert muttered, wilting into his chair. He dragged a hand over his face, then stared unseeingly in front of him. "I coulda killed him and it woulda all been over. We coulda told Sheriff Juilliard he broke in here and tried to steal—"

"No, Daddy." Chauncy moved to place a hand on his father's shoulder. "We couldn't have done that and you know it. It wouldna been right."

Herbert lifted a tear-bright gaze to his son. "I did it all for you, Chauncy. Everything I did was for you . . ."

"Oh, God . . . I suspected as much," Chauncy murmured, then closed his eyes. "The mornin' after the fire, when I passed Lucy Belle on the stairs takin' your clothes down to wash 'em, I smelled smoke."

Chauncy opened his eyes and focused on Cord. "That's why I sent the note to Delia, askin' her to meet me," he told him. "I was afraid somethin' else might happen. And I didn't want her to be caught in the middle of it."

Cord lowered his gaze by degrees to Herbert Bateman. With his eyes twitching and his mouth forming inaudible words, the older man appeared lost in his own troubled thoughts.

Cord directed his next question to Chauncy. "The *gris gris* and the carriage accident, your father, he was responsible for these things as well?"

Chauncy hung his head. "I made the arrangements for the *gris gris* to be put in your bed." He peered at Cord from beneath his brows. "But I don't know nothin' 'bout the buggy accident, I swear. I would never do anything to hurt Delia. Never."

"And what about John Hart? What do you know of him, *hein*?"

"Nothin'," Chauncy replied with a shrug. "I hardly ever spoke to the man."

Cord eyed Chauncy suspiciously. "Did you not deliver a package to him shortly before he disappeared?"

"Well, yes. But just because Daddy asked me to." Chauncy frowned pensively. "I thought at the time the envelope was a little bulky for old bank business papers. Couldn't imagine why Daddy would be sendin' 'em to *him* in the first place, with John bein' retired and all." Chauncy shook his head. "Anyways, John Hart never said a word when he opened the door, just grabbed the—"

"John?" Herbert spoke the name, looking from Chauncy to Cord with clouded eyes. "Is he here? He's s'posed t' be in N'orlens. I paid him well enough to stay outta town."

Cord took swift strides across the room. Stopping in front of Herbert he stooped and caught the arms of the man's chair.

"Why did you pay him, m'sieu?" he asked, meeting Herbert's gaze. "Tell me. John Hart, he was blackmailing you, perhaps?"

"Yes! Damn his hide," Herbert blurted out. He searched Cord's face with only the slightest sign of recognition, then he squinted. "You're that Kibedeaux boy, ain't you? That trash Winston took in."

Cord let go of the sides of the chair and straightened, looking down at Bateman.

Herbert tilted his head back and observed him keenly. "This is all your fault," he hissed. "None a this woulda happened if you hadn't come back t' Boudreaux Parish and started snoopin' around."

"You?" Cord's shoulder blades tightened. "*You* were the one who framed me?" His gaze drifted above Herbert's head for a second. "Of course. You keep the bank's books, do you not? You would naturally have known the combination to the safe." Cord regarded the older Bateman with a mixture of pity and disgust. "And John Hart . . . he was the one who actually took the money for you, was he not?"

"Daddy, is this true?" Chauncy asked.

Herbert glanced at his son, then reached up and patted the hand Chauncy rested on his shoulder.

"Why, m'sieu?" Cord whispered in a hollow voice. "How could you do this to me? I do not understand. What have I ever done to cause you harm?"

"You tried to steal my boy's rightful inheritance," Herbert stated bluntly.

A look of confusion passed between Cord and Chauncy.

"What're you talkin' about, Daddy? Cord here never—"

"He did!" Herbert shifted in his chair and glowered at his son. "*You're* Winston Grayson's legal heir, Chauncy, not *him*," Herbert declared, jutting his chin toward Cord. "I could see things changin' after Winston took him in. Winston was fond of him. *Too* fond of him. Had things kept on going the way they were, Winston woulda made *him* the beneficiary of his will, you mark my word.''

''Good God, Daddy. You mean t' say you sent a man t' prison for somethin' like that?'' Chauncy combed his fingers through his sandy hair. ''Lord. Then when he came back here, you tried to—'' Chauncy let his sentence break off and stared at his father in amazement. ''Good God. You *were* responsible for Delia gettin' hurt when that carriage rolled over, weren't you?''

Making no response, Herbert turned his face away from his son.

Chauncy looked from his father to Cord. ''I . . . I don't know what to say, Kibedeaux,'' he uttered. ''Any regrets I might offer over my father's part in this mess seems so senseless at this point. I just feel so . . . I can't tell you how sorry—''

''I understand.'' Cord nodded, sparing Chauncy any further apologies. Young Bateman had been as shocked and distressed to learn of his father's crimes as he had.

Chauncy took a deep breath and glanced in Herbert's direction. ''You go ahead and do what you gotta do, Kibedeaux,'' he said. ''I can't be a party to takin' my own father in to the sheriff's office. But I won't stop you.''

Cord shook his head slowly. ''It is not for me to decide your father's fate. Only God can judge him. And now that I have the answers I sought, I have no wish to involve the sheriff in this matter.'' Cord settled his gaze on Herbert Bateman again, realizing the secrets the man had kept for so many years had taken their toll on his mind. ''*Non.* I will not take him to the sheriff. But I must insist on him accompanying me to the bank to see M'sieu Grayson.''

* * *

Cord kept a firm grip on Herbert Bateman's upper arm as they walked into the bank together. Ignoring the curious expressions of the tellers, Cord strode past them straight to Winston Grayson's office. Without knocking, he opened the door and hauled Herbert inside.

Seated at his desk, Mr. Grayson looked up from his paperwork with a perplexed frown.

"Cord? Herbert?" he said, then came to his feet, shifting his gaze between the two. "What . . . is something wrong?"

"*Oui*, something has been wrong for a very long time, I'm afraid." Cord nudged Herbert forward. "M'sieu Bateman wishes to tell you all about it himself, I believe."

Herbert hung his head dejectedly.

"Tell him," Cord prompted, and folded his arms over his chest. "You tell M'sieu Grayson the truth."

A soft gurgle escaped Bateman's throat. He sniffled, swiped at his nose, then shifted his weight. "Cord . . . didn't take the money, Winston," he stammered, still staring at the floor. "I . . . I hired John Hart to steal the money and make it look like Cord had done it."

Mr. Grayson's face paled considerably as he pressed a hand to his heart. "*You* . . . stole the money?"

"God's truth," Herbert blurted out. He shook his head, then glanced beneath his brows at Winston. "I never meant t' hurt no one. I just wanted Cord outta the way. With things gettin' as cozy as they were between th' two a y'all, I was afraid you'd end up cuttin' Chauncy outta your will."

Mr. Grayson closed his open mouth abruptly. Narrowing his eyes on his brother-in-law, he moved to stand before the man.

"You never meant to hurt anyone?" he said in a voice trembling with rage. "Herbert, Cord was the son I'd never had. You knew how I felt about that boy. Yet you put us both through the ordeal of that awful trial and sent him off to prison. And *you never meant to hurt anyone?"* Winston reached up and massaged his forehead. "Herbert . . . all these years . . . I've thought of you as my friend, not just my sister's husband. I can't believe you would go and betray me like this."

Covering his face, Herbert sank to his knees and began a soft, pitiful weeping.

Grayson stood looking down at him for several long moments before he lifted his gray eyes to Cord.

"I . . . I'm sorry, son," he murmured. "So . . . sorry. I wish there was something I could say or do to turn back the clock and make all a this right again. Maybe if I'da just had more faith in you . . . if I just woulda listened . . ." Winston's chin quivered and his voice trailed off.

"I too have many regrets, m'sieu." Cord shoved his hands into his pockets, curling his fingers into tight fists. "But I did not come here to exchange apologies. You were once very kind to me. I could not rest until you knew the truth . . . until I proved to you that I did not betray your kindness."

A sentimental stretch of silence lingered between them.

Cord looked at Winston, remembering.

Winston's eyes misted with memories as well. Pain and pride, time and tragedy, had distanced them, making it difficult for either of them to speak. Neither could say how long they stood staring at each other across the room. It seemed like endless hours had passed before Cord turned and walked out the door.

Delia paced across the front veranda, then pivoted, shaded her eyes, and looked down the long drive once more.

Her stomach lurched again, and she pressed a hand to her throat. He wasn't coming back.

Yes, he is, something deep inside her argued.

Then where is he?

The wave of nausea weakened Delia's knees. Closing her eyes, she leaned her forehead against the huge, cool column that supported the upper balcony.

Why hadn't he awakened her this morning? After sharing such a night of tenderness, how could he have left without saying good-bye?

Delia opened her eyes and lifted her head. He couldn't have walked out of her life for good. He simply couldn't have. Something too special had passed between them last night: a giving and receiving that neither of them could deny.

Delia felt her cheeks flush and smiled. *He'll be back.*

As if willing it to be had made it so, she heard the gallop of a horse and turned her head. Picking up her skirt, she flew down the steps and into Cord's arms as he dismounted.

The way he clung to her in an almost desperate embrace made her look up and search his face.

"Cord, what is it?" she asked. "What's happened?"

"It's over," he said with an unreadable expression.

A spike pierced Delia's heart. "Over?"

"*Oui.*" Cord slid his hand beneath her hair, curving his fingers around the back of her neck. "I know who set the fire and caused the accident with the coach . . . and who framed me. But more importantly, Winston Grayson now knows."

Delia wilted against him, so relieved he hadn't been referring to their marriage that a whole moment elapsed before she asked, "Who?"

"Herbert Bateman."

"Herbert . . . ?" Delia blinked, then checked to see if he was serious. "Cord, surely you've made some mistake."

"No mistake, *chère,*" he said, steering her up the steps and into the house.

As they walked up the curved stairway, he briefly relayed the story. She listened intently, her eyes growing wide. By the time they reached their bedroom, she was nearly bursting with questions.

"But what about Chauncy?" she asked as she helped Cord out of his jacket. "Did he know about all this?"

"*Non.*" Cord frowned in the middle of untying his cravat. "*Non,* I truly do not think he was involved."

Delia settled on the side of the bed and watched Cord unbutton his shirt. "But if he wasn't involved, then why—"

"Delia, must we talk of this?" Cord gave her a tired, lopsided grin, and his gaze turned sultry. Crawling on the bed with the movements of a panther, he pushed her backward, then brushed his lips lightly over hers.

"The rest of the day . . . and tonight, they belong to us, *chère.* You and me, *hein?* I do not wish the Batemans or Winston Grayson or anyone to intrude.''

He slid his mouth to her throat and, moving downward, scattered kisses across her breasts. Delia closed her eyes and looped her arms around his neck. And the fire inside flamed high once again.

Chapter Twenty-Three

"**D**elia? Wake up, *chère.*"

Swimming on the edge of consciousness, Delia snuggled closer to the warm body beside her. She pressed her cheek against Cord's furry chest and smiled. "Mmm, good mornin'," she murmured, without opening her eyes.

"Delia?"

"Hmm?"

"I must go now."

She batted her lashes. "What did you say?" she asked, hoping she'd only imagined the strain she'd heard in his voice. Then she nudged her chin up his chest and looked at him.

And she knew.

Ill-concealed agony underscored his expression, but determination held his features hard.

"I must leave you today, *chère,*" he whispered, running his fingertips gently over the planes of her face. "I can no longer stay here."

Delia squeezed her burning eyes shut, absorbing the bittersweet pain of his touch. Because the knot in her throat restrained her voice, she could only wag her head pitifully in a negative manner.

An eruption deep inside pushed upward, outward, until a single phrase broke loose.

"Stay with me," she pleaded softly.

"Delia . . . sweet Delia." Cord caught her wrists and sat up in bed, tugging her to her knees. "Listen to me, *ma petite*. Open your eyes."

She raised her lids and focused a blurry gaze on him.

"Ah, no, *chérie* . . . don't look at me like that. It breaks my heart." Pulling her into his arms, he pressed her cheek against his shoulder. "The world, she has locked too many doors between us," he murmured, and rubbed his chin back and forth across the top of her head. "You are accustomed to a comfortable life. Me, I could not give you the luxuries you are used to. I have no money, no means to support you properly."

She tried to move her head to look up at him, but he held her securely against him. "We'll have my inheritance, Cord. We could—"

He put his fingertip to her lips. "What kind of man would I be if I lived off your money?" he asked.

"You'd be my husband." Her voice quivered with desperation.

"*Oui*. There he is, people would say when I passed them on the street—there goes M'sieu Adelaide Abernathy."

Delia squirmed out of his hold and gazed up at him, despite his effort to keep her from doing so. "Since when do you worry 'bout what people say?"

"Talk never used to affect me," Cord replied, peering deep into her eyes. "Words, they could not hurt me. But you . . . you, *chère*, have awakened something inside me." He lifted her hand

and held her palm against his pulsating heart. "Something here."

Trembling with a mixture of emotions, Delia reached out and lightly traced his mouth . . . his chin . . . his brow. How could she go on without him? She couldn't bear the thought of never touching him . . . never seeing him again. There had to be a way for them to be together.

"We can work this out," she said breathlessly. "I know we can."

"*Non*, you are wrong. I will not live off your money." He folded her hands between his own. "Can you not understand this? I must work to feel worthy. *Oui*, I could get a job as a field hand, but what kind of life would that be for you? You would not be happy for long living in poverty. You would soon grow to hate me."

"No, I wouldn't." Delia shook her head and a tear rolled down her cheek.

"Yes, you would, *chère*. Me, I would feel like a whore if I let you take care of me. And sooner or later, I would resent you."

Cord's hands constricted achingly around Delia's before he turned them loose. Curling a finger beneath her chin, he tilted her face to his.

"Let us part cherishing what we have had together," he whispered against her lips. "Let us always remember each moment . . . every day. This is something, *ma chérie*, that no one can ever take from either of us."

He kissed her so sweetly, so tenderly, that she felt weak when he finally pulled away. She saw her own anguish reflected in his amber eyes . . . saw his throat work convulsively before he rose from the bed.

Too numb to move, Delia stared blankly at Cord

while he dressed. From the corner of her eye she watched him move about the room and gather his few belongings.

Cord paused by the door and looked back at her, but neither of them could say good-bye.

"Now, Delia, aren't you glad I talked you into ridin' into town with me this mornin'?" Milly flicked the reins against the horse's rump, setting the lightweight buggy into motion. She nudged her friend with her elbow. "Well? Isn't this better than sittin' home in your room mopin'? After all, Cord's been gone for—what? Almost a week now."

Delia blinked back her dreary thoughts and turned from idly viewing the passing scenery.

"A week precisely, Milly," she commented. "One week. Seven days. One hundred and sixty-eight hours, and—"

"Oh, hush," Milly snapped with a frown. "However long it's been, it's high time you stopped feelin' sorry for yourself. You shoulda known better than to go messin' around with a man like that in the first place. The ones possessin' those dreamy-lookin' eyes aren't good for nothin' but a heartache."

Despite the pain in Delia's chest, she curved her lips slightly upward. "I s'pose you're right, Milly."

"Well, of course I'm right." Milly tilted her nose smugly. "You mark my word, you just get on with your life, and you'll forget all about Cord Kibedeaux soon enough."

Milly remained respectfully silent for the rest of their ride into town. Delia suspected her friend of providing the quiet time for Delia to ponder her advice. Though she doubted she could ever truly forget Cord, Milly's wise words prompted her to put things in perspective.

Laying her head back against the seat, she fingered the gold, heart-shaped locket Cord had given her for her birthday. Since he'd gone, she'd worn the locket every day, touched the tiny heart as if it were some special part of him he'd left behind.

Milly's philosophy made sense, Delia supposed. She had to go on. She couldn't waste away in her room. She had to come to terms with the fact that the locket was the only fragment of Cord she'd ever have.

Closing her eyes, she inhaled the fresh morning air. The sun fell warm upon her face. She listened to the birds, to the breeze rustling through the trees. And the aching inside eased a little.

Cord had disrupted her life, not ended it. He had swayed her from her path, lured her from all she'd deemed important in the past. He'd left her no reason not to resume her plans to join her father in Europe.

The aroma of fresh-baked pastry infiltrated Delia's senses. She opened her eyes as the buggy passed the bakery edging Boudreaux Parish.

"Milly," she said, straightening her spine, "stop by the bank."

"Oh, Delia, let's not dillydally with business today." Milly puckered her lower lip. "Sedberry's just put out their new hats. There's one in the window that'll just match the pink taffeta I got in N'orlens," she said and rolled her eyes. "I saw Cynthia oglin' it yesterday. And if she gets there first—"

"Milly, please." Delia clutched her friend's

sleeve as they neared Grayson's Bank. "Stop at the bank. I'll just be a minute, I promise."

"Oh, all right." Milly jerked the reins, halting the carriage outside Winston Grayson's prominent establishment. "But I can't see wastin' our time here when your credit's already been reestablished," she remarked, then flounced down from the buggy seat.

Delia stepped onto the walk and immediately noticed that the strength had returned to her legs. Clutching her reticule to her waist, she smiled and waited for Milly to round the rig.

"Milly, I'm finally gonna do it. I'm gonna withdraw the funds to book my passage to Europe," she said with a lift of her chin, then caught her friend's arm and dragged her into the bank.

Delia marched directly to the teller and completed her transaction without a flicker of hesitation.

"There," she said, turning to Milly. "Now see? That didn't take long."

She bustled forward with Milly trailing behind. But at the same moment that she looked down to tuck her withdrawal safely inside her purse, she bumped right into Winston Grayson coming out of his office.

"Oh, my," he exclaimed, catching hold of her shoulders. "Are you all right?"

"Gracious, yes." Delia pressed a hand to her heart. "Do forgive me, Mr. Grayson. I wasn't watchin' where I was goin'."

"No, no, don't apologize, my dear. I'm certain it was all my fault." Winston gave her shoulders a pat, then dropped his hands. "I've had a lot on my mind lately," he added, furrowing his brow.

" 'Mornin', Mr. Grayson," Milly chimed in.

"Why, good mornin', Miss Millicent." He smiled politely and straightened his string tie. "Well, if you two ladies will excuse me, I—"

Winston frowned, his gaze skipping between Delia's face and the center of her chest. "That . . . locket," he uttered. "Where did you get it?"

Delia caught the gold heart between her fingers and glanced down. "Cord gave it to me for my birthday," she answered, a little bewildered by his intense interest.

"May I see it?" he asked, staring at the jewelry with a peculiar gleam in his gray eyes.

Delia thought his request a bit odd, but could find no harm in allowing the man to examine the locket closer. Reaching behind her neck, she unfastened the clasp and dropped the heart and chain into his waiting palm.

He simply held it at first, running his thumb over the engraving. Then he pressed the tiny latch and flipped it open. "M . . . A . . . G," he whispered. His eyes grew misty, and he blinked rapidly.

"Cord gave you this, you say?" He looked up. "Cord Kibedeaux?"

Delia nodded, completely baffled now by his curiosity.

Staring past her, he remained silent for a few moments, obviously deep in thought. Then he excused himself rather absentmindedly and started to walk away.

"Mr. Grayson," Delia called after him. "My locket. May I have it back, please?"

The banker stopped, opened his fist, glanced at the contents, then strode back to Delia. Mumbling an apology, he stuffed the necklace into her hand, then walked briskly out of the bank.

Delia and Milly exchanged a concerned frown.

"Milly, you think poor old Mr. Grayson's gettin' senile?" Delia asked as she refastened the locket around her neck.

Milly shrugged. "Well, he is gettin' on in years. Then again, people claim he's been a tad eccentric since his daughter ran off, you know."

"Well, I hope he don't walk out in front of a carriage or nothin'." Delia compressed her lips. "Maybe we ought to follow him, Milly, just to see he gets home all right."

"Oh, now, I'm sure he'll be fine." Milly looped an arm through hers and steered Delia toward the door. "Come on. Let's get on down to Sedberry's. We need to get home early this afternoon to get prettied up for the Taylors' dinner party, remember?"

Cord awakened to the shrill morning songs of swamp birds. His eyes batted open slowly, focusing on the bright spots of sunlight among the overhead leaves. As long as he didn't move, nothing was real.

Lazily, he ran his hand over his face, down his throat, the stubble of his beard prickling his palm. What had possessed him to come back to the bayou? Why in God's name hadn't he left Boudreaux Parish?

But he already knew the answer.

He felt like he belonged here among the charred rubble of the shanty. He felt foul and dirty. And he had no place else in mind to go.

Cord rose on one elbow, and a bundle slid down his chest. Knowing it was food before he folded back the cloth, he pushed himself into a sitting position and stared at the loaf of bread.

Tante Netha Bea. The old woman had been here again. Cord was glad he'd been asleep. Otherwise, she would have tried to force him to eat . . . and shamed him into shaving.

He broke off a piece of crust and lifted it to his mouth, but his stomach churned and prevented the bread from going any further.

Sleep. All he wanted to do was drift into oblivion.

Cord flung the small loaf aside. Shoving himself up from the ground, he stood and watched a flock of birds descend upon the bread. Though his legs were weak from lack of use, he stretched his arms high over his head, wresting the kink from his back.

He couldn't stay here any longer. He couldn't bear the thought of Delia being so close, yet so far away. It was time he moved on.

But where?

He combed a hand through his tousled hair and glanced around at the marshy swampland. *Texas, maybe?* It didn't matter. Some town where no one knew him. A place where no one had ever heard of Raoul and Anna Kibedeaux would do.

A swish of water broke into Cord's thoughts. He looked up to find a pirogue docking next to what remained of the porch. Then Samuel reached down and helped a gentleman stand, and Winston Grayson stepped onto the bank.

Self-consciously, Cord buttoned his soiled, wrinkled shirt as the man strode purposefully toward him.

Seemingly unaware of Cord's shabby appearance, Winston stopped before him, his expression grave.

"Cord, Adelaide says you gave her a locket," he said without mincing words. "Is that true?"

"*Oui*," Cord replied, then lowered his brow. "The locket belonged to my mother."

Winston's face turned ashen-gray. "Your . . . mother?"

Grayson swayed, and Cord caught his elbow. "M'sieu, are you not well?" Frowning, he studied the man's dazed features. "M'sieu? Why would you come here and ask me such a thing? M'sieu Grayson, can you hear me?"

Winston's knees buckled, and Cord lowered him to the ground. Grayson sat, staring blankly for a long moment. Suddenly he fixed his gaze on Cord and gripped the front of his shirt. "How did your mother get my daughter's locket?"

Cord blinked. "Your daughter's . . . I do not understand."

"I had it made for Mary Ann's sixteenth birthday. It even has her initials in it." Winston's chin quivered and his eyes brightened. "I can't believe she would have sold it . . . but—"

"Maybe the answers you seek are here," *Tante* Netha Bea cut in. Stepping from the cover of the bushes, she held out the battered tin box Cord had given her for safe-keeping.

An incredible possibility flickered in Cord's brain at the sight of his mother's small treasure chest. The notion was almost inconceivable. Yet his scalp tingled with some foreign sensation as Netha Bea handed Grayson the box.

"What the devil—" Winston began.

"You look inside, m'sieu," *Tante* Netha Bea instructed him with a jut of her chin. "And you will see, *hein?*"

Obviously perplexed, Grayson pried open the lid.

"Dear God," he whispered, and lifted the ribbon, rubbing the faded satin strand between his thumb and forefinger. A deep breath escaped him and a tear trickled from the corner of his eye as he picked up the photograph. "Mary Ann," he whimpered softly.

Shakily, he raised his head and looked at Netha Bea. "Where did you get this?"

"These things belonged to my mother," Cord answered, confused by Winston Grayson's reaction.

Winston turned to him, his gray eyes roving over Cord's features and intermittently darting to the picture he held. Slowly, a tremulous smile creased his lips, and he reached out and lightly touched Cord's temple. "Of course," he murmured. "The eyes. They're the same. Why didn't I notice before?"

A warmth rose within Cord's chest. Yet he dangled beyond believing the implications of the old man's rantings.

"There must be a way to prove it," Winston mumbled. Dropping his attention to the box once more, he rummaged through the sparse contents.

Cord's breath lodged in his lungs as he watched Winston unfold the marriage certificate. Even though he knew his mother's maiden name matched Grayson's, fear held hope from surfacing.

Winston Grayson's face broke into a smile, and he lifted his misty gaze to Cord's. "Good God, I have a grandson," he said incredulously. "A grandson," he repeated, then leaned forward and clutched Cord in a hearty embrace.

Cord's arms moved stiffly from his sides. Hesitantly, he wrapped them around the old man's shoulders. Grayson shook with sobs. Cord's eyes stung and his throat swelled shut.

He was Winston Grayson's grandson. In all these years, he'd once never suspected he had a grandfather. At least not one who gave a damn whether he even existed or not.

The two parted and simply looked at each other.

Cord dragged his shirt cuff beneath his nose.

Winston swiped at the stream of tears draining down his cheeks, then burst out laughing.

"Good God," he said, then shook his head. "Who would've thought?"

The corners of Cord's mouth twitched into a grin.

"There's only one thing I don't understand." Grayson picked up the yellowed certificate and arched an eyebrow. "The man my daughter ran off with was named Giffault."

Cord nodded. "My father used that name often. "That is why I was not surprised to see the initials M.A.G. inscribed inside the locket."

"I still can't believe it. Anna Kibedeaux and my Mary Ann were one in the same." Winston closed his eyes, and his throat worked convulsively. "Was she truly as mad as they say?" he asked.

"No . . . not so bad," Cord lied, then dropped his gaze. "She was getting better, I think, before . . . well, before . . . she and my father passed away."

"I know, son." Winston laid a hand on Cord's shoulder. "I'm sorry. I wished I'd known. Maybe I could have prevented him from . . . hurting her, and you."

The breeze rustling through the trees filled an awkward span of silence.

"Cord," Winston said, breaking the stillness, "I want you to come home with me, son. We have a lot to talk about. A lot to catch up on."

Cord met the old man's gray eyes, and the corners of his mouth tipped slightly. "*Oui*, we do have much to discuss. But—" Cord's smile wavered, and he gazed into the distance, seeking the right words. "I will come tomorrow. I need time alone to sort out all that has happened. It does not yet seem quite real."

Grayson nodded. "I understand, son. I'm a bit overwhelmed myself."

For a while they sat together without speaking, each man reveling in a quiet way, and absorbing the notion that he was no longer alone in the world.

Chapter Twenty-Four

D elia sat listlessly at the Taylors' long dining table, feeling miserably out of sync with the other guests. The ride into town with Milly earlier in the day hadn't been quite as tiresome as she'd imagined it would be, but this evening's outing had been a mistake. She pushed her food around the china plate with her fork, wondering what she'd ever found so enticing about such social gatherings.

Why she had allowed Milly to bully her into coming, she would never know. The moment she'd walked through the Taylors' front door, she'd realized she still wasn't ready to face the world. Maybe a few more days of convalescing would heal her battered insides. For the time being, her bruised heart still lagged along at a pitiful pace.

Annoyed by the animated chatter surrounding her, Delia closed her eyes. On impulse, she longed for the peacefulness of the bayou. Unfortunately, thoughts of the bayou brought thoughts of Cord. Pleasurable thoughts. Painful thoughts.

Unbearable yearnings.

"Well, Delia, is it true?"

She lifted her head and looked across the table.

"Parker and I have just been wonderin' . . ." Cynthia leaned closer to her new husband, hugged his arm, and aimed a small, wicked smile at Delia. Parker straightened his string tie. "Well, to put it delicately, Delia, we heard a nasty rumor that Cord's leavin' town." She lowered her lashes coyly. "Not that we want to pry, of course, but . . . that's not so, is it?"

Delia's skin paled. She stared blankly at Cynthia.

"Parker and me, we're simply worried about your welfare, or we wouldn't ask," Cynthia cooed in a voice laced with pity. "Word has it the two of y'all had a fallin'-out."

"Honestly, Delia, if you want my opinion," Parker drawled, "you'll be better off without him. Boudreaux Parish don't need his kind 'round heah. And quite frankly, deah, neither do you."

Fire pricked Delia's cheeks. Shifting a cold glare between Cynthia and Parker, she scraped her chair back, stood up, and clenched her fists in the folds of her skirt.

"Let me tell you somethin', Parker—and *you*, Cynthia, dear, should listen as well." Delia's tightly controlled voice rose above all the others. "My *husband* is more of a gentleman than you could ever hope to be. He's good and kind, and he would *never* be so rude as to speak to me the way you just have."

Delia glanced slowly around the table at the frozen, shocked faces turned her way.

"Let me tell you *all* somethin'." She nudged her chin a little higher, and a slight smile touched her lips. "I'd wager everything I own that my Cord is worth *ten* of every man here."

Looking back at Cynthia, Delia brightened her smile considerably. "And, *no*, Cynthia. To answer your mannerless question, Cord is *not* leavin' town."

With one last, sufficient glower at everyone who dared to meet her gaze, she lifted the hem of her hooped skirt and turned to leave. "Leastways, not if I can help it," she added beneath her breath as she rustled toward the door.

Delia stopped just outside the crackling campfire's yellow ring of light.

Her heart beat a hard, determined rhythm as she viewed Cord's shadowy form. His head in his hands, he sat with his elbows braced on bent knees, a mellow glow from the fire casting gold hues across his dark, tousled hair.

"Cord," Delia called softly. With a deep breath, she took an obstinate step forward.

He raised his head by degrees, then stared at her as if in a trance. "Delia?"

"Well. I s'pose that's a good sign." She clasped her hands behind her back. "Rememberin' my name, I mean. Tell me, Cord, do you remember the names of all the other women you've dallied with?"

"What do you want, *hein?*" Cord's expression flickered between anger and anguish.

Delia dragged her eyes over his bare chest, watching the firelight dance across his muscles. "I want the same thing I wanted the last time you asked me that question."

"Go home, *chère.*" Cord squinted into the fire. "You should not be here."

"Oh, no?" Delia lowered herself to the ground and sat down across from him. "Where else would a wife be but with her husband?" she asked, rearranging her skirt. "Tell me, Cord."

"Do you come here to torture me, Delia?"

"No, Cord. I came here to talk."

He lifted his eyes to hers briefly, then focused on the golden flames again. "Then talk. Do not tease me. I am in no mood for such games to-night."

"I wasn't teasing you, Cord," Delia whispered achingly. Twisting her hands in her lap, she silently prayed for the magic words that would move him. "A woman *should* be with her husband. Through thick and thin. For better or worse."

Cord remained completely still and quiet, broodingly watching the bright yellow flames.

Delia caressed him with her gaze, wanting so badly to wrap her arms around him. Clutching her folded hands tighter, she wet her lips.

"We were married in the church, Cord . . . bound together in holy matrimony. What God has joined together, no man . . . *nothin'* can tear apart. Don't you see? I belong to you. You belong to me."

Cord raised his head slowly and searched her face. "And what of your grand plans to go to Europe, Delia? I thought you wished to go live with your father."

"I thought so too. Once." She focused on the tiny orange sparks that drifted upward from the fire, then vanished into the night. "But I've done a lot of thinkin' lately . . . and an awful lot of growin' up. And I've come to the conclusion that if my father had wanted me to live with him, he would have come to fetch me a long time ago. Oh, I know he loves me. But he has his life. And I have mine. And I have you now." Delia looked at Cord pointedly. "My father used to be the most important person in the world to me until you came along. But it was you, Cord, who taught me the meanin' of love."

Cord laced his fingers loosely between his knees and observed her quietly from across the campfire.

Delia didn't miss the strong emotion in his eyes or the movement of his jaw. Something she'd said had touched him. She could tell he was on the edge of breaking. Only his stubborn pride stood between them now.

Pushing herself up from the ground, Delia stood and dusted off her skirt. Cord's gaze followed her as she walked around the fire and stopped before him.

She reached out her hands to him, and hesitantly, he took them and came to his feet. They stood apart, their fingers tightly entwined, and looked at each other for the count of several heartbeats.

"It will not be easy," Cord murmured, his breath short and labored.

"I know," Delia replied with a slight smile.

Cord edged his tongue along his lower lip and frowned. "Winston Grayson has offered me a job at the bank . . . and I have decided to take it." His features softened as he gazed into her eyes. "I will work hard, Delia."

No longer able to hold herself back, she stepped forward and hugged his waist. "And you'll earn the respect you deserve."

Cord's arms instantly folded around her. He clutched her against his chest. "I . . . I love you, *chère*," he whispered into her hair. "God knows how I love you."

His chest flexed beneath Delia's cheek as if the words had been torn from his heart. Delia's own heart quivered with a tremendous flood of emotions.

"Ah, Delia, sweet Delia." Cord buried his face in the hollow of her neck. "What am I to do, *hein*? I am lost," he admitted in a deep, raw voice, his breath warm spurts against her skin. "I love you so, but I fear I may fail you. I do not wish to shame you. And I *must* not shame Winston Grayson."

"We'll fight those fears together, Cord. You won't fail me, and you won't fail—" Delia creased her brow. "Winston Grayson? Cord, I know you were once fond of the man. But his opinion shouldn't—"

"He is my grandfather, *chère*."

Cord stepped out of her embrace and combed his fingers through his hair. "Mary Ann Grayson was my mother," he said quietly.

"Mary Ann . . . ? Mr. Grayson's daughter?" Delia laid a hand against her breast. "She was—"

"My mother," Cord finished. "*Oui*. M'sieu Grayson and I, we just found out today." He hooked his thumbs in the waistband of his trousers and curled his toes into the dirt beneath his feet, fixing his gaze on the ground. "And now M'sieu Grayson, he wants me in his life. Me, I would like nothing better. I have never had any family to speak of. But surely I cannot be such a desirable grandson. I do not know what to do, Delia. I fear I cannot live up to what he expects of me.''

''Oh, Cord.'' She cupped her hands around his jaw and tilted his face upward. ''The past is dead. Let it lie. Your parents' sins aren't yours. You're a good man, Cord. An honorable man. A man anyone would be proud to call their grandson . . . or their husband.''

She smiled at him with all her love shining in her eyes. ''Things might be difficult in Boudreaux Parish for a while. But folks'll come around, Cord. They always do. And until they do, I'll stand by you. So will Grandy. And Milly. And Winston Grayson. And we'll show 'em all.''

Cord swallowed hard, his eyes bright in the soft yellow glow of the fire. ''But what if—''

Delia pressed her fingertips to his lips, and he closed his eyes. ''You only fail, Cord, if you don't try.''

The brittle wood crackled in the silence. The mingled scents of smoke and wild honeysuckle drifted on the balmy night breeze.

''Actually,'' Delia remarked, tracing Cord's chin with her thumb, ''I came here tonight to discuss a little business with you.''

Cord opened his eyes to half-mast, and the corners of his mouth eased into a weary grin. ''Business, *hein?*''

''Mmm-hmm.'' Delia dragged her hand down his throat to toy with his thick chest hair. ''I'd like to offer you another proposition.''

''Oh, *non, chère.*'' Cord laughed huskily, then

looped his arms around her waist. "Not another proposition. Our first bargain has gotten me into enough trouble. I am not certain my poor heart can withstand another one of your deals."

"No, no. Now just listen." Delia walked her fingers up over his broad shoulders and clasped her hands behind his neck. "What would you think about extendin' our marriage from six months to . . . oh, let's say . . . what? Maybe a lifetime?"

"I don't know." Cord frowned pensively. "I might live an awfully long while yet, and me, I'm not sure I could put up with you for so many years." Curling his lower lip, he shrugged. "You would have to make it worth my time and trouble, would you not?"

Delia cocked her head, tightened the corners of her mouth, and slapped him playfully on the back of the head.

"No, no. Now listen," he mimicked with a teasing light dancing in his dark eyes. "You should give me something special in return for my expert services, should you not?"

Delia eyed him suspiciously. "I'm almost afraid to ask what that might be."

"I would like a son," Cord stated flatly.

Delia's jaw dropped.

"Well, a daughter would do, I suppose. Or perhaps one of each. *Non*, wait." Cord tilted his head back and squinted at the star-ridden sky. "Maybe two or three of each, *hein*?"

Delia shook her head and burst out laughing. "Cord, you're terrible," she quipped.

"*Oui*, so they say."

"I think you've been listenin' too much to Grandy and all her nonsense about a great-grandbaby."

"Mmm. Perhaps." Peering down at her, he arched one slanted dark brow. "Maybe with the money I earn at the bank, I will buy us a nice little house, *hein?*"

"It better be a big house, with as many children as you want." Delia's smile grew wider. "We can use some of my inheritance for furnishings and such." She quickly pressed a finger to his lips. "And don't you say a single word about that money, you hear? We're married, remember? What's yours is mine. What's mine is yours."

Offering no argument, Cord kissed her fingertip, then took her hand in his. He laid his forehead against hers and Delia closed her eyes, her heart swelling.

"You know," she whispered, "that big four-poster is just sittin' useless back at the plantation."

"Ah, now, we cannot allow that, *hein?*"

"I'm afraid not. Not if we're gonna start workin' on gettin' Grandy that great-grandbaby."

Cord chuckled deep in his throat and scooped Delia into his arms. "I love you, *chère,*" he whispered against her temple as he carried her in the direction of the waiting boat.

"I love you too," she whispered back and snuggled against him.

"Do you know what you have given me?" he asked, striding steadily toward the edge of the bayou. "Have you any idea what your sweetness has taught me?"

''No,'' Delia murmured, then kissed his cheek. ''What?''

Cord took a few more steps, then stopped and gazed deeply into her eyes. ''There truly *is* a difference between love and lust, *chère.*''

Avon Romances—
the best in exceptional authors and unforgettable novels!

1 Out Of 5 Women Can't Read.

1 Out Of 5 Women Can't Read.

1 Out Of 5 Women Can't Read.

1 Xvz Xv 5 Xwywv Xvy'z Xvyz.

1 Out Of 5 Women Can't Read.

*As painful as it is to believe, it's true. And it's time we all did something to help. Coors has committed $40 million to fight illiteracy in America. We hope you'll join our efforts by volunteering your time. Giving just a few hours a week to your local literacy center can help teach a woman to read. For more information on literacy volunteering, call **1-800-626-4601.***

LITERACY. PASS IT ON.